The Glass Dagger

By: Kelsey L. Robinson

For TJ.

Without you, none of this would have happened.

Love you endlessly.

CONTENTS

Rairene
Grècia

N
S
Trudel
Vicuria
Evrotia

FOREWORD

The Glass Dagger is an adventure fantasy set in a dark fairytale adaptation world with teenage assassins. It includes elements regarding torture, war, hand-to-hand combat, poisoning, blood, intense situations, death, and mental manipulation through poison that are shown on the page. Readers who may be sensitive to these elements, please be aware that you're entering into the dark fantasy world of the Kingdom of Assassins...

PROLOGUE

Once upon a time, as all stories start, three sisters loved each other, mostly. One was destined to rule, another arranged to wed a foreign prince, and the last didn't know what she was meant to do. But at least they had each other.

Until a diplomatic mission went awry.

The sister destined to rule fell in love.

And two kingdoms were on the verge of war.

To keep the peace, a treaty was established, promising a new marriage to bind the two kingdoms together, and finally, everything would be as it should have been. Or at least, that's how it should have gone. But as is the way with most stories, things are hardly as they seem.

CHAPTER ONE

One at a time, Ella tapped her fingers against her thumb, counting the beats. The beats of her heart, steady if a little raised. The footbeats of the commoners clamoring past her, the beats of the women chasing after children over cobblestones, and the beats of each word on the letter Sophie had sent to her.

I need advice. Meet me at midday in the marketplace.

So, here she was, at midday, in the marketplace, waiting. And Sophie had yet to reveal herself. Ella leaned against the wooden wall of the pub. She stood in the outskirts of the shadows, her dark blue hood pulled up high enough to keep anyone walking by from being able to identify her. At first glance, anyone would think she was a well-off commoner with her plain blue dress, soft leather shoes, and black corset. If anyone had desired to get a closer look, not that she would have let them, they would have seen that her corset was enchanted with metal plates of protection and that hidden beneath her plain blue cotton dress was an assortment of daggers. Of course, she hadn't fully armed herself for what should have been an easy rendezvous with a protégé. The only item on her that would be a hindrance was the shoes. They were extremely comfortable, but not suitable for anything other than walking. As each beat ticked, the hairs on Ella's neck told her she was going to need to go faster than that.

Ella looked at the grand clock in the center of the marketplace. Five past. Sophie should have arrived by now. She knew that being prompt was important. It had been ingrained in her since day one of her tutelage. It had been a grueling and intense year for both of them, but both had come out better for it. Ella was more skilled now, at seventeen, and Sophie was getting better. She had been tested and deemed ready for an assignment. At least, that was what Ella had recommended. She bit the inside of her cheek, gazing around at the townspeople of Riset. All of them moved about with no knowledge of what happened in the shadows to keep them safe.

What Ella and the others had done to ensure the Kingdom of Rairene remained protected.

"Ella," a whisper floated over her shoulder.

She turned to find her protégé, a short fifteen-year-old girl with big brown eyes and even bigger dreams, tip-toe towards her. Her bright red hair was in an elaborate braid that trailed down her back, wispy curls breaking free to frame her face. Her freckles stood out on her pale skin, giving her an innocent look that was not to be underestimated. She wore a dark green dress that belonged to a nobleman's daughter, giving Ella pause. What mark had she been given?

"Sophie—"

"I know. I'm sorry. My mark got held up, and it has delayed the entire morning." Sophie crossed her arms and slouched against the opposite wall.

"What's wrong?" Ella walked over and fixed Sophie's posture. She would never admit it, but she had become quite fond of Sophie. What had begun as a contentious mentorship had blossomed into a strong sisterhood, and Ella would protect her.

"I need your advice...have you ever..." Sophie twisted her hands together. "Have you ever fallen in love with your mark?" Her brown eyes remained downcast, her cheeks flushed.

"No...." Ella watched Sophie wilt. "But I've come close. Isn't your mission ending tonight?"

Sophie nodded her head slowly.

"There's no turning back. The marks we hunt are bad, Sophie. He may present a pleasant mask to the world, but that's to hide how despicable he is on the inside. You know this."

"But, he's not—"

"He is. I promise. Why else would he be marked for death?" Ella watched Sophie, her eyes darting back and forth as she twisted a stray piece of hair, her nervous tick. "Here, take this." Ella took out an enchanted diamond earring. Sophie's eyes lit up. As long as both of them wore one earring from the enchanted pair, they could hear everything that the other said. "Only put it on if you need to. Emergencies only."

"Of course." Sophie grasped it before tucking it into a secure pocket.

"Is there anything else?" Ella looked around the marketplace, making sure no one had seen them.

"No. Everything's fine. I'll do as you say. I know you're right."

Ella turned to look at her. She was slumped again against the side of the building. Her hands limp at her side.

Ella knelt. "This job we have isn't easy. No one will thank us for it. Yet we know that what we do is for the protection of the kingdom we love. We're paid well, we're fed, have a comfortable bed, wonderful friends, and we get to serve. Blood in my veins, right?" Ella held her hand, watching Sophie's eyes dart back and forth.

Gradually Sophie stood up taller, steel in her eyes, all sense of innocence gone.

"Bones of my ancestors," Sophie whispered with confidence.

Ella kissed her forehead and smiled as Sophie turned around and walked away, the diamond earring securely in place on her left ear should Sophie need her. Not that she would.

Ella, are you able to talk? Jaq's silky voice came through on Ella's other diamond earring. She paused at the tense strain in her enchanter's voice.

Jaq—

We have a mark that needs to be taken out immediately.

What's wrong? We've done quick jobs before, Ella glanced around as she picked up her pace, dodging around townspeople.

She loved this part of the city. The sounds of children laughing and women gossiping. The smell of cinnamon and spices swirled around everything, creating a bouquet of scents unique to the city she called home.

This one involves an Earl. They typically give you a few days to plan.

Ella shrugged. She'd never killed an earl with less than two days' notice, but there was always some new challenge to take on, and she would never back down. *It'll be fine. I'm about to leave Riset. The walk home will take about an hour—*

Gus is on his way, Jaq interjected. She could practically feel him tugging on his tunic to calm his nerves.

Alright, so they're in a hurry. I'll see you shortly.

Ella glanced up in time to avoid colliding with a royal guard.

"Watch your step, commoner, or I'll arrest you."

Ella bit back a response, narrowing her eyes as he moved on. The marketplace was admittedly a busy place, but she'd never felt closed in before, not like this. A young man with brilliant red hair stood in the center of it all, his green eyes darting around. Henry.

He had grown so much since she had last seen him. David stood next to him. His black hair swept to the side as he smiled, portraying the perfect prince. A line of commoners had formed before David. Ella examined them, realizing that all of them had some type of ailment, and David was looking each of them over. Once he was done, he handed them an enchanted potion. He was healing them, Ella realized.

"Get in line or move aside." A guard barked at her.

Ella's fingers twitched for a dagger. How she longed to tell him just how much she protected the royal family, too. But she couldn't. No one could know...not even those she defended.

She chanced a glance back at her former friends, catching Henry's eye for a second before she pulled her hood back up and walked away. Her heart hammered in her chest long after she had left their sight. It didn't matter that they were happy without her. It had been nine years, after all. She didn't expect them to wait for her; she certainly hadn't waited for them. Ella had become what she had always wanted to be; a protector of her kingdom. If she had done as the palace had wished, she would have become one of those simpering ladies of the court who followed David everywhere he went.

Gus was waiting for her outside the gate into Riset, horse, and carriage at the ready. The horses galloped home, with Jaq briefing her through her earring. The Earl of Gascony was suspected of selling information to the neighboring Kingdom of Holodal that put Prince David in imminent danger.

Why do they think it's him? Ella sat up straighter at the threat made against David.

The earl fell on hard times recently due to his gambling addiction and incessant need to go to brothels—

That describes about half of the nobility. Ella leaned back. This was probably going to go nowhere.

Do the other members of the nobility have cracks in their mansion walls and uneven cobblestones with an unkempt garden and limited staff?

No. Why do we think he's already sold the information?

He was seen back in some of his usual holes throwing coins around.

I'll check it out. Though it doesn't sound very promising.

As evening laid claim to Riset, Ella darted around her home, changing to ensure she looked the part of a wealthy socialite. She wore her plated black tunic and pants underneath an exquisite dark blue dress.

Gus took her back to Riset, stopping at a pub in the third circle, where he would wait for her return. She bunched her cloak around her, shielding her from the chill that ran off the trees, carrying the smell of mist and beer. If only the enchanted plates of armor stitched into her clothing could heat up. Hidden further within were her seven glass daggers.

Each home she passed was lit with candles that would burn well into the night. The earl's home was not so fortunate. Though he tried to demonstrate wealth, she saw the lies as she approached. Jaq was right about uneven cobblestones, and a dangerously wild garden. However, it was the large cracks that ran up his home that revealed his troubles.

It was a rushed plan of attack. She had confidence she would succeed. David's life depended on it. Per Jaq's report, the earl would head home with the only guard he could keep employed.

Ella eased the gate to the earl's home open. The garden and lack of guards gave her all the cover she needed to go up to the modest mansion unseen.

Ella opened an ornately delicate compact mirror and looked into the tidy reflected glory that was Jaq. His brown hair was perfectly placed, his red tunic wrinkle-free, and his spectacles spotless. *How are the city guards?*

Everything at the city guard's station is quiet. They're about to change shifts. Jaq glanced at one of his enchanted mirrors.

Two years ago, Ella had gotten into the city guard station and sprayed every mirrored surface she could find with Jaq's enchanted potion. Once dried, he could forever see through the mirrors in his 'top secret enchanter room', as he liked to describe it. It had been the only time Ella had taken a potion that would enhance her stealth.

Ella shook herself, bouncing back and forth on her feet until the goosebumps from the memory vanished. Not only were potions addictive, but she had become a ghost in her body after ingesting Callidus. She had been aware, but not quite in control of her actions. Of course, being able to slip past anyone unseen, no matter how out in the open she was, had been a wonderful benefit. However, she never wanted to lose connection with her body like that again.

Ella discarded her cloak and dress, hiding them in the wild lavender bushes. At the back door, Ella pulled the lock picks and tension wrench out of her wig, making sure it stayed securely in place. Beneath it, she had braided back her snow-white hair. She scratched her head, grimacing at the slight movement. The wig never felt secure enough, though her stepmother insisted on it for her protection. Ella stopped her protesting when it was wearing the wig, or changing her hair, the last connection she had to her mother.

She inserted the tension rod and turned the lock to the right, keeping weight on the lock. Ella slid the pick in, feeling each pin release while maintaining pressure. She moved fast, running the pick over each one until she felt the last one release, the knob turning in her hand.

Ella slipped into the dimly lit house. The earl had yet to use his new coin to replenish his candles; she noted. She paused by a side table, picking up a framed portrait of him. He was someone who would not have trouble attracting women. According to Jaq, his list of lovers was almost as long as his list of accusers. As she walked through the house, she sprayed every mirror, ensuring Jaq could see everything and warn her of any intruders.

The guards' room was where she would hide, four doors down from the earl's on the third floor. She would have to make sure taking down the guard was quiet. Hiding in his wardrobe, she kept the door open just enough for the flame light to shine in. She inhaled the smell of his clothes, wrinkling her nose at the sweat.

All set, Jaq. Ella looked into her mirror.

Still no movement out of the usual. Jaq commented.

Ella slipped the mirror into a small pocket and pulled out her diamond earring.

By the time she got her earring on, the sound of hooves on dirt reached her. The earl yelled something profane at his guard. Wonderful, he was drunk. Ella gently hit her head against the wooden closet door. She hated drunk men, and this one was cruel while drunk.

A few minutes later, she heard the guard walk on creaky boards to the earl's room. The guard walked to his bedroom, removed his clothing, and plopped down. Ella smiled.

She eased the wardrobe open. Wisps of beer and food floated off of him. Ella pulled out a thick piece of rope, rolling it between her fingers, its ridges rippling under her gloves. She leapt onto the guard, getting the rope around his neck, and pulling it tight. He attempted to turn around, but she had him pinned between her thighs. Ella didn't want to kill him. He wasn't her mark, and he couldn't help that the man he served was horrible.

The guard's rough hands slid off of her as his body went limp. She gagged and tied him to his bed before moving down to the earl's room and pushing open the heavy wooden door.

"What is it, John?" The earl turned to her, his brow scrunched.

"Lord Edward, I see your house has become a bit...rundown." Ella eased into his room, her fingers tapping a beat against one of the daggers nestled at the base of her back.

"How is that your concern?" Lord Edward moved slowly around his room, heading for a hidden sword, no doubt.

"Don't. Move." Ella removed one of her glass daggers, pointing it at the earl. "You're in a lot of trouble for what you did."

"Pray, what did I do? I do a lot of things. I'm an earl, as you know, and I have to do a lot for this kingdom."

"Do you," Ella whispered. "I'll hazard a guess that it's nothing compared to what others do in service for the crown."

"Because an assassin knows so much about serving the crown?" Lord Edward laughed, taking a side step towards a mirror.

Ella threw a small dagger; impaling his arm. He screamed, collapsing to the floor.

"I do. Tell me, why don't you serve the crown as you should?" Ella crouched down before him, pulling his head back to look at her.

"I've always remained loyal to the Kingdom I love," he spat.

"We'll see about that." Ella gripped his collar and lifted Lord Edward to his feet.

He broke out of her hold, landing hard on the ground. He jumped up, wrapping his arms around her waist, and pushed her against the wall. Spots danced in her eyes as her head bounced off the hard wooden wall. She fought him until she was on his back, legs wrapped around his waist, the crook of her elbow tight under his neck. Lord Edward shot up, lifting her off the ground and ramming Ella's back into the dresser opposite his bed.

Her vision blurred, but she held on. He weakened as he lost air, collapsing to the ground.

Ella held on until he passed out.

She dragged him to one of his cushioned chairs and bound his wrists and ankles. He woke up groaning.

"All this just to kill me?"

Ella leaned in close, setting her hands on his arms. "Oh, I'm not going to kill you," she said. She watched the slight flicker of hope in his eyes. "Well, not yet anyway."

She pushed away from him, pulling out one of her glass daggers.

"If you think I'm going to tell you anything. You're—"

"You're going to do more than talk, you're going to scream," Ella promised. For everything he had done. For putting the Prince's life in danger.

"Now this can be easy," Ella tapped the dagger against his cheek, "or it can be hard," Ella dug her gloved nails into his scalp and pulled, tearing hair from the room. The earl let out a short groan of pain, stomping his feet. "All you have to do is answer my questions."

"What would those be?"

"First, how much coin did you demand to betray your kingdom? What was the price that made it acceptable for you to commit treason?"

He blinked.

"It probably wasn't even a lot, right? It's why you were approached. You're broke, the fifth circle of Riset broke. If you hadn't inherited this home with your title, you would live on the street."

Lord Edward remained silent.

"No? You're not going to answer the easy one?" Ella delicately slid her knife up his arm.

Ella moved before he could figure out what she was going to do. She ripped back his pinky finger, breaking it. This time, the earl did scream. Ella walked away, surveying the almost bare room. He had sold off his furniture. No wonder he had been so easily swayed. She needed to break him. David...Prince David, she corrected herself, was in danger because of him, and she had to find out how.

"Answer my questions and this can be over," Ella murmured.

"You're crazy if you think I'll admit to treason."

"I don't think...I know. You should be more careful about who you go boasting about your good fortunes. Especially in a brothel." Ella looked at him sideways. His chest moved rapidly, as sweat stank up the air.

"I didn't give away any information. I would never sell out Prince David." The earl protested adamantly.

"Was it worth it?" Ella circled the earl an hour later.

His head lolled to the side. He would not take much more. Ella would have to scale back. She needed that information from him. It was her duty to protect the crown by any means necessary. He refused to give it to her, no matter what she did.

"Just tell me what you told Holodal, and I'll end your suffering," Ella whispered, running a dagger lightly up his arm. She applied only enough pressure to scrape his skin.

The earl smiled through blood-stained teeth.

Ella got up and walked over to the torch burning in its sconce. She pulled out a dagger and stuck it in the flame, heating it until she knew it was hot enough to burn. Her lips twitched as she drew closer to him. The blade's handle warmed her calloused hand. She didn't register the heat anymore, having held it so many times before.

Ella let the tip fall and press into his neck. His skin split beneath from the heat as she pulled it down his collarbone.

"What information did you sell to Holodal?" Ella stepped back from him, the earl's fear clouding her senses.

He smiled. "You might want a better enchanter."

Cinderella look out, Jaq's voice burst in her ear, her codename echoing around her.

Ella opened her mouth to respond as two men broke through the door.

Mouse, find me a way out, Ella said as the guard she had tied up charged her. His sword was drawn as another man worked on freeing Lord Edward. Ella armed herself, crouching into a defensive position. She got in close to the guard, using her marginally smaller height to her advantage. He wrapped an arm around her, keeping her from fighting.

Ella bit him, jumping free when he howled.

He lunged for her, got ahold of her wig, and pulled. Ella fell to the floor, hitting her head hard. Her wig was in his hand.

Lord Edward was free, staring at her. Looking at her white hair. She heard more footsteps. More men. She knew she could handle it. She just had to knock all of them out and kill the earl. He had threatened the safety of those she protected.

Mouse? Ella got up into a defensive position, blinking away the double vision.

Get to the alley next to the fence.

Easier said than done, Ella huffed. Her eyes darted around the room as she stepped back again, two more men running in, giving her an odds of five to one. She was near the bed, and all of them were in the middle of the room. The additional guards wavered in and out of her vision the more she tried to concentrate on them. Great, all of them had taken Callidus, giving them the ability to slip past all the mirrors unseen. Though the enchanter hadn't been powerful if she could see them.

Cinderella! Sophie's light voice erupted through Ella's other earring.

Scarlet, I'm a little— Ella whispered, using Sophie's codename. Ella lunged when one guard darted towards her, evading his blade.

I failed—

Ella could hear the tears soaking Sophie's voice.

Scarlet, I don't have time for your crush— Ella ducked as another blade came close.

Screams echoed through Ella. Sophie's screams.

Liquid ice ran down Ella's spine at the fear in Sophie's voice.

Scarlet... Dread weighed Ella down, sinking through to her feet with a weight heavier than her horse. *Scarlet.*

Silence.

Sophie!

Nothing. Ella had to get to Sophie. She had to believe Sophie was still alive and couldn't answer her. Ella glanced at the guards marking their positions. Before she could second guess herself, she grabbed the vial of Velocity from her pocket and gulped it down. It wasn't a lot. Jaq had only ever given her enough to ride the enchantment long enough to get free of a situation.

But it worked. Too well.

The air in the room became frigid as Ella moved, rushing them.

They had seen her. They had heard her. She couldn't let them live. Couldn't let them out of this house before getting to Sophie.

Ella collided with the men. She flipped and twirled around the room in an intricate dance.

She crashed into a wall.

Ella ducked, spun out her legs, and stabbed a man faster than her mind could process. She had to get out. Had to kill them. Had to get to Sophie.

Wait, hadn't she already started killing the guards? Ella thought before looking up from the guard below her. Yes. She had already attacked them. She had to get out. They couldn't live. Not anymore. Had to get to Sophie. Couldn't leave a trace of herself behind.

Pinpricks of pain blossomed in Ella's vision as she fought them. Ribbons of red floated around her, daggers at the ready. Her mind spun with the need to make sure these men did not get away. They couldn't get away. Ella kicked out her legs again, knocking more down. She had to go, run, fight, no run, she had to fight first. Had to...had to get to Sophie.

Cinderella! Jaq's voice reached her, floating in time around her. *Cinderella, focus, Velocity is—*

Ella stopped moving.

For a single heartbeat, her world stopped. She centered herself and focused. Sweat coated her skin, soaking through her clothes. Bile rose from her stomach at the scene before her. She had cut them to shreds. Red mist hung in the air, unsettled as she paused. Ella covered her lips with her hand.

Jaq—

I see. Get out of there. The city guard is coming.

Velocity gripped Ella's heart, and she ran.

She ran through the halls, her body slamming against the building, trying to slow down. She had to slow down. Ella paused in front of a mirror, dragging her hands over her face. Her pale skin was freckled and splattered with blood. Her white hair is in knots. But it was her eyes that froze her. Her ice-blue eyes were ringed in the same sickly yellow color of Velocity, and it was barely shrinking in size as her body absorbed it.

Ella's mind jumped. She needed to grab her dress and get to Sophie. She needed her clothes. She had to remember those.

Ella sprinted across the earl's unkempt gardens and snatched her clothes right as she caught the sound of horses running to the house. She dashed for the side of the stone fence Jaq had instructed her to get to. She leaped, the Velocity in her body carrying her the extra distance to make it over the top.

Ella landed hard and rolled. She stood up, wincing. Why was she wincing? What had happened? Ella slowed down, trying to take stock of her body, but her mind refused. It wanted to run, run, run. Run as fast as she could, never looking back. She had to get to Sophie.

A large gruff man got out of a very well-made carriage and mockingly bowed to her, a glimmer of mischief in his eyes. "Your carriage awaits, my lady." Gus dropped his smile. "Let's get you home."

Ella barreled into the carriage, rocking it back and forth.

"I have to get to Sophie." Her screams were trapped in Ella's mind.

"I have orders to bring you home."

"But—"

"We'll figure it out when we get there." He settled a hand on her shoulder.

Ella nodded, gripping the side of the carriage as she lifted one foot, followed by another. If she was deliberate in her movements, she could think, react, and process.

"I'm going to be sick," Ella said, her legs jumping up and down with unspent energy.

"Ella—" Gus twisted towards her as he drove the horses, pacing them at a normal trot.

"It all went so bad." Ella gripped her head in her hands, willing the Velocity to process through her. The sooner it was gone, the sooner she would feel comfortable in her skin and could figure out what had happened with Sophie.

"Focus on your surroundings. Let Riset help ground you. With Velocity, you have to focus on something other than running. If you don't, you'll fall into a manic spiral."

"Too late," Ella moaned, her stomach revolting again. She kept it down.

"Focus on the streets."

So she did. Ella leaned dejectedly against the carriage, looking out through the window. The streets were dark, the torches low. All the nobility and their households would be in bed. Only other unseemly people, such as herself, were out. Riset was peaceful, the dim lighting casting an ethereal glow over the streets. Ella fell into the feel of the cobbled roads that rumbled beneath her feet, making her legs bounce. The fog had rolled in and was kissing the ground, bringing the smell of fresh air and new life with it. Her favorite smell, the smell of wet stones coming to life, swirled around her.

She closed her eyes, focusing on the wind blowing through the redwoods, and the crickets slowly chirping around her, letting her mind jump to each fresh, beautiful, and disgusting scent. She did all of this instead of letting her body jump out of the carriage and run and run and run.

CHAPTER TWO

They rode up the dirt pathway to the dominating Aumont Hold, home to the Duchess of Aumont, Ella's stepmother. Ivy covered more than half of its yellowed four-story walls. To the outside world, it was Lady Tremaine's Finishing Academy for Young Women. To Ella it was her childhood home, and now, a place where assassins in service to the King of Rairene were trained.

Ella stumbled out of the carriage, her body moving faster than her mind could process.

"Steady yourself. Remember to focus." Gus gripped her shoulders, planting her on the ground.

"Right. Focus. Sophie." Ella rolled her shoulders and ran. She ran right up to the doors and inside.

She raced past the few who were still awake. She walked down the dark hall to where her stepmother commanded everything. Her office.

The first and only thing Ella noticed was the quiet.

She didn't pay attention to the empty dark room lined with bookshelves. Or the empty cushioned chairs and dying fireplace. All Ella noticed were her stepmother's four large mirrors against the far wall which were normally filled with images of current missions. Tonight, they were veiled with thick black drapes.

"Where's Sophie? I need to see her," Ella demanded. She had to focus. She had to get to her.

Lady Tremaine stood up from behind her black wooden desk and walked around it, with her head held high. Her blonde hair, streaked with gray, was coiffed on top of her head. Her green eyes, which usually held such fierce determination and confidence, were overwhelmed with sorrow. However, it was the disorderly skirts that gave her away. Her stepmother prided herself on perfection, and right now, she was anything but perfect.

"Ella, I'm so sorry—"

"No. She's alive. She was alive when I got out of that house." Ella paced the room, her laced-up boots leaving a trail of dirt in their wake.

"El—" Lady Tremaine walked over to Ella and lightly gripped her shoulders, keeping her still.

"What happened?" Ella balled her hands, staring into her stepmother's green eyes, choking back the tears welling in her throat. The Velocity rampaged through her, demanding movement, demanding action. Action she could not give.

"Sophie knew the risks of her assignment. Going after a mark always comes with a steep price," Lady Tremaine whispered, gently forcing Ella to sit down.

"She's not dead. She's good. I trained her myself. I would know if she wasn't ready. She knows how to handle herself." Ella spoke through gritted teeth, her shoulders slumping the longer she looked at Lady Tremaine.

"She was good. But tonight, someone was better. I'm so sorry, Ella."

"I need to see." Ella walked towards the door. "Where did it happen?"

"You don't need to go to the site. It's right there." Lady Tremaine pointed to one of the covered mirrors.

Ella ripped the drape off and stepped back.

A body lay on the floor of a luxurious room, the rugs below stained with her blood. Her red hair was strewn across her face. The death blow, a knife to the heart, was on full display for Ella. She tried to analyze the scene, memorize the blade, the handle, and the carpet, any detail that would help her find the person responsible for her friend's death. But the Velocity wouldn't let her focus long enough.

All she could see was her friend, not a scene to be reviewed. The girl she had trained for the last year, and known for the last three. She had been good. Sophie had been ready for assignments. She was always eager to help and prove herself. She knew what to do if something went wrong. And something had, and now...Ella gazed up at the mirror, sinking to the floor as it hit her.

Sophie was dead.

"We'll discuss it in the morning." Lady Tremaine sat beside Ella on the floor, wrapping her arms around her.

"I uh..." Ella paused, then shook her head. "I apologize. I don't know what's come over me. I'll head to the attic for the night." Ella shuddered. She had failed in her mission tonight. She had failed Sophie. That meant spending the night in the attic...in the dark...tied to the wooden table in the center. She would suffer that punishment, knowing it was rightly deserved.

"Not tonight. You've suffered enough."

"But...I failed. My mission was a failure, and my training capabilities were also a failure." Ella motioned to the mirror.

"You made an error. We will discuss how to proceed in the morning. For now, you're going to rest. The Velocity is about to wear off, and you're going to deal with those side effects soon enough."

"Would you like assistance back to your room?" A thick voice that wrapped itself around the room asked.

Ella jerked in Lady Tremaine's arms. Lucifer. Her stepmother's right-hand man. How he was of service to the crown in any manner Ella could never comprehend. But she also wasn't someone to question her stepmother.

"I can manage." Ella bolted to her feet, stumbling as fire raced up her side. There was no way she was letting Lucifer or his grimy hands touch her. She stumbled forward with momentum, her head spinning as blood rushed to it. She blinked, reaching out a hand to steady herself. It didn't matter that the world tilted as she walked. All that mattered was getting past Lucifer and up the stairs to her room.

"Let Lucifer help. You're clearly in pain and the Velocity is running out of you quickly." Lady Tremaine steadied Ella.

"Truly, I'm alright," she reassured her stepmother, as she tried to keep moving. If she stopped, she wouldn't be able to force her legs to move, and if she couldn't move, Lucifer would be there. Ella moved until she got to the door, resting on it for a second.

"At least let him escort you in case you fall into an enchanted sleep."

"I can take her mother." A velvet voice washed over Ella as the sound of a cane coming down on the hard wooden floor echoed through the room.

Ella slowly looked over at Drea, her stepsister, and retired assassin, Nightshade. She walked over and grasped Ella's arm, her cane lightly touching down with each step. Ella nodded her thanks as Drea supported her up the stairs and down the long, carpeted hallway to her room. She used to be the best of them. Better than her sister, Anastasia. Better than Ella and her closest friend Raven. Until she had made an error and paid dearly for it. The two of them didn't speak a word, focused as they were on achieving the task at hand while Lucifer waited in the shadows. Ella wouldn't have known where to begin, anyway. She and Drea seldom spoke to each other.

As Ella walked into her room, eucalyptus and lilac swirled around, her body relaxing. Drea went straight to the washroom, limping on her left leg.

Mira, an assassin known to the world as Siren, stood up in front of the enormous fireplace that sat opposite Ella's large bed. "I got a fire going as soon as I heard you were here. I'm so sorry about Sophie."

Her dark red hair and golden skin glowed in the light, her emerald eyes full of emotion as she helped Ella into a comfy blue cushioned high-back chair. It was part of a set of four in her room. They surrounded the fireplace, the wood burning brightly, leaving only a few small shadows. A wardrobe full of training clothes, enchanted clothes, and a vanity sat off to the left of Ella's bed, an assortment of wigs and cosmetics on display. Large windows overlooked a massive estate garden in the back. The plush, dark blue carpet beneath Ella's feet was especially welcome as she wiggled her toes in it. The light blue floral wallpaper was a perfect contrast in hues

Mira continued to fuss around her.

"Mira, clean the cuts on Ella's face and then put some of the healing serum on her." Drea sat down and peeled off Ella's clothes, wiping away the blood that had marked her.

"Drea—"

"Stop talking. You're going to make the cut on your face worse."

Ella reached up to feel it, only now realizing its burning presence.

"We know how much Mother hates us having scars on our faces." As if to emphasize her point, Drea pulled back her own thick curly brown hair into a leather strap, revealing her scar. A thick line of scarred red skin jaggedly cracked along her face from the left side of her forehead and down to her jaw. Though she was prone to argue the fact, Drea was ethereal despite it. Ella had never seen a portrait of Drea's father but knew she must closely resemble him. She barely looked like her mother, their only common feature being their discerning green eyes.

She didn't speak as Drea continued to examine more wounds on Ella's body. Images of her dagger slicing through those men assaulted Ella's mind. Her stomach rolled, and she had to hold back the vomit. Even though Ella had done plenty of horrible things, nothing had been as bad as tonight. She would never take another enchanted potion again, not even if her life depended on it. Mira was delicate, using a warm washcloth to rub the blood off of the single slice on her cheek.

"Before we put this revolting serum on you, do you think you're able to stand and rinse off?"

Ella looked at Drea, her brow furrowed.

"You look like our worst nightmares come to life from one of our books."

"You should see the other men," Ella choked out, their images rising with her stomach.

Ella willed herself to stand and take one step, and then another. By the time she had taken the fifteen steps to her washroom, her legs were shaking, her vision clouded. But she had made it. Ella looked in the large circular mirror, assessing the damage. She was a horror creature that came to life. She had come back from missions bruised and bloodied before, wearing her marks' blood, bruised from their struggles. Never her own. Her pale skin was tinged pink.

Her naked body was a testament to her triumphs and her pain. She rubbed the thick red scars that wrapped around her wrists, her constant reminder of what awaited her in the attic when she failed. Her back was an odyssey of her failures, filled with scars that even she couldn't force herself to examine, lest the phantom touch of a whip come back to lick her skin. Then there was the burn on her neck. The one she pretended didn't exist. Ella stepped into the bath, the heat burning her cuts. The soap only made it worse, its coarse exterior scraping off skin.

Her body convulsed, a shudder running through her as everything struck her at once. Ella punched the stone wall, a single soul-wracking sob escaping. Just one. That was all she allowed before taking back control. She scraped back at her composure and finished washing.

Ella walked out of her washroom, clean and wet, her black silk pajamas clinging to her. Mira and Drea spoke in hushed voices as she walked over to her bed, the Velocity clouding her eyes as it wore off.

"The two of you don't have to stay. I'm perfectly capable of taking care of myself." Ella fell forward onto her bed, her body shaking. Waves of ice rippled through her as Ella found herself unable to move.

"I'll put that serum on your cheek, and then you can fall asleep. It looks as though Velocity has finally run its course." Drea walked over, carrying a jar of orange goop that smelled worse than a dead animal.

"Will she force me to retire if the cut scars?" Ella whispered, her eyes wide. Drea applied the serum, her hands gentle.

Drea stepped back from her. Though Ella couldn't see her as Velocity pulled her under, she knew she was giving her a look. "There is so much more to life than being an assassin, Ella. Even one that serves the crown, there are other ways to do that."

Ella snorted, instantly regretting it. She looked up at the ceiling, embarrassment coloring her cheeks. Drea didn't kill anymore. She could barely get around.

"We're going to let you sleep." Mira kissed Ella's forehead as she squeezed her hand.

"Ella," Drea's voice softened as she moved towards the door. "I know we don't talk, but you went through a lot tonight. If you ever...need to talk...let me know." Ella nodded as Velocity finally left her and everything went black.

CHAPTER THREE

"Who was her mark?" Ella didn't wait to be invited into Lady Tremaine's office as the afternoon sun shined in. She walked in, dressed for war in her enchanted armor.

"Eleanor." Lady Tremaine sat behind her desk, Jaq in front. His posture was anything but relaxed. "I'm glad to see you're awake. How are you feeling?"

Ella ignored the question. "I need to know who her mark is. I'll finish it."

"Ella—"

An emergency enchantment flashed on the four mirrors. Three white flashes indicated it was a message sent out on all enchanted mirrors. They only ever did that if something had gone wrong. Lady Tremaine walked over and covered the mirrors, stopping the message from being heard.

"Last night was a hard night for everyone," she sighed, rolling back her shoulders and massaging her neck.

"What else happened?" Ella sat down next to Jaq.

"Part of Sophie's assignment was at the palace. Unfortunately, while she was away attempting her mission, the Prince was attacked."

"David was attacked?" Ella leaned forward, her hands fisted in her black training pants.

"He's alive," Jaq reassured her quietly.

"But injured. The palace hasn't said how badly. They caught the would-be-killer, and have dispensed with their body already."

"Do we know where they were from?" Ella asked, trying to put the pieces together.

"Holodal, they want to put a stop to the treaty being renewed in three weeks."

"Renewed?" Ella knew about the treaty. It had been established twenty years prior between the Kingdoms of Rairene and Trudel. Both kingdoms were wealthy. Their alliance all those years ago had helped to prevent a war. As Ella had been taught, it had been to keep the King of Trudel from invading Rairene and expanding his kingdom.

"Yes, renewed. It was agreed that upon the eighteenth birthday of the King's first-born child, the treaty would be renewed. The two kingdoms united permanently. The king of Trudel has always thirsted for this land, and unfortunately, a war between us would leave us open to Holodal as well. Both kingdoms have fierce climates that are not the most suitable for living a content life. Trudel is covered in snow for half the year, and Holodal bakes in the sun."

"I know. I remember my history," Ella grumbled, crossing her arms as she leaned back in the chair.

"Then remember this: if the treaty is broken, Trudel will invade immediately. They're power-hungry and have been building up their army for just such a moment. They do not easily forgive being reneged on. After the last treaty was established, I'm afraid no mistakes can be made this time."

"What happened last time?" Ella scoured her memory for any mention of a scandal in her history lessons. Nothing coming to mind.

"Nothing to worry about." Lady Tremaine turned away, looking at her black-draped mirrors. "We need to focus on figuring out who else in the palace is a risk and take them out."

"I'll go." Ella twisted her hands together. She hadn't been back at the palace since...since that disastrous night nine years prior. But she wouldn't...couldn't...focus on that night. It could have no bearing right now.

"Ella—"

"Send me in. I'll find them and protect David." Ella straightened her back. If she went in, she could also learn who had killed Sophie, and pay them back in kind.

Lady Tremaine steepled her fingers in front as she locked eyes with Ella. Her emerald eyes enchanted Ella, their intelligence and kindness pulling her in like a siren singing at sea. After a minute, she nodded stiffly, pressing her fingers to the bridge of her nose. Ella leaped up, ready to leave.

"Before you go prepare, there are some things you need to know."

Ella froze at the tone of her voice, the way it lashed around her like a whip, and held her in place.

"Okay." She sat down, her back tight. Ella spared a glance for Jaq, who had sat up straighter, adjusting his spectacles.

"First, you will not show up today—"

Ella opened her mouth to protest.

"Or tomorrow."

"But my mission with the earl indicated that information had been sold about David. He needs protection now—"

"Which he has. In the form of his guards." Lady Tremaine spoke slowly as she calmed Ella. "As you are aware, the crown employs us to eliminate its current threats while protecting the kingdom. As you are also aware, we are not acknowledged by the crown as an entity that exists. No one knows who we are or what we do. Therefore, when you go to the palace, it will not be in the crown's service as an additional protector."

"But, that's—"

"Let me finish," Lady Tremaine snapped. "You will protect from the shadows. To the kingdom, the crown, and especially to David, your role will be that of a returning nobleman's daughter after being away for the last nine years. You will watch over David without him, or anyone else knowing, until the outside threats are eliminated, and the person who killed Sophie is caught."

"Fine." Ella crossed her arms. "Where am I telling them I've been?"

"Exactly where they believe you've been."

Ella raised a brow. When Lady Tremaine had offered her a chance at her dream nine years ago, she had been told that she would have to turn her back on her friends. She could never return to the palace. She had happily agreed. They had turned on her, so she had no problem turning on them. And at eight, she hadn't bothered to ask if the palace would care about her disappearance, or even wonder where she had gone.

"How much do you remember about that night? When you had your big fight with Queen Charisse?"

"Everything," Ella whispered, staring a hole into the carpet. That night was not only her greatest triumph but her greatest shame. Ella shied away from the memory, refusing to relive it. It haunted her enough in her dreams.

"Then you remember where the queen wanted to send you." Lady Tremaine supplied, leaning back once more as she let Ella put the pieces together.

Ella twisted her lips, summoning the name of the kingdom that Queen Charisse had chosen for Ella to learn how to be a proper lady of the court. "The Kingdom of Evrotia."

Ella pondered the life she would have had if she'd chosen to go there instead of choosing to become a protector of the kingdom. Evrotia was a kingdom known for a court stuck in old traditions and a queen who had staged a coup and killed her husband. Her best friend Raven, known as Snow White, was there, reporting on the Evil Queen, as she liked to call her.

"Exactly. Per Queen Charisse's request, you were sent to Evrotia to become a lady of the Court, and now you've returned home." Lady Tremaine stood up and walked over to Ella. She knelt beside her. "It will be difficult. Much has changed, especially after...after the queen died."

While Queen Charisse had sent her away, Ella had loved her as a mother. Even though her mother died when she was three, Queen Charisse had stepped into the role. Her death two years ago had been too much for Ella to bear, and she had not dared to face it.

"I'll be fine." Ella squared her shoulders, standing up. "I'll spend the next two days getting a wardrobe and any other essential items prepared for my arrival home. I'm assuming that I'll have become so homesick that I'll request to stay at the palace as I adjust to life back in Rairene."

"You assume correctly. They will welcome you back with open arms, Ella."

Ella scoffed, "I highly doubt that since I never heard from them."

"There is one last piece of information you should know."

Ella turned to look at her stepmother, who stood closer to her, pleading with her eyes.

"The queen...she changed her mind about sending you to Evrotia the following day. You'd already agreed to leave them behind, and I...I was selfish. I wanted the bond you and Charisse shared, so I didn't tell you. I knew it was my chance to give you something you wanted that she could never supply. So I took it." Lady Tremaine grabbed Ella's hand.

Ella's heart hammered in her chest, near to imploding at the suggestion that Charisse had wanted her to stay...she took a breath and asked. "Would she have let me train as a knight in the palace?"

"No. She had remained resolute in that decision."

"Then you did the right thing." Ella pulled herself away and walked out the door, her mind a thunderstorm of thoughts and emotions. Ella grappled with each bolt of emotion that struck her and shoved them to the furthest recesses of her mind. She would not focus on the new, earth-breaking information she had just received. No, she would focus on the mission and make sure she had everything she would need before walking back into the one place she had thought she would never return.

"You can't go back there." Jaq followed her out of Lady Tremaine's room and down the hall to his mage's workshop. The scents of spiced magic and vanilla filled the air as Ella sat down on the large cushioned chair that had seen better days. Jaq headed to the wooden desk built between a wall of bookshelves stuffed with books and bottles filled with various enchantments. The rest of his room was immaculate, with a wall of enchanted mirrors across from Ella. Each one was filled with people milling about, going about their lives, unwittingly being watched. There were even some in the palace. Ella had tried to count all the mirrors one day but had lost track and grown bored by the time she reached seventy-five. How Jaq kept track, she had no idea.

"Lady Tremaine seemed to think it was plausible for me to return."

"What if..."

Ella raised an eyebrow at him. He turned away from her, muttering an incantation over an amulet. His hands lit up with wisps of silver starlight wrapping around the amulet. The casting got tighter around the amulet as its intention solidified. Jaq's power brightened until the enchantment was complete. Ella blinked against the light, clearing out the black spots in her eyes.

"What if they make you think you don't want to protect the kingdom anymore?" He asked, rubbing his hair and avoiding eye contact.

Ella straightened. "I'm going to try to not be offended that you think I'm so weak that I could change my mind so easily."

"I don't think you're weak. I know you loved them—"

"Loved. As in the past. Not anymore. I've just healed my heart from Luca. I don't need to go looking for someone else to break it." Ella reassured him. "Besides, I know I always have you around to remind me of who I am."

"I'll always be there for you," Jaq affirmed, handing over the amulet. "This will protect you."

The amulet was beautiful. A ruby framed in silver filigree that twisted and spiraled around down to a sharp point.

"I would love to take it with me, but I can't." Ella ignored Jaq's open mouth of protest. "I'm returning from Evrotia, a kingdom that has banned all use of enchantments and kills any enchanter they discover. I'm so sorry, I do love it. I'll grab it when I 'visit home for the first time'," Ella said when she saw his eyes dim.

"Sure." Jaq moved away from her, going to other enchanted items he had already imbued with his magic. Items that didn't seem to be enchanted, at least not at first. Once he had given her an assortment of her glass daggers, boots, and corsets, Ella left to get the rest of her cover together.

She bit her lip as she looked at her wardrobe minutes later. Since she had never gone back to court, she had never needed to keep a supply of court-worthy dresses. So she went to the one place she knew would have some, and wouldn't miss them, Raven's room. It was easy enough to pick the lock, not that any of them truly had any privacy living in a house of people who knew how to pick locks. Her best friend's room had been left untouched for the last five months. The bright room in hues of green was a contrast to her friend's dark personality. Everything was spotless and tidy, just like Raven, who prided herself on keeping everything in its place. Ella opened up the double wooden doors leading to Raven's closet. It was stuffed with gowns for any occasion, in any kingdom. After Drea's downfall two years ago, and Anastasia's inability to grow in skill, Raven had become Lady Tremaine's heir apparent. Ella held no ill will towards her friend. They were all there for the same thing; protecting the crown. Raven was superb at it. Ella went straight to the gowns styled in Evrotia's latest trends and grabbed enough to fill a trunk.

As she left, she glanced over at Raven's enchanter workstation. It still held an assortment of her most deadly enchanted poisons. Ella spied one that was completely black, with sparks of red spinning throughout the liquid. She shuddered and turned away, remembering how much pain had been funneled into that particular poison.

Ella.

She froze as Raven's smoky smooth voice swirled through the room. She turned towards a large mirror over Raven's desk, dropping the armload of dresses to the floor as her best friend looked down at her through the enchanted mirror.

Raven, what...how...you could be killed. Ella walked over to look closer at her friend. Raven's pitch-black hair was normally so well kept and chin length had grown to her shoulders, with the curls rebelling against Raven's attempts. She stood stiffly, her shoulders pulled back too far, her sea-blue eyes weary and full of shadows.

It's early enough, and I'm in my room. No one will know. But I don't have a lot of time. Lady Tremaine contacted me. I'm sorry about Sophie, she would have been good one day. Raven glanced around. *You need to know that Evrotia is a very different court from Rairene.*

I know. It's very traditional—

It's more than that. It's all about manipulation and survival. Everyone fears Queen Lyanna and will do anything to stay out of her way so that she doesn't kill them.

Raven, are you—

I'm fine. I'm strong. Raven smiled, though it could barely be considered one. *And that's my point. We need to convince the crown that you're not sunshine and rainbows.*

Now there's a sentence I never thought I would hear from you. Have I ever been sunshine and rainbows? Ella cocked a hip and analyzed her soul sister. It all made sense now. The disorderly hair, the weariness, all of it. She was exhausted, and she needed to come home.

Of course not. But you will need to present a strong front at first if you're going to pull off claiming that you lived here.

Ella nodded in agreement. *When are you coming home?*

Raven's eyes dimmed even more. Ella hadn't thought that was even remotely possible. *I don't know. Lady Tremaine won't tell me.*

Well, once this is done, I'm coming to you.

Raven nodded briefly. *Tell the others I say hi. I have to go. I've already been too long.*

Bones of my ancestors— Ella whispered.

Blood in my veins.

Raven's mirror returned to its normal reflection, showing Ella herself. The orange goop on her cheek had dried and turned chalky, indicating it was almost time to peel it off. Ella touched one of the other scars on her face. There were only two, neither one disfiguring her face. One was half the length of her finger, slashing just above her left eye. The other was smaller, past the length of a fingernail, resting at the edge of her hairline. Ella's fingers hovered over it. She had gotten it when she was five while playing with David and Henry. Ella shook her head, sending the memory away.

The last thing she had to do was run an errand to a bookshop that also dealt in dark market trades. Then she would be all set for her biggest mission yet, protect David, and kill the person responsible for Sophie's death.

CHAPTER FOUR

Ella gazed at herself, her fingers tapping a slow rhythm against her side as she looked into the full-length mirror two days later. She could do this. She would be so radiant that they wouldn't know what hit them. Ella took a breath and shook out her hands. Raven's dress fit perfectly. The dark green bodice hugged her tight, the corset plated on the outside to represent decorative armor. Somehow, it was the current fashion in the Court of Evrotia. The sleeves wrapped around her wrists with black embroidery on the edges of the off-the-shoulder neckline. Ella rubbed her wrists, thankful for the long sleeves. At least the scars from the shackles in the attic would be covered. The dark green fabric swirled around her as she swished her hips from side to side. Ella's eyes narrowed at her hips, and then her arms, observing their width. She wasn't mopstick thin like other girls at court. Never had been. But her training at least had honed her arms and legs.

Ella rolled the serum off her face with a wooden dowel, examining the faint mark on her cheek. It was almost invisible.

"Shine bright," Ella whispered Queen Charisse's words to herself, looking into her eyes. "You were born for this," Ella added before smiling one last time at herself.

Gus drove Ella up to the palace. It was the middle of the day, which meant that whoever was at court would eat their midday meal on the terrace overlooking the royal gardens. At least, that was how it had been when Ella had been part of the crown's family.

As they rode up to the palace, Ella noted that almost nothing had changed in the nine years since. The palace's faded yellow stone walls had always loomed before her. The imposing five stories had smoothed with time, ivy laying claim to sections. The gardens leading up to the palace were as impeccable as always, their roses and irises coming up to bloom in the early spring. It was the smell of the gardens that struck Ella, flashing memories of running through the garden into her mind.

Ella paused at the foot of the carriage, waiting for the memories to fade. Ice crawled up her veins, giving her strength. She squared her shoulders and began the steep climb up the palace steps. Each new smell was another memory she had tucked away, each one forcing her to fight with herself, to rein in her emotions. Ella let the cold beneath her skin thicken in the attempt.

Cinnamon and vanilla washed over her from the kitchens, and suddenly, she was throwing flour at Henry and David before getting covered in it herself, laughing as the kitchen staff shooed them out. Ella shook her head.

Roses encircled her, just like the warm embrace of Queen Charisse.

What she wouldn't have given for a hug from her.

Ella took a breath, looking down at her feet, her wavy hair obscuring her face. She was thankful, it let her compose herself once more. Ella forced herself to stay focused on putting one foot in front of the other.

Warm wood from the blacksmith's forge outside stroked her memories. Ella stumbled on the last step as the image of sitting on the king's lap, reading her a story tunneled into her mind.

Ella squeezed her eyes tight.

She had gotten to become what she had always dreamed of a protector. But...none of that mattered. All that mattered was finding Sophie's killer and protecting David. No matter the costs.

Nerves bounced through her as she approached the court. She could picture it. King Matthias would be in the center with David and Princess Celeste. Henry would be beside them, if not at a table nearby. All other members of the court would preen for attention from the royal family. Ella stared at the two doors. They were made of thick glass with elegant gold twirling around them in intricate designs.

All she had to do was walk through the door.

Just walk through the door, Ella thought.

She rested her hand on the cold handle, her heart pounding a rapid beat in her fingertips. Just turn the damn handle, Ella, she scolded herself.

The handle turned before she could touch it, and the door swung open to a startled maid. Show time. This was what she had prepared for. Raven's opinion of the court in Evrotia had helped her understand exactly what she needed to do.

Ella squared her shoulders and turned to the footman, whispering her name to him. He nodded as he closed his mouth before announcing her.

"Lady Eleanor of House Aumont, Majesty." He took Ella's hand and led her into the room.

Where there had been chatter before, Ella found silence. Several young ladies sat to the side, all of them frozen as they gazed at her. One of them even held a cup of tea halfway to her mouth. Ella let the smallest smirk escape before composing herself.

The terrace was extensive, expanding behind the second floor of the palace, where it overlooked the massive royal gardens. She walked slowly and with the grace expected of someone of her status. A lady of the court, indeed. Ella scoffed internally. This was really whom they wanted? She shuddered internally.

King Matthias was at a long wooden table closer to the edge of the terrace, where Queen Charisse had loved to watch everything. Ella smiled, curtseying low to him. Lower than was necessary, but it had been nine years.

"King Matthias." Ella had to wait to be invited to join. She was interrupting, after all. It was good manners, even in Evrotia. Her heart hammered so loud, she was sure everyone could hear its betrayal. For the first time, fear trickled through her mind. What if he didn't invite her? The thought had never crossed her mind until this moment. She remained in a curtsey, not daring to move as the king remained silent.

"My dear daughter." A calloused hand gently lifted her chin to raise her out of the curtsey. "You need never curtsey to me."

Ella looked up into the light blue eyes of King Matthias and found that she had forgotten how much kindness they held. Before she could respond, he hugged her, the smell of warm wood enveloping her once again.

"Welcome home. Now you must tell us about your journey over a wonderful lunch." King Matthias said, guiding Ella to the table and pulling out a chair for her.

"It's lovely to be back." Ella remained standing, looking around. "Where's David?"

King Matthias's face fell. David hadn't died. Ella knew that, yet looking at the king, you would think he had.

"David was attacked recently—"

"Attacked?" Ella kept her voice low, portraying a perfectly surprised lady.

"He survived. He's recovering, but alive. That's why he's not here."

"Hello, Ella, you probably don't—"

"Hello, Pumpkin," Ella squeezed Princess Celeste's hand as she took in the young girl before her. She had grown so much. Her brown hair cascaded around her, framing her light brown eyes filled with innocence.

Celeste hugged her. "We've missed you," she whispered. All of them sat, the niceties completed, and resumed their meal as a maid brought out Ella's plate. Everyone else resumed eating as well now that the show was over.

"What's the court of Evrotia like?" Celeste leaned forward, her eyes dancing.

"Cruel."

Celeste's face paled as the king coughed, pressing a napkin to his mouth.

"I'm kidding," Ella smiled. "It served its purpose."

"It must have been amazing to have gotten to see the world," Celeste sighed, leaning back in her chair, her eyes closed.

King Matthias tensed beside Ella, "Celeste—"

"Ella."

She had thought the room was silent before. But nothing compared to the silence that fell next. Not even an assassin could move about unheard. She looked up at the person who'd said her name, freezing as her eyes locked onto golden brown eyes that, no matter what time of day it was, seemed to shine with light. Except now. They were dim, and the wound on his face was part of the reason. Prince David stood before her, wearing disheveled pants and a tunic that was wrinkled from sleep. Yet, there he stood. Tall and uncertain as he continued to stare.

"Prince David, you should be—"

The man who walked up behind him stopped as well. She was frozen. Just like them, unable to figure out how to move. These had been her closest friends for the first eight years of her life. And then they had forgotten her. Her heart didn't know what to do, sing or scream. But she couldn't do either because the entire court was watching them.

"It's true...you're home...." David found his feet, stepping slowly.

Ella realized a second later that he didn't move slowly of his own volition, but that it was simply as fast as he could go after the injuries he had sustained. As an enchanter, David could not take any enchanted potion to help with the healing or the pain, lest it poison his magic. She got up and walked over briskly, ensuring he didn't tire himself.

"It's true. Surprise." She laughed, her hands hovering at her sides, lest she touch a wound.

"When? Why didn't you write?" David's eyes pulled her into a hug, and she felt herself unable to think of a single word.

"Oh, you know me, always looking to make my grand entrance. I thought a surprise after nine years would be more fun." Ella smiled shakily, glancing between David and Henry.

"Welcome home, Eleanor." Anastasia, Ella's step-sister glided over, smirking as she pointedly glanced between David and Ella.

"Thank you, Lady Anastasia," Ella responded in Evrotian, hoping to hide the disdain in her voice behind the harder accents of the language.

"I hope you enjoy this court now that you're home as a proper lady. I think you'll find it to differ greatly from the type of court you're used to," Anastasia replied in Evrotian, her accent thick and sloppy. She had never been one to excel at the languages they'd been taught growing up.

Ella straightened. She was certain Henry and David at least knew what Anastasia was saying.

"I think you'll find that the courts of Evrotia prepare a lady for anything. At the very least, I learned the proper way to address another member of the court, Lady Anastasia," Ella spoke without a single stutter in her voice. It was a good thing she was fluent in it and two other languages.

"Come on now, Anastasia, surely you missed your sister after all of these years?" David reasoned as he angled his body between them.

Anastasia scoffed. She would thrive in Evrotia, Ella noted.

"Not really. It feels as though it were only yesterday that I saw her." She sighed as she walked away, joining a group of other young ladies.

"Don't listen to her. She's always had it out for you." David whispered. "Now—"

Ella glanced back at him in time to see the wince of pain as he held his chest. Henry was there in an instant, using his body to shield the prince from observant eyes.

It wasn't until then that Ella realized how much Henry had grown. He was broad-chested and had the body of a warrior who had trained his entire life. His red hair still burned like fire in the night, while his green eyes held a level of severity that she hadn't expected to find as he looked at David.

"Let's get you to your room. That's enough excitement for one day." Ella straightened her skirts and guided David out of the room with Henry.

None of them said a word as they walked. David breathed heavily, his steps slowing. Eventually, Henry supported him the rest of the way to his room. Ella stayed outside. A proper lady wouldn't go into another man's room, even if he had been a childhood friend.

Henry closed David's door, his dark green eyes constantly assessing her. He didn't look at her like a friend, but a threat to be analyzed.

"So, are you back permanently, or is there a suitor waiting for you back in Evrotia?" He escorted her outside towards the royal gardens.

Ella stumbled at the suitor's idea. "No, no suitors...and I hope I'm back permanently. I did as the queen and king desired." Ella attempted a half smile. Henry had changed. His carefree spirit was completely gone. "Aren't you happy to see me? The last time..." Ella didn't want to think about the last time she had seen any of the people she had once considered family. "I hope you—"

"I am...you just seem different."

"Well, I think all of us have changed. Evrotia is...cruel. It makes you do horrible things, and treat people who are nice and honorable with contempt. It molds you into the very thing you never want to be, just to survive."

"I think you'll find that this court has changed little. You should be able to adjust quickly."

"Being here...being home...already in just one day...I want to be me, whoever that is now." Ella walked through the gardens with Henry, her hands behind her dress. She felt the weight of her dagger pressing into her back should she need it.

"I hope you do," Henry replied.

Ella watched him think, his eyes shifting as he pieced together her story. She needed them to come together for him. Needed him to believe she had been in a place so horrible, that it had changed much of who she used to be. She had changed, after all, all of them had. She needed them to believe it was from being in Evrotia, not from training. Henry must have seen enough in her, enough of the truth to take it and move on.

They walked back to the palace, and Ella found she remembered every route there was within its stone walls. She knew that if she turned down the hallway to their right, went down the stairs, and made a hard left, she would be in the kitchen. She could go down there and get something sweet for herself, as the smell of sweet bread wafted up to her nose. Then it was gone, replaced with the smell of soap and water as maids cleaned every inch of the palace.

"Getting ready for something?" she questioned.

"As if you didn't know, surely it's why you've returned home?" Henry sidestepped the question.

"I completed my training. That's why I've returned home. I thought I would put my royally requested skills to the test in a new court. You can only withstand so much death and dictatorship in a court for so long, Henry." Ella tilted her head to look at him, his face confused. "You didn't know that Queen Lyanna rips the hearts out of those in her court that displease her?"

Henry blanched.

"I'm sorry that you had to experience that. It must have been hard to avoid angering her," Henry whispered.

Ella chuckled. Raven had been very clear about how to stay on the queen's good side. "Not too much. All I had to do was agree with every single thing she said. It was the other members of her court that you had to watch."

"That sounds like a lonely place to be," Henry said as they neared the royal wing again.

"Yes...it was."

"I'm glad you're back, and that you survived in Evrotia." Henry motioned to the medal on his chest, the champion's mark. He was David's champion, his second in command. He could do anything to protect him, and no one would question it. Henry leaned forward and whispered to her in a language she had hoped no one else would have understood. "If you wish to survive in this court, you will learn to adjust to how we operate. Which is not through threats or complaining." His Evrotian was almost as perfect as hers.

"Henry—"

"You should know better than to be baited by her." His message was simple. If she imagined that cruelty would win her any favors here, any sign of preference, she was wrong, and she would be gone.

Ella and Henry walked back to court. The midday meal would be over, which meant King Matthias would hold court for anyone who wished to bring a grievance to his attention. All she wanted to do was go wandering around to locate Sophie's room and figure out where she had died. She just needed to find the right person to manipulate into telling her all about it. The throne room was, as Ella remembered it, grand and filled with members of the court. The cathedral ceiling still left her in awe of its architects, the stone window frames letting in a welcome breeze on the warm spring day. Ella had always loved this room, especially the way the sunlight poured in through the windows, a place where no shadows could hide. The smell of eucalyptus and roses floated around everyone as King Matthias dealt out fair punishment and listened to inquiries. The entire court was enraptured by him. But all she could see was the man who used to read her stories at night while curled up on the queen's lap. The man who had thought she had left, and had done nothing to bring her home.

Ella inched closer to Henry and whispered, "How's he truly doing?"

"Who?"

"David...it must have been quite a shock." Ella kept her gaze facing forward, trying to not be too obvious about her information digging.

"He's recovering. Ever since the queen...he's a very different David. These last few weeks he had been more like himself and then that assassin...I'm worried he'll go back to hiding in his room again."

"What do you mean? David would never hide in his—"

"I told you, we all changed. Especially him. He hasn't been to the midday meal with all the court in two years."

"Well, that doesn't—" Ella stopped talking when King Matthias rose.

Court was over, and he was walking straight towards her. Ella curtsied low, Henry standing tall beside her.

"My dear, please, you don't have to curtsy to me." King Matthias gently raised her.

"Habits." Ella smiled. It would have been demanded in any other court.

"Ella, do you mind joining this old man for a walk?" The King held out his arm to her. Ella fixated on the way his eyes waited for her to say no, to turn down the king. She noted the fear there, the rejection, and her heart ached while her spirit smiled. At least he was concerned about what their choices had done.

"Of course." Ella smiled at him, her heart unable to break him today.

He gently wrapped her arm around his before leading her out of the room. Ella couldn't help but look up at him, the touch of his hand on hers bringing her more comfort than she wanted. The need to tell him she had done what she had always dreamed of, and was serving the crown tugged at her, while at the same time, she shrank inside, wondering what his reaction would be if he knew.

"My Evrotian is a little rusty. Do you mind speaking in Rairenian? I know it's been years for you—"

"Of course," Ella reassured him, his shoulders relaxing at her words. It was a kind gesture she wouldn't have expected from a king, especially not the Queen of Evrotia based on Raven's report.

"I am truly thrilled to have you back. I know the boys have missed you. Celeste is looking forward to getting to know you. She was so young when you left for your education," he added.

Ella held her tongue. No complaining. They were walking back towards the royal wing. It was different walking down the hall with the king than with Henry. Henry had been brisk and direct, while King Matthias was slow, taking his time as they walked. It gave her the chance to gaze at the portraits and paintings on the wall. She averted her gaze from one of Queen Charisse. Not yet. She couldn't face that...not yet.

They stopped at a door further down the hall, past Henry and David, past Celeste, but it was a door she had known well as a child.

It was her door.

King Matthias paused at the threshold, his arm tense beneath hers. Ella couldn't do it. She couldn't go in. As the door opened, so did the memories of her very last night in the palace. The smells of her room, lavender and vanilla hit her, and she was transported to being eight years old again, playing in the room before her. The same bed was opposite the door, a trunk full of toys at its base. A small vanity and towering wardrobe were near the washroom on the right. To the left was a nook window with the perfect spot to sit and read a book. As Ella's eyes wandered, she saw her eight-year-old self throw a toy across the room, tears running down her face.

"I hate you!" she yelled. She had yelled it so loud, she was certain the windows would shatter. But they hadn't.

"Ella?"

She shook herself free of the memory as she stepped away from the threshold.

"Sorry, did you ask me something?" She turned sideways to face him, ignoring the room.

"I asked the maids to come here after you left with Henry and David. They've been cleaning it out, and of course, we'll get a new bed in here..." King Matthias looked around the hall. "If you wanted to stay here, of course. You are under no obligation to do so. I understand you may wish to reacquaint yourself with your sisters." His hands twisted in front of him as he spoke less and less like a king.

"I would like to stay here for a bit. I may go back home to Aumont at some point, but right now...I've missed my true home."

All tension left the king as his brown eyes glistened with joy.

"But...can I stay in a different room? That one maybe?" Ella pointed to a random room, one she knew was most likely unoccupied.

King Matthias winced, his shoulders straightening. "We will find you another room. Just not that one. No one is allowed in there."

"Oh?" Ella raised her eyebrows. She certainly hadn't expected that response.

"Someone died in that room recently. There's an investigation happening, and that room is to remain undisturbed."

Well, at least now she knew where Sophie had been killed. Why so close to the prince? What had she been doing? Ella nodded to the king. They wandered around the palace, watching the staff move about their day, content in the silence.

"Ella, I'm so glad you returned safely home." Lady Tremaine walked over to them as they rounded a corner at the entrance to the palace.

"I take it you knew she was arriving home after all these years?" King Matthias barely tensed under Ella's arm, but it was enough for her to notice.

"I did. She begged me to keep it a surprise. I hope you don't mind."

King Matthias made a noncommittal noise as the three of them walked towards the steps Ella had ascended to gain access to the palace just a few hours ago. Had she only been back for a few hours? It felt like days, and it felt like home.

"Ella has agreed to stay with us in the palace for a little while unless you oppose?"

"Of course not. She always mentioned in her letters how much she missed everyone. And she's returned just in time for the ball." Lady Tremaine was downright gleeful.

Ella had to keep herself from looking at her stepmother. She never displayed so much emotion at home.

"Though I have one request. I'm very glad Ella has been welcomed back to Rairene. I do hope you'll understand my need for caution regarding her safety. Her father loved her so much, and with the recent...attempt on the prince's life—"

King Matthias's arm twitched.

"I hope you won't be offended if I insist on assigning Ella a personal guard until everything is settled."

"Need I remind you that the would-be-killer was dealt with?"

"But the problem with Holodal hasn't been—"

"There's no concrete proof it was them. To suggest otherwise would instigate a war we do not need nor desire. However, I will allow Ella to have a personal guard until everything is resolved. Did you have someone in mind?"

Ella fumed. Lady Tremaine was going to give her guard? She was fine on her own, and a guard would only make her job harder. Ella was sure she had her reasons—

Luca walked out from around the corner. He probably had an enchanted earring in place, so he'd know when it was okay to reveal himself. Ella was glad King Matthias was unable to see her jaw drop. Luca was the epitome of beauty, as though the gods had carved him themselves. His golden skin was flawless, and his shoulder-length black hair was pulled back with a couple of braids showing off his dark emerald eyes. Though none of those reasons were why Ella's jaw had dropped.

Her ex was away on an assignment last she knew and wasn't meant to be back for at least another two weeks.

Luca walked over wearing the uniform of her father's house. It was entirely black, with her father's house emblem emblazoned on the left breast, a silver stallion rearing on a battlefield. He was pure excellence, and every woman Ella had ever seen look his way knew it. Luca left women swooning with his smile. It lit up his face into an undeniable charm, despite being almost nineteen. His true defining feature, though, was the crescent scar that cut across his left eye. She decided that this was a partnership she wouldn't mind in the slightest. Their relationship had ended on good terms.

"Your majesty, I'm sure you recognize my personal guard, Luca. I've decided to have him shadow Ella—"

"You mention the threat from Holodal and in the same breath bring in a Holodonian to guard a ward of my palace?" King Matthias's face reddened as he balled his hands.

"I didn't think his heritage would be a matter of concern. Luca has no ties to that kingdom. He hasn't been there for over four years, not since entering my employ. Surely you don't discriminate against him because of his race?" Lady Tremaine gently challenged.

"Of course not." King Matthias pinched the bridge of his nose. "He may stay."

Lady Tremaine let the briefest of smiles flit across her face. "Wonderful. Ella, try to not lose Luca. I know you and David used to do that as children, torturing your poor guards. Hopefully, Evrotia worked that out of your system."

Ella grinned. "He'll just have to keep up."

King Matthias quickly covered his smile with a hand.

"Ella, if you don't mind coming home this evening? You could pick up some things and then come back tonight with Luca."

Ella nodded as King Matthias looked ready to protest. "I'll be back before anyone notices I went missing." She hugged him quickly and followed Lady Tremaine and Luca out of the palace. She had to wait until they were in the carriage to hug Luca. His spiced cinnamon scent washed over her, creating a safety net around her instantly.

"I leave for four months and come back early to find out you've entered the lion's den without a partner?" he whispered. His deep voice brought her to life as she leaned into him.

"I'm glad you're home. Why are you home?"

Luca stiffened beside her. Ella opened her eyes to look up at him before looking at Lady Tremaine.

"I requested he come home—"

"I could have handled myself. There was no reason to pull him away." Ella snapped, "I'm sorry," she said, running her hands through her braided hair.

Lady Tremaine didn't acknowledge the outburst. "I just lost...we just lost Sophie. I know you're experienced, Ella, but I wanted to make sure I didn't lose you."

CHAPTER FIVE

Ella ran through an endless black hall. The earl's men caught her, strapped her down, and dragged her heated daggers over her skin. Enchanted poison was forced through her lips, the hallucinations instantaneous. The attackers multiplied, each one inflicting a different pain. Ella screamed for help, for someone to hear her. She wanted to get away before she lost control. Before she killed all of them. Why couldn't she break free? Ella tried to pull her arms free, but the ropes only tightened as poisons rolled through her. Her worst nightmare was coming true, and she wouldn't be able to control her actions once they took full effect. Ella's heart raced with the anticipation of what would happen, fear sliding down with the sweat on her back. What she was sure was only seconds felt like hours as she broke free. Ella got her daggers in hand. And all control was lost. Again. She couldn't keep herself from killing all of them. Sophie's screams echoed in her head.

Ella dragged herself from the nightmare.

She made it to the bathroom right before she lost the contents of her stomach. She crashed to her knees, her legs liquid beneath her. Sweat coated her body.

"Ella?" Drea's voice floated through her room.

She couldn't respond as her stomach heaved again. A foot dragged over the carpet. Hands gently grabbed Ella's hair, pulling it back as more came up. Sticky sweat and the bitter cold of emptiness shook her body as she leaned away from the toilet, trying to breathe through her ravaged throat. Drea filled a glass with water and handed it over. Ella's fingers shook as she gargled half and spat it out. The rest burned as it slid down.

"Thank you." Ella handed the glass back as her hands continued to shake.

"Aren't you supposed to be at the palace?" Drea sat on the lip of Ella's tub, resting her head on her cane.

"Time got away from us last night. We informed the palace I was catching up with you and would arrive in the morning. Why are you up?" Ella asked.

"I'm always up this early. It's peaceful." Drea clasped her hands together. "Ella, are you alright?"

Ella stared at the scratched-up wooden washroom floor. She must look quite the mess if Drea was concerned.

"Do you remember that time when we were kids and you and Anastasia were arguing—"

"Was there a time we didn't argue?" Ella groaned. She leaned her head back until it rested against the wall.

"Touché. Well, this time, Ana argued with you outside. It had just rained, and you refused to come in and help with the chores. She was so mad." Drea sat up taller. "I'll never forget the look on her face when you pushed her into a giant puddle of mud."

Ella laughed at the memory.

"Those were simpler times," Drea murmured. "I knew right then that I liked you. That I wanted us to be friends."

"I didn't know that." Ella looked up at the girl who sat before her, broken yet stronger with the cracks. "Drea...do you...dream about it? That night..." Ella lowered her eyes to the wooden slats below her. She didn't have to say anything else. Drea would know which night she meant. The one where she almost died and obtained her scars.

"At first...I dreamed about it nightly. Sometimes more than once. I always dreamed about being kidnapped, waking up in a different location, fighting both men...even now...two years later...I still dream about it." Drea touched her cheek, her fingers running along the scar. "I was the best Ella. Mother was proud, and a lapse in judgment...all to protect someone...it cost me everything." Her hand fell limply at her side, her large green eyes fixated on the ceiling.

"What did you do to help with the dreams?" Ella mumbled.

"I got myself so exhausted that I didn't dream at all—"

"You stayed away from potions, right?"

"Of course. I'm an enchanter Ella, I can't risk the addiction. Not even to make myself sleep." Drea put her hands behind her head, where her eight-pointed star mark identifying her as an enchanter would be. Just like Jaq, she had not received a formal education from the Enchanter's Academy. Ella wondered if Drea ever wished she could have spent those four years there instead.

"Any other advice?"

"Keep your head down, as much as you can in court. From what I remember, it's quite the place to navigate, and you've been out of practice for nine years."

Ella clenched her jaw, thinking about how she had already misstepped.

"I can't fail, Drea. I won't let Sophie or Lady Tremaine down."

"Be your charming self, and you'll be fine. You won't fail. You've always found a way." Drea stood up and walked past her. "I have to go. I get to train some novices on how to properly eat at a table. You should get some sleep."

Ella nodded. She bent her knees and rested her hands on them, relaxing on the wooden floor. Her body shook less, and she could drink more water. Eventually, she got up on shaky feet and filled the bath, letting steam fill the room. She stripped out of her nightgown and climbed in, hoping her legs wouldn't give out.

Ella walked up to Jaq's mage room an hour later to find his door closed, indicating he was in the middle of an enchantment. Shrugging, Ella opened it. He didn't hear her as she entered, too lost in his enchantments to notice anything but the daggers in his hands. He stood tall and confident, his hands glowing, his power wrapping and writhing around the blades.

Jaq was a highly—specialized enchanter, one of the best, and he was her partner. His object enchantments were stronger than most others could ever produce. His mark was one of the darkest she'd ever seen. She had seen it once, tracing its lines in fascination. The edges looked like scarred skin, though when she'd touched it, there was no lift in the skin, nothing to show that something was there.

"Corpus in aera incidi." Jaq repeated the phrase five more times, the blades brightening with each enchantment. He had tried to explain enchanting to Ella once. All the phrases he had to learn boggled her mind. What made it worse was the concentration they had to maintain, depending on the enchantment, and how strong they wanted it to be. Given that he was working on daggers, Jaq had to form an intention of harm and incredible strength. Most enchanters could only enchant two to five objects over several hours. Jaq, however, could enchant ten or more in two hours.

Ella sat down and watched, mouth open. His brown hair stuck up at all angles, his normally smooth tunic was wrinkled, and his glasses smudged. After a couple of minutes, his hands dimmed, and he set the daggers down. He slumped into his chair.

He fell back in the chair when he saw Ella.

She laughed as she helped him back up. "Sorry, I didn't think I would scare you."

"Uh-huh, you know I frighten easily." Jaq towered over her. "What brings you here?"

"I can't stop by and see you?" Ella peered at the mirrors.

"Don't you need to be at court?" Jaq scrunched his face.

"I do, but I missed you." Ella leaned forward. "How many more en-chantments do you have to do?" She eyed all the pendants and potion bottles on his desk. Most of them held a clear liquid that would change color depending on the potion Jaq created.

"Too many. Are there any you need?"

"I'm good," Ella replied, leaning back.

"I'm sorry that you have to live at the palace—"

"It's fine."

Luca walked in as he knocked on the door, dressed in his finest uniform. "Ella, we should go."

Ella kissed Jaq's cheek lightly. "Could I have a set of earrings so that we can stay in communication?"

Jaq handed them over. Ella put one in her ear and handed the other over to Luca.

"For me? You flatter me," Luca smiled, making sure the earring was hidden behind his hair.

"Of course. I have to keep tabs on you. Make sure the maids stay away," Ella joked, blushing at his smile. In all of their years as friends, he had always been a charmer. He could charm anyone into anything, even Ella. However, after some big fights, they decided it was better to leave his flirting with everyone but Ella.

They rode next to each other in the carriage as Luca guided it. The people of Riset were already awake and thriving as they passed through the circles. Ella wondered what would be in store for her in the court today, and if she could navigate it.

Ella walked into the dining hall to find that most spots were taken. No one offered her a spot, not that she had expected them to. She was new, and everyone wanted to wait and see what she was like before inviting her in. She had succeeded in selling the idea that she had spent time in a court vastly different from this one. Ella walked to the buffet piled high with breakfast, her head held high. It was too late to pretend she could behave otherwise. Luca was by the door, watching everything unfold. She noticed he stood taller under everyone's gaze, especially the young women who tried to divert his attention with their fake smiles.

The smell of freshly baked bread and pastries swirled around her as she looked at everything before her. Lady Tremaine had kept all of them on a strict diet for years, and Ella hadn't had fresh bread in Gods knows how long. She grabbed three small loaves, planning to hide one in her dress for later. Ella grabbed some pastries, smiling as she imagined the taste of the almond paste that would melt in her mouth. With a full plate, Ella turned and found the one person who would let her join their table.

"Can I join you?" Ella whispered to Celeste as the dining hall buzzed around them.

"Of course! I was hoping you would join me." Celeste smiled as she moved over to give Ella more room. Her plate was almost empty, indicating she would probably have to leave for something in court soon.

"Did you have anything fun planned for today?" Ella asked, looking at Celeste.

"Just some royal duties..."

"Could you miss them today? I've been dying to go shopping ever since I returned home. I need some dresses in Rairenian fashion. No more of this armored clothing." Ella glanced at her gown. She loved it. The way the metal of the bodice curled around her waist and supported her chest. She felt ready for battle. But that wouldn't do in this court, not if Henry's warning yesterday was any sign. What better way to bond with Celeste and get more information out of her than to go shopping?

"I will always miss royal duties for a shopping trip." Celeste beamed.

Ella finished her meal quickly, ignoring the sideways glances at not eating slowly and delicately. She barely avoided giving an eye roll. The two of them left arm in arm, Luca walking close behind. Ella felt Celeste briefly tense beneath her once the princess noticed Luca. Ella's head snapped to look at her, wondering if she would also hold a grudge against Luca for his heritage. Nope, that was a blush creeping up the princess's cheeks.

Luca drove them to the second circle of Riset, where Celeste's favorite dress shop was located. The shop was busy with a flurry of women and daughters. Dresses lined the walls, while pedestals and mirrors stood in designated areas for each group of women. The shop's owner, a formidable woman with a hooked nose and spectacles that highlighted her blue eyes, gazed at them, one eyebrow arched high. Her stern features shifted to kindness when she noticed Celeste in the center. The shop owner strode over to them, her dress swirling around her.

"Princess Celeste, we weren't expecting you today."

"I know. I'm sorry for not giving you a warning. It was rather last minute, my friend—"

"Lyra?" The woman's mouth dropped when she looked at Ella. "Sorry, I know you're not Lyra, you...you look just like her." The shop owner paled as she took in Ella.

"Lyra was my mother."

"Oh, you must be Eleanor. She spoke of you every time she came here. Come, let's get you two settled in our best suite." The shop owner didn't look at Ella again.

Ella took a steadying breath as she watched the shop owner bustle around. The woman had known her mom. She had known her mom well enough that she knew about her personal life. Which was almost more than Ella could boast. Her heart longed to ask questions, to dig deeper and find out more about her mother. But she couldn't. Not while she was on assignment.

As they walked through the shop, Ella couldn't help but notice the stares. Why was everyone interested in her return? Was life truly so dull that only someone new could bring entertainment?

The shop owner sat them down near the back, in a private suite where two seamstresses were waiting. Celeste lost herself in the dress shop as she scoured for items to try on. Ella hesitated before all of them. Where Evrotian fashion showed strength and confidence, Rairenian fashion was all about grace and beauty. Most of the necklines were off the shoulder, which Ella didn't mind. She could never cover up that burn on her collarbone, anyway.

Nor did she mind the corset bodices or flowing skirts.

Ella scrunched her lips as she gazed at a beautiful gown of the deepest green with black embroidery. Her hands fidgeted with the sleeves of the gown she wore, pulling on them. A hand gently wrapped around her fingers, covering her wrist even more. Ella kept herself from turning towards Luca. He knew all about the visible and invisible scars she had, the ones that needed to stay hidden. Luca gave her a gentle squeeze before releasing his hold on her.

"It would be perfect for the ball," he whispered, making sure no one heard.

"Is something wrong with it?" Celeste stood on her other side, looking between the dress, Ella, and Luca.

"No, it's beautiful...I just...I was hoping there would be some dresses with sleeves?" Ella looked around the shop again, her hopes slightly rising.

"We can always add sleeves to any gown. Or we can provide gloves," one seamstress said. "Would you like to try this one on?"

The intricate black and silver embroidery called to Ella, its satin fabrics welcoming her in. The sleeves were capped and could settle delicately around her shoulders. It would be a shame to change it for her.

"Try it on, Ella, I insist, and I'm the princess, so you can't say no." Celeste smiled, motioning for the seamstress to take the gown with her.

Ella and Celeste turned to go back to their suite filled with gowns. They found several young women surrounding them. Luca was beside them in an instant. All the girls were in some stage of curiosity. They were either wide-eyed or judgemental. Ella positioned herself in front of Celeste. None of them were going to attack, right? They wouldn't—

"Are you going to marry the prince?" One girl, who could barely stay still, burst out before clapping her hand over her mouth.

"I'm sorry?" Ella glanced between all of them. Celeste's shoulders shook beside her as she, too, covered her mouth. Luca, Ella noticed, raised a fisted hand to his mouth to clear his throat.

"That's why you're back, right? You're going to marry Prince David?"

Several other women turned to listen to the conversation.

Ella sorted through her memories as a child, trying to remember if the conversation had ever come up. They had been children, and their parents had let them be children, well, mostly.

"I'm back for Prince David's birthday. Nothing else." Ella grabbed Celeste's hand and navigated past the girls, ignoring the shake in Celeste's hands as she tried to hide her laughter. Once they were back in their private room, Celeste burst out laughing, Luca remaining outside.

"Why is it so funny? David is engaged to someone else because of the treaty. As if I could break a treaty." Ella sighed.

"It's part of the reason the court is intrigued. They think you're here to do just that and throw us into a war. You're also a mystery. Everyone here knows everyone except you. You've been gone, so none of them know what to say to you, or how you'll react. But don't worry, in a few days they'll ignore you, just like they do to me."

"I'm sure that's not true—"

"It is. They didn't know how to treat me after Mom..." Celeste paused, "so they opted to ignore me."

"We'll have to fix that. Remind them of who you are. David too."

Celeste snorted. "Good luck with that one. Yesterday was the first time he's ever come to midday since...everything. Though maybe the small celebration we're having in your honor will bring him out." Celeste walked over to the dresses she had chosen and tried one on.

"The small celebration?" Ella questioned as she picked one and brought it behind a curtain.

"We're having a tiny celebration in honor of your return...which means we need to find you a dress to take home today."

"Why?" and why didn't they ask her? Ella wanted to add, but she held back.

"It's tomorrow. No one told you?" Celeste stuck her head out from between the curtains, her brow furrowed.

"No, I'm used to being kept in the dark. So, tell me about this small celebration we're having." Ella smiled, shoving down the anxiety building in her chest. She rubbed her wrists again, not daring to glance at the two thick, dark red lines that encircled them, hoping Celeste wouldn't notice.

CHAPTER SIX

"D avid, can I come in?" Ella called through his door. "Maybe we could go riding?" She waited for him to answer. "I'm not going away until you promise to ride with me. Even if it's tomorrow."

Ella listened for any sound. Nothing. There was nothing. Which wasn't right. Henry had confirmed that David was in his room, taking tea and biscuits with his head between his books.

"David?" Ella called louder in case he was in a different room.

The pain that ripped through David's scream had Ella tearing the door open.

David lay on the floor, his body contorted as he writhed. The vein in his neck stood out, pulsing in the candlelight. His brown eyes were so wide, that she thought they might burst.

"El—" He screamed.

"Someone get help!" Ella roared so loud her lungs could burst. She ran to David, her hands hovering over him. "David—" She stopped when he pointed to the broken teacup on the ground. Ella scrambled for it, picked up a shard, and smelled it.

She dropped it, her face twisted at the smell of sickly sweet apples twisted with lavender. While the apples were the more potent smell, it was the lavender that gave her pause. Ella noted the sweat coating David's skin, the fever that had taken over, and how he could barely speak. Wraith. Shit. Someone had spiked his tea with one of the poisons Raven had developed.

"El—" David groaned as he vomited on the floor, his arms wrapped around his stomach. Whoever enchanted it wasn't very good. David shouldn't have been able to form a coherent word given what Wraith did. Ella knew what a strong version of Wraith looked like, and this wasn't it, but his reaction still sent tremors down her fingers.

What had Raven said helped ease the fever? She frantically gazed at David's room, locating a cloth, bowl of water, and some pillows near his work table. By the time she turned to look at him, his entire body was paralyzed at a twisted angle, his brown eyes fixated on her, pleading for the pain to go away. Ella's heart stopped. Whoever had poisoned him, she was going to find them, and she would make them answer for this.

"Ella!" His voice cut through her.

David's body convulsed, his magic flaring around his hands as he fought for control.

"I'm here." Ella landed on her knees beside him, cupping his face in her hands. "I'm here." She had to remain focused. For him. She could do this. She hadn't sat through all of those nights with Raven, helping her through the fear and pain of the poisoning for nothing. Ella watched David's eyes shift from pure terror to emptiness as the pain became too much, and David lost his sight.

"Ella?" he questioned, his voice wobbly as tears rolled down his face.

"I'm here. I'm here." She squeezed his hand gently, her fingers shaking as she positioned a pillow under his head. Where was the help? Hours seemed to have passed since she had arrived.

"Stay awake David. Fight it. You have to." She pressed the wet cloth to his forehead, cooling him down, brushing her hands through his hair. David moved a finger, letting her know he was trying.

"Henry!"

Where were the servants? Why didn't anyone come down this freaking hall? Why couldn't she have been an enchanter as well? She could have done something. Could have made Vivifica or Solacium, something to help.

Ella leaned down, pressing her hand to David's forehead, slick with sweat. "Please David, I just got back home. Fight it. For your mom...for yourself," she whispered. His pulse fluttered too fast, faster than she liked.

"Ella?" Her name echoed down the hall.

"Help, please," Ella begged, her voice hoarse.

"What happened?" Henry skidded into the room. His hands glowed as his grip on his power slipped for a few seconds before he regained control.

"He was poisoned. I don't know what it is. Is there an antidote? David pointed to the teacup before..."

Henry would know what it was. She prayed he would recognize the smell of lavender. Please know what it means. Henry picked up the cup and dropped it as soon as he took in the smells.

"Shit." Henry leaped towards David's worktable and began tearing it apart. "Why couldn't he have organized it just once? Just once I would like to find — yes!" Henry walked back, triumph in his eyes as he held a bottle with a thick red liquid inside. The antidote. Ella would know it anywhere. Except, how did they have it? Raven was the only one who knew how to create it.

Henry turned David onto his back, opened his mouth, and poured half of the bottle down his throat. "It's going to get—"

David's body spasmed, throwing him against Ella. She fell backward, letting the spasm pass before she tried to move him off of her.

"Help me get him to his bed." Henry sprinted over, picking up David's torso before Ella could scramble to her feet. She picked up his lower half and carried him, knowing they had a minute before the next spasm would take hold. That was the downside to the antidote. Sure, it let you live, but the process... was brutal. They got David settled right as the next one hit with Henry there to help him through it.

Ella's pulse raced as she watched David in pain. She hadn't expected to feel this much fear trickling down her face with the sweat on her brow. It was a nauseous sensation that continued to crawl up her stomach as she watched his skin pale, sweat covering his body. She wanted it to end. Who had done this to him? He looked so alone, so sick...just like her mom. For a moment, Ella was transported back in time to when she was three years old, and her mom was lying in bed, barely breathing, eyes closed, unresponsive.

She sank to the floor, her knees folded up against her chest. Would he die like her mom? Frightened and barely able to breathe? No. Ella asserted. This was Wraith. It wasn't the fever that had swept through the kingdom. He would be fine. Yet Ella couldn't move.

"You don't have to stay, Ella. You can go."

She snapped her head up at the pity and understanding in Henry's voice. He was sitting beside David, looking down at her over the ledge of the large bed. She had ended up pressed against the wall; the stones cooling her back. When had she gotten here? She didn't know. But she knew she couldn't leave.

Ella wiped a stray strand of hair out of her face. "I'm content right here," she spoke with conviction, though her heart said otherwise.

Henry nodded, turning back to David as his spasms settled. His antidote seemed to be stronger than whatever enchanter had made the poison. One more person for Ella to add to her list of people. Henry walked to the door to leave.

"Where are you going?"

"It's going to take a bit for David to become conscious. So while the two of us wait for him, I'm going to have some food brought to us—"

"Make sure someone tastes it in front of us," Ella added, her eyes fixated on the bed.

Henry paused. "Of course."

King Matthias charged in shortly after, a flurry of guards and high-ranking members of the court behind him, demanding answers. Henry intercepted all of them as Ella remained in her seat, observing. She had never thought of King Matthias as a king until that moment when he commanded an entire room of men without raising his voice. He thrived, and they all acted in unison to make a plan. Several times she heard the word Holodal whispered in the background.

Ella remained in the room, unobtrusive to everything. When the food arrived for her and Henry, she moved with lethargic grace, stretching out stiff muscles. Once everything had been sampled by the food taster, she dug in, not realizing how hungry she had gotten.

The two ate as they watched David. Henry was on constant alert despite the four guards that had been posted outside the door.

"Are you okay? You seemed a bit shaken?" Henry commented as he finished eating.

"I will be. I'm not used to seeing—"

Both of them stopped talking when David groaned. Henry moved from the table and over to his friend's side in a blink. Ella could tell from his complexion and breathing that the worst had passed. David mumbled something unintelligible.

"You're going to have the worst headache tomorrow," Henry said.

"But I owe Ella a horseback ride tomorrow, and I'm supposed to go into Riset to—" he groaned.

"The people of Riset understand their prince is busy and may not always be there to treat them," Henry soothed him. "I'll have someone go down today to let everyone know you can't come tomorrow."

"Henry, it's important. You know it is. They need to know that their prince will take care of them." David fought to sit up in his bed.

"And they will. They already do, David. Give yourself a break. You've been going into Riset for two years now. They'll understand."

Ella remained silent, absorbing the information she had learned. She looked at David with kinder eyes. At least he had some priorities that got him out of the palace.

Ella didn't leave until Luca arrived. He frowned when the guards outside questioned him. Reassuring them, Ella got up and said goodbye to David before leaving. They walked down the hall and past her new room. She unclenched her hands, stretching out her fingers. All the terror and anger had built up, and she had to get rid of it. Seeing David lying on the floor had brought up emotions she didn't want to deal with. Fears she had kept shut down deep within, and all of them chomped to be set free.

Ella didn't stop walking until they got to the stables and got a horse hitched to a carriage. Luca raised his eyebrows at her, sitting next to her as she drove aimlessly through Riset. Her legs jiggled up and down, shaking the carriage. This wasn't working...she had to do something else.

"Ella, where are we going?" Luca watched the alleys go by until he was lost.

She drove to the fifth circle, in one of the most rundown parts of Riset. Ella tied up the carriage, pulled the hood of her cloak over her head, and walked to a wooden door that barely stood.

"You can't be serious. We're not going in there." Luca put himself between Ella and the small greasy man in front of the door.

"Yes, I am. You don't have to come. I need to stay sharp and clear my head, and I can't do that in the palace," Ella growled.

"Ella—"

She opened the door and walked around Luca before he could grab her. He followed her, trying to hide the insignia on his armored tunic beneath his cloak and pulling his hood up over his braided hair. Luca came up short as the fighting ring came into view. Ella continued barreling down the aisle, heading straight for the ring, where two men were beating each other up.

"I thought that after you saved Snow from here you were banned?" Luca spoke gruffly.

Ella ignored him, not stopping until she got to the edge and spoke with the stage master, an older scrawny man, who had seen too much, and based on the malicious glint in his smile, been the cause of a lot of people's pain.

"No." The stage master glared down at her.

Ella put her hands on her hips. "You're going to let me into that ring, master."

"After that little stunt, you and your friend pulled on my partner, I should have you killed—"

"My friend and I made you and your friend more coin that night than any other fighter in this ring. Besides, don't you want a new Noble Lady, for one night, and one fight only?"

"They won't see your face?" Greed gleamed in the man's black eyes and Ella knew she had won.

"I wouldn't have it any other way," Ella replied, pulling the hood firmer over her.

"Then, by all means." The stage master motioned for Ella to join the ring, now that the other fight was completed.

Ella scampered into the ring in her dress with no weapons. She would not let the stage master change his mind. Two fighters were let in, two large fighters.

Ella grinned.

She watched them as the stage master called out their names, waiting for everyone to place their bets.

She waited for them to make their move before she unleashed herself. She knew she couldn't get injured, couldn't have David or Henry asking questions. So she dodged their punches and kicks, not that she found it hard. These men weren't a match for her. They were novices who'd learned most of their inadequate skills in pubs by picking fights with people who didn't know how to defend themselves. Pathetic.

Ella knocked one out quickly with a hard punch right under his jaw. She took her time with the second one. She wanted to make sure her skills remained at peak performance levels. The crowd had gone wild at the sound of her name being announced, the 'Noble Lady'. That had been Raven's stage name, and they had missed her. Ella played with the second fighter, letting the crowd fuel her. No wonder Raven had gotten addicted to fighting. By the time Ella knocked out her second opponent, her cheeks hurt from all the smiling. She leaped off the stage, collected some coins that she wouldn't tell Lady Tremaine about, and walked away. Raucous cheers followed her out the door.

She let the crowd's energy fuel her, shooting energy back into her veins. Ella couldn't afford to feel anything but clarity, and being back at the palace only provided haze. She had almost failed today in her mission to protect the crown. To be their protector in the shadows. Seeing David like that...it shouldn't have, but it had affected her. She didn't like that. She needed to succeed and to make sure he remained alive.

"El, you can't do that. Someone could have recognized you. That was—"

"Fun? Exhilarating?" Ella twirled on her feet, dancing on the cobblestones.

"It was dangerous and stupid. What were you thinking? I know I'm assigned to be your guard, but I didn't think I'd have to protect you from yourself."

"Please, you enjoyed it. I won't go back, I promise." The cheers still echoed in her ears, chanting her 'name'. Blood rushed through her heart at a pace she was sure would make her faint.

"Ella," Luca paused at their carriage, his hands holding her still, "how are you?"

She noted the concern in his green eyes, the way the edges crinkled with worry. She didn't want to think about what had happened, what had made her anything but fine.

"I'm fine." She shrugged. And she would continue to feel fine as she pushed everything else down. Ella didn't acknowledge the crawling in her stomach or the tightening pain in her lungs that threatened to make even breathing feel impossible. She wouldn't voice them into being, and because of that, she was fine. She knew Luca didn't believe her, but he remained silent.

Luca's hands seemed to press her into the ground, holding her firm.

"If you ever need to talk about anything—"

"I know." Ella studied her feet, realizing for the first time that day how much they ached. She wasn't used to wearing soft court shoes.

Luca gently kissed her forehead before ruffling her hair and getting into the carriage. He grabbed the reins, making sure they were truly going back to the palace. Both of them were quiet as Ella rested her head on his shoulder and fell asleep.

CHAPTER SEVEN

Ella's new room was large and luxurious, the smell of vanilla and eucalyptus swirling around her the moment she entered. Her favorite smells, and they had remembered. A large four-poster bed was situated right across from the door against the back wall, covered in pillows and a comfy dark blue blanket that she would sink into. A fireplace roared to the left of her room, heating the cool night air. Two chairs sat beside it, looking almost as comfortable as her bed. To the right was a vanity next to a large window overlooking a hidden courtyard that was perfect for sneaking in and out of. The butler who had taken Ella to her room took Luca to his right next door.

Ella walked over to her trunk, happy to see that no one had unpacked it. She had, of course, not put anything incriminating in it, but she still preferred to do her unpacking. Luca was the one who had all their gear.

Once Ella had unpacked the following morning, she got into one of her new dresses, a dark blue off-the-shoulder gown that was fitted down to her waist with skirts that swished around her. Silver embroidery in the shapes of vines twisted and curled around the bodice with the light sleeves she had requested. The vines thickened at the wrists, the two unexplainable scars hidden. Wearing the dress was like slipping into another person, one she hadn't been in a long time. Years. Sure, she had worn dresses to blend into her surroundings, but her armor had always been on underneath, now...it was gone, and she had never felt more exposed.

Ella stepped out of her room, prepared for battle and to protect the crown, all the while hopefully looking like a true Lady of Rairene for the first time. She walked over to David's room and nodded at the two guards stationed outside. They didn't stop her, and she didn't bother to knock as she let herself in. He wouldn't have been able to get out of bed easily, anyway. The first day after Wraith was the worst, with vicious headaches and muscles that wouldn't stop screaming. David lay in bed, propped up by an obscene amount of pillows.

"You know, I was wondering where my pillows had gone. It seems you cleared out the entire palace." Ella laughed as David continued to be swallowed up.

"Ha. Ha. Celeste...she uh...was a little overzealous in her need to take care of me." David slowly turned his head to look at her.

"A little overzealous?" She raised an eyebrow. "How are you feeling?"

"Better than I was this morning. Remind me, if I ever want to get poisoned again, Wraith is not the one for me."

"You plan on being poisoned again?" Ella leaned against his bedpost, crossing her arms. She had done a peripheral search of his room and saw no shadows, no hidden people waiting to attack.

"Not if I can help it." David tried to sit up taller in his bed, grimacing as his muscles spasmed. "Thank you, by the way."

"For what?" She tilted her head, trying to remember what she had done. She'd been completely useless yesterday. A feeling she would rather not experience ever again.

"For getting help, for staying with me...when I lost my vision...when I couldn't think..." David shuddered at the memory. "It was hearing your voice, feeling your hand in mine, that kept me from losing control. They train us, all the time, about poisons, especially enchanted ones. They train us on how to help, how to assess which poison it was, and what to do if you've been poisoned. But they don't tell you that almost all of that training vanishes the moment that poison hits your system, and all you're left with is instincts." David grabbed her hand, shocks of ice cracking up her arm. "So thank you for keeping me from losing control of my magic. I would have died."

"Does that mean you'll go horseback riding with me?"

David dropped her hand. "Someday. Soon. I promise. I'm so close to figuring out this one enchantment. I can feel it."

Ella watched grief bloom in his dark brown eyes, deepening their depths. Ella slumped, though at least here in his room he would be safer. Well, safe-ish, she amended. He had just been poisoned there.

"You know, when I was in Evrotia, I would pretend to be someone else...just like when we were children on one of our adventures."

"Oh? Why?"

"I loved the idea of being someone else, anyone else, if only for a moment to get me through the current pain I was in."

"I see." David glanced away. "I learned a while ago that we're not children anymore, Ella. We live a life where we're meant to behave and lead our people, not have fantastical dreams of a normal world."

Ella walked over and sat on his bed. The carefree David she'd known was hidden away, and hopefully, she could get some of him back.

"If we could be those people, though, what do you think they would be doing right now?"

"Ella, I don't—"

"Come on, just pretend for a little bit. What would you, or Kit, as you called yourself, be doing?"

"I don't know...something with enchanting? Probably still working at the palace. Maybe as a healer. What would Diana do?" David questioned, indulging her. "Would you teach singing lessons?"

"No." Ella straightened her spine. "No...no singing." She hadn't sung since...Ella shook her head. "I would work in a cafe where I could listen to all the gossip and eat all the pastries I wanted without a lady looking down on me." Ella smiled. "What's something you wish you could do as Kit that you can't as a prince?"

David thought for a long moment. She already knew the answer. He was just trying to find a diplomatic, princely way to say it. "Everyone expects so much of me. Sometimes, I need a break. Kit has his freedom, while I do not." David fisted his hands in his blankets, looking away from her.

"That's what Diana did for me in Evrotia. Everything I went through..." Ella thought of her training. It had been punishing, and tiresome, but she had loved it. She loved every minute as she grew stronger and became the person who could protect her kingdom. "Everything was a lot, but she helped on the hard days."

Ella brushed back her hair, trying to locate a ribbon to tie it back with. She glanced towards him when he remained silent. "What?"

"The burn...on your neck. How did that happen?" David leaned forward enough to touch her. His hand was rough, but still gentle as he surveyed the burn that had marred her neck for years. Ella closed her eyes as his fingers lightly grazed it, sending shivers down her whole body.

She lost herself in his touch, all words forgotten. The smell of books and magic swirled around him, engulfing her as she attempted to remember how to talk. She didn't like to think about her scar, let alone speak about how she got it. The concern in his eyes wasn't helping, either. Ella swallowed, took a breath, and spoke.

"I uh...I misspoke once to Queen Lyanna. Even though I was young, she didn't tolerate insolence. So, she uh..." Ella paused, finding air in her lungs to help her function. Just say it and be done with it. It was nine years ago. But the memories wouldn't leave her alone. Ella shut them down, squeezing her eyes shut. "She had two guards hold me down as she poured liquified wax onto me. I learned my lesson and never spoke out of turn again." Ella spoke so softly that the words barely lived. She risked a glance at David, trying to smile.

"Ella, I'm—"

Ella stood up and paced across his room. "It's not a concern. Nothing to worry about." She closed her eyes, steadying herself on shaking feet.

She had gotten used to seeing that scar. She could look at it in the mirror every day and not feel a thing. But talking about how she had been so scared she'd wet herself, or how Lady Tremaine had been so mad as she poured the wax onto Ella's neck, reminding her it was Ella's fault this had happened. The embarrassment, the shame she carried with her daily for receiving that scar. She had learned her lesson that day. If she didn't know how to hide her emotions, and how to feel nothing, then she would not last in their world. She would not be worthy of protecting the crown. So she had to hide everything, and she would continue to do so until she had served her purpose.

"I'm sad that you won't be able to join us tonight. Maybe if you feel better, you'll make an appearance?"

"Maybe." David's shoulders fell as Ella turned away from him, her hands twisting in her dress. Ella left his room, closing the door softly.

She flopped onto her enormous bed as soon as she was back in the depths of her room, absentmindedly rubbing the scar.

"He asked about the scar, didn't he?" Luca stood in her doorframe. His guard's uniform was impeccable. Luca walked in when she remained silent and sat beside her. "You know that no matter how hard you try, it will always be there."

"I know," Ella snapped. "It doesn't hurt to try, though." She leaned back against the headboard and looked sideways at him. He was always so perfect in everything he did. He had never failed. Unlike her.

"It's part of you. You can no more remove it than you can remove your passion to protect the crown and those you love. The sooner you accept it, the sooner you can grow from it."

"What would I do without you?" Ella forced a smile and rested her head on his shoulder. Heat radiated off of him, comforting her.

"Probably wither and die of boredom." Luca rested his head on top of hers.

Ella snorted. "Yeah, that's definitely it."

Luca stood up and pulled Ella to her feet. She stood there and watched him go through her trunk, pulling out clothing for her. "Come on, we're going to go for a ride." Luca tossed the clothes at her.

"Luca, we can't. I have the dumb celebration in my honor to go to in my honor."

"Trust me, you need this. We'll be fast."

Ella and Luca guided the horses out to the open forest beyond the palace walls. The sun was high enough in the sky that Ella knew they could get a delightful ride in before it was too late. Her horse Dream pranced in anticipation of the open ground before her. It had been too long since they had gone for a ride, and Ella wasn't sure which of them was more excited. Fresh grass and flowers chased around them as swirls of trees and plants blurred past them, the smell of warm wood giving her new life. Ella and Dream were one being in that moment, in perfect synchronicity. Luca was close behind, his stallion charging after them.

Ella turned around and looked up at the palace in the distance.

"I know you want to make sure he stays safe, so isn't his room the best spot to do that? Why do you want him to leave it?"

Ella frowned. Why was it so important? "I think he's forgotten a bit about how to live. He's so focused on his enchantments that he doesn't join in his royal duties anymore. He needs to remember that there's more to life than his books."

"Says the woman, who is determined to be the best protector." Luca laughed.

Ella's lips twisted to the side. "At least I get out. Celeste commented how he never comes out anymore. His appearance at the midday meal I was at was the first one in years."

"Ella, your idea of getting out is going to a fighting ring. My idea is to go to a pub, have some drinks, and then have some fun. Why do you think going riding is going to get him out?" Luca questioned. They had begun riding back, making sure it truly was a quick ride.

"Riding was always what the two of us did as children. Henry came along sometimes, but otherwise, it was the two of us, and our guards, of course. But riding was our thing. We both love horses and the thrill of riding one at full speed without a care in the world. I want to remind him of that life."

Luca brought his stallion next to Ella and leaned over, his hand softly resting against her cheek. "I see, so if he was looking out his window right now, and saw me touch you like this," Luca ran his thumb over her skin before moving his hand behind her neck, tilting her head up at him. "You think it would make him come out of his room?"

Ella swallowed. Mischief and laughter danced in his green and gold-flecked eyes, though everything else about him was confident and serious. He would kiss her just to make David jealous, she was certain. He hadn't teased her with a kiss in a year.

"Uh..." Ella's heart hammered in her chest at the thought of kissing him again. "I do...but..."

"We have an agreement." Luca smiled, kissing her cheek. "I know. I won't break it, I promised. But if you ever want to go out like I do...let me know." Luca backed away, a smile pulling on his lips as Ella's cheeks flushed.

"I get out. I go shopping for jewelry, shoes, and weapons all the time." Ella crossed her arms and tilted her head at him as she *tried* to get her face to stop turning red.

They rode back quickly, stabling the horses as the sun began its descent. They dashed through the palace as the welcome event crept closer.

The gown she wore was the one chosen by Celeste, its red fabric shimmering in the firelight as she spun around in its depths. Her hair was braided back, the horse ride tangling it too much to be kept down. She wore one of her favorite necklaces, a large obsidian gem nestled right below her collarbone on a silver chain. It was simple and elegant, just what she liked.

Luca escorted her down the hall to the small ballroom where her celebration was being held. Only the advisors and inner circle of King Matthias were invited. Maybe one of them could shed some light on the person who killed Sophie.

Ella always thought the idea of this ballroom being considered small was laughable. By any other description, it was massive, roughly the same size as the one in Aumont. Stone pillars bordered the edges to support the roof. Stained glass windows separated their world from the city of Riset outside. Several tables were in the back, waiting for food to be brought out before the guests could sit to eat. The dance floor was currently crowded with everyone milling around, waiting for dinner. Luca and Ella entered as the court crier called out their names. Celeste was instantly by their side, wearing a deep purple down with gold embroidery dancing around her shoulders. King Matthias smiled as he escorted Ella to her seat of honor at the head table.

"Ladies and gentlemen of the court, it brings me great pleasure to welcome back Lady Eleanor of House Aumont to our halls once more. Her absence has been felt these long years, and I am honored to have her grace us with her presence again. So, let's have some excellent food and dance." King Matthias sat down, one chair over, leaving room for Celeste.

David wasn't coming then.

She hadn't expected him to. He had just survived a poisoning. But Henry's earlier statement that David was a recluse sent rocks sinking to the bottom of her stomach. He was a mark and nothing more. Never before had she had the privilege of protecting the royal crown so closely. Except that being back around him...it was as though no time had passed, yet the tingles running down her spine were new and exciting.

"Celeste...why does David..."

"Hide?" She regarded Ella, her expressions reserved. "When you first left, he hid for a bit. But then he had to begin his studies as an enchanter, but mom...ever since then..." She fell quiet, transforming into a little girl who was lost and vulnerable, not the strong young woman Ella was getting to know. Celeste straightened her back and turned to her food.

"It's hard for them." Henry sat down on Ella's right, a full plate in front of him.

Ella leaned towards him as he lowered his voice.

"Losing the queen...it hit everyone. But especially them. I will say this, though. I haven't seen David this alive in a long time."

Ella bit her lip. What would happen when she had to leave? Once they sorted out the threat with Holodal and signed a new treaty, she would move on and continue protecting them from the shadows. Would they be fine? They'd been fine without her for years. They hadn't once asked for her to come home, so why would they need her now?

Henry spoke again, switching to Evrotian. "So how different is this court from Evrotia, truly?" His accent was near perfect, though it reflected his Rairenian heritage in the way he lowered his voice on some vowels.

She set her fork down and tilted her head as she spoke in Evrotian, pulling on the stories Raven had shared with her, "Well, the queen didn't always have the court around. She likes to have time to herself. On those nights, the court is much like this celebration right now, relaxed and flowing with conversation." Ella analyzed him, wondering why he felt the need to speak in a different language.

"On the nights she was there?"

"Those nights—" Ella paused mid-sentence as she watched Lady Tremaine and Lucifer walk into the room. Her eyes followed them as she continued. "There was always a sense of impending trepidation. It could be someone saying something at the wrong time, or simply because she was in a bad mood." Ella followed Lady Tremaine as she walked to the head table and she made her grand entrance, making sure she passed by as many tables as possible. She ensured she drew as much attention as possible. Ella should have expected her to be here. Why wouldn't she come to her step—daughter's welcome home ball? Lucifer preened at the attention, standing tall in his uniform beside Lady Tremaine.

"I see," Henry stilled beside her, glancing between her and Lady Tremaine.

Ella got up and walked around the head table to greet her stepmother. Ella hugged her.

"Lady Tremaine, welcome to the celebration. I'm glad you could make it." King Matthias spoke softly as he added. "Though, I assure you, a guard was unnecessary."

"Until the situation with Holodal is resolved, I will bring Lucifer with me. We would hate for the Queen of Trudel to worry so close to the treaty being signed."

Ella raised an eyebrow. Why would the queen of another kingdom worry about her stepmother?

"Of course not, Ambassador Tremaine."

Lady Tremaine curtsied gave Ella one more hug, and went to her table. Ambassador? Ella's brow furrowed as she went to her seat. She'd never heard her stepmother referred to as an ambassador before.

"She's the Ambassador for Trudel, didn't you know that?" Henry leaned over and whispered.

Ella shook her head, earning a frown from Henry as she looked over at her stepmother. Why had she never mentioned it before? Was it because what she did to protect the crown went against what the queen from another kingdom wished? That had to be it.

Ella monitored them, especially Lucifer, as dinner wore on, waiting to see if he would slink off anywhere. Henry pulled her onto the dance floor, opening the dancing up for everyone else. Since Henry was David's Champion, his role was to also perform certain duties when David wasn't present.

"What's wrong?" Henry pulled Ella closer, making sure his lips barely moved as they danced over the marble floor.

"Nothing's wrong, why?" She took a second. His dark green eyes assessed her, looking for her secrets.

"You haven't stopped following Lady Tremaine's guard since the moment they walked into the room."

"I'm...not a fan of his." Ella's back tensed at the thought of Lucifer. Each scar he had given her with a whip tingled. She had always earned their punishment, but could never quite shake the feeling that Lucifer had not been allowed to do that to anyone else. Ella closed her eyes, pulling away from the memories that threatened to undo her in front of Henry. The ones that haunted her.

"No one likes him, though haven't you barely gotten to know him?" Henry tightened his grip on her hand.

"Aren't a few interactions with him enough? Believe me, living in Evrotia means you have to learn how to assess someone quickly, and those select moments with him have been more than enough." Ella couldn't stop the shudder. It was, of course, more than a few moments. If she added up all the time she had spent locked up in the attic for misbehaving and being shown the error of her ways...she didn't want to do the math. She'd learned during those first few years when rebellion had begun to strike.

Halfway through their dance, the rest of the court joined them. Ella danced with several other members of the court, including the king, who made her laugh and spun her around like she was six years old again.

She stumbled towards her seat when her feet screamed at her, needing a reprieve. She stopped at the edge, Lucifer blocking her path.

Ella froze, staring up at him through narrowed blue eyes.

"Where are you going? Won't you dance with me?" Lucifer stepped closer, and Ella stopped breathing.

"You're in my way." Ella didn't break eye contact with his light brown eyes. To do so would only make him happier. It would show her fear, and that she could never do. Not with him.

"Well, if you would agree to a dance, I wouldn't be," Lucifer purred.

They were far enough removed from the dance floor to be noticed. Ella twisted her shaking fingers together behind her back, wishing she had a knife with her. Lucifer had the slightest advantage right now. He was armed, and she wasn't. Nor could she reveal herself in front of everyone. At least she knew his game was his usual brand of fear and intimidation. At least there was no whip present. Not that he could do anything here. That fact kept Ella from panicking. He couldn't do anything, not here. But if she pissed him off, she knew he would make her pay for it later. He always did.

"You're out of line," Ella whispered. "I'll never dance with you."

Why didn't she have one fucking dagger with her? Ella backed up a single step.

"Is there a problem?" David's voice whispered calm gentle thoughts over her as she sensed him step beside her.

She dropped her hands to her side, waiting for Lucifer to say something, to back down to the prince, as befitting of his station. Lucifer kept his brown eyes focused on Ella, daring her to say something. He smiled a Cheshire grin. Ella fixed her attention on her father's emblem instead of locking her eyes with Lucifer again.

"I asked you a question, Guard." David took a step forward, a hand resting on Ella's wrist.

Lucifer smirked at her, raising an eyebrow at David's challenge.

"Ella, would you like to dance with me?" David turned so that his back was to Lucifer.

She paled.

Lucifer would never forget the slight, or the complete disregard for him, as a threat to David's life. Ella watched Lucifer's eyes darken as David remained facing her. She nodded slowly, reaching out for him and bringing him to the floor before anything else could happen, her aching feet forgotten.

"You came." Ella faked a smile, her nerves wreaking havoc in her heart. She genuinely thought she would faint at the confrontation.

"Well, I heard there was dancing." David shrugged, wincing.

"You're still sore from the antidote. You should be resting, David," Ella whispered. If Raven's past complaining was any indication, she knew he was in a lot of pain.

"Dancing, Ella." He smiled, spinning them around.

"Just the dancing, huh?" Her heart stuttered as he continued to look at her. His brown eyes were highlighted with shimmers of gold and green in the candlelight, laughter dancing in their depths.

"Well, and you, of course." David stepped closer. "I have to make sure my friend is supported at events like these."

"It seems to be the correct thing to do." She tore her gaze away from David's eyes, focusing on his shoulder.

"I didn't miss a front-row seat to a classic Henry scolding for going without an escort, did I?" David winked.

"Luca was with me. I was completely safe." Let alone the fact that she could take care of herself, but she couldn't tell him that. Could never tell him that.

"I saw that." David adjusted his grip, his hand pressing into her lower back. Warmth shot through her. Especially when he brushed aside a stray piece of hair. Ella almost looked into his eyes again. "But with what's been going on, Henry wants to make sure we aren't being needlessly careless with our safety."

"I see." Ella adjusted her hold on his hand, well aware of just how close they had gotten. "So if you and I wanted to go riding without an escort, that would be completely out of the realm of possibilities," Ella whispered, her breathing hitched.

"Definitely out of the question," David confirmed with a nod, a forced grimace playing on his face, but then she looked into his eyes and saw the glimmer of mischief in their depths fighting free of the shadows. "But that's only if Henry finds out."

"Well, when you think of a solution, let me know." Ella smiled back as she curtsied at the end of the song.

CHAPTER EIGHT

Ella and Luca walked down the palace halls wearing specially designed 'sneak suits'. Ella shifted in hers, pulling at the tight fabric until it lay against her comfortably. Luca looked at her sideways, his lips twitching just enough for her to notice. She once again adjusted the black material that contained pieces of metal enchanted to deceive the eye. The metalwork was beautiful and intricately placed outside of her corset. The enchantment deceived the eye, blending Ella into shadows, making her almost invisible. In the dark of the night, she couldn't be seen by anyone, but if a flame came her way, shadows would ripple around her, masking her features and body as best as they could. Only someone with a piece of her uniform could see her. Luca held a piece of hers, just as she held a piece of his.

Their footsteps remained silent as they surveyed the palace and its security, finding some holes, but nothing too egregious. Ella craved her bed, her feet complaining with each step she took. Her nerves danced under her skin as they patrolled, her heart racing with excitement. Walking through the corridors while everyone slept, listening for any noise out of the ordinary, electrified her. She was doing what she was trained to do: protect the crown. Her senses heightened and the adrenaline rushing through her body gave her a new life. There was no better feeling, apart from sparing, of course. Ella pulled the black hood up higher over her head, obscuring her face in its enchanted shadows. Not that it mattered too much, she'd worn a black wig...just in case.

The hair on Ella's neck stood up as they rounded a corner leading to the wing where the royal family slept. Ella looked at Luca. He sensed it too, the current in the air that told them something was wrong. Very wrong.

David's door was unguarded.

A shadow caught Ella's eye as it slipped into his room.

She sprinted down the hall.

She got to David's room and saw the shadow slinking in the dying firelight. If she went in there, she could be revealed as well, but the shadow was creeping towards David's bed. Ella shook her head, focusing. She had one job: to keep David alive. And she would. The Callidus the would-be-killer had taken was very good. But not good enough if Ella could make out their silhouette.

She didn't have time to be quiet. Trusting in her enchantments to conceal her, Ella barreled into them.

Warm skin pressed against her as they collided with the wall. The would-be-killers sweat and a hint of rum assaulting her. Great, they'd had some liquid courage before taking the potion. That wasn't going to end well...for them. Ella found his arms and hauled him out of David's room, back into the hallway where torches flickered.

Ella grunted as David's killer sliced her leg with a small knife, letting go long enough for it to break out of her grip. Pain blinded her for a moment as she gathered herself, groaning in frustration. He had to be completely naked for her to not be able to see any aspect but his shadow.

Luca ran up the opposite end of the hallway in his nightclothes. Good call, Ella acknowledged. They couldn't be found fighting assassins. Ella positioned herself in front of David's room, knowing the killer's escape was cut off. They would have to go past one of them. A glint of metal flashed right in time for her to dodge the blade slashing towards her face. She pulled out her glass daggers, palming one in each hand as she faced off against them.

"What's happening?"

David's voice froze her. She didn't dare take her eye off of the shadow, her back facing David. She couldn't speak. If she did, David would know exactly who was standing in front of him. As it was, she was lucky enough that her enchantments still writhed around her, trying to shield her from the torches. The killer thankfully didn't give her the chance to think of a solution before moving towards her. Ella blocked him. She wondered what it looked like to David to see a mass of shadows facing off against...well...what appeared to be nothing.

"Look out!" His voice shook the ground as the shadow tried to get past her, causing her to stumble. Well, at least he could track the shadow as well.

"Your Highness, you should stay—" Luca was near David, standing in a defensive position.

"The hell I will," David growled.

Ella shook herself, refocusing on the man and ignoring David. She had to. She knew he would be protected. Her heart pounded frantically against her ribs. She wasn't sure if she was excited to be fighting an almost invisible opponent and proving herself to David, or scared witless that he was behind her.

Ella smiled as the man's potion diminished. The killer should have been done by now, so the effects were wearing off, and she could take her shot. She engaged the man in hand-to-hand combat, unleashing herself. She shoved him farther down the hall, away from David and any chance of him seeing her face.

The killer couldn't get in any shots, backing up against a wall, fear pulsing in his black eyes. Ella's grin widened as she cornered him. It was just the two of them, the hunter and its prey. Nothing would get between her and accomplishing her mission. No one would survive her. She knew that. Now, so did this man.

Ella took her glass dagger and shoved it into his chest, right between his ribs, and straight into his heart. Red clouded her vision as she breathed, calming her pulse down. No one would get through her.

"What have you done?" David's voice was quiet.

Ella remained motionless as his steps stopped right behind her. Where was Luca? She could use a distraction. But all she felt was David, looking at her back, and the dead man on the floor, his blood pooling.

So she ran, her cloak flying behind her as David yelled for her to stop. Ordered her to stop. She kept running, not daring a glance behind her as the night swallowed her whole.

"Your majesty, we need to get the guards." Luca's voice carried down the hall. Good, he would keep David there, make sure he was safe. Because now...she had to sneak back into her room and change, all while the palace would go on high alert. Just perfect.

Ella looped around the palace until she got to her hidden courtyard. Luckily, she always left her window open a crack. The moment she got into her room, she unlaced her corset. Next were her boots and all of their strings. She was out of her clothes and scrambling into her nightgown when she noticed the blood dripping down her leg. Shit.

Ella limped to her washroom and tore at a tunic. She wrapped it tightly around her leg. She had to get out into the hallway. There had been little sound, though she could imagine that the earlier noises would have woken her up. They had to see her and know that she had been in her room. Ella ripped off her wig, wincing at the pins scraping her head as she peered into a mirror. Ella paused. Her cheeks were flushed, and sweat was on her brow, but no blood was in sight. Her blue eyes were wide with shock from David's anger. Ella shook her hands out, trying to calm her nerves. That had been close. Too close.

Deep breaths, Ella, deep breaths.

She repeated it over and over, walking in slow circles around her room until she was steady. Red no longer coated her vision. She could open her door and no one would suspect a thing.

The silence outside of her room confused her. Henry and his father, Lord Andrew, were there, along with the king. David was still near the dead assassin. Celeste was nowhere to be seen, though her room was only four doors down. Luca stood guard near David, on constant alert.

"David? What happened? Are you okay?" Ella walked over, holding her arms close, keeping her fingers from touching him. Oh, how she wanted to touch him. Make sure he was in one piece. A wave of panic hit her right then that his life had been in danger. Again. If she hadn't been there.... horror washed through her, numbing her.

But she had been there. He was safe. She just needed to confirm that he was indeed in one piece.

He hugged her first.

"I'm glad they didn't try to hurt you," he whispered. His arms tightened around her, pulling her closer. Ella wrapped hers around him, closing her eyes as she breathed him in. He was fine. His heartbeat was strong, shaky, but strong.

"Is he an assassin?"

"He was, but another assassin killed him...in front of me."

Ella waited for the praise. For the adoration of her fighting abilities. For the gratitude. After all this time, he would say she was a great fighter. Of course, he wouldn't know it was her, but it would still have the same meaning. Only, it didn't come. David continued to stare at the man. Young boy Ella realized. He couldn't be much older than her.

"Do you know who the other assassin was?" Ella looked around. "We should thank them—"

"No." David's voice dropped an octave, rumbling through her bones. "I detest killing. There's always a different solution to taking a life. I tried to get them to stop, but they didn't listen to me." David locked eyes on the body, grief filled for the person who had been going to kill him. Disgust churned in Ella's stomach.

"You tried to get her to stop?"

"I did. Yet she still killed him. We could have at least questioned him. But now we'll never know who is truly trying to have me killed." David's magic flared for a second before quickly being snuffed out.

"I'd heard it was Holodal. Is that not correct?"

"Does that man look like he's from Holodal?" David furiously rubbed his hair. "If he looked like Luca, sure, I would say yes. But he's from Riset, and we don't know who hired him."

Luca shifted, drawing Ella's attention to him. He was wearing his serious face, she noted, not letting anyone know what he was thinking, being the perfect guard. King Matthias and Lord Andrew assessed them as they walked over. Lord Andrew's green eyes locked on Ella, surveying her. Had she missed something? Was there a speck of blood somewhere?

"Lord Andrew, I want to make sure only the most discreet servants are up here to assist with cleaning once your unit has done their work," King Matthias spoke softly. "We don't want this getting out. And find out what happened to those guards." His eyes flicked to the door where Sophie had once slept.

"Of course," Lord Andrew nodded his head, his eyes latching onto the door as well.

"Now, we should all try to sleep. We all have early mornings." King Matthias rubbed the bridge of his nose as he motioned for all of them to disperse.

Ella watched everyone go back to their rooms as four men dressed in black uniforms walked up, one of them beginning an enchantment. His power flickered around his hands. They brushed past her, surrounding the body. Jealousy tickled Ella's spine as she watched the man cast his spell. Ever since David and Henry had been identified as Enchanters, the jealousy had been there, the need to be just as successful, just as important. But she could never protect the kingdom as well as they could, but she would be damned if she didn't try. Getting into Sophie's room would be the first step. Next would be getting enchanted items to help her figure out who had murdered her friend, and who was trying to kill David.

Ella ran through the palace, outrunning the shadows. The walls dripped with black blood, her heart frantic as she tried to find them. She had to find them. They were in danger, and she needed to see them...had to warn them. Queen Charisse was nowhere to be found, and she was about to be hurt in a way that would forever scar her. Ella had to reach her. Tell her it wasn't too late, that things could still be fixed. The shadows had crept in, their arms reaching out for Ella.

The monster was here.

It would get her. But not if she found the queen first. The queen would make everything go away, she always did. Ella's hand scraped over the hard stone walls, cutting her palm open. The shadows licked it, thickening before her, gathering to swallow her. A torch flickered at the end of the hall. Ella sprinted for it, tripping over the layers of skirts she wore. But they wouldn't stop her. Nothing would keep her from that door and the light at the end. She knew the queen was on the other side, waiting for her. Queen Charisse would make it alright. All she had to do was walk through the door.

The shadows swarmed like a hive of angry bees.

The torch was extinguished.

And darkness reigned.

Ella jolted awake, falling out of her bed. Sweat coated her skin, sticky with fear. She gripped the side of her bed and pulled herself up, falling hard on the mattress. The sun had just risen over the hills behind the palace, painting the sky with hues of pink and purple, when Ella glanced over at her enchanted mirror as it softly glowed. She rolled over in bed and opened it, smiling as she looked at Jaq. Her smile turned into a frown when Ella took in his tousled hair and wrinkled tunic.

What's wrong? Ella held the mirror closer to her, as though that would allow her a better look at her friend. Jaq rubbed his eyes, blinking away the exhaustion. *Why were you enchanting?*

You stopped another attack. You need more protection—

Jaq, I'm fine. I wasn't the one who was about to be assassinated.

No, you're just the person protecting the prince everyone wants to kill. Jaq pounded a fist on his desk.

Ella raised her eyebrows, waiting for him to calm down. She crossed her arms and leaned back, watching as the red in his face cooled down to his normal tan complexion, and his brown eyes filled with timid shame instead of anger.

Why did you scry me? It has to be important.

I have some enchantments for you. Are you able to come to Aumont?

Ella chewed her bottom lip. She didn't like the idea of leaving the palace for a long period. Even for the few hours it would take to get to Aumont and back. It would be too risky.

Could you have Mira bring it to me? I can't leave.

She's under house containment....again... Jaq glanced away. Their friend was constantly rebelling and getting into trouble. She was probably in the house more than outside of it for the stunts she liked to pull.

I don't even want to know what Siren did this time. Ella paused, her next question hanging in the air, waiting to be spoken. It would not be an easy one. *Could you ask...Drea?* The question hovered, waiting to strike. Drea hadn't been up to court in two years. Ever since her injury, she had, as far as Ella knew, refused to come near the palace. It would be a huge ask and one that wouldn't come without a price.

I'll—

Ella. Drea came into the mirror, giving Jaq a withering glare. *I'll meet you in Riset at your favorite cafe. But I won't go to the palace. If Jaq's enchantments are that necessary, meet me there in an hour.*

Ella looked at Jaq for an answer. He nodded, pushing his spectacles back up his nose.

I guess I'll see you in an hour.

Ella moved quickly, getting out of the palace with some time to spare. She told Luca where she was going and headed out before any guards were aware of where she was going. That was something she would have to mention to Henry. The guards should not have been so complacent about ignoring her. Her favorite cafe, the Bird and Mouse, was small and often went unnoticed, making it ideal. The stones had yellowed with age as ivy crawled up its sides. The owner had been the same for as long as Ella could remember, a tiny old man with thick gray hair, who was sweeter than the pastries he made.

She walked up right as he was setting out his two small wooden tables and chairs, the open sign reading *"Fresh croissants flakier than your fairy godmother!"* sat out for all to see.

"Fairy godmothers, huh?" Ella walked in after him, breathing in the fresh scent of warm dough and more sugar than any one person could eat.

"Everyone has one. It just depends on whether you're looking or not. Don't you ever wonder why something worked out just perfectly to make it possible?" Despite his age and fantastical ideas, his voice was always firm and confident.

Ella chuckled. "I call that luck."

"And I call it fairy godmothers." He smiled. "Your usual, I presume?"

Ella nodded and said, "Plus one more," as she watched him waddle over to his glass case containing an array of delicacies. He stopped in front of the rows of croissants and pulled out three. Ella never could help herself when croissants were involved.

Drea waited for her outside, already sitting down at one of the tables. Villagers filled up the small marketplace where Bird and Mouse resided. Some went in for pastries, and everyone else foolishly went about their days.

"Here," Drea pushed over a small black satchel, its contents tinkling inside.

"Thank you," Ella held onto it, not bothering to look inside. She would examine them later. "Is there anything—"

"Just be careful at court, Ella," Drea said.

"I am." Ella bit into her croissant. "Henry has turned into quite the responsible adult. It's annoying. I didn't think Henry of all people would—"

"He's been through a lot...more than anyone should have to go through." Drea inserted, her green eyes narrowing.

Ella leaned back in her chair, looking over at her stepsister. Drea sat with a stiff back, hands clutching her cane.

"What do you know about Henry?"

"I.... just remember that from when I went to the palace and attended court...he seemed to have a lot." Drea fidgeted with a bracelet. It was simple, nothing special to the eye, so Ella had never noticed it. The silver wrapped around her wrist delicately, clasping together with two intertwined leaves. Small sapphires twinkling in the middle.

"Why don't you attend court? I know you'd be welcome there. Anastasia certainly is." Ella looked at the surrounding people, monitoring Drea's reaction out of the corner of her eye.

Drea touched the scar on her face and slowly closed her eyes before straightening her back. "I can't."

It was all she said before standing up and turning her back on Ella.

"You're beautiful Drea, I hope you know that."

Drea adjusted her grip on her cane before moving away, her cane seeming to shout her pain with every cobblestone it touched.

Ella grabbed the bag and rushed quickly back to the palace.

Henry was waiting for her outside of her bedroom. "Where did you go?"

"I went to Riset. Drea wanted to see me and she wasn't comfortable coming here, not that it's any of your business—"

"It is actually. With everything going on, it is part of my responsibility to ensure the safety of Prince David and you. So you or Luca *will* inform me the next time you decide to go anywhere that's not on palace grounds so that a proper escort—"

"Luca is more than capable of taking care of me. I also learned some self-defense in Evrotia—"

"Self-defense will not get you anywhere if someone—"

Ella moved quickly, looping a leg behind him. She held onto his arm and twisted, sending his body straight onto the stone floor. Henry inspected her, blinking rapidly as he rubbed his head.

"You were saying?" She crossed her arms and walked into her room.

"Ella, stop." Henry rubbed the bump that was forming. "Yes, you know self—defense, but I need to protect you—"

"You used to be so much fun, Henry. What happened to the eight-year-old boy who used to run down these halls with me chasing invisible assailants?" Ella smiled.

"They became real, Ella." Henry's hand rested on her arm, keeping her from turning away from him. "Those invisible 'bad men' we used to laugh about fighting?" Henry covered his face for a second, and in that moment Ella saw her old friend turn into someone carrying a weight they didn't deserve to bear. A responsibility shouldered too young. "I know you've been gone, and that you don't know what's happened. But know that the changes you find confining are for everyone's safety, especially yours. Please, the next time you leave, let me know. At least Drea had the sense to scry me—"

"She did? Why?" Ella raised a brow, trying to keep her jaw from dropping.

"She knew I would be worried about you—"

"But why would she know that?" Ella stepped in front of Henry when he tried to turn away. "Henry?"

"It's a long story. I need to get to a meeting with my assassin unit. I'll see you at dinner."

"You're in charge of assassins?"

"No, I'm in charge of hunting them down." Henry walked away, brushing past Luca and turning quickly down a hall.

CHAPTER NINE

Ella stood in the hallway, watching her friend walk away, his cloak snapping in the wind. Good thing they were on the same side. Henry just didn't know it. At least none of her kills would anger him. She needed to find out who had killed Sophie and stop the next attempt on David's life. If the past few days were any indicator, they would not ease up. Ella opened the satchel from Jaq and pulled out a few small enchanted earrings, an enchanted mirror, and a slim corset that she could wear underneath any outfit and be protected. The pale boning and fabric didn't look like much, but it would stop any blade from reaching her.

Luca knocked on her door, quickly coming inside.

"I know that look," he sighed.

"What look?" She smiled, a mischievous gleam filling her blue eyes.

"It's a look that is typically followed by a dose of rebellion and some minor form of injury."

"Huh, I didn't realize I had a look. Remind me to let you know when you're having one of yours." Ella smirked. "I'm not going to leave the palace. Henry has ordered us to stay here, so I will. And I'll be close enough to hear if anything happens to David."

After a few hours of restless sleep, Ella put on her leather black suit, strapped on two daggers, and braided her hair. The sky had yet to signal the rise of the sun as she opened her window and looked at the uneven stones of the palace wall. Luca was looking out his window next to hers as well, assessing the likelihood of being able to scale it over to Sophie's window. Unfortunately, they didn't have another way in. After all the attacks, David constantly had guards outside of his door, and Ella couldn't very well waltz past them.

"Should be fun?" she whispered to him as she put her foot on the first uneven stone.

"Yes, fun is exactly what I would call this," Luca commented as they climbed along the inner wall of the palace.

Ella made it past multiple rooms, coming to a stop outside of Sophie's room. She examined the window as closely as she could for any sign of enchantment. There was none that she could see from her angle. She removed her lock picks from her braided hair and opened the latch. Ella tiptoed into the room, listening for any sound on the other side of the door. She moved away from the door, turning around to examine the room.

How Sophie had gotten a room this close to the royal family was a feat. Who had she been sent to kill? The room itself, though, was nothing much of note when compared to hers, or others. It was more of an elite servant's room than anything else. The bed was smaller, if not very well made, with a thick decorative wooden frame and headboard. The blankets had been left tangled as though its occupant had been quickly removed from sleep.

The vanity had been knocked over, its contents left on the plush red rug beneath it. The wardrobe in the corner was untouched, along with the small washroom and single lounge chair. It was as though she had been a recent addition and the royal family had placed her there until they'd found a better spot for her to dwell in. Ella stopped cold at the large dried pool of blood on the rug below the bed. She knelt, pressing her knees into the thick rug as she got down to Sophie's vantage point. Indentations showed Ella where Sophie had pleaded for her life to be spared. Her fingers hovered over the dried blood, not daring to touch the last place her friend had laid. A glint caught Ella's attention from under the edge of the bed. A small piece of silver rested there, hidden in the shadows. It was sharp, though no bigger than the end tip of her fingernail. How she would ever find its owner, she did not know. But at least she had something.

"Did you find anything?" Luca remained sitting in the window, eyeing the door and listening for any sound.

"Just this." She showed him the silver fragment with a small line in the center. "I just need one more minute. I want to locate her journal."

"She wouldn't keep a journal with her. That's too risky."

"Knowing Sophie, she would have. I taught her a special code so no one could read it," Ella explained as she looked for any good hiding spots. But no matter where she looked, it was nowhere to be found.

Ella glanced at the bed. There's no way her protégé would be so foolish as to—

"What are you doing up at this hour?"

Ella froze at Celeste's voice on the other side. Luca stood, giving her a clear exit.

"Don't. We have to go," Luca whispered.

"I need to know." Ella darted to the bed, rifling under the mattress.

"I couldn't sleep, and wanted to check something in here," Henry responded on the other side. The sound of a key sliding into the lock sent Ella's nerves into a panic.

"Ella," Luca commanded in hushed tones.

"What do you need from that cursed room?" Celeste's voice shook. Why would Celeste be frightened of this room?

Ella didn't have time to ponder as she found the flimsy leather book and yanked it free.

"I think I misplaced something in there," Henry said, the knob turning.

Ella jumped out the window and closed the glass window quickly. She didn't bother trying to lock it. She didn't stop moving along the stone ledge until she got to her room and could collapse on the floor inside.

"Was it worth it?" Luca spoke softly, lying next to her on the cool stone floor.

"I hope so." Ella waved the book before closing her eyes for a minute and calming her heart as it hammered in panic. That had been close. Closer than she would have liked. Though now she knew two things: Henry had left something in the room, and Celeste had been afraid of what was in the room, or who had lived in it. She wasn't sure which one she wanted the answer to be, that Celeste had been afraid of the room for a supernatural reason, or because Sophie had been its occupant.

By the time Ella had calmed down, and taken some time to look at Sophie's journal, with no results, the midday meal had snuck up on her. She rushed to change into a loose floral green dress, with her hair twisted up at the nap of her neck. But she wasn't going to bother with the dining hall. That's not where David was. He hadn't taken part in his royal duties in a long time, and instead found reasons to always be in his room, and she was going to find out why.

"David?" Ella knocked on his door and waited for a response. None came. "I'm coming in."

His room was barely lit. He had moved books around, putting them in the way of any natural path through his room. Other items had been placed in strategic spots as well, forcing Ella to stop in the middle of his room and look around. He had made it hard for someone to sneak up on him. Ella's chest ached. The weight of the effort he had gone through to protect himself weighed her down. She wished she could tell him he was safe. As long as she was around, she would always protect him. But she couldn't. She could never tell him. Not only had Lady Tremaine forbidden it, but David wouldn't approve of her. She knew that now.

"Can we go for a ride? I need a break from court life."

"Is court life not as entertaining here as in Evrotia?" he called from an attached room.

"Something like that," Ella muttered. "Please come riding. Henry's demanding escorts and I would rather have your company than just some boring guards."

"You don't want to go with your *guard*?"

Ella heard the eye roll in his tone.

"No, I want to go with you. Come on, you need some fresh air, especially after the last few days...a good ride will do wonders for you."

"Oh, it will?" David walked out of the adjoining room, a small smile on his face. He wore basic trousers and a black tunic. Nothing fancy, but his simple clothing made him more handsome to Ella than any uppity royal uniform.

"Can we talk about the other night—"

"Let's talk about it while we're out riding." She practically begged him, and he still didn't want to go. He had never been so reclusive before.

"Give me ten minutes to get ready."

Their escort comprised five guards, to Ella's dismay. How much trouble did Henry think they could get into while out riding horses? It's not as though attackers were laid in wait out in the forest. All of it faded from her mind as they took off over the sprawling fields bordering the forest. The forest itself stretched the length of the Emerald Mountain, filled with redwoods. One could get lost in there if they ventured too far. She had barely gone into its depths as a child, always making sure she could see the forest's edge.

The large hills provided an excellent place for horses without fear of running into a low-hanging branch. The two of them charged forward, not bothering to make sure their escorts could keep up. As long as they were within eyesight, that was all that mattered. Ella looked over at David, who smiled, a truly genuine 'eyes lit up with life' smile. The shadows that had plagued him receded. His pale skin was flushed. But it was the eyes that made her heart stop. His warm brown eyes which were normally shadowed were now filled with light. Eyes that belonged to someone who was turning eighteen, not someone who had experienced so much pain that it had sucked the life out of them.

Ella laughed, startling David into a soft laugh as well. Laughing for joy, laughing for fun, as the horses continued to run.

"Gods, I love riding. Don't you love the feel of the wind on your face and in your hair?" Ella glowed. If she had been an enchanter, she would have been oozing over with energy.

"It has been a while for me," David smiled, patting his stallion. "Thank you for making me come. I don't think I realized how much I had missed it." He steered his horse closer to hers, guiding them further out in the hills. Their guards, Ella noticed, were still trying to catch up, though they remained in view.

"David, the other night—"

"I'm sorry you had to see that boy's body. I can only imagine how traumatic it must have been for you."

"It wasn't."

David's head whipped around to look at her, his brow furrowed.

"I lived in Evrotia for nine years, David. Queen Lyanna killed people in front of me all the time. That was one of the least traumatic deaths I've seen."

"I'm...sorry," David mumbled. He stopped his horse, grabbing hers as well. Ella turned to look at him, a brow raised. He gently held her hand, shocks of liquid fire racing along her fingers as his touch warmed her. "I've heard how...hard it was there. I had half a mind last night to send you back to Aumont to keep you safe," he confessed.

Ella's heart sputtered and her muscles tensed. He couldn't send her away.

"I would rather stay here...with you...than go anywhere else...I feel safer."

"I won't make you leave. I just want to keep you safe." David moved away from her, whispering, "I've missed my friend." It was as though he hoped she wouldn't hear, yet spoke loudly enough for her to understand.

"David, will you come to midday meals with me? I could use a friend." It wasn't until she asked that she realized how alone she felt. She missed hers. But she wouldn't be able to see them for a while still. They were usually always close by, yet recently they had been sent away.

David's shoulders slumped as he gazed out over the hills before them. It was beautiful as the clouds lightly covered the tops of the mountains in mist, but all Ella wanted to do was stare at him. She couldn't tell what he was thinking, and she desperately wanted to know.

"David, talk to me." Ella guided her horse around to face him. The escorts had finally caught up but stayed out of earshot. "Why don't you join the court anymore? You don't interact with them at all, and you should be learning from your father right now. Not hiding away—"

"I'm not hiding," David interjected.

"You are. You are hiding in your books, you are hiding in your studies, you are hiding David, and I want to know why." Ella made sure she stayed in front of him when he tried to turn away.

"I'm not hiding," David stood up in his stirrups and quickly sat back down. He fisted his hands in his hair, yelling, "I'm studying to be a better enchanter. If I had been better..." David locked eyes with Ella. "I study to be the best. I have to be better. I have to protect my people...my mom didn't have to die..." David shook himself. "So while you think I'm hiding, I'm learning for the betterment of my kingdom. Of my people. You do not get to judge me for what I do as I prepare to be king."

Ella leaned back in her saddle. "That's why you and Henry go into Riset every week. To practice and make sure the people are taken care of."

"Leave it alone, Ella." He lightly kicked his horse, getting him to walk over the hills.

She kept pace with him, watching the treeline for any threats as she switched topics, "How are *you* doing after...everything?"

David grunted. "I'm processing. I'm not used to someone wanting me dead, at least not someone this proactive."

"Why do they want you dead? You can tell me." Ella reached out a hand, stopping before she touched him.

David flicked his eyes at her, their depths softening as he looked. "It's nothing for you to worry about."

Ella groaned internally. Even though she knew what the reason was, it grated on her that he wouldn't trust her enough to tell her.

"David—"

"Let's go home." He turned away from her, kicking his horse into a canter. She followed shortly behind.

As they rode back, Ella processed all that he had said or hadn't said. Did he think that if he didn't talk about the assassinations they would just go away? Or did he think that the queen died because he hadn't been able to save her? She had passed away from a fever, a fever that had swept through the entire kingdom. The enchanters couldn't create enough potions fast enough to save everyone. She understood his desire to protect his people. It was all she wanted to do. She longed to tell him how much she understood. That she had hidden herself away for nine years to be able to protect him. Her friends and training were all that she knew. Most of her time was spent training with them. Everyone else she ignored. Just like him. Above all, though, she was more annoyed that he didn't think she was worthy enough to know why someone was trying to kill him. That she could not stand, nor ignore.

CHAPTER TEN

Luca was waiting for Ella at the stables when they got back. David took off quickly, leaving Ella to walk back to her room and lie down in bed. Luca followed suit. The smell of spices and metal washed over her as he scooted closer. He held his hands together on his stomach and peered at her. She'd remained in her riding gear, white hair a tangled mess spread out beneath her.

"What are you looking at?" Luca asked, his voice raised as he rapidly looked between Ella and the spot in the ceiling that she was burning a hole through with her gaze.

"Is it worth it?" She tilted her head to look at him. "Is it worth protecting him if I end up alone?"

"Where is this coming from?" Luca turned on his side and rested his head on his hand. He reached out and swept away a rebellious piece of Ella's hair.

"David hides away to learn how to be the best enchanter to protect his people. And like me, he's isolated himself. So is it worth it? To be the best protector, yet alone?"

"You, my dear, are anything but alone. You have your friends, Jaq, you have people..." Luca's hand rested on her cheek. "You have me. You haven't isolated yourself. There's a difference between having many people in your life and having a select group of quality people in your life. You and David have both chosen who to let into your lives. Right now, it appears he's trying to decide on whether to let you in. So maybe you need to let him in first."

"I have let him in—"

Luca raised a brow. "Oh? You've talked to him about how much it hurt you that he never reached out? Or have you talked about...the queen...with him?"

Ella turned her head away. No, she had not spoken about those things with him. She didn't want the frozen lake inside of her to crack. She had worked hard to freeze over those tumultuous waves. Already she could feel the violent currents beneath the thick layer of ice, and she knew they would have the power to drown her should she fall through. They would swallow her, pull her down, and never let her go.

"I need to get ready for dinner." Ella rolled out of bed and took off her riding clothes. It didn't matter to her that Luca was in the room. He had seen her in less before. He continued to lie on the bed, eyes closed as she went into the washroom and bathed.

"Luca, can you help me?" She stood before him, clean and wearing a deep red gown that covered all the scars. Her back was to him, the lacing on her dress open, waiting for him to tighten it. "You didn't answer my question, you know," she spoke softly as he worked on her gown. "Is it worth it? To be the best?"

"You tell me. After all of these years, you finally get to protect the most important person in the kingdom. Has all of this pain you've gone through been worth it?" Luca finished lacing her up.

She turned to look at him, reaching up to braid her hair. "It's all I've ever wanted."

"Then it's been worth it." Luca hugged her, resting his head on hers.

Ella hugged him, her shoulders relaxed as he held her. The safety he had always provided wrapped around her. It sang a song she knew so well.

The two of them walked to the dining room. The cold of the stone seeped into Ella's soft shoes. Though they were the proper attire to wear, she longed for the sturdy feeling of her lace-up boots. These weak slippers wouldn't benefit her in any fight, not even one with another noblewoman.

The towering wooden doors opened before them as they entered the dining hall. The hall was cavernous, and everyone's voice danced around the room. Three long wooden tables lead up to the head table, where there are two levels. The top was where King Matthias entertained his advisors and ranking officials. Princess Celeste sat on his right, an empty chair between them. Being the daughter of the Grand Duke of Aumont meant Ella always sat at the second head table. Had her father been alive, he would have been sitting beside King Matthias. Luca took up his position along the wall, where he could watch and hear everything. Ella ignored the surrounding chattering, focusing on her food. It always made her nervous to be so far away from David. But she had to play the role of a good obedient noblewoman who returned to court.

As Ella's mind wandered, her eyes landed on the queen's empty throne. One of the last times she had seen the queen, she had been on that throne. She had worn the most breathtaking gown Ella had ever seen. It was midnight blue with silver details along the corseted bodice and throughout the skirts and flowing sleeves. Her midnight black hair had cascaded in curls down to her waist, her silver crown glinting in the candlelight. Everyone had been ready for the ball to begin once dinner was done, especially Ella, who loved it when the queen smiled as she twirled around the dance floor. That night had been so magical—

"Ella, can I sit with you?"

"Hmmm?" Ella turned to find David standing next to her. "David, what are you doing here?"

"I believe I live here." He smiled softly as Ella turned scarlet. "Besides, a friend of mine told me that my court missed me."

"Well, I wasn't wrong," Ella whispered. The entire hall had fallen silent when David sat beside her. He fidgeted next to her as all eyes watched. He placed his fisted hands in his lap as the hall continued to observe them. Ella reached over and gently squeezed his hand. "Luca, can you find a servant and inform them that the prince will take his meal here with us tonight?"

Luca bowed his head before heading to the kitchen. His movement broke the spell that had descended over the people, and their droning chatter consumed the hall once again. Ella caught King Matthias's gaze out of the corner of her eye. She moved just enough to look at him as he smiled, toasting her. If she hadn't known any better, she could have sworn there was a slight glimmer in his eyes as he watched his son. Celeste did not hide her emotions as several tears worked their way down her cheeks. She dried them with her napkin before going back to her dinner.

"Stop fidgeting, David, you're fine. There are so many guards—"

"It's not that, it's all the staring. I can feel it. This is why I don't enjoy coming here. They can't stop looking at the poor prince who lost his mother," he grumbled, his eyes once again filled with shadows.

"Maybe if you made it more of a habit to attend to your duties and be social, they wouldn't stare at you. You've made yourself a novelty. Someone to be pitied. So sit up straight and pretend that you don't care what they think. It's what I do." Ella cut into her chicken and took a small bite.

There were still many members of the noble class looking at them, whispering behind their hands. Let them gossip. Let them be entertained. It didn't matter to her. As dinner went on, David's meal was brought out. At least she had somehow gotten David to come out, if only for one meal.

"David, do you still train?"

"Of course. Why?" He looked up from his food, his face open and curious.

"I was wondering...well, you know how I always wanted to train when we were younger..." Ella paused. She was treading on that frozen lake. How much stomping did she dare create with this request? With this test? How much would his rejection hurt her?

"I remember. You wanted to be a knight like me and Henry." David smiled.

"Right...it was a.... point of contention..." She furrowed her brow and bit her lip. Why was this so hard? So what if she didn't know how to do what she was going to ask? She was allowed to learn new skills. Plus, she was simply trying to think of something that would get him out of his room again. "Would you be willing to teach me archery? I know it's not something women are allowed to do, but I would love to learn, and—"

"Sure—"

"I know you may not say yes, but please hear me out. I think that—" She stopped talking to look at David when he laughed. He was laughing. At *her.* But he was still laughing.

"I said, sure." He grinned, taking a bite filled with rice and chicken.

"Yes...you said yes?" Her mouth had yet to close.

"Of course, a little archery never hurt anyone," David commented. "Come to the practice yard tomorrow morning, right after sunrise. That's when Henry and I train with the soldiers. I'll be able to step away then."

"Thank you, David."

He reached over and squeezed her hands. Warmth spread throughout Ella, thawing a small layer of ice that had coated her heart.

Ella stumbled through the palace. Darkness engulfed the walls and covered them in a layer of black slime she knew the monster would crawl out of. The hair on the back of her neck stood at attention as green eyes grew out of the wall beside her. They blocked her again and again from every room that contained safety. Her heart ruptured as she tried to get away. Sweat dripped down her face as she continued stumbling into the walls. The world tilted as her vision blurred. Panic had fully found residence within her. It had crawled in and set her heart racing, pumping blood through faster than anyone could bear. The monster was going to catch her. She was completely isolated, and nothing was stopping it from getting to her. Why wasn't anyone helping her? The monster prowled out of the shadows, coalescing into a large black leopard, its green eyes ever watchful, devouring her. It was going to do it. It would make its final killstrike.

"Please. Stop." Ella had cornered herself and all she could do was make herself smaller as the cat grew to five times its size and laughed. "Stop."

"Ella."

Pounding reached her ears on the other side of the palace doors.

The leopard got closer, its rancid breath brushing over her face. Death poured out of its maw, converging on her, covering her in a cloak of darkness.

Ella screamed, the darkness leaping inside and choking her.

Her body seized, oxygen fleeing as her mind went dark. Empty.

"Ella!"

Her world shook as the last dredges of the leopard slid out of her. She opened her eyes, her body gripped in a vice. The cat still had her. Even awake, it still clutched her. Ella's eyes darted around for the light. There had to be light. It couldn't get her if candles were lit. Ella refocused on the thing clutching her arms hard enough to bruise.

David was gripping her.

He was inches away from her. His brown eyes were wide, his face pale as he looked at her. Why was he so worried? What had happened? Had there been another attack? Why was he without a tunic?

"What happened?" Ella gasped for breath, looking around the room. Where was the intruder? There had to be a threat. Except there was nothing. She heaved a sigh, her heart steadying. "David, what happened? Is everyone alright?"

He dropped her arms and stepped away. "Are you alright?" His eyes assessed her.

Ella ran her hands through her hair, her scalp sticky with sweat. She grimaced. Why was she so sweaty? "I uh..." Was she fine? The monster...it was here. It had followed her. "I..." Ella surveyed her room again. Her hands were clammy as she shook. "David, please don't let it get me." Ella leaned into her pillows, pulling the blankets up high.

David was by her side, brushing her hair out of her face before his arms wrapped around her. If she hadn't been in such a state of fear, her one weakness, Ella would have taken the moment to savor David being this close to her. The hypnotizing smell of magic and books wiggled their way into her nose, steadying her.

"Why won't it leave me alone?" Ella whispered.

"What won't leave you alone?" David's voice was tight, though his hands remained gentle as they slowly rubbed up and down her arms.

"My nightmares. The monster that stalks me in the dark."

"How long have you been having them?"

"Ever since I was..." Ella paused, her hand resting over David's heart and the fresh wound that angrily stood out over seven inches long. Ella narrowed her eyes. "Who did this to you?" Her voice thickened as she fisted her hands. She noticed just how close the assassin had gotten. How dare anyone—

"It's not important. They're no longer a problem." David captured her hand and removed it from his chest, holding it instead. "You've been having these nightmares since you were..." he left the question open, waiting for her.

All Ella could focus on, though, was protecting him and keeping him close. She wanted to tear the kingdom apart to find the person trying to kill him. She would find them, but for now, she had to keep him close, and that meant letting him in.

"I've had them since I was sent away and told I couldn't come back until I was a lady." It was only a half-truth. They'd begun after the first time Lady Tremaine had sent Ella to stay in the attic for a night as punishment.

"I hate that you were sent away. I missed you. Everyone did. I wrote you so many letters, El—"

"Why didn't you send them?" Ella kept her eyes fixated on the wound over his heart. Not only did it give her more rage, but it fueled the hurt she knew she would feel when he told her why he had never tried to communicate with her.

"I did."

All pent-up anguish left at those two simple words. Who would have known that two syllables could have such an impact on one's ability to breathe, or think?

"Why didn't you respond?" he questioned.

"I never got them, David, I swear."

David pulled back, looking down at her. His brow furrowed, his lips twisted as he thought, "Henry would give them to Drea. We didn't think they would get to you if they came from the palace. Evrotia isn't the best at passing along information. But don't worry about it right now. At this moment, you need to rest. Your screams could have woken the dead."

"Not. No one else is here," Ella motioned to the empty room.

"I sent them away. I didn't think you would want to wake up to a room filled with a bunch of people. Though your guard Luca put up a good fight."

"I'll bet he did," Ella mumbled, a small smile on her lips. "I'm sorry that my nightmare woke everyone up."

"As long as you're safe, we'll be okay." David didn't let go of her hand. "Would you like me to stay for a bit?"

Ella nodded. She let her gaze drift over his bare chest, trying to hide her shock at the red scars around his waist. Five jagged marks on each side of his body. Scars that were just like the ones on Drea's face. Scars that a person could only get when an enchanter lost control.

"David? What happened?" She leaned forward to get a better look.

"It's nothing," he snapped. David haphazardly put a tunic on. "Don't worry about me. I just want to make sure you're comfortable. I'll stay until you fall asleep."

Ella let him fuss over her as she sat in a chair by the fireplace. However, the image of those scars, in the exact place hands would go when someone was bent over, holding themselves in pain while losing control, refused to leave her mind.

CHAPTER ELEVEN

Ella woke up, and David was gone. She frowned for a moment before she saw the note. He had gone to training, and she was expected there as well if she still wanted to learn how to shoot a bow and arrow. A set of training clothes rested at the foot of her bed. Ella breathed deeply. She clutched her throat. The phantom whisper of whatever had slid into her pressed against her chords. Rubbing her neck, Ella eased out of bed before pulling on the training clothes. The black cotton fabric hung loose on her frame, so loose she had to laugh. David was not good at sizing a person.

Luca walked in, a grin instantly spreading on his face.

"Stop laughing. It's not too bad, right?" Ella pulled on the fabric, looking down.

"Ella, you could cut off a third of that and still be comfortable. You'll never train well."

"Well, if anything, the loose clothing will help sell the idea that I don't know what I'm doing." She smiled, braiding back her hair.

"You *don't* know what you're doing." Luca crossed his arms. Ella was treading on dangerous ground by learning something without Lady Tremaine's approval.

"I have to go. Do you want to escort me?" Ella confidently walked past Luca, ignoring his watch-where-you-tread-stance.

His eyes softened, his hand resting on her shoulder to stop her. "How are you? You scared me half to death, Ashes." Ella scrunched her nose at the nickname. "Last night...it hasn't been that bad...since the queen died."

Ella grimaced. "Was it that bad?"

"Yeah, it was Ash-Ella...last night, seeing you, not being able to help you...I want to help you—"

"You are. By being my friend. We were a disaster together and you know it. We're so much better as friends."

Luca let out a sigh, his body slumping. "I know. Just don't scare me like that again."

Ella chuckled. "I wish it was that easy. Now, let's go, and no more nicknames, *Scar*." Ella winked before walking out of the room and towards the training fields.

The training fields were in the back of the palace grounds, hidden from normal court life. However, that never stopped the ladies of court from watching. There were several groups of soldiers warming up and going through their rounds. Ella noted they were novices, getting the pleasure of learning under the strictest of instructors. As a little girl, she had been as close as she could. David and Henry had accompanied her as well until eventually they could pick up a wooden sword or spear and play with them.

She had not.

While the novices practiced, Ella noticed that many of them kept getting distracted and shifting their gaze to the main training ring, where the experienced knights had gathered. The novice's instructors got pissed off and were now making them line up to run laps around the palace. That was not something she envied. Luca got closer to her, his hand on the small of her back. Not the spot a normal guard would put his hand on. Ella gently removed it, making sure it went unnoticed by anyone watching them. She took his arm and wrapped it around hers, a proper way to escort a lady. Her curiosity got the better of her and led her to the group of soldiers cheering around the ring. Several moved, bowing their heads, when they noticed who she was before they went back to hollering. There were two fighters in the ring, and from the sounds of it, they had been sparring for a while. Powerful muscles chorded their biceps, sweat soaking through the back of their sleeveless tunic. His red hair was matted to his head. Henry. It was Henry moving in the ring, and he was excellent.

Ella's jaw dropped as she watched her friend take on his opponent. Henry was breathing heavily, sword at the ready. Both of them moved swiftly and with precision. However, his opponent, who had a smaller frame and more graceful build, made up with speed what he lacked in strength. They were a perfect match. Ella stood on her toes, trying to get a good enough angle to see Henry's adversary.

If Ella's jaw hadn't already come unhinged, it would have fallen wide open when the two fighters paused long enough for her to see David on the other side. The ten-plus years of training the two men had endured had more than paid off. Before her, the yelling soldiers fought their future king and his champion. Both are worthy fighters. Both are capable of inspiring their men into battle and to victory.

She could envision it so clearly. Henry and David were side by side on a battlefield, bloodied and bruised, but still full of the will to fight, to persevere. To win. They would be even more inspiring to watch in battle than they were now, should the time ever come. Luckily, David was going to sign that treaty and avoid the war. But should the day ever come, it would be anyone's honor to stand behind these two and defend Rairene with them. Ella's heart raced with the need to get into that ring and join them. It had always been the three of them, together, and all she had to do was jump over the wooden barricade and throw herself into battle and show all that she had learned.

Ella bounced up and down on her feet, her hands clutching the wooden barrier enough to feel it biting into her skin. She wrapped her arms around herself, moving back and forth on her feet. She had to get into that ring. It had been so long since she had gotten into a good fight, and this would fix that. She could do it. She could get in there. Show them that a woman was as capable of fighting as any man.

Warm hands landed on her shoulder. Luca stilled her, his charming green eyes apologizing. He shook his head just enough to stop her. All of her pent-up energy fled, her shoulders slumping as she looked at the ground. She would obey. She wouldn't ruin everything. But it didn't keep her from watching David and Henry. By the time they walked off, both of them glowed with life.

"Ella." David's face brightened as they walked off, the men parting before them. All of them went back to their drills now that the two were done.

"You two have certainly come a long way from playing with sticking and maiming friends." Ella laughed, touching the scar on her forehead.

"We've come along a bit since then," David commented.

"Though he doesn't know how to size someone properly." Henry laughed as he grinned at Ella. "Even with that belt on, it's too big. Good thing we're only teaching you archery," Henry attempted to adjust her tunic, and despite his best efforts, and Ella's from earlier, neither of them could get a better fit. "You thought she needed this much fabric?" Henry chided, as David turned red.

Ella smiled before walking to the archery field. Luca was right in step with her, the other two following quickly behind. "It's still in the same spot from when we were children?" Ella asked, looking back. David nodded as he drank water from a leather waterskin.

The archers were already in full swing, each of them practicing their shots at varying degrees of difficulty. She slowed down when one instructor gripped a handful of arrows and tossed them down in front of one novice before harassing them for missing so many times.

"Oh, will he be punished for failing?" Ella asked David, wondering where they took those who failed.

"Punished how?" David questioned, looking closely at her.

"Well, there are a couple of different ways, poisoned, cut, tortured... whipped..." Ella whispered the last one. She felt pity for the novice's failure, but at least their punishment would encourage them to do better next time. It had always done that for her. Every time she failed, she knew she would be in the attic overnight, surviving her nightmares after an afternoon of being on the wrong side of a whip in Lucifer or Lady Tremaine's hand. But she had gotten better. So would this archer.

"Isn't it punishment enough to be chastised by your instructor in front of everyone?" Henry said, drawing Ella's gaze over to his critical one.

Ella nodded. "I keep forgetting how different things are here."

"No one should ever be tortured or whipped for failing a lesson. That's cruel." David remarked, "I'm sorry you had to see that happen to someone."

"Me too," Ella muttered as she pulled harder on her sleeves, making sure her scars remained hidden. They walked to the very end of the range, away from the rest of the archers. None of them noticed their passing, too focused on their task at hand.

"The Master already warmed the bow and strung it for us. Since we're doing basics, we're going to be in the beginners' range, away from the others, in case a stray arrow gets away from us," David explained. They were indeed very far away from everyone else, their range pointing away from the others.

"David and I will demonstrate a couple of shots first, and then guide you through some." Henry stepped up to the line, bow in hand. David brought over a bucket filled with arrows, their edges dulled from practice and time. Henry pulled an arrow out and set it on the arrow's rest. As he drew back, his entire chest expanded, his fingers anchoring against his mouth. He rested his shoulders, took aim, and released, his left arm following through. His arrow landed dead center on the bullseye.

Ella smiled, showing them she was impressed. David and Henry showed to her several times, each one talking through their processes. Ella was bouncing on her feet by the time they walked over to her. She was going to do it. She was going to practice archery, and not only that but with her friends.

David led her over to the line and stood behind her. Ella picked up an arrow, gripping the bow tightly. She made sure her feet were shoulder width apart, making sure her hips were positioned wrong. The perk of doing this, she realized, was that David would need to correct her stance. Ella smiled as his hands rested on her waist, goosebumps rising on her arms.

"Before you draw, let's correct a couple of things," he whispered. David stood directly behind her, his lips inches from her neck. His hands did land on her hips, adjusting them to be perpendicular to the bullseye before lightly grazing up her side to her shoulders, making sure she stood straight and didn't lean back.

Her heart was a wreck at his touch.

"Relax your grip, like this." David adjusted her fingers. "Now, pull back and remember three fingers under the arrow, and your index finger anchors in the corner of your mouth." His voice dropped an octave. Ella did as she was told. Her breathing hitched as he continued to touch her. "Now," David cleared his throat, "relax your shoulders...like that." He laid his hands on her shoulders until they lowered. "Look at the bullseye, and when you're ready and have your target in mind, let go and make sure you follow through at the end with your right elbow coming back."

Ella breathed in. She would have to miss it. The target was so close she knew she could make the shot, even though it was her first time. Ella took another breath and breathed out through her mouth, focusing on missing the target. She let go, making sure to not follow through as the arrow sailed and lodged itself in a tree behind the target. She morphed her face into disappointment.

"It's not a bad shot for the first time," David reassured her. "Let's try another."

Ella took five more shorts, some getting closer, others missing entirely. She didn't know what was more exhausting, having to miss on purpose or pretend that she kept forgetting how to position her body.

"Can I have some practice?" Luca walked over, his eyes guarded on approach.

"Of course." David handed the bow over, a smile on his lips, shadows in his eyes. "Did you get to learn in Holodal?"

"I did. I was lucky enough to have some of the emperor's men take pity on me and show me."

Ella wondered what Luca was trying to accomplish. Did he want the practice? He was an expert marksman. You didn't grow up in Holodal and not know how to shoot a bow, though learning from the emperor's men was new information to her.

Luca drew the arrow and, in quick succession, aimed and released. His shot was perfect, landing dead center. He quickly followed with another, splitting the first arrow in half. Luca grinned as he looked at her.

"Show off." Ella smiled as she took the bow from him and, with no help from David, aimed. She wanted to show them a little bit that she could do this. Prove that if she had been given the chance when they were younger, she could have become something other than a shadow in the dark for them. She could have been more than a wallflower to be summoned at parties.

Ella drew the bow, took aim, and released.

It landed true, splitting both of Luca's arrows.

She jumped up, smiling as she turned to look at the others. Luca grinned, David's jaw was open, and Henry...he smiled meekly, head tilted to the side.

"I think I'm ready for the next target." Ella laughed, leaning forward on the bow.

"When you can make the same shot twenty times in a row, then you can move to the next one," David said.

Henry looked up at the sun. "We have to go." He gave David a look that invited no arguments.

David sighed, nodding. "I know. You know I wouldn't miss it."

"What is this top secret important thing you have to do?" Ella joked, hoping they revealed something. They were both so good at keeping everything close to the chest. She needed them to give up something.

"We might have a lead on the assassin who killed the queen," Henry whispered.

The bow in Ella's hand fell to the ground when her limp hands couldn't hold it. All sensation rushed out of her as those last five words plunged her into a river of ice. She didn't dare move. Couldn't dare breathe.

"What?" Ella blinked. It was all she was capable of as her heart spasmed and her nerves shook her.

"We heard she passed from the fever." Luca stepped up, not touching Ella, but lending her his support.

"We didn't want the people to panic, or for her killer to get credit, so we spread a lie. Had Ella decided to come to her funeral, we would have told you then. We have to go. Hopefully, now you understand. We'll talk more when I see you later," David said.

Ella nodded absentmindedly as she processed the words that had come out of Henry's mouth and David's. The edges of Ella's vision went black as they jogged away, neither one of them looking back at her. Which she preferred. She didn't want them to see her. To see the grief rippling through her, threatening to reveal itself.

The queen...she had...Ella shook her head, covering her face with her hands. She couldn't think about it. All Ella felt was the rapid pulse of her heart, as those words pounded into her over and over again, 'the assassin that killed her'. Whoever that assassin was...Ella would make them regret it.

CHAPTER TWELVE

"How can I do this?" Ella whispered. Her wall had deep cracks splintering, and she had to rebuild it. With Sophie's death, and now the queen's revelation...she had to repair it. If she didn't, she wouldn't survive.

"Come on, we're getting out of here." Luca stood up and pulled Ella to her feet. He lightly rested his hand under her chin and tilted her face to look at him.

Ella sniffled, wiping the tears off her cheeks. "I can't go anywhere Luca, I need to protect him. I have to." She looked up at where David had gone, taking all the answers she needed with him.

"He's with Henry, he'll be fine." Luca held her hand and escorted her towards the stables.

"No, Luca. I have a responsibility—"

"You're too emotional right now."

"Oh, I am?" Ella snatched her hand out of his and stopped walking. "Since when have I ever let my emotions impede completing an assignment?"

"That's not what I meant."

"It is." Ella stood taller. "Now, I am going to go back to my room to freshen up and then talk with Celeste until David's out of his meeting. As for you...you can do whatever you want." She turned around and headed back into the palace, ignoring Luca as he called after her.

Ella rebuilt her walls as she walked back inside. One stone was placed over in the far corner of her mind where the nightmare had gotten through. Another was replaced and patched where cracks had formed over Sophie's death. That one had yet to be fully solidified, not until her killer was found. Then Ella's mind turned to the wall in the darkest corner, the one she hadn't dared go near in two years. The fortress she had built around her memories of the queen.

"I hate you." Slithered out from one of the cracks, striking Ella.

She looked all over for anything to patch up the crack.

"I hate you."

Those three words repeated over and over as she tried to cover it up. Her resolve acted as a sealant in the fortress. She harnessed a will more powerful than the crumbling stones of her wall, to solve the death of the woman who loved her like a daughter, and the girl who had been more than a friend.

By the time she reached her room, everything was fortified once again, and she could focus on what needed to be done. The first of which was a bath. Once refreshed, Ella took out her compact mirror and thought of Lady Tremaine. She pictured her stern, motherly face, her always perfectly placed blond hair, and her dagger-sharp green eyes.

Ella, I wasn't expecting communication from you. Are you alright? Lady Tremaine got larger in Ella's mirror.

I'm processing. Did you know the queen was assassinated? Ella examined her stepmother. She had to have known. How could she have not? Why hadn't the king used them to hunt down the queen's killer?

Nothing had been confirmed. The king wanted to keep everything private. So private that he established his own unit to look for the killer, not that it's done them any good. Lady Tremaine crossed her arms and cocked a hip.

Could I be allowed to look into her death? I know the king hasn't asked for our help, but maybe Jaq could help me? Ella trailed off, biting her lower lip. She already had so much to do, but she had to know.

Are you up to that? Lady Tremaine turned away from the mirror, bringing Ella's attention to Jaq sitting behind her.

I'll always help. Jaq smiled. *I hope we're able to figure it out.*

Ella nodded in thanks.

On that note, we have to go. There are several critical assignments. But Ella, please reach out if you need me. You know I'm always here for you. Oh, and I'm glad you and David are getting along well, it makes me happy.

Ella nodded as Lady Tremaine ended the communication. Ella didn't close hers though, instead, she thought of Drea and instantly saw her stepsister in the mirror.

I know you won't come to the palace, but could you meet me at the bakery again? I need to ask you about some letters. Ella rushed. It was almost midday, and she would need to have a good excuse for missing it. Once that was done, she could go back to David.

Ella—

Please, it's important.

Drea nodded and ended the communication.

Somehow, Drea had arrived at the bakery before Ella.

"I figured you wanted to be fast, so I took a carriage with two horses."

"No one is with you, though?" Ella looked around for anyone else from Aumont, especially Lucifer.

"Of course not. I know an off-the-books request when I see one." Drea raised an eyebrow.

"When you were at court...did David ever ask you about any letters he had sent me?"

"Why is this important?" Drea adjusted her crossed arms.

"I need to know if David's lying...so did he ask?"

"No. He didn't ask," Drea spoke softly.

Disappointment weighed Ella to the cobblestones.

"But he didn't lie to you." Drea handed her cane to Ella. "I'm going to give you something, but before I do, I need you to tell me something. Do you care for David?"

Ella laughed, "As a friend? Yes. As anything beyond that? No. He's an assignment. My entire life, all I've wanted to do was to protect and fight with him. I need to know if I can believe him when he tells me things."

Drea's eyes conveyed skepticism before she dug into a satchel on her shoulder. "I know you'll be mad at me, but I was told to destroy them, and I could never bring myself to do that. So now that you're asking, I'm handing them over to you. Henry was the one who delivered the letters, hoping I could get them to you." She handed Ella a large stack of neatly bundled, unopened envelopes.

Ella grabbed the letters with one hand and handed Drea's cane back to her with the other. "If I had never asked about them?"

"I would have never told you."

"You had no right—"

"I was disobeying direct orders by saving those. I thought you didn't care—"

"I don't...I just want to know why," Ella snapped, pressing the letters to her chest.

"You would have to ask Mother. It was her decision. Maybe she thought you would change your mind." Drea shrugged. "Just remember, you're here to protect him and as soon as that's done, you're going away again. They can never know who you are, or what we do. It's what we swore. Remember your goal, don't let yourself become attached, or emotional, you'll make a mistake—"

"What would you know about getting emotional? You've never displayed a single emotion—"

"I know more about the *devastating effects* of becoming emotionally involved in an assignment than you'll *ever* understand," Drea spoke softly, her velvet voice low as her green eyes cut through Ella. Her hands glowed lightly as she clutched her injured leg, her control over her magic wavering.

"Did Henry—"

"Leave. Henry. Out of this. I...survived...and I cannot go back, Ella. Please stop bringing it up." Drea turned around and headed towards an alley.

"Drea, I didn't mean—"

"Ella...I'm tired, and I'm going home. I think it's about time you figured out exactly what home means to you."

Ella turned around and headed back to the palace, hoping to get there right as the midday meal ended, and hopefully have her absence go unnoticed. Everything blurred around her as she walked back. All she could feel were the letters pressing into her hands, screaming to be read. David had told her the truth, and Lady Tremaine had lied.

CHAPTER THIRTEEN

Ella hid the letters in her room. She would read one later when she didn't need to speak to David. She went to his room and discovered it was vacant. Sugar and chocolate wafted around the corner, pulling Ella into a detour to the kitchens. Someone was baking cookies, and if David was still the person she remembered, he would be there, waiting to eat all of them. Ella walked past the two guards posted outside and looked inside. The kitchen, when she found it, was a disaster. She was certain that at any moment a child would come running out covered in more flour than what was currently on the counters and walls.

"Well, I guess it might bring Henry solace to know you're just as messy in the kitchen as you are with your enchanting," Ella remarked as she leaned against the kitchen doorway. David turned to face her. "I didn't think flour could get into so many places, especially the...ceiling?" She looked up at the flour track marks that swirled around the room.

"I may have gotten a little carried away." David winced.

"Just a little." Ella smiled. "I didn't know you liked to cook."

"Bake," he clarified, "I can't cook to save my life. But I can bake. It helps me focus."

"I see." She stole some dough with a finger. She licked it off before he could stop her. "That's great." Her eyes widened in surprise as she stole some more, grinning when David tucked the bowl close against his chest.

"Placing it there will not stop me," Ella smirked, walking closer to him as he backed up against the wall.

She stood up on her tiptoes, locking eyes with him as she reached in for more dough. The sweet smell of his magic and chocolate hugged her. She leaned forward, and David flinched, blocking her with the bowl.

"I need to get the rest of this in the oven," David muttered.

"Fine, bake it." Ella scooted to the side, allowing him to pass.

"Did you need something?" David spoke with his back to her.

"I uh..." She had come here for a reason outside of protecting him. "I wanted to apologize...for not writing back—"

"You said you never got the letters." He looked at her over his shoulder for a second before going back to his cookies.

"I didn't, but I could have reached out as well." Ella fiddled with her dress.

"Why didn't you?" David turned away from the cookies as he focused on her.

"I thought I smelled cookies." Henry walked into the room and paused at the tension. "What's going on?"

"Nothing," Ella said too quickly.

Henry surveyed the two of them as he smiled. He went over to David and swiped the bowl from him.

"Hey. Those need to be baked." David leaped over to Henry as he put himself on the other side of the counter.

"They need to be in my belly now." Henry grinned.

David grabbed some flour and tossed it at Henry, laughing when it dusted his hair. Ella slunk over and grabbed the bowl, getting some dough for herself.

"Come on, they're meant for Celeste," David ground out.

Ella instantly set the bowl down as she and Henry both apologized.

"Ha. Fooled you." David ripped the bowl back. "They're for me." He grinned.

The soft sound of feet on stone silenced her...and Henry, she noticed.

"Sorry, you can have some—"

Before she could further assess the situation, a blade flew towards them.

It sliced Ella's arm.

David was beside her in an instant, pulling her down to the ground. The wound was shallow, and nothing major. She had experienced worse, not that he knew that. David's hand rested for a second on her shoulder before he moved into action beside Henry. He grabbed two knives from the butcher's block. Ella watched as he lowered his head and moved his lips. His hands lit up with his magic, his power writhing up around and into the blades. Ella had never seen anyone enchant under pressure, let alone while being attacked. Her jaw dropped. She didn't think Jaq would have ever attempted it. Enchanting required intense focus and intent, and to hold that focus while under stress was impressive. Henry enchanted nothing as he removed his sword and engaged with the attacker.

She clutched her arm, blood running through her fingers. Any other woman would be in hysterics, but she had to remain calm. She had to focus and make sure David remained alive, while hopefully not giving herself away.

She didn't know if enchanting an object right then would tire David out. And she wasn't the type of woman to play the sit-around and wait game. Their attacker jumped over the table away from Henry, instantly engaging David with his daggers, forcing him to go on the defensive. As the two men fought, she rapidly assessed the kitchen for anything she could use. All she saw were knives, and those were currently not an option. At least not yet. David was holding his own, not even breaking a sweat. His enchantment had finished casting, his blades now coated in a light glow of power that strengthened them. Henry kept trying to find a way in between the men but to no avail. Each time he tried, the man expected it and turned so that David was in the way.

"How did he get past the guards?" Henry questioned, not once removing his eyes from the assailant.

Ella ran to the kitchen archway. Both guards were unconscious. "He must have poisoned them or knocked them out somehow."

She turned back to find Henry enchanting his sword as his patience frayed and David climbing up onto a kitchen counter so that the assailant wouldn't have him pinned. Ella's eyes landed on an object that would have to do to end the fight. She shrugged and picked up the frying pan, spinning it in her hand. It was weighted well. Why had she never thought to use one before? Oh well, she was going to now. The cast iron was heavy, straining her wrist as she hefted it, waiting for the perfect opportunity. David's would-be-killer had dressed as a guard, and he fought well. Very well. She observed David's defensive style, as she realized David had put himself into a compromised position, a weaker position, multiple times...all to protect her. He was trying to make sure the assassin didn't notice her, while also avoiding killing the person.

Ella rolled her shoulders and used the moment they got off of the counter to her advantage.

She swung with one arm, the frying pan connecting squarely with the man's skull. He collapsed to the ground in a limp pile of limbs and flesh. She knew he was dead.

Ella stared, mouth open in shock like any frightened court lady would look.

"Ella?" David moved out of his stance, looking between her and the man on the ground.

Henry knelt to check, shaking his head as he, too, assessed Ella, a frown on his face.

"At least you can never say I don't know how to take care of myself," she joked, a quivering smile on her lips. She dropped the frying pan, not knowing what else to do with it. It's not like she could just sheath it. David eyed it like he was about to grab it from her, anyway.

"Are you okay?" David stepped over the body, turning Ella from it, his hand resting gently on her shoulder.

"I think so...are you? You enchanted two kitchen knives and fought him. Aren't you tired?"

"You will never need to worry that I'll tire after enchanting. That would take...a lot..." he smiled.

"Oh....good...."

"I'm going to find reinforcements," Henry said as he hurried down the hall.

"El, are you sure you're fine?" David walked them out of the kitchen. "Let's get that wound examined."

"I'm fine, David. I'm more worried about you. Please, let me in, let me help." Ella stopped them at the door and turned to look at him.

"I will, but first we need to wait for Henry to come back," David held her hand, gripping it tightly. She wasn't sure if he held on that tightly to reassure himself she was there, or to let her know she was safe. Either way, she didn't care.

The moment guards were located, action and chaos ensued. The body of the would-be-killer was left on the ground to be examined by Henry's unit. Lord Andrew's private unit searched for any other intruders. Ella and David found themselves sequestered in a private drawing room filled with light, books, and chairs. A thin layer of dust covered almost every surface. It was decorated in soft greens and grays. The chairs were large and comfy. The wall against the door was lined from floor to ceiling with books, while the opposite wall held a nook for reading that overlooked part of the royal garden. It was the perfect room. Ella sighed as she sat down in a chair and draped her legs over the arms.

"Lady Eleanor?" Luca opened the door, stepping inside. "I'm going to be outside on guard should you need anything while the palace is searched."

"Thank you, Luca," Ella nodded.

"Are you hurt? Do you need anything?"

"I'm fine, thank you for—"

"The Lady suffered a minor injury. Would you mind asking a maid to bring me some wrappings and a bowl of water?" David interjected.

Luca, she noticed, glowered at her for lying. He knew she would have said something if it was anything major. She had promised him she would. And this wasn't major. Luca nodded and left, returning several minutes later with everything David had requested, along with a tray of food that Ella was more than happy to stuff into her face.

"I'm going to pull up your sleeve so that I can get to the cut on your arm." David knelt in front of her, knife poised.

"No." Ella ripped her arm away, wincing at the pain.

"Ella, it's fine. I've seen worse, I promise." David reached for her arm again.

"David, I can take care of it myself—"

"It's in a hard spot, please Ella—" His hand caught the edge of her sleeve.

"David, really it's not." Ella twisted her arm away. "Here, look at it this way." She ripped the sleeve at her shoulder, exposing the wound on her biceps.

David sat back on his heels, his jaw open slightly as he gaped between her and the ruined sleeve. Ella refused to look at him, examining the wall to her right, her cheeks red. She continued to gaze at the room as David moved slowly, cautiously. Gently, he washed off the slice in her arm. She flinched when he rubbed away the dried blood. Once it was clean and David could get a good look, he sighed, leaning back.

"It's not infected, and there wasn't any poison on the blade. I'm going to wrap it lightly until it heals on its own. I could put some Solacium on—"

"No," she snapped.

He sat backward in shock.

"What did I do?" Ella moved to his side, helping David off the ground. Ella rested her hand over his heart to steady herself as she looked at him. The pain in his eyes sliced deeper than any wound or rejection could.

"El...I would never force you to take an enchantment—"

"I know." She closed her eyes, gathering her thoughts as she stepped away from him. "In Evrotia...some courtiers were addicted to enchantments. It's even more of a rarity there since being banished, and...some of them took advantage... I've seen what it does when you get addicted. I don't...I never want to feel that." Ella shuddered.

She could count on two hands the number of assassins they had lost due to them going into a manic rage while addicted to an enchantment, or killing themselves from constantly chasing the bliss of being on enchantments like Solacium of Vivifica.

"That's...awful." David rubbed his head. "So, no enchantments will be offered." David stepped back and looked at her. "Does it bother you I'm in an enchanter?"

"No. I promise. Some of my closest friends...know other enchanters, and I mean, I know you and Henry." Ella bit her lip. She had to stop talking. She was going to ruin everything with a single sentence. She wouldn't know any enchanters in Evrotia. "I always wanted to be one, do you remember?" Ella walked away from him, hiding her face. She went to grab some bandages and brought it over to him.

"I do." David slowly wrapped the bandage around her biceps. If he noticed how defined her muscles were, he didn't comment on it. "You were so disappointed when you found out you were born without a star at the base of your neck. Remember when Henry and I drew one on you and tried to convince our parents it was real?" David laughed.

They had been six, and Ella five, when they realized that the symbols at the base of their necks meant something, something special, and Ella didn't have one. So they had drawn one for her. Of course, their parents didn't believe them that the star had been there all along and that the squiggles were extra special additions, a new special enchanter. Being wonderful parents, though, they had indulged them, playing along with Ella's fantasy of being an enchanter.

"Those were the best years of my life," Ella whispered. "I wanted so badly to make sure you never left my life. I would have done anything." The confession left her lips before she could stop it.

"El...I would have gone with you—"

She looked up at him, finding longing and a promise in his eyes. She leaned closer to him, moving in to finally kiss him. Finally, kiss the man she'd sworn to protect.

David shoved away, fear widening his hazel eyes.

"What was it we were talking about earlier?" David rubbed his head, not looking at her.

Ella remained silent for a moment. She knew she wasn't misreading the situation. Yet he pulled away. "Uh..." She searched her memory for the moments leading up to the attack. "I was about to tell you why I never wrote to you," Ella whispered. Now that the excitement was done, she didn't want this conversation. But she knew she had to let him in somehow, and this was the only path she could see.

"Right...why again?"

"Does it matter now?" She huffed, crossing her arms.

"It does to me. I've missed my friend."

"I didn't write because....I think I felt too much time had passed. I had been so angry, and she had been," Ella stopped short. She didn't want to talk about the queen. "And it got to a point that it seemed stranger to reach out than to remain silent."

"I wish you had written...no matter the time. It wouldn't have mattered. Not to me." David lightly brushed the hair out of her face and tucked it behind an ear. "Do you know what I wish for?"

Ella swallowed and shook her head. She didn't deserve it. Here she was, lying to him about who she was as she got him to open up to her.

"I wish that you and I could be normal people. That we could leave this place, and just...exist, in our world." David crossed his arms, leaning against a wall.

"What would we do in this normal world of ours?" Ella barely got the words past her lips.

"Be happy? Whatever that means..." David shrugged.

Ella didn't get a chance to comment. The search was over, and they were free to go back into the palace. David was pulled into a meeting with his father, Henry, and Lord Andrew. Ella was promptly shut out of it.

Ella lay down in bed. She had tried to kiss David. And he had rejected her. Flinched away from her. She had seen the longing in his eyes. Maybe he held back because he was going to be engaged to another in a few weeks.

She couldn't fault him for that.

Then there was the would-be-assassin. He had been wearing a palace guard's uniform, so someone had helped him, and she would need Jaq to figure out who in the palace was a rat. While everyone went to bed, Ella changed into her black suit and grabbed Jaq's enchanted potion that would let him see through mirrors. She was extremely selective, choosing only certain mirrors and small patches at that. She couldn't have an enchanter or guard noticing anything. Now Jaq could see all the hidden places people wouldn't want to be seen, and Ella would hopefully get some answers.

Before getting sleep of her own, she pulled out Sophie's journal and the stack of letters from David. Opening Sophie's journal, and flipped to the last entry, hoping that whatever hesitation Sophie had would be written out. It wasn't. It was a half-page scribble about how she was in love with her mark, and that she needed to speak to Ella. Sophie went on in other entries about her mark and David. Ella would have thought Sophie was in love with him. Too tired to decipher more, Ella selected one of David's letters. Curling up in bed, she opened it slowly, the old paper crinkling in her hands.

Ella,

I know you've never responded to my other letters, but I guess I've gotten into the habit of writing to you. Even though you're so far away, it's comforting to talk to my friend. Your thirteenth birthday just passed, and I miss you. Lena, Princess Superior is coming back in a month. It'll be her fourteenth birthday. What should I get her? A boat ride home? Mom says I can't do that, though Celeste agrees. Should we stage a coup? Just kidding...sort of. Next time you visit Aumont, please come to the palace. Do you visit Aumont? Lady Tremaine constantly tells us how much she misses your presence. Please write back...please come home soon. I hope the training you're undergoing is at least fun. Is it fun to train as a lady of the court? I don't know how the ones here enjoy it. I know that it's not as fun here without you. Happy birthday, Ella. When you get home, we'll have to go riding, just the two of us.

Forever,

David

Ella folded the letter slowly, absorbing what she had read. Her need to read the others increased but lost to the need for sleep. At least one thing was certain to her: David hadn't lied.

CHAPTER FOURTEEN

The next day, Ella wore a dress she had that was in the Evrotian style, relaying strength and armor without uttering a word. The dark blue skirts of the dress swirled around her, their depths comforting her. The bodice fit her well, with thick silver vines resembling armor working their way around her chest and up her back. The sleeves were loose enough for effortless movement while covering her wrists. She had braided her hair into its crown across her head and a chignon at the base of her neck.

Ella strode into the large courtroom with David beside her, and Luca behind. The massive room's arched ceilings were bathed in the afternoon sun's light. The entire room was filled with members of the court. Most of them were present to see what judgments would be ruled on by King Matthias. Very few were there to learn or to advise. David would be there to do both.

Ella couldn't help but stare at the two thrones that stood vacant at the end of the room. They were a pair carved out of the same pure white marble. Each one had minor distinctions to its partner. The king's throne was slightly larger, with vines carved into the head and a stallion on top. The queen's throne was carved with flowers, and a horse was engraved into the top as well. Next to them sat two wooden chairs, both ornately carved, one for David and one for Celeste. Celeste already occupied hers, smiling at Ella. She was resplendent in her purple gown and golden circle around her forehead, her black hair falling in curling waves.

Ella paused next to Celeste, motioning for David to continue to his seat. She squeezed Celeste's shoulder in reassurance, kneeling to be at her level.

"Hi, Pumpkin," Ella whispered, mindful of the eyes watching them.

"I'm glad you two came today. Court's been so boring recently. It will be much more entertaining with you and David here."

"Especially if it means Luca is here as well?" Ella smiled as Celeste blushed. "You should talk to him sometime. Practice flirting with him. He's very good at it."

"El." Celeste covered her mouth, her cheeks flaming. Ella grinned as she stood, King Matthias walking towards them.

"What were you two conspiring about?" David leaned back in his chair.

"Oh, you know, boys and flirting." Ella winked.

As soon as King Matthias sat down on his throne, his gold crown on top of his head, the court began. Ella had never realized before how similar David and the king were. They both carried themselves the same way, even tilting their heads the same as they listened to their concerned citizens. The crown King Matthias wore was intricately crafted. It held only four gems, each one a diamond embedded into strategic places around the crown. The rest of the crown matched the throne with decorative vines creating the circlet. David's crown was a simple piece of gold that rested on his forehead. Though he was handsomely dressed for court, Ella found that her heart raced more when they were on the training field, wearing their plain homespun tunics, and no posturing was needed.

Celeste was correct about the court being boring. Ella wondered if this was why Queen Lyanna of Evrotia always did something wild. Though Ella never would have guessed that Matthia was bored. He leaned forward to listen to his people, his hands always at his side or gently clasped in front of him. Whoever was before him, no matter if they wore clothes barely stitched together, or walked in wearing everything made from gold, they got the same treatment from their king. David, too, leaned in, listening to them, weighing in, and asking questions when he wanted more information. Though he may have shut himself off from the kingdom, at least he still remembered how to be in court.

She observed the room, noting who paid attention and who had fallen asleep. Anastasia seemed to be interested in what was happening. She had remained silent, leaning against a column, ignoring the gaggle of girls behind her. Luca remained behind Ella, next to the other guards. Henry was behind Celeste, her constant protection.

Ella watched the next woman approach. She wore clothes that were hanging off her frame. They had been stitched together, her feet bare. Her black hair was knotted on top of her head, her steps timid. The hairs on Ella's neck stood tall, her gut twisting to react, to jump into the middle of the court and strike the woman down.

Ella shifted, glancing around. Henry moved, his feet changing position, but he didn't move into any defensive position. David remained calm, one leg crossed over the other as he leaned forward.

"Please, I need food for my family. We have no food in so long." She stood close, almost at the base of the five stairs leading up to them.

Ella folded her hand behind her back, snapping her fingers once. She was certain Luca was paying attention, but on the off chance he wasn't, that sound would alert him.

"I am sorry for your hunger. Have you been able to find work anywhere?" King Matthias sat back on his throne.

"No, no one will hire me." She looked at her feet, and so did Ella.

They were firm feet and legs, from what Ella could see. The woman stood in a wider, well-balanced stance, and though her hair appeared dirty and tangled, it was also pulled out of her face. Ella positioned herself a step closer between the woman and David, just enough to have a better reaction time should anything happen. Ella noted the shield at the base of King Matthias's throne, within her reach.

"We'll arrange for some food to be sent to you, and possibly have you talk with our chief housekeeper about a position here until you find something else," David commented. He too had leaned back as the woman had gotten closer to them. No other citizen had dared even approach the base of the steps, let alone step onto one of them.

"Oh, thank you." The woman collapsed to her knees, moving up towards David.

"That's far enough." Henry strode around the back of the throne to put himself between David and the women, sword drawn. His blade glowed as Henry actively enchanted it, the glow its own form of threat. One most people backed away from.

"Of course, of course." The woman moved backward, standing up to regain her footing. "I have a gift for the prince, that is all."

Henry remained in his spot, sword at the ready, as she slowly reached into a pocket in her tunic.

Ella strained against the stillness she had to endure. She needed to move. Needed to fight and take her out. Her heart thrummed a battle cry against her ribcage, demanding recognition, demanding Ella to react.

"It's from Holodal—"

The woman moved, and so did Ella.

She grabbed the shield, jumping in front of David as the woman pulled out a dagger and flung it at him. The enchanted blade cut into the shield, stopping only when the hilt would let it go no further. Ella stared down at the point of the blade that was mere inches from her face. Red coated her vision as she reached into the small of her back, where she always kept a dagger. This wanna-be murderer would know what it was like to tangle and die at the hands of a true assassin.

Her hand almost touched her dagger when Henry took charge. He forced the woman down the stairs as she defended with another blade. Guards ran into the room, weapons drawn as the other guards positioned themselves between the nobility and their threat.

Ella spared a glance at Celeste, who remained in her chair with the King and Luca beside her. Both men had weapons drawn. Luca locked eyes with her, a question burning in their depths. Ella nodded. She could protect David. Someone had to watch over the others.

Henry grunted as the woman sliced open his arm.

He moved faster, striking quickly.

Henry ran his sword through her chest, the enchanted metal easily cutting through muscles and bone.

The woman laughed. "Oops."

Henry backed away, sword following. The woman's entire body lit up with magic as she stumbled. Ella kept her defensive position in front of David as the enchanter turned towards them. All motion slowed down as Henry turned, running towards them, his mouth open, yelling something, but all Ella could do was watch. She'd never seen an enchanter die before, but she knew what would happen. The raw power that the enchanter held within would explode throughout the room.

The enchanter's glow grew as she collapsed to her knees, her entire chest painted red as she hemorrhaged.

Fire tingled down Ella's spine as David stood beside her.

"David—"

He could not be this close. The enchanter was dying, and her magic...it was about to burst free from her.

David muttered under his breath rapidly, his hands glowing as he clutched the shield in Ella's hands. His magic flashed as the enchantment completed.

David stood beside her, his hand resting on her back, as he pulled them behind the hefty shield. Ella turned back to the enchanter. She had stopped moving right as Henry reached the bottom step.

Her entire body lit up the room, her arms pointing directly at David.

All of her magic was expelled through her hands in a burst of raw lightning.

Ella planted her feet, holding the shield with David as the current blasted them. They lifted the shield, their feet sliding on the stone as the power pushed into them. David tightened his hold on her, shifting into a defensive position as his enchantment took effect on the shield.

"Protegen et defendant vim mentis," David whispered the enchantment over and over for what seemed to be hours.

Screaming echoed in Ella's head, the sound returning as the attack faded.

Charred magic swirled in Ella's nose as she breathed in. The noblewomen of the court were chaotic, as she and David continued to stand there, shield in hand.

"Did that... happen?" Ella whispered. Safety wrapped around Ella as she stayed behind the shield with David. It was just the two of them, holding their protective barrier.

"Are you hurt?" David's voice was rough in her ear, low and husky.

Ella shook her head, setting the shield down slowly, avoiding the dagger.

"Are you?" She turned to look him over. His skin was pale, his brown eyes lit with an inner fire as he surveyed the scene before them. He nodded tersely.

Ella turned back to the assassin on the ground. She knew she shouldn't be looking. Any respectable lady of the court would look away. But not her. The assassin's hands were rippled with streaks of red from her uncontrolled power. A smirk on her face. Guards encircled her, forming a loose perimeter. Ella assessed her. She had been good. To a point. Ella would have tried nothing so openly. Only a fool wanting to die would be so brazen. Or someone wanting to make a statement. A very loud political statement. What had she said? She had a gift for David from Holodal. Only someone looking to start a war would do that.

"David, why does—" Ella stopped when Henry reached them, his face pale. "Henry, you're bleeding." She whispered.

The room remained in chaos. Ella wasn't sure which was more annoying, the women unable to leave because of crying, or those who wanted to see what unfolded next.

"It's nothing—"

"Let me be the judge of that." David grabbed Henry's wrist, sliding the sleeve up his arm.

"Why would Holodal want to kill you, David? I thought there were no poor relations with them?" Ella sat on the steps, shield beside her. The attack wasn't adding up. Lady Tremaine had, of course, assigned Ella because of the threat from Holodal, but based on what Luca had told her about his home kingdom, they wouldn't behave in such an obvious manner. For all she knew someone was trying to make it look like Holodal was responsible.

"They wouldn't," Luca spoke before David or Henry could answer. Both of them glanced up. He had walked over, his hand resting on the hilt of his sword.

Luca had never looked more imposing, or confident.

"Excuse me, Guard Luca, I know you hail from Holodal, but what would you know about the inner workings of that kingdom's ruler?" Henry winced as David cleaned his injury.

"I may have left my home kingdom several years ago, but I doubt the emperor's opinions on how to engage in subterfuge have changed. He would see this as cowardly."

"Well, the woman certainly looks to be from Holodal," David commented, sparing the body a glance.

"That may be—"

"Doesn't the emperor there have a stranglehold on enchanters in his kingdom?" David frowned.

"Yes, but not all remain in Holodal. I'm simply pointing out that he has nothing to gain by attacking you. Who else does?" Luca's eyes darkened at the challenge he was receiving from Henry and David.

Both men remained silent, refusing to debate who was trying to kill David any further.

"You were handy with that shield, Ella. We're lucky you have such fast instincts." Henry looked away from the slice on his arm as David got a closer look.

Ella blinked at the topic change. "I, uh...saw someone do something similar in Evrotia. I'm just glad that the dagger's hilt stopped it." Ella rubbed her head.

"I'm glad you're both safe." Celeste threw herself into Ella's arms, holding on tight. The thirteen-year-old shook in Ella's arms.

Ella wrapped her arms around her, squeezing tight. Celeste's face was pressed against her chest, tears soaking through.

"I'm glad you're safe, Pumpkin. I'm happy Luca was by your side." Ella glanced over at him, thanking him silently.

David leaned away from Henry, apparently satisfied with his examination. "Well, the blade she had wasn't coated in any poison, luckily, but you're still going to need stitches, and no healing tonics, unfortunately," David surmised. He had ripped off Henry's sleeve and cut it into strips before wrapping them around the wound.

"I didn't realize you were such an expert already," Ella commented, watching as David deftly took care of Henry.

"Well, it is his specialty." Henry grimaced as David tightened the bandage. "Everyone thought he would have specialized in defense or combat. How surprised our instructor was when you told him you, the prince, had been deemed a healer." Henry smiled.

"The look on his face was worth it. I can still hear him yelling down the hall that the evaluator was mistaken, that no prince before had ever specialized as a healer." David grinned.

"Why is it a bad thing? Wouldn't being a healer be good?" Ella tilted her head.

"The instructor was upset that he didn't get the honor of instructing the future king, and was instead left with me," Henry remarked.

Celeste had yet to let go of Ella, her arms holding on tight. Ella rested her head on top, realizing that this was probably the first time the princess had seen anything violent. Envy slid down Ella's back at how innocent Celeste's life had been up to this moment. She grieved for the loss. Ella rubbed Celeste's arms and gently pulled back for the young princess to look up at her.

"Let's go for a little walk. Get the jitters out of us," Ella whispered. David would be fine on his own for a little bit. She didn't anticipate anyone else attacking today.

Celeste nodded her head vigorously, spinning both of them around towards a back door. Ella kept pace with her as she led the way through a series of hidden passageways until they were outside in the royal garden maze.

"How's Celeste?" David stood at the entrance to Ella's room.

The walk with Celeste had lasted hours. The heels of her feet had pounded in her head with every step. Luca had been close behind the entire time. But no matter how much walking they had done, Celeste had continued to shake. Ella had held her soft hand in her own, talking about nothing for hours. Celeste had talked when Ella mentioned sailing across the ocean. She had lit up in front of Ella's eyes as she expressed her desire to forge better relationships with other kingdoms and begin opening new alliances. Ella was awed by her dream of their kingdom.

"She will be." Ella folded up a wool blanket and set it on the trunk at the base of her bed. "It's the first time she's seen someone killed, or seen her big brother attacked...it was...a lot."

Ella walked across her room to the fireplace and sat down in one of the comfy chairs, sighing in relief. She motioned for David to come in, watching him as he got closer to her. He moved with confident grace; the door closing behind him.

David had been attacked today.

The words washed over Ella, dousing her in a pool of frozen water. Her heart sped up, remembering the power that had confronted them as the enchanter died. If David hadn't enchanted that shield...

Why did this one feel any different to her? She shook her head and smiled at him as he sat down and leaned back in the chair.

"What are you smiling about? Today was...long." David observed her, his face heavy with exhaustion.

Ella clutched the armrests, keeping herself in place instead of by his side. "I'm smiling because my friend is alive." She forced herself to lean back in the chair, putting a little bit more distance between them.

"I'm glad you're safe." David ran a hand through his hair, briefly covering his eyes. When he looked back at her, the anguish flooding them was almost enough to undo her will to stay away from him. As it was, he stood up and crouched before her, his hand taking hers into his. "I was so..." His hand shook as he grasped hers. "You blocked the brunt force of her magic. I can't believe you did that...or knew to do that. You're incredible."

David moved their hands so that they covered his heart, both of them sitting still for a moment. Ella's eyes remained fixed on their hands.

"I saw a lot in Evrotia. It became second nature, I guess...to protect those I care about." Ella bit her lip.

David met her eyes, his hand slipping free of hers to touch her cheek.

"David..." Ella's heart cracked at what she was about to say. She was going to leave once this assignment was over, so she had to do it now. "You're engaged. It's part of the treaty you're signing in eight days."

His fingers fell away slowly before lying limply by his side.

"Ella...I don't....I don't want to marry her. I want—"

"What do you want, David?"

"I want time. I want time to figure everything out." David got up and paced around her room. "I want to know why Holodal is trying to kill me. Why assassins keep cropping up in the most...random of places..." David's eyes darted to her door as though there was one lurking outside for him. "I want to keep the peace between our kingdoms, yet someone is determined to make sure I can't..." He stopped moving long enough to look at her.

Ella's heart demanded to be heard by her, ordering her to go to him and kiss him. Hug him. *Anything* that would get the look of pain and conflict off his face and out of his grief-stricken hazel eyes. But she clamped it down. She would not listen to her heart. Not right now.

"You're telling me that you want to break the treaty?" Ella did her best to keep a straight face. Her entire mission was about the treaty and making sure he was alive to sign it. If he didn't...David would put the entire kingdom at risk.

"Yes. No. I don't know. I'm talking to my friend about what's going through my head." David sat down heavily in the chair opposite hers and covered his face with a hand.

"One thing I've learned throughout all of this is that we have to be willing to make sacrifices for our duties. Yours is just a little bit bigger than the rest of ours." Ella said, staying firmly in her chair. She couldn't listen to the frantic beating of her heart telling her to make him agree to the treaty, nor could she do anything about his engagement.

"Sometimes I think the burden is too much, that my parents put too much on me before I was even born." David chuckled. "I'll think about what you said. Thank you for talking with me."

"Of course, David, I'll always be here for you," Ella said before she could stop herself.

"Will you?" David walked over and again held her hand. Tingles of an emotion Ella refused to recognize shot up her arm. "If there's one thing the events of today make me realize, it's just how much I've missed you. And how much I've enjoyed having you around again...if I had lost you today..." David looked around her room. "I couldn't...not again..."

"David..." Ella looked at him. After all of these years, this was what she had wanted to hear. That she had been missed, that they needed her. Just not in the way she wanted to be needed.

David shook himself and walked towards her door.

"David," Ella bit her lip, wondering if she was pushing her luck. But David was opening up to her, and she had to ask the question that had been burning a bright hole in her heart. "Why is Celeste afraid of the room down the hall from me?"

David visibly froze before her, his tan skin going three shades whiter. "The person who used to be in there...died tragically...she did something that hurt us...that's all. Just ghosts." David whispered before leaving quicker than Ella could blink.

Ella didn't move when David left, shutting the door behind him. Ella sat in her chair for a few minutes, absorbing what she had learned, and wondering not for the first and certainly not the last time. What exactly had Sophie done?

Ella unlaced her corset and dress to pull on her sneak suit. She had to process everything that had happened, and the only way to do that was by doing something else. She twisted her hair up in a tight braid and crawled out of her window. Sneaking through the garden, she avoided guards and any late-night members of the noble class taking a stroll in the moonlight. Though Ella wanted to follow them and see where they were going, she resisted her curiosity and walked to a path that only two other people knew about. They had discovered it one day when David and Henry were helping her avoid Anastasia and Drea. The three of them had sworn each other to secrecy. Ella approached the wooden door covered in ivy between a grove of trees hidden in the ground and pulled it open to let Mira out of the passageway below.

"This better be worth me walking through that disgusting, slimy, mold-infested route," Mira complained as she stepped out, a torch in her hand, illuminating her fiery hair.

"You have no problem swimming in freezing ocean waters filled with seaweed, yet this you have an issue with?" Ella smiled, relaxing in the glow of the flames.

"Uh yes, the ocean does not feel like that, or make me come out covered in filth."

Ella remained silent, leading her farther into the gardens. Once they were far enough away, Ella relayed all the day's events, her hands twisting in her suit as she paced around.

"Shit, El, what are you going to do?" Mira curled her hair around a finger before braiding it into a fishtail and leaning forward to get a better look at her friend.

"I'm not sure...all I've ever wanted is to protect David and our kingdom. I feel as though I'm protecting him with my eyes closed, and a hand tied behind my back." Ella walked around the small alcove they had sequestered themselves in, making sure to never leave the glow of the flame's light. "I will do *anything* to make sure he's protected, and once I'm gone...I don't know."

"You're willing to leave now that you've gotten the chance at your dream assignment?"

"We both know she's not going to let me stay. Lady Tremaine has a lot of work for us, and if protecting the kingdom means leaving David—"

"You mean leaving someone you care deeply about?" Mira remarked.

"I have a child's crush, that's all. I can't let myself feel anything more. He's an assignment, Mira."

"Of course," Mira nodded a small smirk on her lips. "So, if I kissed him, or...if I seduced him, you would have no problem with that?" Mira crossed her arms, arching a brow.

"None it might help me solve Sophie's murder if you did." Ella held herself tall as Mira spoke about using her own particular skill set. Mira was excellent at her job, being the Siren, seducing men, and getting them to reveal their secrets. She had no problem if Mira turned those skills on David.

"Are you going to tell Lady Tremaine about the possible threat to the treaty?"

"No. He's just being emotional and will come to his senses. He knows he has his oath. He'll follow through."

"Then I think you know what to do. You'll stay, be his friend and protector, and in eight days when he signs the treaty, you'll leave."

"You make it sound so easy," Ella said.

"It is when you think about it logically. David will always be in danger. It comes with being part of a royal family."

"What if I told him?"

"Told him what?" Mira locked eyes with her.

"Everything? Maybe he would let me stay and protect him? The king could command Lady Tremaine. It's not as though she can tell her king no."

"Ella, part of our oath is that we can't tell them. We operate in the shadows so that they--"

"Don't have to. I know that's normally my line." Ella replied.

Mira and Ella walked back towards the garden, their steps even and silent, avoiding any detection. Mira put the flame out, holding Ella's hand as they looked up at the full moon shining down on them, offering Ella just enough light. As Mira left, Ella wondered if she was right about not telling David everything. But her fear of rejection weighed heavily on her mind as she kept her flame of hope low.

CHAPTER FIFTEEN

Ella sat on the windowsill of her room, a cup of hot chocolate in her hands. She had barely slept all night. What had Sophie been doing in the palace? Ella pulled out Sophie's journal and read more. Her protégé never mentioned her mark by name. She was obsessed with David and mentioned being weary of Henry and forming a good bond with Celeste. But not once did she talk about her plan of attack or who her mark was. If Ella was going to discover her killer, then she needed to know, and Lady Tremaine wasn't going to tell her. All she could do right now was to continue with her assignment. It was the best she could do. But that didn't mean she was useless.

Ella? Jaq smiled at her. His glasses were smudge-free in the early morning.

How are you? Ella leaned back against the wall of her nook, an easy grin lighting her face.

Better with seeing you. When do you get to come home? Jaq pinched the space between his light brown eyes.

What happened? Ella held the mirror closer, her hands gentle as though she were holding him.

I've been doing a lot of enchanting. A lot...so I'm a bit more drained than usual. Jaq rubbed his hair, the black ends sticking up in all kinds of angles.

You should tell her—

I can't. You know that's not how it works here, and with Calla gone, I'm the strongest enchanter here. I'll manage it. For the crown.

I wish you didn't...I saw what happens when. Ella paused. Her heart crawled into her throat. *I saw an enchanter die—*

Are you hurt? How strong were they? Jaq leaned in so close to the mirror, that all she could see was the top half of his face.

I'm fine. Everyone's fine. Ella was not going to tell him she had taken the brunt force of that blast.

He blew out a breath as he slumped. He gazed around his room, and Ella couldn't help but wonder what was going through his genius mind. The way his lips pressed together told her he wanted to say something, but didn't know how.

Is there something you need from me? Jaq sat up straighter.

I was wondering if there's been any progress on discovering who killed the queen. Or Sophie?

He hung his head and shook it slowly. Jaq pressed his hands to his face before looking up at her, all hope gone. *I'm sorry, but no, to either. The queen died so long ago that finding anything that could have a remaining memory imprinted on it will be hard, which means scrying will be more difficult.*

Ella scrunched up her face. She had been worried about that. Most imprinted memories only lasted a few months on objects unless it was a memory imprinted with intent, and that wouldn't have happened while the assassin was killing her. The only place that might hold something of use...with memories, would be...Ella didn't...couldn't...go near the queen's rooms. She wasn't ready to face that.

I don't, but I could ask Luca to get something for me... Ella didn't like it. She would be putting him at risk, but she didn't see any other option. *Would you be able to come into Riset to get it from him today if I got him to agree?*

I think I can make that work.

Ella nodded, closing the mirror. She looked up and over to where Luca leaned against the door frame, a frown on his face.

"What are you convincing me to do?" Luca walked in and closed the door behind him.

She remained in the window, Luca coming to sit across from her. She continued to look out to the courtyard below, fog rolling around the hedges as the sun lit up the gray sky. "Do you think you'd be able to get something that belonged to the queen out of the palace and into Riset to give to Jaq? I know that I'm asking you to put yourself at risk of being caught."

"I can do it, but if I'm caught, you could also be implicated."

"I know, but it's important to help solve the queen's murder. I'll make sure David's out of the palace, and Henry will be so busy trying to find us that no one will pay attention to you."

"Where should I look?"

"The queen's study. That's where....it all happened," Ella couldn't bring herself to say killed out loud.

Ella put on her riding gear and went to David's room. He opened his door, rubbing the sleep from his eyes. She took the moment to admire the lean muscles on his chest as he stood in nothing but his undershorts. The dagger's wound on his chest had finally begun to heal.

"It's a little early, don't you think?"

"Or is it the perfect time to go for a ride? Before everyone else is awake?" Ella wiggled her eyebrows at him. "I smuggled some hot croissants out of the kitchen."

"Give 'em." David grinned, grabbing a croissant from her. "I need a few minutes." David left the door open for her as he walked into his room to change. A loud thud vibrated throughout the room. "I'm okay."

"What did you do?" Ella was halfway across the room by the time he had called out. She rounded the door to find David on the floor, a pile of books on top of him.

"I may have one too many books." David sheepishly smiled.

"Just a few. At least it wasn't too bad. We wouldn't want you taken out by your books just to make all of those other kingdoms happy." Ella smiled as she walked back to one of the chairs in front of his fireplace and sat down to eat a croissant, its warm flakes getting all over her pants.

"Should we notify Henry?"

"It's so early we don't want to disturb the guards. Besides, it's a horseback ride through the palace grounds. We'll be back before they'll know we're gone." Ella assured him as David walked out, tucking in his tunic.

The stablehand's mouth dropped when he walked out to find Ella and David saddling their horses before he could get to them. Both horses were warmed and ready to go by the time they got to the open fields behind the walls of Riset. Ella and David let them run, soaking up the smell of warm wood and fresh spring flowers. The tall grass rippled around them on the wind, turning the fields into an ocean full of currents. By the time they slowed down, the fog had begun to lift, letting the sunlight stream over them.

"Let's give them a rest." David stopped his horse and dismounted, pulling out a blanket and laying it on the grass for them. As the horses grazed nearby, the two of them lay in silence, looking up at the clouds. Ella hoped Luca was done with his task. They would need to head back soon.

"How has it been being back at court here?" David spoke softly, as though he didn't want to know her answer.

"It's been okay. All the attacks and snide comments from courtiers have made me truly feel at home." Ella laughed.

"Is it so bad?" David asked. "The attacks and snide comments aside...is it so bad to imagine a life at court with Henry and Celeste...and...me?"

"That's the only good part about being at court."

"So you won't be leaving soon?" Davids rose in pitch with his hope.

"Court was very educational, but...all the politics, David...I don't want to have to constantly be on my guard that if I say one thing incorrectly at the wrong time, I'll never recover my public standing. That kind of pressure..." Ella shivered. "I would rather learn how to do something else that would contribute to our kingdom other than being a talking puppet."

"You could do that. Your Mom did that as a duchess. It would be the same for you. Your father's title is yours to inherit. You have the opportunity to make an impact. If you ever want to talk about what that would look like, I'm here."

"I know, but like you, I need time. I've only been back for a few weeks. I want to make sure we get you through to this ball first." Ella laughed.

"Where I get to officially be engaged to Princess Lena." David shuddered. "I didn't talk to my parents for a week when I first found out."

"Sometimes we have to—"

"Sacrifice for our duty. I remember. I just don't understand why I'm the one sacrificing because of our parents."

"Do you know what happened? I know nothing." Ella ignored the sinking pit in her stomach. Maybe David would back out of the treaty.

"It was quite the scandal back then. Dad was supposed to marry Queen Laila but fell in love with Mom instead. Dad scrambled to save the treaty he was meant to sign, which is why there's so much importance for me signing this one."

"And you think being in court is fun?" Ella tried to laugh. None of it sounded fun. It was the exact thing she hated about courts coming to life and dragging her into it.

"Most of the time, it's informative. It lets us see how people are doing, and monitor those we've entrusted to run various towns or villages of Rairene. If they step out of line, we have an easier time removing them from their post."

Ella remained silent, soaking up what David had said, and weighing her options, even though she knew Lady Tremaine wouldn't let her walk away from Aumont. They had too much to do, and she played a vital role in that.

"David, what do you think our normal selves would be doing right now?" Ella turned on her side to face him as he gazed up at the giant redwoods, the sun shining through, highlighting his face.

"Let's go find out." David smiled as he stood up and walked to his saddlebags. Ella got to her feet, tilting her head. She frowned when he pulled out two wigs.

"David—"

"Let's go explore Riset as normal people. I've been thinking about it a lot, and I want you there with me."

"It's not safe, David." Panic pooled in Ella's stomach as ice drenched her like a bucket of water being poured over her head. She was about to see him willingly put himself in danger. She couldn't do it. Wouldn't allow it.

"Come on, I'm going to go whether or not you come with me." David pulled back his hair and put the wig on.

"It's not safe for you. What if something happens?" Ella tried to get the wig out of his hands.

"Nothing is going to happen. Come on Ella, where's the rebellious girl I grew up with who would try to see how quickly we could lose our guards? Bring her out. I miss those days."

"David, we grew up, that's what happened. Henry will—"

"Henry is not my keeper, and I want to get out of the palace walls for a little bit. Now you're coming with me or not, that choice is up to you.

Either way, by the time you get to the palace, I'll have snuck into Riset." David shrugged as he walked to his stallion.

She couldn't leave him to his own devices. That would only be worse. She had to go. She knew she did. It was a lose-lose situation, but at least this one had David in constant protection. Ella held out her hand for the wig, ignoring the light in his eyes as he gave it to her.

They got on their horses and rode towards the wall. As soon as they were within sight of the palace, they dismounted and left the horses tied at the edge of the gates. David grabbed Ella's hand and led her into Riset. Her fingers tingled where he touched hers, sending warmth cascading throughout.

The two of them weaved through back alleys covered in dirt and an everlasting smell of waste and human filth. No longer did they look like they belonged at the palace by the time they walked out into the streets of the fourth circle. David released Ella's hand, and for one second, her heart stopped. It was quickly replaced with giddy nerves when he wrapped her arm around his, escorting her through the city, his thumb rubbing over her hand. Ella smiled as they walked leisurely between people who had no idea who they were.

"So, where should we go first?"

David looked around, a mischievous glint in his eyes. "Do you trust me?"

It was such an innocent question. One meant in jest as they played out their alter—personas. But it hit Ella deep in the chest, down where all the powerful truths lived. Ella nodded, unable to voice her truth. She hadn't expected the 'yes' that instantly rose. She did trust him. David grinned and led her through more streets, not stopping until they got to a small nondescript shop. If it hadn't been for the line of people, Ella would have sworn the store was closed. Its front door hinges barely held on to the frame and cracked windows lined the storefront.

"What is this place?" Ella asked as they got in line two storefronts down.

"I'm not giving you any hints."

"Evil man." Ella smiled. A whiff of a smell went past her, tickling her nose with the barest of whispers. "No." Her eyes widened. The sweet smell of cinnamon, sugar, and dough wafted over her. David's smile somehow grew larger as she saw a patron walking by carrying a box full of cinnamon rolls.

"I know they're a treat in Evrotia, and it looks as though their love of them passed to you." David was practically glowing. So much so, that Ella wondered if part of his magic was responding.

"My best friend makes them. They're incredibly delicious. I haven't had one in...so long." Since Raven had left five months ago, Ella added silently.

"You never talk about it, you know."

Ella looked at him quizzically.

"You only mention the horrible things you went through, and none of the good. Such as your friends. You had to have had many friends, maybe even suitors. I would love to learn about all of it...the bad and the good."

"Really?" Ella surveyed him, searching for the reason. Did he want to use it against her later? But all she found was genuine curiosity.

"Of course. I want to learn about the people important to you. They helped you become the amazing woman you are." David leaned in close. So close that all she had to do was take half a step and she could kiss him.

Ella gazed into his brown eyes, fell into their depths, the flecks of green and hazel, and couldn't stop the blush rising on her cheeks.

"Hey, move along."

Ella stumbled sideways as the woman behind yelled at them. Ella looked over. The line had indeed moved. A lot. David smiled, grasping her hand as they moved closer to the desserts, waiting for them.

"So, your friend, what's she like?" David whispered, his hand playing with hers.

"Well, she's extremely tough. You have to be there...in Evrotia...so she adapted quickly." Ella paused, choosing to take the moment to truly let David in. "You know those relationships that you have where there's a bond that goes beyond friendship? Beyond even that of siblings? It's as though part of your soul is linked to them in a way you never knew was possible."

David nodded. "I think so? I've always felt that way with Henry, but we've been friends since birth."

Ella smiled. "It's similar. I have the same relationship with two others outside of her. I don't know what I would do without them." Ella thought of Mira and Calla, her heart clenching. It had been so long.

"I hope I can meet them all one day. I would like to thank them for being by your side. From what you've said, it sounds like a cruel place to learn how to be a lady."

"Why isn't there a better relationship with the kingdoms near us?"

The woman behind them harrumphed. Ella spun to look at her, storm clouds darkening her light blue eyes. "You have an opinion?" Ella's voice was icy as she appraised the woman, who paled under her gaze.

"I would love to hear what you think." David smiled. The woman relaxed, her tense shoulders slumping. He was so very good at that, putting people at ease.

"We don't have any relations no more because our king, bless his soul, is too busy tryin' to take care of 'is heart and those of the prince and princess. Losing our beloved queen to the fever like that can't 'ave been easy for any of them. I don't blame 'im, of course. But that's why. Grief destroys those left behind."

Ella and David blinked.

"I completely agree." Ella stepped between the woman and David, who had gone whiter than her hair. "Grief impacts us all in so many ways." She turned David away right in time to step through the door and get their cinnamon rolls.

All thoughts about the woman's comments vanished as Ella and David dug into their treats. The sweet rolls melted in their mouths.

"So, I take it you like them?" David smiled when Ella bit her lip and studied the line, debating on going back for more.

"Thank you for bringing me here." Ella held David's hand, this time squeezing tightly. "I think one day we'll have to come here as ourselves. Though I am enjoying our 'normal life'. Should we figure out what they would have done next?"

"We shall."

David and Ella spent the day wandering the streets, doing anything they thought their counterparts would do. They went into bookshops and dress shops, tasting different foods along the way. As the sun descended, they walked into a small, crowded pub. It was in amazing condition, the stone walls and wood ceiling flawless, though that wasn't why the location was bustling. Entertainers in the far corner played their instruments with joy and precision. Ella swayed with the music as she and David found a small table in the corner.

Ella closed her eyes and let the melodies and harmonies brush against her. She leaned against David, smiling as the tune took hold and captured her spirit. She never wanted to leave as the world fell away and music became an encapsulating world.

"I wish we could stay in this moment forever," Ella whispered. The song had come to its bridge, carrying Ella up with it.

"I forgot how much you love music," David replied.

"I haven't listened to it since..." She hadn't listened, truly listened, since the queen had died. She hadn't listened to anything powerful enough to move her to tears because once they came, they would never stop. So she didn't think about music, because Queen Charisse loved music just as much.

"She did love it," David mumbled.

"The effects of grief." Ella breathed. The songs weighed them down, the gravity of one wrong word, one misstep, and everything would come tumbling down.

"Would you like to come up and sing?"

Ella looked at the young man smiling down at them.

"What?" Ella shrunk against David.

"I saw you. Someone who gets that lost in music must be able to sing. Would you like to perform with us?"

"She's fine, thank you for—"

Ella elbowed him.

"What?" David leaned in close to her, his brow furrowed. "You don't have to go up there. I know what this means for you—"

"I know you do." Before she could stop herself, and before David could move, Ella kissed David's cheek and got up. "But I owe it to her...to at least try."

Ella shook her fingers as nerves danced in her stomach. She followed the player up to the small stage as the others looked at her for the song. Ella twisted her hands in front of her, smiled timidly at the players, and turned her back to them. They wouldn't know the song she was going to sing. It was an Evrotian love song, one of the queen's favorites. The crowd hushed as Ella took a breath. Her heart pounded so fast she was sure she would faint. Ella closed her eyes, taking a moment to center herself. This song was just another kill. It would get her closer to her goal, therefore, she could do it. She could do this. She killed people, stalked them, and became their worst nightmare. She could face this down. Face her grief, or at least begin to look down upon the black pit inside.

The crowd murmured as she took her time. Ella opened her eyes and didn't dare think about the pain welling up in the back of her eyes. Taking one final breath, she began.

Ella sang four chords and stopped, her voice catching.

She swallowed, her heart fluttering as her hands gripped her riding pants. The crowd stirred, impatient. Ella closed her eyes and began again.

The pub held still for Ella as she sang, her voice ringing soft and true.

As the song built, so did her voice, becoming more urgent and filled with passion.

She remained in complete control over her voice, wavering only once on the demanding scales and slides in the song. She wove a love song that was rarely heard by the people of Rairene, and even though none of them could understand what she sang, they all knew what the song was about. Not a single dry eye looked up at her as Ella reached the crescendo. Her voice faded off as the two lovers lived the rest of their lives with each other.

Her throat was thick with saliva, tears blurring her vision as she sang the final chord.

Ella's heart soared over the lyrics, bursting with happiness and sorrow, the two emotions clashing within. As Ella stepped off the stage, the room was still quiet. She breathed a small sigh of relief as a small piece of her grief dimmed.

The pub didn't seem to know what to do with her performance. Everyone remained in abject silence, as though waiting for her to vanish before their eyes, for surely someone who sounded like that was a gift from the gods who needed her to return home. But no deity came to reclaim their prize, and once everyone realized that the room imploded with cheers for her.

Ella smiled meekly at David as she returned to his side. He remained thoughtful, his eyes wide as the room continued to cheer before the players began a new song. As the pub turned away from them, they sat togeth-er, absorbing all that had happened.

The players began a joyous song, contradicting Ella's pain. But she didn't mind. She stayed in the moment, settling into the emotions of singing once again.

"If we were somewhere private, I would—"

"Eleanor. David." Henry's voice hit them like a heat rod to a cow.

Both of them jolted at their table to look up at him. Henry's anger billowed off of him, seeming to encase the two of them in a shroud of darkness. The writhing glow of his power faded as he regained his control.

The surrounding patrons went silent as they noticed Henry. He was not one to be easily missed and was well-known in the city. They all then turned their eyes onto David and Ella, their faces going white as they realized whose presence they were in. A few even bowed before David motioned for them to stop. David's glower could have killed Henry. The three of them walked out of the pub quickly, removing their wigs as they did.

"Henry—" Ella began.

"I don't want to hear it. The two of you knew...you knew you needed an escort. Both of you. I didn't think both of you would lose your minds and decide to pull a stunt like this," Henry got on his horse, Dream, and David's horse were behind with a unit of guards.

"It's my fault, Henry. I take responsibility, the day got away from us—" David started.

"I don't care. Let's get to the palace. All of us have been searching for the two of you for hours. Luca's been frantic," Henry cut in, stabbing Ella right through the heart.

"Luca?" Realization washed over Ella. Sneaking into Riset had never been part of the plan.

"Why didn't you scry—"

Henry tossed a mirror at David. He caught it before pocketing it.

"You didn't bring it with you, or any other type of weapon that would let me scry you. We'll discuss this more when we get home." Henry clicked his horse, all of them taking off at a steady trot.

Ella and David remained quiet in their shame. The entire ride up to the palace, everyone stopped to look at them and smile, and they waved back. They couldn't display any weakness or any sign of trouble, so they smiled and waved. Henry didn't stop for anyone. The sun had made way for the moon by the time they got back and unsaddled their horses. The guards left them at the entrance to the palace, going back to their stations. Meanwhile, Ella and David were greeted by King Matthias and Luca, both of whom looked ready to strangle them.

David opened his mouth, stopping when the king spoke. "If you ever disregarded your life or that of Eleanor's again, you will be severely punished, David. What were you thinking? You didn't even inform Henry that you were going out—"

"It's my fault—" Ella said. David didn't need to get into any more trouble.

"It doesn't matter who did what. What does matter is that the two of you willingly put your lives at risk. I expect better from the two of you.

How can I expect my son to lead and for Ella to be protected when you do something this reckless?"

"We just..." Ella felt the heat rising on her cheeks as David remained stoic. "We wanted to be ourselves. The two of us, for a minute, and yes, we lost track of time, and we apologize, but I will not apologize for us taking a break from having to be perfect all the damn time. I am *not* some helpless—"

"Ella," David whispered, instantly stopping her. "Father, I'm sorry. We didn't mean to be gone that long. It won't happen again."

Ella stormed off. If she could only tell them who she truly was. They would know that David was never in any danger so long as she was there. She'd already saved his life three times. When she reached her room, she slammed her door and instantly went to light a candle.

"Ella." Celeste launched herself into Ella, holding her.

"Pumpkin...everything okay?" Ella glanced down, wincing at the tracks of tears on Celeste's cheeks. "I'm sorry if we frightened you. The day got away from us."

"I'm glad you're alright, angry, but glad," Celeste whispered, burying her head.

"I won't do it again, I promise," Ella mumbled.

"Princess Celeste, do you mind if Lady Eleanor and I have a moment?" The ice in Luca's voice was decidedly more terrifying than Henry's fire. Ella had never heard such a tone from Luca before, and she didn't think she ever wanted to again.

Celeste gave Ella a sympathetic smile before scurrying out of the room. Luca slammed the door shut behind her. He prowled over and held Ella's arms as his eyes burned with anger. Yet his hands were gentle.

"I could kill you for the panic you caused today. I swear you took years off of my life. I'm sure my hair is turning gray from today's events."

"I know. I'm sorry. He was going to go into Riset with or without me. I had to make sure he stayed protected. I didn't realize the time."

"You could have made him stay here. You could have kissed him, something, Ella. There's enough tension between the two of you to light hundreds of fires."

"We're only friends. Especially in his eyes. I didn't want to try anything that would push him away. I had to go. Besides...it was nice." Ella slid out of his grip and walked to her bed. "No one cared about what we said, or did, or how we looked. It was just the two of us...surely you can understand that?"

Luca moved to lie beside her, grabbing her hand gently and squeezing it. "I do...just let me know next time. I know everyone was worried about David, but Ella, the thought of you being in trouble because I helped you with something...I couldn't bear it. I'm solely here to protect you."

"I can take care of myself, Luca."

Luca laughed, "I know, Ashes...believe me...I know. That doesn't mean I'm not allowed to worry."

"I'll be careful next time. I promise." And she meant it. She knew there were a lot of promises made recently that she had no way of keeping, but this one, she would do her best to keep.

Ella patted his shoulder as she went to her armoire and pulled out a dress suitable to wear down to the kitchens. A light glowed on top of her dresser, pulling her away from any notion of changing. Her mirror was demanding to be answered with Jaq on the other side.

Jaq—

I've found something about Sophie.

CHAPTER SIXTEEN

What did you find? Ella almost dropped the mirror. Finally, she had a break.

I can't tell you this way. Can you meet me in person? It was then that Ella realized Jaq wasn't in his mage room, or in any discernible place that she knew. Darkness surrounded him, the only illumination coming from the glow of his mirror.

Where are you?

The fifth circle of Riset and a pub called The Lion's Den. Meet me here.

Ella looked at Luca, who had stayed behind, an idea forming. She nodded and closed the mirror.

"Want to do something fun?" Ella asked, a small smile forming.

"Always, though sneaking out right now is going to be...interesting."

"I have a plan. I just get to look like an ungrateful bitch." She scrunched her face.

Luca nodded.

Ella walked over to him quickly and shoved him out of her door. He stumbled into the hallway and landed against the opposite wall, his eyes wide before he pretended to be angry.

"I said I was sorry. Now leave me alone," Ella screamed as loud as she could. Loud enough for the entire city of Riset to hear her. David and Henry walked down the hall as Celeste's door opened. "I want to be alone for the rest of the night." Ella glanced at David and Henry, staring them down for a second before turning on her heel and slamming the door behind her.

She groaned, her skin crawling at the display. She shook out her arms. No one annoyed her more than someone who made a scene.

"Ella?" David asked as he knocked on her door.

Ella leaned against it. "I want to be left alone, David. Please...I'm sorry about today. Can we talk tomorrow?"

"Sure."

She had never heard someone sound so defeated uttering a single word, but there it was. Total defeat. Ella took a deep, quivering breath and collected herself as she leaned against the door, listening for David's departing footsteps.

Slipping one of her unenchanted suits on was like stepping into herself and becoming who she was meant to be: a protector. Someone who didn't have to be a perfect lady of the court, but a weapon of the crown. Ella's entire body relaxed, as though she had been drowning in the skirts and now she was free. She braided her hair and donned a black cloak, covering her hair and face.

Ella dug to the bottom of her trunk and pulled out her set of glass daggers. She ran her hands over the cool smooth blue glass, warming them. Each one was special and unique. Three were short and curved to resemble claws. Two were standard daggers with curved sharp edges. One was bigger than the rest, with several curved edges and thicker glass to handle the pressure of being stabbed into someone's heart. The last one was Ella's favorite, with a single curve and wide middle. It was thinner, but sharper and could make thin, painful cuts. Ella looked over each one, making sure there were no imperfections.

By the time Ella opened her window and crawled out, Luca was doing the same, turning to look at her. They climbed down the side of the palace, using its uneven stones to navigate their path. They dropped the last eight feet and landed quietly on the grass. The two of them walked beside each other, listening for any sound that was out of place. The guards on night patrol weren't paying attention to who was already inside the walls and only looked for those who might want to get in. Ella and Luca pulled their hoods over, obscuring their faces.

The walk to the fifth circle was quick as they kept to the shadows. The Lion's Den was a very well-kept pub that seemed out of place in the fifth circle. The ground beneath their feet had long ago turned from stone to mud. There were no horses down here with riders. Everyone walked to their destinations. The children that were out this late were wearing clothing stitched together more times than Ella could count. This pub was standing well compared to its neighbors, with their leaning walls and hay-filled roofs. The stonework was excellent.

Upon entering, Ella and Luca found a pub bursting with patrons. Luca stiffened the moment he surveyed the room. Ella arched her brow, noting that most of the wait staff were from Holodal. It wasn't their darker golden skin that gave away, but rather the braids some of them donned that revealed their heritage.

Ella thought Luca was going to snap in half when two warriors got up from a table and approached them. A man and woman stood in their way as Ella located Jaq at a secluded corner table. The man had the sternest facial expression she'd ever seen. He could give Henry a run for his money when it came down to being overly serious. His physique and stature suggested a life of battles. The woman wore her hair in braids tightly pulled against her head, the ends of which trailed down her spine. Both were prepared for a battle of any kind.

"Shen, what brings you here?" Luca was borderline friendly, his hands clenched.

"We need to speak privately, your—"

"Fine." Luca cut her off. "I'll meet up with you in a few minutes," Luca whispered to Ella.

She nodded as Luca rushed the two warriors out the door. She shrugged. He would tell her later if he wanted to. She made her way over to Jaq, ordering a drink and some food.

"Hey—"

Jaq hugged her tightly before she could say anything else. His usually calm demeanor was anything but as he squeezed her. He held on for a few seconds longer before stepping away. His tunic was wrinkled and dark circles had formed under his eyes. His spectacles were a little dirty.

"What have you been up to?"

"Enchanting. It appears there's little time for anything else." Jaq sat down heavily.

"If I'm keeping you from something, my inquiries can wait—"

"They can't. Your life might depend on it." Jaq clenched Ella's hands, desperation in his eyes.

"What did you learn? Why did you need me out here?" Ella rubbed his hand, trying to calm him down. She'd never seen him be so protective before. Something was different about him this time.

"I wanted to make sure you were...unharmed."

"I'm fine." Ella motioned to herself. "Now, what's happening?" Her fingers shook as she took him in. Jaq was genuinely rattled.

"I found someone who witnessed what happened to Sophie's body."

Ella leaned forward, her heart pounding. Finally, she could seek her retribution.

"I was also able to procure some of her blood from a piece of clothing."

"You know who did it." Ella gripped the table.

"I have to let you know that I'm not as skilled as Calla is at reading blood, and that this sample was degraded, but based on what my witness saw, who I confirmed, and this sample..." Jaq took a breath. Ella was about to strangle the answer out of him. She didn't need all the prefacing, she needed answers. Now. "The person who oversaw the disposal of her body was Henry."

"What." Ella leaned back, all life sucked out of her. "No. Henry protects the crown. He oversees a unit that hunts down assassins, he would never—"

"I heard him. In Sophie's blood. I couldn't see much, but I could hear her pleading for her life, and then I could hear him talking to her before he stabbed her. Henry killed her."

Ella absorbed the blow. Disbelief swamped her, making her hearing fuzzy. She let the emotion roll through her, processing it as her hearing sharpened and all sounds came back. Internally, she burned, her nerves lighting up with a need to react to the information.

"I don't believe it," she whispered. "There has to be a mistake, Henry would never—"

"You said there was someone on the inside helping the assassins?"

Ella nodded slowly as the pieces fell together.

"And you just said that he oversees a unit that hunts down assassins. What if that's a cover? What if Lady Tremaine found out and assigned Sophie to him? If he was her mark, and he found out, given his status at the palace, he would kill to keep it safe."

"But *why*? It makes little sense. I read her journal. She only ever seemed weary about Henry, not in love." Ella furrowed her brow as she ran a hand over her face. It didn't make sense.

"Money? Power? Why do any of them do what they do? But if he's the one you need to keep David safe from...Ella, I'm worried about your safety." Jaq grabbed her hand again.

Ella's eyes were focused on the wooden table beneath her hands, the smooth grain rubbing against her skin. She didn't even notice when the waitress brought over the food she had ordered.

Henry? Nausea rushed over her in waves, each one stronger than the last. He had killed her friend? He was trying to kill David? Ella was frozen. She was going to have to kill her friend. For the first time in her life, she didn't want this role. She didn't want to take out a friend.

But she would to protect the kingdom.

To protect David.

"Ella?" Jaq shook her. She looked up into his mousy brown eyes and all the concern they held. "You know I would do anything to keep you safe."

"I know."

"What did I miss?" Luca asked as he approached the table.

"I'll fill you in on the way back. If Jaq's intel is correct, we can never leave David unattended." Ella stood up, making sure she remained hidden. "Thank you, Jaq. I know it must have been hard to tell me. I appreciate the work you do for me. Always."

Luca raised his eyebrows but remained silent as they left. With each step closer to the palace they took, the more Ella's heart broke. Henry was going to regret the day he became a traitor.

Ella looked at herself in the mirror. Dark circles lined her eyes in the candlelight. Sneaking back in had been easy. Too easy, in her opinion. Probably part of Henry's plan to kill David. The security, though, was going to be the least of her problems. A light knock had Ella adjusting the robe she had on.

Another timid knock came through.

"Ella, I know you said you wanted to be left alone...but..." David's voice broke, followed by silence.

Ella stared at the door, one eyebrow raised, wondering what he could need this late at night. "What's wrong?"

Ella cracked open the door to peek out. David was slumped against the wall, his eyes closed, tears on his cheeks, and defeat in every inch of his slackened body.

"How do you do it?" he whispered, slowly turning his head to look at her through brown eyes covered in unshed tears.

"Do you want to come in?" Ella adjusted her robe, pulling the sleeves down.

David walked in, his shoulders hunched over. He collapsed in one of Ella's chairs by the fireplace, rubbing a hand over his face.

"How do you do it?" he questioned again.

"Do what? I'm a little confused." Ella closed the door and watched him as he tried to sink further and further into her chair. She was certain if it could, it would have swallowed him up.

"How have you grieved for her? How did you move past it?" David's voice was grounded in anger, and a desperation so strong it nearly sent Ella to her knees.

She leaned against her other chair. "Why are we talking about this?" Ella kept her voice level despite the rapid wings fluttering in her chest, threatening to break the walls inside her.

"You *sang* today El—"

"David, I haven't—" The wall was cracking, splintering out from her core as he confronted her.

"How did you do it?" David's voice quivered as he tangled his hands in his hair. "I'm so tired. All the time. I'm tired of carrying this grief that paralyzes me to my core. Please..." David gazed at her with eyes clouded in darkness. "Tell me how you did it."

"I haven't."

David scoffed, rubbing his nose. Ella walked over and held his hands.

"I haven't grieved David...I—I don't know how." She ignored the pain swelling in her eyes, closing them for a second before continuing. "When I found out..." Ella shut her eyes again, the tears about to reach a spilling point, her heart flooding with a pain that she had been suppressing for years.

The memory sprung to mind as if it had been only yesterday when Lady Tremaine had told Ella the queen was dead.

"When I was told...I stayed in my room for weeks." She opened her eyes, gazing at the fire as memories danced before her. "I haven't spoken to anyone...I haven't even..." Ella paused. She had to do this. For him. For herself. "I haven't even spoken her name in two years, because I know what will happen..." Ella blinked as the tears continued to build up, her throat thick with them. "It will make it real, and I'm not," her voice hitched, stuck on the words. "I'm not ready."

Ella sat down in front of David, the weight of her grief consuming her.

"It will make it real and that *pain*...that weight of despair that has held me together...it will crumble..." Ella pressed a hand to her chest as the reality of their loss hit her. "I haven't allowed myself to even think about the idea of never seeing her again. I'll never hear her voice call my name. I'll never get to hug her again." Ella squeezed her eyes shut, burying her face in her hands.

"I don't know how to do it, Ella."

"We do it together. One day at a time. We honor her by thinking about her and living our lives the best that we can. All of this grief we have—"

"I wish I didn't feel any of it. I hate it." David slid down to the floor beside her.

"Don't say that. You can't live a life of happiness without pain, otherwise, how would you know you were happy? Or loved? This pain we have..." Ella rested her hand on David's arm, drawing his attention to her. "It's up to us to figure out how to turn that pain back into a joy that honors her."

"I miss her, El...I miss my mom." It was the hitch in David's voice that broke the dam in both of them.

Ella pulled David to her and wrapped her arms around him, hiding her face in David's nightshirt. "I miss her too...Charisse..." Ella choked on her name. "She's dead," Ella spoke the words she had kept hidden at the back of her mind for two years. A new round of body-wracking sobs enveloped her. "Charisse is gone."

David held her close until both of them fell into tear-drenched sleep.

This time when Ella woke up, David was still there, pressed against her, sleeping soundly. She reached up to brush some hair out of his face, marveling at being so close to him. Her heart fluttered at seeing him in bed with her, peaceful and content. He opened his eyes, smiling at her.

"Not to ruin anything, but don't you have training to get to?" She smiled, resting her hand on his chest, feeling his steady heartbeat.

"Trying to get rid of me?" David mumbled.

"Never, but I would rather not get on Henry's bad side if I can avoid it."

"That is a very valid point, but I am going to be late today for training." David sat up and got out of bed, stretching in front of her. Ella soaked it all in. David arched a brow when he caught her.

Ella blushed, turning away.

She got up and sat in her nook, resting her head on her knees, and closed her eyes, needing to ignore David. This was a simple assignment. Keep David alive. Do her duty, and uphold her oath. That was it. There was nothing else. Now Henry was the one who killed Sophie. David's Champion was trying to kill him? She still didn't quite believe it. Henry would only ever kill someone who posed a threat to David, and Sophie was also there to protect David, right? Nothing made sense anymore, but she was going to do all that she could to protect him. No matter what.

CHAPTER SEVENTEEN

"Here, have some of this," David whispered.

The smell of chocolate with a touch of cinnamon wafted around her, rousing Ella from her thoughts. She opened her eyes as the sunlight broke through the thick layer of fog, casting rays over the grounds below in shades of gray. She didn't dare clutch her head as a headache grew from the never-ending parade of thoughts vying for attention.

"Hot chocolate is still your favorite drink, right?" David asked after she took too long to respond.

"Hmmm? Oh yes, it is, thank you." Ella grasped the steaming mug in her hands, her gaze drifting out over the gardens. She couldn't look at him. She couldn't tell him that Henry was trying to kill him. Or that she had killed people and was there to guard him. She had never thought keeping a secret could ever be so hard.

"What's on your mind?" David sat down on the other side of her cushioned window seat, his eyes open and curious.

"Nothing..."

David gave her a look that clearly said he didn't believe her. "About yesterday—"

"It was my fault—"

"It wasn't. I'm the one who put you in a difficult position. We both got caught up in the moment and as much as Henry would love to strangle me for it, I don't regret it."

"You don't?" Ella paused as she looked at him, realizing how close he was again, and waiting this time for him to close the gap. She wouldn't put her heart on the line anymore now there was too much at stake.

"No. I got to see you as yourself, and I...I fell into the moment. Whenever I'm around you...the entire world around me seems to fall away." David reached over and rested a hand on her knee. "All there is is you and me. Maybe it's because I missed nine years of us being friends, but I swear time slows down and the world is brighter with you in it."

"David—"

He stopped her with a finger to her lips. "I know I'm engaged, and that everything is complicated right now," David mumbled, rubbing her hand. The scent of his bookish magic swirled over her, wrapping her in its safety.

Ella clutched her mug, using the heat to ground her, to keep her from saying everything that her heart was demanding to be spoken. Ella opened her mouth—

"Training is starting." Henry stood at her door, armed and wearing his training clothes. He didn't smile at them.

"I had hoped that rebelling would get me out of it somehow." David sighed. "I want to talk more about last night." He patted her knee as he got up and walked towards Henry.

"Wait." Ella bolted to her feet, sprinting to be next to him. "Could I join?"

"Join?" David lightly laughed.

"You know...watch...I know I can't join...obviously." Ella ground out, her jaw tense. She could easily spar with them. However, today was not the day to reveal that. Especially to Henry, but she also couldn't have their practice going unsupervised anymore. That just wouldn't do.

"Of course," Henry said as he waited for David to get ready. "Though didn't it upset you when we were younger because you couldn't get in the ring?"

"It did, but I was eight. I've grown a lot since then, Henry." Ella stood taller, and even though she was shorter than him, she felt him shrink just a little bit under her gaze.

The walk to the grounds was quiet and quick. Ella itched for one of her daggers. She would pin Henry to a wall and demand answers. She would make him admit to killing Sophie and hiring all the other would-be-killers. He would not get away with this. Ella ground her nails into her palms, fighting the urge. It was not her place. It was not her role. All she had was a degraded blood sample from her protégé begging for her life, and Henry's voice denying her. She would need to have Lady Tremaine pass the information along to the King. He could handle the traitor however he saw fit, though she wished to deal with it now.

Ella stood outside of the training ring as David and Henry went through their morning routine. Others eventually came around as well to watch, including the master at arms. Ella glanced up at him. He had been an imposing giant when she was little. His black hair was now streaked with silver. But the same cunning intelligence was in his brown eyes. The queen's brother.

"Lady Eleanor, I hope you're still not trying to convince the boys to let you train with them." Lord Dominic's gravelly voice grated over her skin. Here was someone she had never gotten along with. He had always been the biggest voice opposed to her obsession.

"I'm not. The horrors of Evrotia have diminished that request." Ella stood up to her full height. She was as tall as him now. Though he was stronger, she knew he would be hard-pressed to beat her.

"Good. I'm glad something came out of that excursion. Even though the queen regretted it, I had always told her it was for the best." Lord Dominic looked away from Ella.

Ella balled her fists, her muscles vibrating with restraint.

"Though, I have to admit that even I did not expect how much of an impact your absence would negatively affect my nephew." He didn't look at her once. "It pains me to say that I'm glad you're back if only to see him smile again...it's almost as though Charisse is here again."

Ella relaxed her stance as she saw Lord Dominic as the old, battle-worn, sad man who loved his nephew he was. Even if that meant he would always be negative towards her.

"Lady Eleanor, your presence is requested." Luca came up behind her before she could say anything to Lord Dominic.

"Whoever it is can come here," Ella dismissed. Luca knew she couldn't leave David now.

"It's Lady Tremaine making the request," Luca muttered.

Ella froze as she formulated her response. "I'm sure Lady Tremaine can understand my hesitation in departing right now, given all that's happened."

"Go to her, Ella. I'll watch over your prince," Lord Dominic assured her. "I promise," he added when he looked over and saw her hesitation.

Ella nodded before walking away. She didn't like it. But she couldn't exactly say no without giving a reason.

"Doesn't Lady Tremaine know what we found?" Ella asked once they were out of earshot.

"No," Luca whispered, "Jaq hasn't told anyone—"

"You're certain?"

"You doubt his loyalty to you?" Luca raised his eyebrows.

"No, never. But he's not the best at keeping things to himself."

"Jaq hasn't told Lady Tremaine. He thought more evidence was needed."

"Good, it'll buy us time."

The ride was silent as Ella watched the city turn into forests and hills. She missed being out in the country. Riset had its charms, but out here, in the green hills with nothing around her but animals and trees, Ella could relax.

The stronghold was washed in the early morning gray light. Servants had begun to move around the property as Luca and Ella approached. Luca stopped the carriage out front, untying his horse from the hitch to allow a stable hand to take him away. Stepping up the stairs, tension flared in her back. Ella touched the two daggers hidden on her body, calming at their weight. She was fine. David would be fine. Lady Tremaine wouldn't keep her long, especially once she knew the danger all of them were in.

Jaq waited right inside for her, arms open wide. Ella walked directly into them, breathing in the smell of minty magic. She clung to him, holding on tight. Jaq tightened his hold, resting his head on hers.

"It's good to see you." Ella kept him close for a second longer before stepping away. "Any idea why I'm here?"

"All I know is it's about the prince," Jaq whispered.

Ella straightened her spine as the two of them walked down the central hall under the grand staircase. Lady Tremaine's office loomed large in front of her. The black door cracked open. Was she going to remove Ella from David's protection? Or add someone else? Either way, the skin on her neck hadn't stopped crawling since she'd walked through the doors. Ella took a breath and walked through unannounced.

"I don't agree—"

"I don't need you to agree," Lady Tremaine had her back to Ella, facing the giant gilded mirrors behind her desk.

Raven looked back from one of them. She had gotten worse since Ella had spoken to her two weeks ago. Raven opened her mouth to say something to Ella, but Lady Tremaine severed the connection.

"Please take a seat, Ella." Lady Tremaine motioned to the large black chair. "And next time, please knock." She sat down, pinching the bridge of her nose.

"Is everything okay?" Ella asked.

"Yes, everything is fine. Raven simply doesn't want to do something." Lady Tremaine waved her hands, dismissing all thoughts of the situation.

"What did you need me for? David is—"

"There's been a change in your assignment." Lady Tremaine stood up and crossed her arms behind her back.

"What kind of change?" Ella asked. Had she also learned about Henry? Was she about to tell her to kill him?

"There comes a moment in all our journeys where a choice has to be made. Are we going to protect the crown and do whatever is in its best interest? Or are we going to do what is in our best interest?"

"I have always served the crown—"

"I know. It is that undying faith and will you have to serve the crown that I know will aid you in this sacrifice you will have to make." Lady Tremaine stood behind Ella, her hands pressed into the sides of the chair.

Ella didn't dare turn around, as the entire world seemed to have shifted in the space of a second. Chills ran down Ella's spine. Even though the sun was rising, the room seemed to grow darker before her eyes.

"I know you have invested a lot in this current assignment, Ella, and it has not gone unnoticed by me. I have a lot more work for you to do, and being successful in this assignment means you'll be able to take an even more active role in protecting our kingdom."

"What is changing in my assignment? Do I need to protect Celeste as well?"

"No. Nothing like that. I'm afraid that our treaty is even more at risk right now, and that our sources have been informed that David has no intention of signing it. He is going to throw us into a war."

"David would never—" Ella stopped. How did she know? Mira was the only person she had told, and Ella trusted her with her life. Ella's heart pounded in her ears. Had David gone to the king? Had he asked for the treaty to be rewritten? Horror washed through Ella. All of King Matthias's advisors would view that as a threat to the peace that had been maintained. Even the king might—

"You now have to kill David, Ella. This will be no easy feat. I know that the two of you are close, but you've sworn an oath to protect the kingdom and crown. And David has put himself in the way of that."

Ella didn't move. She had to absorb all the information that was being pummeled into her. Too many pieces were in motion, and if she wanted to figure them out, she could not, for one moment, show any amount of resistance to this new plan.

"Is there no other way?" Ella whispered.

"None. The night of the ball, you're going to kill him before he breaks it, preventing a war. You'll be a hero, Ella."

Being a hero was all Ella had ever wanted. To be a protector, to be seen for who she truly was. Yet right now, all she wanted to do was vomit. In less than a day, her entire world, and what everything in that world meant, had been thrown into chaos.

Ella nodded, her hands limp in her lap.

"Is there anything else you need from me?"

"No. Though I must admit, I expected more of a fight." Lady Tremaine moved back around her desk.

Ella straightened her back and looked her stepmother right in the eye. "As you said, we all eventually have a choice to make. Are we in service to the crown or ourselves? I'll always choose the crown."

Lady Tremaine bowed her head in acknowledgment before dismissing her.

Ella left, walking in a blur throughout Aumont. Blindly she wandered, her mind spinning. She walked to her bedroom, finding that everything had been left as though she had only stepped out a few moments before. The curtains were open wide; the sun illuminating her bed and dark blue walls. The floral silver accents glinted, welcoming her home. Ella stepped in further, rubbing her arms. All the training clothes she'd left behind still hung in her closet. Her books were still untouched. Her traveling packs out on the floor. Ella walked over to the old large wooden trunk at the base of her bed and opened it. Bundles of gowns lay inside, delicately folded. She reached past the gowns that she had hoped to wear in her mother's honor and pulled out her father's sword instead.

She had taken it shortly after his death, hiding it before Lady Tremaine could touch it. It had been passed down for generations in her family, and she would let no one but herself wield it. Legend said it could cut through anything with no resistance. Ella knew that meant it was enchanted, but she had always loved the idea of wielding a blade that no person could stop.

Its handle had the head of a horse molded out of pure silver with sapphire eyes. Despite its age, it had never dulled. She slid it out of its sheath, admiring the metal's glint in the light. Ella held it before her, looking at its perfection. She hoped one day to mirror the same perfection and be worthy of using it. Only a true warrior of the Aumont Family could ever dream of holding this sword on a battlefield, and Ella knew she would be the next one to spill blood with its blade. Her father depended on her to carry forth the family name, their legacy, their ferocity.

"Ella?"

Ella sheathed the sword and tucked it away. "Drea."

"You look...contemplative."

"What's your dream?" Ella touched one of the dresses in her trunk, rubbing the silk fabric between her fingers.

"I'm sorry?"

"What do you want more than anything else in the world?" she asked as she pulled the gown out. Its golden detail sparkled in the sun, the green fabric revealing its shades.

"I want to be free." It was a whisper in Ella's ears, but she heard it nonetheless.

"And would you do anything possible to be free?" Ella turned to look at her stepsister, formally known as Nightshade, the most feared assassin, now a rejected, reclusive enchanter.

"I would." Drea stood tall, her hand lightly holding onto her cane, her back ramrod straight as the two looked each other over. "Why do you ask?"

"Just thinking something through." Ella shrugged.

"It's a beautiful gown. You should wear it sometime." Drea walked over, her cane thudding on the carpet.

"You wear it. Let it be your first step in being free. Come to the ball, Drea."

Drea remained thoughtful as Ella handed it to her, closed the trunk, and walked out of the room. It may have once been her bedroom, but it no longer felt like home.

Ella turned around the corner, too distracted with a busy mind.

"Ella." Lucifer's voice slid down her spine.

"Lucifer. You're in my way." She would not look up at him.

"You're in my way. But it's no trouble. I enjoy our conversations." Lucifer tilted Ella's head until she was forced to look at him. His black eyes reflected no light. Her fingers twitched at her side, waiting for the moment she could grab her daggers and slit his throat. He smiled, his pointed nail digging into her chin.

"Funny, I thought the only thing you enjoyed was following Lady Tremaine like an attention-deprived cat."

Lucifer laughed, releasing his hold on her. "I enjoy so many things. Remember all of those times we had our fun in the attic? You would get in trouble, be chained up there, and I would come to keep you company with that whip. I'm sure you would do anything to avoid that happening again." He pouted, his eyes filled with mirth.

"That will never happen." Ella stepped away from him.

"We'll see."

"Ella, what's going on?" Luca walked over and stopped so that he stood right behind her.

"Let's go." She turned around and walked out of Aumont, with Luca directly behind her. She wiped away the small bead of blood under her chin and got into the carriage.

"Are you sure you're okay?" Luca looked over at her, his brow furrowed. "Something's changed."

"I'm sure. I'll tell you everything tonight, I promise. For now, let's get back." Ella rubbed her arms, massaging them as a slow ache built.

Ella walked up the palace steps slowly. Her mind reeling with all the information it was trying to process. All she knew was that she couldn't trust anyone. Only her friends, and had been sent away. With each step Ella took, the closer she got to those doors, the more twisted her stomach became. By the time she reached the top, she was going to vomit or collapse into a heap of useless appendages. She didn't know which would come first, just that they would. The palace she reacquainted herself with was muted in her ears. She no longer heard the roar of the horses pulling carriages or smelled the cinnamon that wafted from the kitchen. Everything had narrowed in on the way her muscles ached. It felt like tiny daggers were being stabbed into her.

The ground shifted beneath her feet.

The stone below tilted, rushing towards her.

Why are the stones rushing towards her?

She stopped moving. The stone steps were a few inches away from her face when a warm arm wrapped around her waist, sending shocks of warmth throughout her body, and bringing her back to herself.

"Are you alright?" David continued to hold her, his brown eyes searching. All she saw was the deep green streaking within their depths, highlighted in the morning sun.

Ella nodded. She was fine. She would be...she had sworn an oath.

"Are you sure? That stone was about to meet your face, and not in a way I think either of you would enjoy." David had yet to remove his arm.

"I'm fine." Ella mentally shook herself, standing up straighter. What was wrong with her? "I don't know what happened."

"You look like you need to talk, want to—"

"Go horseback riding? That's what I would like to do. No talking. Just riding." Ella stepped, ignored the pain in her body, and forced a smile. If she pretended the pain wasn't there, then she wouldn't feel it. Right?

"Horseback riding? You're sure?"

"Yes, now let's get changed."

Ella didn't let her mind settle as she dressed. She didn't think about taking David out alone. They were only going riding through the palace grounds.

Their horses were prepared and waiting, both steeds more than happy to run. Ella let Dream run free, not once looking over at David. They ran and ran, and if she could have continued to run, at that moment, Ella never would have stopped. She would have taken Dream and never looked back.

By the time they slowed down, both of them were breathless, pulses racing.

"Will you tell me what's on your mind? I can be a great listener." David pulled up beside her.

"It's complicated, and I don't want to discuss it right now." Ella massaged her arms. She squeezed them, wondering why they were sore. She went riding all the time.

"That's..." David dismounted, his brow furrowed as he gazed at her. "We're rebuilding something, and I'm trying to be open, to tell you things, but when I ask...I feel the hesitation and I see you building your walls higher. All I'm asking is that you work on lowering them. I want you to know that you can keep putting those walls up, but I will always do my best to jump over them...every time."

Ella got off of Dream, her heart pounding. "I am trying, David. This...this is me trying. Being here, coming back, taking part in this ball, I am trying. I'm sorry that it's not to your standards." She held Dream's leather reins in her hand, twisting them into her palm as she bit the inside of her cheek. "I'm a talented dancer, but David...this ball, means something to you, and I don't want to ruin it." There that was a lie he could believe. It's not as if she could tell him she had been assigned to kill him. Ella ran her hands through her braided hair, grimacing at the pain.

"That's what this is about? Dancing?" He walked over to her and cradled her hand in his. Fire tingled up her arm.

"Maybe?" Ella glanced at her feet. "It's been a while since I've danced anything that wasn't Evrotian."

"Then let's practice." David wrapped her arm around his and led her into the towering forest.

"Now? There's no music, and we're without an escort already. Is it a good idea?" She spoke rapidly, her heart beating quicker, and she didn't think her nerves had anything to do with it. She looked around them at the sun rays streaking through the trees, highlighting the massive grove of ferns and clovers beneath their feet.

"Don't you hear it?" David moved so that they faced each other. He rested a hand on her hip, the other gripping her fingers. "It's in the wind rustling through the trees. The birds are singing. Everything around us can be the song that we need." David moved them through a waltz, his hand running up and down her back, lighting up her nerves in their melody.

Ella stopped gazing at the forest, turning her attention to him.

David knew exactly where to go and how to apply pressure in the right spots on her to get her body to move. Dancing to their own song as life went on around them, Ella tumbled into the moment, forgetting her aches and pains. It was like when she'd rolled down hills with David as a child. Slow and a little bumpy at first, but then the hill gets steeper, and you fall faster, but you aren't scared because you're having too much fun. The grass beneath cheers you on, until you get to the bottom, breathless, and full of life. That's what dancing with David was, pure unadulterated joy, and she never wanted it to end.

Ella didn't pause or flinch away when David leaned his head towards hers.

Before his lips could brush against hers, a branch snapped.

CHAPTER EIGHTEEN

Ella fisted her hands in David's tunic and tossed him to the ground before the dagger found its mark. It embedded itself in the tree behind them, vibrating in the trunk. All sense of peace fractured as Ella scrutinized their surroundings. David flipped onto his stomach, lying low as they tried to locate their assailant.

"We have to go." Ella loosened one of the smaller daggers that she kept on her. It was made of obsidian stone and would remain hidden in her pants until necessary.

"Let's get to the horses." David's hands lightly glowed his grip on his magic either close to flaring out or preparing to be used. "Do you have anything enchanted with you?"

Ella nodded, touching the corset she always wore.

"Good, now's the time to use it. We need to get to a defensible position, learn where the attacker is, and figure out a way to get you home."

"We're going home together, David," Ella whispered. They remained low and exposed. She moved first, sprinting for a fallen log that they could hide behind. David was fast behind, both of them leaping over it as an arrow flew overhead.

"We need to get to the horses." David peeked out over the trunk of the tree.

Ella looked back at the forest that lay behind them. No one was back there. Their only escape route to the horses was cut off. "We can't. We need to go further into the forest and loop around."

Ella heard the leather of their assailants shift as an arrow was pulled. Her eyes darted over to David, who was still trying to see over the log. She dragged him down, ignoring the anger in his eyes that demanded answers. An arrow flew by before she could say anything.

"We can't sit here—"

"I know," David ground out.

"What should we do?" Ella asked. She knew what she wanted to do. But David was the prince, and he needed to think strategically because she would not be killed like this. She would go out in a blaze of fire if she had to. She would expose *exactly* who she was to stay alive. Of course, she had another choice, and that was to live to fight another day, and not die defending a prince already marked for death.

David's eyes flicked toward her and the forest multiple times. She saw him fight with himself over protecting her and getting out alive. He would always put her safety above his, the fool.

"Do you trust me?" She spoke the same words he'd said to her only yesterday, her palms slick as she tensed for the answer that would hurt her. She tossed up an extra wall around herself, bracing for impact.

"Of course."

Tension plummeted out of her body, her vision blurring as the world swayed for a second. "Then let's go." Ella took his hand and squeezed it once before they jumped to their feet and sprinted for the forest.

They ran in crisscross lines, avoiding the arrows that flew by. Ella's lungs burned as they leaped over fallen trees and avoided roots rising from the ground. Not once did she look back, though she could hear their assailant's footsteps crunching the leaves. She wasn't about to chance falling to the ground, because if she did, the attackers would be on her. She did, however, take reassurance in the snapping twigs that David was still there. Soon they were going to have to find a place to stop.

Each step sent shocks of pain coursing up her muscles and into her spine. Her legs screamed as they burned, pleading for water, for rest. Her lungs ached. But they couldn't stop, not yet. Her arms weighed her down, the movement sending tears down her cheeks. She continued to run, getting lost in the dense forest, not bothering to watch where they went as the thundering footsteps behind them continued. Ella counted at least five distinct sounds. Each one coming from various directions, trying to surround them, pin them in. Wolves did the same thing. Unfortunately for these attackers, they were hunting a fellow wolf, and she would not be cornered.

Ella looked ahead for an advantage. Anything to get them to rest and avoid their assailants. She couldn't force her body to move through the pain for much longer. It had only increased the more exertion she put out. What had been a faint tingling pain in her muscles while dancing with David was now a full-force tear in her ligaments. She ran on her toes, as each time she landed was like landing on a bed of needles. Ella ran through their options. They couldn't climb the redwoods. Their bark was too soft and their branches too high. Ella also had to acknowledge that they were lost, and even though David could probably keep moving, she no longer could. Her one salvation that these particular redwoods would have, was shelter in the base of some of the burned-out trunks. That was what they needed. It was a risk, Ella knew that. It would corner them. But until Ella and David could figure out where they were, they would have to either stop or keep running.

Ella's muscles contracted tightly, growing heavy with exhaustion and pain.

Her muscles were a glaring mass of red in her vision as she tried to remain on her feet.

Ella let out a small squeal when she saw a tree that had a hole in its base. David glanced over at her, eyebrows raised. She stopped running, her chest heaving as she allowed it to rest.

David gripped her arm, his eyes searching for an explanation. She pointed to the tree. It eclipsed them, its body so tall they had to crane their necks to see its top. At the bottom, though, was a small hole, just big enough to crawl through. Ella let herself hope it would be big enough inside for both of them.

Not waiting to give him a chance to debate it, Ella walked over, careful to not leave a trail of snapped twigs or leaves in her wake. She knelt, angled her body under the opening, and crawled inside with David right behind her. It was now or never.

Ella closed her eyes, her hands above her head as she cautiously stood up, feeling for the ceiling of the tree. If there was one, it was high enough that her arm, even fully extended, couldn't touch it. Yet she kept her eyes closed. She wanted to make sure that when she opened them, they would adjust quickly to the dimmed interior.

Ella turned around in the tree, opening her eyes to look at the interior as sunlight crawled in under the opening. The wood was black, its edges charcoaled and worn from years of exposure. David turned to face her, his arms out in a 'now what' gesture. Ella walked around until she was near the mouth of the tree and sat down. Her muscles tightened, spasming. But she could see the sunlight, and that was what mattered. Sunlight was still around her. Ella grimaced in pain, squeezing her eyes shut, and waited for it to pass. Waited for the throbbing that consumed her entire body to just...pause.

David sat opposite her, leaning against the base.

Neither one spoke, both of them listening for any sounds. Any snap or rustle of fabric. Metal sliding out of a scabbard. Voices calling out. Anything to tell them where their attackers were. But there was nothing.

Ella stretched her legs, massaging her muscles. David did the same, watching her. Her cheeks flushed as he continued to gaze at her.

"David." Ella paused, her voice barely over the sound of a whisper. "We should go. I think they're gone." Ella looked towards the entrance where the sunlight had vanished. It had continued to recede during the last hour until she could no longer see it. Her pulse quickened, sweat beading on her forehead.

"We need to stay. It's getting dark and—"

"Exactly. We need to get home before that. Henry must be going crazy."

"I'm sure he is. He's probably out there looking for us. If we stay here, he will find us. It may not happen until tomorrow." David shrugged, closing his eyes.

"We have to get back." Ella's voice spiked an octave, her hands twisting together. "We can't even light a fire in here, David, please—"

"Do you know where we are in the forest?" David opened his eyes as Ella stood up and paced the small distance. "Because I don't. I lost track of where we were once we started sprinting. If we leave right now, we'll end up wandering in the forest all night. So we're staying here."

He had an excellent point. Ella hated that. She needed to leave. She needed to be around the light. But David was right. She would rather be stuck in a tree at night with him than wandering around the forest in the dark. Ella sat down in the dirt, unbraided her hair, and finger-combed it, hoping that it would stop her fingers from shaking. It didn't.

Ella brought her knees to her chest and wrapped her arms around them, burying her head between them and her chest. Darkness settled over Ella and David, crickets and owls creating their song. Ella's knuckles turned white, the tips of her nails impressing crescent moons into her palms. She would survive. She'd survived other nights in the attic. She would make it through this. She had to.

"I can do this," Ella whispered, her throat tight. "I can do this." she looked up to complete darkness, and her heart stopped for a second. "David?" the tremble in her voice shook her.

"I'm here."

"I can't do this." A sob wracked Ella's body. "I can't...I can't...please...I need to leave." Everything shook. The ground swallowed her up. She could feel it. The monster was getting ready to pounce.

"El? What's wrong?"

Ella heard shifting beside her, but her eyes refused to see. Something, a creature, lashed out and gripped her arm. It held on tight, rubbing circles on her sleeve. A hand. It was David's hand. Ella slapped her hand over her mouth before she could scream. Tears welled up in her eyes as she squeezed them tight. Stars exploded in her vision, dancing before her.

"Ella, what's happening?" His voice was calm.

"I can't, David…" Ella spoke through the saliva coating her throat. She gasped for air as she tried to breathe, trying to maintain control. Her hands gripped her head, tangling in her hair. "I'm terrified, David," she whispered it…this deepest confession. She could hardly voice it to him, this failing of hers. "I…I always sleep with a candle burning…I have to, I can't…" Ella fumbled, grappling for the right words to describe the way her heart beat so fast she was sure the entire forest could hear it. How the smallest sound rippled through her like thunder, strong and quick. How she knew that at any moment, the creature in the night would prowl through that entrance and kill her.

"Ella, why didn't you say something? We could have left—"

"No. You were right—" Ella's hands gripped David's arm as he rubbed hers. "You were right. It was better to be here, hidden, than out there exposed."

"But if I had known—"

"There's nothing we can do. Just…help me get through the night?" She jumped when a sound blasted through her ears. It was an owl. An owl calling in the night.

"I'll do my best." David moved so that Ella could lie back against him, wrapping his arms around her.

Tears ran down her cheeks as the noises of the night paraded past them. She kept her face hidden in David's chest, his tunic wet from her fear. But she kept her face hidden, making sure any noise she made was muffled. Each twitch of her body, each time a muscle stiffened, David rubbed her arms, or her back, drawing slow circles on her.

"Everything hurts, David. What's wrong with me?"

"We did a lot of running." David rested his head on top of hers, his pulse calm.

"I think...it's more than that, David...something's wrong." Ella's arms pulled her down, her legs seeming to melt into the ground. If she could have, Ella would have let the dirt swallow her whole.

"Everything will be okay. You'll see. We'll make it through this." David ran his hand through her hair, kissing her head.

Ella kept her eyes open as every nerve pulsed, and the darkness crept closer.

CHAPTER NINETEEN

Ella twitched in David's arms all night, sleep evading her. As darkness wore on, Ella didn't know if the erratic pulse was because of her fear or whatever was coursing through her body. She hadn't had this many aches since she had begun her training. All those years ago, her muscles had screamed at her all day and night, but she had persevered and carried on through the pain. Two weeks of only moderate activity wouldn't account for this fatigue. She had to have been poisoned. But when? And why? Ella's mind swirled with the possibilities as night gradually turned over to daylight, and the sun began to rise.

"Did you get any sleep?" David whispered. He shifted his body, making both of them more comfortable.

Ella chuckled in pain. "Did you?"

"Not at all. Should we go out and see if we can figure out how to get home?"

Ella nodded, moving stiff muscles. She eased off of David and moved slowly as she crawled towards the entrance. Birds had begun to sing, but other than that, not a sound could be heard. Ella confirmed her dagger's placement and ducked out from under the tree. Ferns glittered with morning dew in the sun, birds chirping around them. Ella closed her eyes as she took in the fresh air, soaking it up through every fiber. Then she turned to look at David and laughed.

"I'm sorry, it's just..." Ella bent over with laughter. "You look—"

David's hair stuck up, dust and cobwebs coating him. Charcoal was smeared over his face and clothes, while dirt covered his pants.

"You should see yourself." David laughed. "I don't think I've ever seen your hair look so ashy before. Or," David paused, stepping closer to her. Ella's heart sputtered. "Don't move. You have a spider on you." His brown eyes focused on her shoulder.

"That's not funny David. You know how I feel about—"

David slapped her shoulder, sending it flying.

"All done." He smiled.

Ella relaxed her shoulders, looking down at herself. She was a mess as well. Nothing was clean, and both of them were covered in a thick layer of dirt.

"We should go back to Riset like this. They'll never believe who we are."

"It would be nice, but I think everyone deserves a break from worrying." David looked glum as he rested an arm around Ella's shoulders. "You don't have a mirror or anything on you, do you?"

"David Oakwell, what kind of lady do you think carries a mirror while horseback riding?"

"One who's vain? I need it to scry Henry." David said.

"I don't. Why don't you keep one on you?" Ella raised a brow as they walked towards the sun and the direct location of the palace.

"I do. But it must have fallen out." David checked his pockets again, finding nothing. "Hopefully—" David tackled Ella to the ground at the sound of horses.

They crawled behind a fallen tree and crouched on the other side. Both of them controlled their breathing, listening for any more sounds.

"Dammit, where could they have gotten to?" Henry's voice carried over to them, the horses pausing nearby.

Ella bit her lip, resisting the urge to stop David as he stood up.

"Henry, we're here." He pulled Ella with him.

"If you two ever disappear like that again, I swear I will kill the two of you," Henry charged over, Luca close behind.

Ella positioned herself in front of David as Henry rode up to them.

"I promise it wasn't on purpose. We were trying to not get killed, though I'm glad to hear how much you care about us." Ella smiled. "Did you find our assailants?"

Henry opened his mouth as David interrupted him. "Truly Henry, we were ambushed. If it wasn't for Ella's quick thinking, I don't know what we would have done." David walked over to his friend, the enemy, and hugged him. "How did you know we were out here?"

Another thing Ella wanted to know as well. Henry assessed her with a critical eye before responding.

"Your horses came back in a panic. It's the only reason I knew something was wrong, and not another stunt."

Ella scoffed when Henry looked at her.

"But I'm glad you two are alive and unharmed. There's no sign of your attackers, though we found where they ambushed you. Maybe now you'll believe me about taking an armed guard with you. I know better than to suggest no more riding at all—"

"No more riding for now seems best," David replied. Henry's jaw dropped. Ella wondered if they had just wrecked one of his schemes, or if the guards were the scheme. "The ball is all of four days away. I think the two of us will survive. Besides, we need to practice our dancing. We were so rudely interrupted yesterday." David walked over to Ella and gently held her hand, looking her over.

Ella smiled, her lips wavering with exhaustion when David's eyes narrowed.

Ella felt Luca step closer to her as David's face shifted from adoration to suspicion as he gazed at her.

"David?"

"Tilt your head back," he commanded.

"What?" Ella took half a step back, bumping into Luca. "Why?"

"Please." David opened his hands wide, his eyes no longer filled with suspicion but concern. "Let me see."

Ella gripped Luca's hand as she looked up at the trees above. David's fingers softly ran up her neck until his thumb grazed over her jaw and then her chin.

Searing pain ripped through Ella's body in a flash of white. Ella kept her mouth shut, her eyes closed as everything inside burned. Her lungs forgot how to breathe, preventing any noise from coming out. Her hand was fisted with Luca's, her nails digging in as he stood behind her.

"What the fuck was that?" she gasped. Ella delicately extracted her fingers from Luca's, shaking them out.

"Poison...you were poisoned, Ella," David knelt before her, his hands glowing, "I can get it out—"

"No." Ella scooted back into Luca. "I can't...David...I—"

"I know. I won't. Luckily, the dose was tiny. It would have been on something smaller than a fingernail and should wear off in a day or so. But until then, with no treatment, you will be sore."

"I can handle it." Ella blinked back the tears in her eyes, ignoring the pain in the back of her head. "I *will* handle it."

"Why would anyone want to poison you, Ella?" Henry stood over the three of them, his face twisted into a look of suspicion.

"I don't know. How did anyone know we were going riding yesterday when it was a spur-of-the-moment decision?" Ella stood up with assistance from Luca, her muscles spasming. She didn't add that no matter what they did for the next three days, she was still meant to kill David.

Ella eased up onto Luca's horse and leaned into him when he got behind her.

"These are all questions we need to solve, but for now, I think we could all benefit from several hours of sleep. Should we go home?" David spoke as he mounted Henry's horse, and they took off for the palace.

Luca positioned his head so that David and Henry couldn't see his lips move. "Ella, isn't that where—"

"Lucifer touched me yesterday? Yes. It is. You and I have much to discuss." Ella said nothing else when she glanced over and found Henry assessing her once again. She smiled lazily at him and closed her eyes, trusting Luca to get her home.

"Shit Ella, you couldn't have told me this change yesterday?"

"Luca, I was going to when—" Ella gestured at her filthy clothing. "I didn't think it was a conversation to have at Aumont, or in a carriage."

"But why poison you? What was the point of that?"

"For me to fail? If I hadn't taken David riding yesterday, where would he have been? In his room, and I would have been lying in bed."

"Did you give any indication that you wouldn't complete your assignment?" Luca sat on her bed as she untied her corset and flung it to the ground.

"How could I? The change had happened only an hour before. That attack was pre-planned, Luca. What I don't understand is who is truly trying to kill David, and why. Lady Tremaine says it's because he won't sign the treaty anymore, and the kingdom needs to avoid a war. But if Henry was also trying to kill David, the reason would be different, because Sophie was here before that decision. I just don't know what to do." Ella sat down heavily on her bed. She wrapped a blanket around her legs and pulled them up to her chest.

"I'm worried about you, Ella. All of this is unraveling rapidly." Luca sat down opposite her at the foot of the bed.

"I'll be okay. I always am, so long as I have you and Jaq, everything will be fine. You'll see. Now, I don't know about you, but I need a little bit of sleep." Ella closed her eyes and fell asleep before Luca could even form a response.

As she slept, her mind wandered, trying to play the complex chess game before her. Everything had shifted, and the pieces kept changing their roles and rules. By the time she woke up, the sun was shining on her face and a hot bath waited for her. Ella squealed in delight as the water engulfed her. It had been so long since she could lie in a tub and soak. Not that she could relax and turn off her mind. All it did was spin and spin. She couldn't confront Lady Tremaine. Not that she even knew what to confront her about. She was doing the king's bidding, and he wanted his son dead to avoid a war. She couldn't talk to Henry, who might also be trying to kill David. Ella was paralyzed with indecision and uncertainty. Someone was lying to her, and she was going to find out who, but first she needed to know why Lucifer had been allowed to poison her. Her muscles protested as she got out of bed, aching from the enchantment wreaking havoc on their nerves.

Ella donned plain clothing, a simple training tunic, and pants. Gone were the elaborate gowns and shoes with complex hairdos. She needed stealth and invisibility, more than any enchantment could offer her in the light of day. The entire palace was abuzz with ball preparations. Servants were everywhere, along with members of the noble class, all of them nosing around. She slipped into the gardens and made her way to the secret passage. Mira had been right. It was disgusting. But it did the charm of disguising who she was when she walked out on the other side covered in mold and slime. The streets of Riset bustled around her as she walked out and into the masses, heading straight for the countryside pastures Aumont was nestled on.

Ella arrived as the afternoon sun began its slow descent. The only thing she was certain of was that David had to be protected. It was the first time in the last nine years she had ever questioned her mistress, and Ella's stomach twisted at the thought. Maybe she was being threatened with something if she didn't have Ella kill David? There had to be a reason for it.

She crept through a long-forgotten side door in the stone wall guarding Aumont. It was well hidden behind ivy, older than her. Ella walked silently through the halls, avoiding any lingering novices who weren't in their lessons. Lady Tremaine's office was empty when she opened the door. Most of the house felt empty. Ella walked upstairs, listening for any sound, any sign of where someone was. She found it outside of her parent's bedroom, now Lady Tremaine's room. Ella took two steps towards it and stopped. She hadn't entered this room in...years. But now she needed some answers.

The door opened before she could knock. Lucifer stood on the other side. A smirk adorned his face as he took her in before he left. She hoped he couldn't see the slight shake in her legs. The room was nothing like how Ella remembered it. What was once a bright airy room filled with light hues of green was now covered in dark reds. Ella stood still for a moment, absorbing the changes.

"Ella, what brings you here? I heard about the attack. Are you alright?" Lady Tremaine questioned from her seat in front of the large floor-to-ceiling windows overlooking the back training field. All the novices were down there running their drills. Anastasia sat beside her mother, sipping tea, a small smile curling the side of her lips.

"I'm fine. Though I wonder why we're still being attacked if I'm to kill him anyway," Ella muttered.

"They're attacking to start a war, my dear. We're killing him to prevent one." Lady Tremaine grabbed her saucer and sipped from her cup.

"Then why poison me? If I'm to help avoid a war, surely having me in good health is part of that?"

"Poison?" Lady Tremaine set down her cup and stood up. She walked over to Ella and searched her eyes.

"Yes, why did you allow Lucifer to poison me?" Ella stared her step-mother down, watching her dark green eyes narrow at the challenge before hardening.

"I did not allow that, but I will deal with it."

"I can't wait to see the look on David's face, that look of shock..." Anastasia leaned back and smiled. "It will be priceless."

Ella ignored her, examining her nails. "It will be one to remember."

"Yes, now, Ella, I need you at the palace. No more field trips down here. You need to recover and start planning with Luca. Do check in with Jaq before you go. He has some items for you."

Ella left, feeling more like a pawn than ever before.

Jaq was in his workshop, enchanting more objects. He slumped down in his chair as he finished; the arrows glowing with his power. He removed his spectacles and rubbed his eyes, leaning forward on his knees.

"Long day?" Ella sat across from him, her legs stretched out to ease the ache. "I was informed you have something for me."

"I'm still working on it. It's not quite ready for you." He yawned, sitting back to stare at his mirrors.

"Let's go for a walk. Your mirrors are making me sick." Ella stood up and left, ignoring the dizzying array of homes Jaq had access to.

She looped Jaq's arm over her shoulder, leaning into him. They walked past rooms with recruited street urchins, learning how to hone their skills. Some would never become protectors of Rairene, and would instead go back to the streets to listen and report, knowing they would be paid. Others, the special ones, would continue. Ella paid none of them any attention as she and Jaq walked to oversee the training yard. Gus was out there, his brutish voice echoing across the field. Ella allowed herself a smile for her friend. She had been so terrified of him at first, but now she knew he was a cuddly mouse who loved his cheese and to make novices wet themselves. She nodded to him as he put several through their paces. He smiled back at her before snapping at a novice who had stumbled at seeing Ella.

"Ella, come jump in here and help me show them some fighting routines," Gus hollered. Even though he could no longer command her, she still would do as he asked. She owed him that much. Plus, she needed to work off some of her anxiety and there was no better way than through drills.

Ella walked into the middle of the field where Gus had a novice flat on their back in the grass, his sword pointed at them. Gus nudged the novice out of the area and had Ella work through some training moves with him. Once the novices saw it, Gus summoned one over to spar against Ella. She knocked them flat on their back within seconds, dagger pressed to their neck. The drill went on for several minutes, all ten of them getting their shot at her. None of them succeeded. None of them came close.

Gus sent all of them out, running laps around Aumont as punishment. Ella walked back to Jaq, who had observed a smile on his slim face.

"I wanted to give this back to you." Jaq handed her a necklace with three sapphires glinting in the center. Ella's heart lurched at the sight.

"Where did...who..." Ella delicately held the necklace that the queen had given her shortly after her father had died. It was a symbol of her love. The three sapphires represented the queen's children, David, Celeste, and Ella. She cradled the necklace in her hands.

"Luca brought it after his snooping in the queen's study. Thought it might help solve some mysteries. The memories were too distorted, unfortunately."

"I see." Ella's vision blurred as she continued to stare at it. The last time she had seen this necklace...Ella shook her head. She couldn't think about that.

"Any thoughts on the recent change in your assignment?"

"I am a little concerned about the shift."

Jaq raised his eyebrows.

"Not in accomplishing it." Ella clarified. "But...it doesn't feel like I'm upholding my oath...it feels like I'm breaking it instead."

"Sometimes we have to do something we don't like in service of the crown," Jaq acknowledged.

"I know. Could you help me with my escape? I don't want to take Callidus, but it's the only solution I can think of." Ella shuddered.

"We could enchant a cloak of disguise for you. You would need to be able to get out of the room, but I don't think that should be a problem for you...if you do it at the right time, you could kill him and be walking away and out of the room before anyone notices. You would have to wait for other dancers to be on the floor, but that shouldn't be a problem. Bring one of the daggers I've enchanted with you. One quick stab into a lung to prevent him calling for help, and the other into his heart." Jaq shrugged.

"What about his power? He's an enchanter."

"The result of his foolish behavior and put us at risk for war."

"Hmmm," Ella trailed off at Jaq's nonchalance to innocent bystanders dying. He wasn't usually so callous about others. She would have to be careful of Henry over the next couple of days. She didn't like how he'd been looking at her this morning. Henry was—

Ella froze.

Henry stood at the side entrance to the hedge maze.

He wore clothing that hid him, but she could see him flickering in and out of her vision. He was here, watching her.

"Jaq...I'm going to go for a walk before heading to the palace...alone. I'll see you back inside." She didn't wait for a response before walking around the training yard, across the field, and into the maze.

CHAPTER TWENTY

Ella didn't head directly for Henry. That would have been foolish. Instead, she went to the one place both of them had loved as children, her mother's fountain near the back of the garden. It was a five-minute walk directly, but she didn't go the direct route. Ella walked into the sitting area. It was a rejected part of the hedge maze, overgrown with flowers and ivy crawling over the hedges itself. Henry walked through the other side, sword at his side. But not in his hands. Yet.

"Henry, why are you here?"

"I followed you. You've been acting...different."

"I've been acting differently?" Ella scoffed.

"Why are there children learning how to fight?"

"That's not your concern," Ella snapped.

"There are boys and girls—"

"Are you upset that they're children? Or that girls are learning?"

"Eleanor, I've had it up to gods knows where with your lies. Give me a truthful answer. What is this place?"

"I'm sorry, Henry, but that's the crown's business. Not yours." Ella crossed her arms, holding firm. Maybe he realized he wouldn't be able to kill David now. That even though he had killed Sophie, he would now have to go through her, and everyone else.

"The crown's business is my business," Henry ground out.

"Then you're informed on what this place is, or at least smart enough to figure it out." Ella challenged. Not that she wanted him to figure it out. But she would not be the one to tell him. If Lady Tremaine found him...Ella would have to kill him. She brushed aside the grief that surged forward at that thought. Though she had been playing with it in the back of her mind, the sudden realization that she might genuinely have to kill a friend was almost overwhelming.

"I don't believe you could be a part of what I think this place is."

"All I can say is that we're on the same side, Henry, if only you knew—"

Henry laughed. "I very much doubt that."

"You suspect something, but, Henry, if I wasn't sworn—"

"Sworn. Who have you sworn an oath to?" Henry assessed her. There was no laughter in his eyes anymore. There was nothing in his eyes. "Eleanor, who are you sworn to?"

"Was it so hard to trust me again?" She looked at the ground, bracing herself. Not only was she about to be crushed with distrust, but she was preparing to fight a close friend.

"I don't trust anyone, Ella. You know that. But I didn't...nothing was adding up..." Henry's eyes roved over her, searching, pleading with her to tell him.

"Henry, I can't tell you." Gods, she wished she could sit down. Her legs weighed her down as the enchantment continued to run its course. "There are...choices...we all have to make in life—" Ella began pulling from Lady Tremaine.

"We always have choices to make, Ella. We may not like them, but there is always more than one way to solve a problem."

"Is that why you killed Sophie?" Ella blurted out. Now she would truly have to kill him.

"Sophie? You knew Sophie?" Henry stepped away from her, pulling out his sword. "You are no longer my friend. You are an enemy of the future king and a traitor to the Kingdom of Rairene, and it is my duty to protect them and bring you in."

"I didn't realize you had considered me a friend," Ella snarled. She blinked at the pain in her eyes, refusing to cry. She couldn't explain, but she had hoped, against all odds, that he would deny killing Sophie.

Ella watched Henry shift from the boy she had known into the Champion of Rairene he had become. He stood taller, and was more confident in himself, as though figuring out who she was, had clicked all the pieces together for him. He was ready to fight and die for the people he protected. Those he loved. She was on the other side of that line...would always be on the other side. Yet...she still had to protect David.

"If you kill me...no one will be left to protect David. More people will be sent after him. People that you won't be able to stop—"

"And you will?" Henry challenged. He moved towards her. He was so fast. Faster than she had anticipated after seeing him spar with David. His years of training had perfected him. Henry didn't hold back in his attack, raising his sword in an attack position, not a single sign of hesitation.

She had meant nothing to him.

Ella grabbed her daggers, crossing them in time to catch his sword.

"Yes, Henry, I would stop them. I've stopped all of them so far, haven't I?" Ella spoke through gritted teeth, her arms protesting. Gus had never held back. He had trained her to always expect the unexpected. To never hesitate. So she didn't. Ella pushed forward, blocking out the way her legs felt like lead. It was her turn to take the offensive with Henry.

"The person who stopped those other attacks...the assassin that killed that boy, that was—"

"Me, Henry. I've been there the whole time—"

"I don't believe you. You can't be *her*, Ella. You can't be. You cannot tell me you're the assassin I've been hunting for *years*. She is ruthless, cold, and doesn't care about who gets in her way." It was the pain in Henry's voice that gave her pause.

Ella stumbled backward, Henry taking advantage. They traded blow after blow, their blades slicing against each other in a rapid, smooth motion. Henry's sword slipped between her daggers, cutting through her trousers and into her left thigh.

Ella fell to her knee, groaning as sweat dripped in her eyes. If she hadn't been poisoned, they would have been on equal ground, but she wasn't going to win this fight. So she had to get through to him, had to make him stop and see that she was on his side. Burning heat pierced every nerve in her leg as she blew strands of hair out of her eyes and tried to stand. She would not die like this.

"I have only ever served and protected the crown's wishes." Ella grimaced. "I've only ever killed those whom I've been sent to kill. I promise." Ella's vision blurred, and she wasn't sure if it was from sweat or tears. Henry's sword had done more damage than she had thought.

"You would think that with your training, you would be a better liar." Henry pushed her until she was up against a hedge. "I'll ask you again, whom did you swear an oath to?"

"Did it occur to you that I'm not lying? I swore an oath to the King of Rairene."

Henry pressed his sword near her neck, Ella's daggers the only thing keeping it from pressing against her skin.

"How could I ever believe you?" Henry choked on his soft words as though he could barely get them past his lips. His eyes were narrowed. But it wasn't loathing that Ella found within their green depths. It was sorrow.

Ella almost fell against his blade as the pain of his distrust in her swamped her. She never thought something would hurt more than the stinging rip of a whip up in the attic. Hurt more than losing her mom. Or stab deeper than any blade could. All of them paled compared to those simple syllables.

Ella worked her way through Henry's defenses until he was backed into a corner, his green eyes burning, his magic flaring in his hands. Henry pulled out a dagger and sliced open her right arm. Ella dropped the blade as Henry shoved her to the ground.

He held his foot against her chest, keeping her pinned.

"Henry...please." Ella's vision darkened, his distorted face fading in and out. He kept the pressure on her chest as he knelt, pressing a dagger to her neck.

"I'm not going to kill you. I'm going to give you a chance to explain everything to me."

"I did—"

"I don't think so. I don't think you swore an oath to our king, Cinderella."

Ella's eyes widened.

"I knew it. You're going to get to my room this evening and tell me everything."

"Why are you letting me live?" Ella heaved.

Henry's eyes softened. "Because I think you've been misled for the last nine years, and I owe it to you to hear what you have to say. I'll make your excuses for you to David and the King." Henry stood up and turned his back on her.

Before Ella could fathom a response, Henry disappeared down a long-forgotten path.

Ella coughed, her body a glaring mass of pain. She had to get up. She needed to move. But not until she assessed all of her injuries and processed Henry's parting words. Why would Henry think she had killed the queen? Before she could ponder that, her leg reminded her of the gaping gash in it. Ella moved her hand, reaching in blindly through the tear in her clothes. She groaned, her vision going black at the featherlight touch of her fingers. Her skin clammed up as everything in her went cold.

Ella sunk into the ground as her mind drifted. She tried to open her eyes; her lashes fluttering against the weight. Ella willed her head to turn, opening her eyes long enough to see a pair of boots walk through the archway.

"Ella?"

Her name came to her in whispers in the air, but she couldn't be bothered to call back.

"Ella?" Gentle, calloused fingers brushed over her cheek, pushing back her sweaty hair. "Open your eyes."

She knew that voice. Safety and spices enveloped her as they spoke to her, murmuring soft things to her.

"Luca..." Ella tried to open her eyes. Tried to look at her friend. His blurred face slowly came into focus, his green eyes wide as he continued to stroke her hair.

"What happened? Henry scried me, which was...interesting, he said you needed help."

"Henry...he...scried you?" Ella tried to sit. She had to focus. She needed to do something...be somewhere. "We have to get back to the palace. He knows..." Ella closed her eyes against tears. Ella's pulse quickened, sweat beading on her forehead. She *had* to get to the palace. Right. Now.

"He knows what?" Luca helped her sit, holding her shoulders.

Ella looked around, her vision slowly clearing. "He *knows*. Please, Luca, take me to the palace." She gripped his tunic, pulling him close, looking into his beautiful eyes that had always been there for her.

"We have to get you patched up first. I'll take you to the healer—"

"No." She tightened her hold on him. "No one can know, Luca. Not even Jaq...not yet. Please. Take me to my room. I have supplies there."

Luca nodded grimly, picking her up in his arms. Ella tried to cling to him, pushing past the aches in her muscles as best as she could. As it was, her right arm was becoming more and more useless from straining against the stab wound. Ella didn't know if it was the gods working in their favor, but all of the novices were in their instruction rooms when they walked into the house.

Only one person stepped out before they reached the stairs, Tressa, one of the senior recruits. Luca saw her first, hurrying Ella into a different position. He pushed her up against a wall, wrapping her legs around his waist, obscuring Tressa's view of Ella's left side. Ella smiled at him, remembering the other times Luca had pressed her up against a wall like this. She ran her hands through his hair, savoring the feel of his soft black hair.

"Is it the best idea for the two of you to be back together?" Tressa commented as she went from one room to another, barely sparing them a glance.

"You're hardly one to talk. Still chasing after Lucifer?" Ella snapped as Luca leaned in and kissed her cheek. Ella watched Tressa walk away.

She patted his shoulder once Tressa was gone. Luca held her tightly once again in his arms, carrying her up to her room. He paused in front of her door, unable to set Ella down.

"Let me get that for you." Drea walked over and opened the door quickly.

Luca carefully set Ella down on her bed. She winced as she looked down at her bloodstained trousers. Her arm was okay, the bleeding had stopped, but her leg...she did not want to know what it looked like underneath the fabric.

"I'm not even going to ask," Drea spoke softly, her eyes downcast. She went into the washroom and brought out Ella's supply kit, a bowl of water, and some rags before heading for the door.

"Drea." Ella looked over at her, watching her stepsister battle with herself over staying. "Thank you."

Drea nodded briskly and left, leaving Ella in her cold dark room with Luca and an injury that pounded in her head. She laid down against her pillows, bracing herself for whatever was next.

"What happened?" Luca stood over her, rags and knife in hand, ready to cut away her clothing.

"Not here. I will tell you, but first, we have to get to the palace."

"Then I better clean this wound. I don't think you're walking anywhere, let alone riding anywhere until it's patched." Luca twisted his lips, looking at her trousers.

"You might be able to pull them off. They should be loose enough." Ella unlaced the front strings, groaning as the smallest movements sent fire racing down her leg.

Luca moved methodically as he eased her undergarments past her hips and rolled them down, exposing the damage Henry had caused. Even covered in blood drying like melted wax, Ella knew it was bad. He had sliced through muscle and somehow had avoided bone. They wouldn't know any more until it was clean.

"This is going to hurt. Ready?" Luca held the rags and bowl of water in front of him.

Ella nodded, biting her lip. She couldn't make a sound. If she screamed, someone would hear, and Lady Tremaine would be informed.

Luca was kind and gentle as he worked his way up her leg to her thigh. Each inch closer was another blinding flash, quickly followed by heat scorching through her body. The sheets beneath her were covered in sweat as Ella pulled a pillow over her head and groaned into it. All of her muscles spasmed in protest as she ordered them to stay still. If they moved, she could make the injury worse, and that was the last thing she needed. Time ticked by in small drops of blood as Luca diligently took care of her. Ella's stomach twisted in warning. Giving her enough time to sit up and grab a bowl as she threw up, her body was no longer able to cope with the pain. Sweat poured down her back and forehead as her vision darkened.

"Here, drink this. You need to stay hydrated." Luca pressed a cup of water to her lips, removing the bowl of her sick. He helped her drink, her arms useless at her side.

"How bad is it?"

"Well, it's not great, El. We'll have to use some serum, and then stitch you up later." Luca pinched the bridge of his nose. "You're sure—"

"We have to go, Luca." Ella sat up and looked down at her leg. The cut was deep, stretching over half the length of her thigh. At least it wasn't jagged. Stitching it up would be easier. But until then, the serum would have to do.

Luca grabbed Ella's jar of healing serum, scrunching his nose at the smell. "You know, I wish Calla had found a way to make this smell better."

"She tried. But whenever she added scent, the entire serum would turn to liquid and be useless."

Ella grabbed a cloth and soaked it before rubbing circles on her right arm, breaking off the dried blood to examine her other cut. It was short and shallow and would probably scar, but at least she would only need to wrap it to let it heal. As Luca spread the serum on her leg, firming up the gap in her body, Ella gently wrapped her arm. She was silent, not giving in to Luca's frequent question-filled glances. Questions she didn't know how to answer. All she could do was trust herself, and that meant doing anything she could do to survive the night.

"How does it feel?" Luca wrapped cloth strips firmly around the serum.

"I think I can walk through the hall without falling. Now we need to get some clean clothes and head out of here."

"I don't think this is a good idea. Let me go instead—"

"Luca, please trust me—"

"I do. But it doesn't mean I'll do so blindly, or let you walk into a dangerous situation. Ella, tell me what happened." Luca held her hand in his, squeezing them.

Ella closed her eyes, leaning heavily on her right leg as her muscles shook. Why did everything still have to ache? "I appreciate that, and I will tell you. Just not here. Now, let's go. The sun is going down, and we don't have much time."

Ella took several steps, gaining confidence with each one as her leg held. She exhaled and walked to her door, not waiting to see if Luca followed. The stairs were the hardest part and the slowest. By the time she had reached the bottom, sweat had started coating her back, but she ignored it.

"You weren't going to leave without saying goodbye, were you?" Jaq walked out of his mage room, sealing the door with an enchantment. "Everything okay?" He furrowed his brow as he got closer.

Ella straightened her back and shifted her weight to both legs. They would not give out on her. They couldn't. "I'm fine." Ella smiled. "I would never dream of leaving without saying goodbye." She hugged him, breathing in his magic, her muscles relaxing in his embrace. Here she was safe, but she couldn't involve him. Not yet.

"Ready, Ella?" Luca walked up behind her and rested a steadying hand on her back.

Jaq rubbed his spectacles clean and put them on before looking at her one last time. "You're sure you're fine?"

Ella nodded with a shaky smile.

"Blood in my veins," Jaq spoke softly.

"Bones of my ancestors," Ella whispered. Never had she felt revolted at the phrase she'd uttered in such reverence before. Luca's hand never left her back, keeping her from falling to the ground. They got onto his horse, with Ella leaning heavily on him as they rode.

CHAPTER TWENTY-ONE

Riset was full of life as the day shifted into evening and everyone was going home or going out. Ella tapped her fingers on the pommel of their saddle.

Luca began navigating his horse through side streets and alleys. By the time they got to the gates, the sky had changed from hues of pastel oranges and purples to midnight blue. Luca dismounted first, putting his hands under Ella's arms to help her slide down. Ella and Luca ducked down when two voices echoed down the hall.

"I know I promised no more riding, but I had to take him on a walk of the grounds." David laughed as he guided his stallion to his stall.

"I don't mean to be the worst friend ever and get between you and Ella, or the horses. I hope you know that." Henry walked beside David. He had changed out of his enchanted clothing, wearing a standard military uniform.

"You're certain she was okay when you saw her? She's had to go through a lot recently." David's voice was thick with concern.

"I promise, Ella just needed a day. It was one of her woman's days, I think."

Ella looked over the stable to see Henry resting a hand on David's shoulder.

"I just...I keep waiting for her to disappear on us again, Henry. Having her back...it's almost like..."

Ella's mouth dropped. Henry gave him a reassuring look before gazing at the stable. David shook himself. "She's been acting differently recently...I can't figure it out."

"She mentioned nothing to me."

David nodded and paused. "Have you been able to find anything about Cinderella?"

"I think I finally have a useful lead."

"Good. You know what it would mean to catch her."

David's voice dropped an octave, and for someone who hated violence, that's all Ella could see in him. She felt his words like chains wrapping around her neck and pulling her down. If she could have, she would have laid down and never gotten back up. Who would have guessed that words could have such an impact? How could he hate her? She'd only ever served the crown. What did they think she had done? She had to find out. The rattling of her nerves demanded it.

"I know, David." Henry led him towards the stable door. "I have to finish up some work here, but I'll see you tomorrow."

"Let me know if I can assist with anything."

"With all the work you already have as the crowned prince, in addition to Princess Lena arriving soon, I don't think you'll have any time to spare." Henry laughed. "But I appreciate the offer."

Henry heaved a sigh, rubbing his hands over his face. He looked around the stable, his eyes landing on the stall Luca and Ella occupied.

"He's left. Now come out before I have you arrested or killed where you stand."

Ella stumbled at his words. Luca stepped in front of her, armed with a dagger. She rested a hand on his shoulder, leaning on him as she shook her head. They needed this to work. She needed Henry to believe that she was on his side, that she had always been on his side.

"I need to know Henry...why does he hate me?" Ella took a step towards him, arms open.

"We need to get somewhere more private first." Henry moved away right as Ella fell. She didn't bother trying to stop herself.

Fire blinded her as she landed on her leg, stifling a moan. The last thing she needed was a bunch of guards streaming in. Luca knelt beside her, offering her a hand, an offer she pushed away.

"Stand up, let's go." Henry stood over her, his eyes burning brighter than his hair.

"It's harder than it looks, given that you almost fatally wounded me earlier," Ella said.

"When we get to my room, you're letting me look," Henry ordered as he picked Ella up into his arms and rushed into the palace. Luca moved fast enough to pull the hood over her head before they got inside and went up the stairs.

As they walked through the palace, Ella rebuilt her walls. She had allowed herself to break, to convince Henry, but now...she needed their strength. By the time they were done weaving their way through the palace, Henry's arms shook beneath her. Luca opened the door and got out of the way quickly as Henry carried her. He was surprisingly careful as he set Ella down.

"Do you mind if I move your skirt aside?" Henry questioned.

Ella shook her head as Henry carefully pushed the skirt up her leg. The bandages turned pink as blood soaked through the serum.

"I might need David to come—"

"No." Ella almost shoved Henry to the ground.

"He needs to be told anyway, Ella, and he's a better healer than I am."

"Please, Henry. Not yet." Ella hated herself at that moment. Hated the way she had to plead with him when she was sworn under oath to never reveal herself.

"He deserves to know. We have to tell him, Ella."

"I can't, Henry. I can't...I'm sworn under oath...and...he'll look at me differently—" Ella gripped her tunic, twisting it. David abhorred killing. As of that moment, that was the only thing she was confident about.

"You don't know that, Ella." Henry tossed his hands in the air.

"I do. I *do* know that." Ella blinked against the tears.

Henry scoffed.

"You...*you*, Henry..." Ella stopped to breathe. "You should have seen the look on your face when you figured out who I am...what I do. And I don't even know yet why everyone hates me...I can't...the pain...the hatred I'll see on David's face...I can't...he will never trust me." Ella sucked in a breath, her mind spinning. All she had wanted to do this entire time was to prove to him that she could fight and defend him just as well, if not better than everyone else, and now...now she didn't know what she wanted.

"It will happen eventually." Henry crossed his arms. "So tell me why I shouldn't kill you."

"First, I want to say out loud that you are making me break my oath to the king. I've never been allowed to speak about what I do out of a necessity to protect the crown and its interests." Ella fiddled with her tunic before turning her eyes on Henry. "I dislike being ordered to do this."

"And I'll say again that I think you've sworn an oath to the wrong king." Henry unfolded his arms and sat beside her legs. "Ella...don't you know who you've killed in the crown's name?"

"Yes. I know all of them. None of them would warrant being personally hunted by the prince's champion."

"It might surprise you to know then that Cinderella is wanted for murdering the queen."

"I could never kill—" Ella choked on her words. She clutched the spot over her heart as though that gesture alone would keep her from falling apart. "I never..."

"I don't believe you. You kill people, Ella." Henry didn't even try to contain his disgust as he looked at her.

"All I ever wanted was to be yours and David's equal. To fight beside you and protect the kingdom, not be some spoiled lady you had to protect. All I wanted was to defend *with* you the kingdom that we love. It was made *very clear* to me that I would never be allowed that dream here, so when I had the chance, I took it." Ella's hands shook. She didn't know what he would do.

"And how did that dream turn out for you? You killed—"

"I didn't kill her!" Ella's scream echoed around them. "Can't you see that? Do you think so poorly of me you would believe me capable of killing someone I considered a mother?" Ella rested a hand on Henry's arm.

"I don't know what I think anymore. What I know is that you better have one hell of an explanation." Henry's voice was gruff, though his hands were kind as they cut off the pink-stained bandages.

Henry paused, looking at the serum encasing her leg, his brow furrowed. As Henry examined her injury, Ella took the moment to pause and observe his room. Ornate swords and weapons decorated one wall, each one Ella knew he could expertly wield. The far wall was covered in overstuffed bookshelves. Portraits decorated the room as well. Henry and his sister Tiana, with his parents, and one of his horses. She froze when she saw a small portrait almost hidden on the bookshelf. Her jaw dropped as she realized it was a portrait of Drea before her accident. Ella snapped her mouth shut when Henry straightened and walked over to his mage desk.

"Statu sano corpore instauretis," Henry repeated the enchantment several times, the clear liquid turning blue. His hands glowed brighter the longer he held it until it flared with a white, blinding light that left stars dancing in her eyes. Henry walked over with a potion full of Solacium in hand.

"How dark is your mark?" Ella asked, knowing he must be almost as powerful as Jaq for his enchantment to have shone so brightly.

"It's dark enough."

"I'm not taking that. I don't put those anywhere near me." Ella tried to push away from him.

"It's not for you to ingest. Who would ever ingest a potion? That's not at all safe. This is only for surface injuries. I'm going to put it on your wound." Henry raised a brow at her.

"You're going to put it on my wound?" Ella questioned. This was news to her.

"You take a potion like this one," Henry held up the bottle as he swirled the contents, "and you mix it with a powdered compound. In liquid form, it's too potent. Putting it in a hardened state dilutes it and makes it easier for your system to digest."

"Does that change how addictive they are?" Ella eyed the potion. Henry had yet to use it.

"No, unfortunately not. However, in that hardened form, it would take a lot more of it to become addicted...so, do you want it?"

"Why are you helping me?" Ella desperately wanted to know. She had yet to figure out his motives, and she knew it was critical.

"Curiosity..." Henry kept his eyes downcast, "and you're my friend...I know I may not be the best friend, but until today, I've enjoyed having you back. No matter what you think of me."

"I've enjoyed being back too," Ella confessed, biting her lip. "Do it. But just a little bit." Ella closed her eyes and looked away. She sighed in relief as the pulsing pain slowly quieted while Henry's hands gently messaged it in.

"All done." Henry tightened the fresh bandage on her leg before pulling her skirt back down. "Now, both of us have some stories to tell beginning with how my childhood best friend went from being a lady to an assassin." Henry motioned for her to begin as he pulled a chair over and sat in it.

Luca leaned against the wall next to Henry's window, his arms crossed as he looked over at Ella. She debated on exactly how much to say, though she had to admit that she didn't know the truth from a lie, and might learn something from Henry if she fully revealed everything.

"When I was going to be sent away...after...everything that had happened..." Ella twisted her hands as she ignored the memories fighting to be released. Not yet. She couldn't face those wounds...not yet. "Lady Tremaine gave me an opportunity. I could go to Evrotia as the Queen desired...or I could train, take an oath, and be a sworn secret protector for the kingdom. I didn't ask questions. Why would I? I was eight...all I knew was that I could do what I had always wanted, and I was *excellent* at it." Ella closed her eyes for a moment. She was great. So were Drea and Anastasia, all of their training at such an early age had led to their success.

"But why were you kept away from court? Drizzie...Drea and Anastasia weren't."

"They hadn't been sent away by the queen. For me to do as I wished...everyone had to believe I was gone. I didn't know that she had taken back her order days later, or that David had written to me. I knew nothing, Henry. I have devoted my life to protecting the crown, however they saw fit, knowing that I would never be recognized for it, knowing that I would never see you two again. But at least I would do what I was meant to do...even if I felt banished." Ella glanced over at Luca as he scowled. He had been banished, too. Ella looked at her hands, waiting for Luca to mention her 'special training,' her nightmares, her scars. But he didn't, and she wasn't going to.

"If you thought that—"

"I still do. You have yet to prove to me that I'm wrong. I refuse to believe that all of us aren't working for the King. Are you sure you just aren't privy to the information?"

"I'm positive, Ella. Though it makes me wonder why you're back now." Henry raised his eyebrows and waited.

"Someone tried to kill David. Lady Tremaine assigned me as a private guard until the culprit could be caught and David's life was assured." Ella shrugged. "I was more than happy to protect him, no matter our history."

"Ella...we caught the person who tried to kill David." Henry leaned forward and lightly grabbed Ella's hand.

She raised a brow. "Who was it? Why wasn't Lady Tremaine informed? I mean, people kept trying to kill him, so I had to stay. But that's beside the point. Who was it?"

"It was Sophie, Ella."

"You're lying. Sophie would never...we swore an oath, and David wasn't a threat to the treaty and keeping peace." Ella got out of Henry's bed and paced, her hands clasped together.

"Ella, it was her. I was there the night it happened." Henry remained seated, watching her.

"What happened? Tell me everything—"

"Ella, are you sure?" Luca interrupted.

"Yes. I need to know how my protégé died. I'm owed that."

Henry closed his mouth as he took in what Ella was telling him. He rubbed the bridge of his nose before looking her straight in the eye. Henry's face was impassive and unforgiving, but his green eyes held a level of kindness she had never witnessed before as he spoke the words she had hoped weren't true.

"I killed Sophie," Henry paused for a moment, waiting for it to sink in before continuing. "She had arrived a few weeks earlier, claiming to be the cousin of one of Celeste's friends from Trudel. Even had a letter from her, asking if we could look out for her for a few weeks until she arrived. None of us thoroughly questioned her. Why would we? Sophie got along with Celeste well, barely paying any attention to David. He was withdrawn into his room most of the time, anyway. Eventually, Sophie and David talked more and formed their bond." Henry took a moment, letting Ella process. "I was on my way to my room when I heard a crash in Davids. By the time I got there, David was lying on the floor bleeding and Sophie was standing over him, dagger in hand. She bolted past as I summoned guards. I was able to chase her to her room. I could tell she was speaking to someone through an enchantment, but it ended by the time I got to her."

"She was talking to me..." Ella whispered. Sophie's cries and terror had never stopped ringing through her head. "She was terrified, Henry."

"She was anything but terrified, Ella. She engaged me as well, giving me this lovely parting gift." Henry lifted his tunic, revealing a long scar down his chest. "I truly didn't mean to kill her, but I had to stop her, Ella. She wouldn't have stopped—"

"Our Enchanter said she was begging for her life, Henry."

"She did not. She never had the chance," Henry uttered.

"Why kill her? Why should I believe you? Surely, keeping her alive would have been better for you?" Let him deny that, Ella thought. Let him prove he hadn't killed her to keep Sophie from her true goal: protecting David.

"You're right. Keeping her alive would have been better. I would have found out about you and everyone in your little house of assassins." Henry stood up and paced. "She didn't give me the chance. She made sure I killed her, Ella. She grabbed me and plunged the dagger I held into her heart as I held on before I could think of stopping her. Who would willingly kill themselves?"

"You're lying. She wouldn't...she would never...she was trying to keep you from killing David. That's the only—" Ella stopped as Henry gripped her arms tightly, his fingers digging in.

"Do not ever think I would kill David. I am sworn to protect him. I would do anything to keep him safe. Even if I have to kill you, Ella, I will. Never level an accusation like that against me again." Henry's green eyes glowed with power, his magic flaring brightly around his hands. It crawled up around Ella as he attempted to rein it in, to control his emotions.

But she didn't let it cow her.

"I too have sworn an oath to protect the crown, Henry, and whether you like it or not, I too will do what I have to uphold that vow. My path may be covered in a trail of blood, but just because I got down in the trenches and dirtied my hands so that yours and the crowns may stay clean, doesn't mean I am any less of a worthy protector for David. I'm probably better. Now, let. Go. Of. Me." Ella broke out of Henry's grip, maintaining eye contact the entire time. She would not cower in front of him. She'd done enough of that growing up. "You may not approve of who I've become, but I love who I am, no matter what I've had to endure to achieve it."

Henry turned away from her, running his hands through his hair.

He groaned, "I can tell that you've had extensive training, and you're a great fighter. I will never take that away from you. I know you've always wanted to protect Rairene beside us, but I promise, Ella, your oath was not to our king. My father runs all covert operations, and I would know about you. I would not be *hunting* you—"

"You're wrong Henry. I would never...I *protect* our kingdom," Ella ground out. Tears welled in the back of her eyes and climbed up her throat.

"Ella—" Henry began.

She wasn't sure whether it was the pity in Henry's eyes, or the soft concern in his voice that broke her, but she couldn't take it. Not anymore.

"You're *lying*. I protect *Rairene*. I protect *David*. I do not *harm* the kingdom I love. I keep it safe. I swear, by the blood in my veins, and the bones of my ancestors, to protect the kingdom and the crown, or may the gods strike me down. That was the oath I took. You do not get to tell me that everything I have done for the last nine years has been a lie. I refuse." Ella could no longer see through the tears as the truth of what Henry had been saying hit her. She fell to her knees, ignoring the pain, sending fire down her leg. She deserved it.

"I'm so sorry." Henry knelt beside her, arms open.

Without thinking, Ella wrapped herself within them, her heart breaking as the world she had known fell apart quicker than a novice first learning how to hold a dagger.

CHAPTER TWENTY-TWO

Ella remained on the floor of Henry's room for several minutes as she let herself fall apart. All she had known had been a lie. Everything she had endured to better prepare her...to mold her into the best assassin...it had never been needed. Those nights spent in the attic, cold, alone, and covered in her own dried blood... had all been for someone else's pleasure.

Ella shook herself. She had to pull herself together. She had been trained to withstand more than this, and she would *not* let it pull her down. She would not drown under the revelation that she had been a weapon for the wrong kingdom. She just needed to figure out which kingdom she was going to burn to the ground.

"Henry." Ella rubbed her eyes and adjusted to lean away from him and against the base of his bed frame. "Who do you think I'm truly sworn to?"

Luca walked over with a glass of water, his golden brown eyes void of all emotion.

"Do you know?" she asked him.

Luca shook his head. "No," he paused, crossing his arms behind his back.

Henry ran his hands over his face. "I don't know either. What can you tell me? I know who you've killed. But they're pretty sporadic and impact multiple kingdoms, so I can't form a guess on that. Did anything change for you recently that might help me narrow it down?"

Ella pulled her attention away from Luca, who had become resolutely quiet and focused back on Henry. "Who would want David dead? Truly and completely dead?"

"Why?" Henry leaned forward, his eyes piercing her soul.

"Because that's what has changed. It's the first thing that confused me about my assignment."

"What changed?"

"I've been told that the king wants me to kill David the night of the ball before he signs the treaty."

Henry laughed. "They didn't think that would raise any red banners for you?"

"Lady Tremaine explained David had become a threat to Rairene. He had spoken about not signing the treaty to be with someone else, and that it was more of a threat to keep him alive than let him throw us into a war we may not win."

"That is...a reason..." Henry lay down on his floor, looking up at his ceiling, unblinkingly. "My head hurts."

"Tell me how she died," Ella laid down on the floor beside Henry, looking up at the wooden beams.

"El—"

"Tell me why you think I killed her," she whispered, her fingers playing with her tunic, pulling at the thread. "Let me prove you wrong."

"The queen was in her study. Alone. She was always there during the afternoon. There was an eruption of...raw power...it shook half the palace.

To be honest, we thought the assassin had died in the blast. The room was burned, and everything that had held an enchantment was shattered. The queen was found by…a servant who got there first. She was in her chair, a glass dagger in her heart. By then we had seen other kills by Cinderella, and you always leave behind the same glass dagger, and it was perfect. There was zero doubt you had killed her."

"That's all there was? Nothing else?" Ella bit her lip. There was no way. The only people who had access to her weapons were herself and Jaq…he would never…

"Nothing. Should there have been?"

"No. Not if they wanted to frame me…when you scried it—"

"You can't scry glass, El. Memories don't stick to them. I always figured that's why you used them."

The daggers had always been Jaq and Lady Tremaine's idea. Ella bit her lip. None of it was right. Jaq would never betray her, not like that.

"Hmmm." Ella sat up. "Well, that doesn't help explain why someone would frame me."

"We'll figure it out. We'll figure out all of it." Henry rubbed his head, squeezing his eyes shut. "All I know is you can't kill David—"

"I wasn't going to, but is there a particular reason—"

"War, Ella. You would start a war. You would be blamed for a war."

Ella and Henry talked for over an hour, debating their options. She had to bring herself back to the conversation as her mind wandered, processing and trying to not let the weight of the day's revelations overwhelm her. How could it have gone to shit so quickly? Her mind spun with the implications of starting a war instead of preventing one. How was she going to protect David from so many unknown forces? Unless...there was only one?

"Can't we arrest Lady Tremaine for treason and make her reveal who she's working for?" Ella questioned, looking between both men. "Wouldn't that solve all our problems?"

"I wish, but we can't—"

"Why?" Luca asked. He had remained silent throughout the entire conversation, sitting in the corner of Henry's room.

"She's the Ambassador to Trudel. Lady Tremaine acts on behalf of the queen here. Doing that would start a war. A war we do not want. Not only does Trudel boast a large, well-trained army, but Queen Laila's sister is the Queen of Evrotia, who also boasts a large army."

"Shit." Ella laid down on Henry's bed, a small laugh breaking free. "We're so screwed. Don't you see? She's set it up perfectly." Ella continued to laugh. There was no other appropriate response to the situation. "She framed me for the queen's death, knowing I would come here. That murder is unforgivable, and David will never...he doesn't want to marry Princess Lena. He'll break the treaty, giving them their war. Now, add in the fact that I've been instructed to kill him, and it's a win-win. Either way, they get what they want." Ella devolved into fits of giggles as her world turned dark. "We're so fucked."

"So you think you're working for Trudel?" Henry murmured. "It makes the most logical sense. They've always been angry about the last treaty. Now we need to figure out what to do with this information. It's all hearsay."

"What if there was something you could do?" Luca muttered. He had bent his knees up to his chest, his head resting on his arms as he looked between the two of them. Ella noted how his green eyes were weighed down with sadness.

The energy in the room changed as Luca remained silent. Henry continued to pace as he looked between Ella and Luca, his face growing red in the candlelight.

"You need allies...and, Ella, as much as you want to keep your true self hidden from David, what if that's the answer?"

"I'm sorry, you're suggesting—"

"Tell David and the king. Come clean to them. At the ball. Princess Lena will be there, acting on behalf of her mother. When this evidence is brought to light, they will have to adjust the treaty. Exposing a ring of assassins meant solely for taking down another kingdom will be a public embarrassment for them. They'll have to do whatever the king wants to do to save face—"

"Or they'll just declare war," Henry inserted.

"They could. That would have to be a risk you're willing to take. Even if they declared war, there would still be time to gather your army, and to send someone on a diplomatic mission to your bordering kingdoms and ally with them." Luca rubbed his chin.

"I don't....they would never believe me. Henry already has a hard time believing me. I would need proof that I didn't kill the queen, and I have a feeling that will be in short supply."

"How do you know so much about the inner workings of a court? I know you didn't pick it up guarding Lady Tremaine," Henry questioned Luca, his arms crossed.

"I have my history," Luca dismissed. "It's not important for this. After the ball, send David to Holodal with a few trusted guards and have him ally with the emperor there."

Henry laughed. "We've tried. The emperor will not have an audience with us. We're just lucky that the mountains between us are too difficult for any army to cross."

"That doesn't sound..." Luca stopped himself. "It's the only option we have. Doing this will give you the most amount of time to form an alliance and to keep David alive."

"Luca..." Ella twisted her hands together, grounding herself in the pain. "That's a lot to pull off in four days."

"I need to think this all through, and we need to sleep." Henry yawned.

Ella got out of Henry's bed, swaying.

"One moment, El." Henry got up and walked into an adjoining room.

Luca waited by the door, listening for any sounds.

"Here." Henry handed Ella a stack of letters. She furrowed her brow. Drea had already given her the letters. "I didn't give them all to Drea. You weren't responding, and...things had gotten...strained between the two of us. But I know he would have wanted you to have them."

Ella nodded, unable to speak. She turned around, holding them close as she walked out of Henry's room and down the hall to hers.

Ella woke to the smell of bacon and coffee wafting into her room. And pancakes. There were pancakes involved. Ella bolted to her feet, her nose moving faster than her body. She paused on her leg, waiting for it to collapse. When it didn't, she hastened to her door and opened it as David set down a tray of food.

"David? Did I miss breakfast?" She didn't think she had slept in that late.

"No. I...wanted to surprise you." He smiled sheepishly, his eyes focused on the tray.

"You made it for me, didn't you?" She leaned against the door, inviting him in. Her mouth salivated at the smell, her stomach rumbling. How long had it been since she had eaten? David set the tray down on a small table in front of her fireplace. He relaxed into one of the large comfy chairs.

"What got you up early enough to make all of this?" Ella began by grabbing a pancake smothered in syrup.

"Well, the last time we saw each other, we were interrupted." David smiled as both of them thought about the almost kiss in the woods. "And I wanted to see how you were doing. We've gone through a lot the last few days."

"We have been through a lot," more than he knew. "I'm doing okay, though. Almost feels like I'm back in Evrotia," Ella laughed lightly, "but enough sorrow. Are you looking forward to the ball?" Maybe he would tell her he was breaking the treaty and she could move forward with that information.

"I would be if I knew what to do. Have you thought any more about staying?" David looked at her with brown eyes that told Ella he might hope for more. She couldn't take him down that path. Despite what her heart wanted, or what her false oath had been, she couldn't willingly let him put the kingdom at risk of war.

"I don't know. This isn't the life that I wanted, David. All the politics and the posturing. All I've ever wanted was to defend the kingdom. To fight beside you and Henry—"

"Can't you see how this is a battlefield? It's just one that doesn't involve violence. Well...typically no violence." David attempted to joke.

"I know." Ella twisted her hands in her lap. "David, if I stayed, if I chose you...could I train with the knights and guards? Learn from them?" She held her breath.

David laughed. Ella crossed her arms, waiting for him to stop as her walls strengthened against him. Of course, nothing had changed. She had been a fool to hope.

"Oh, you were serious? I know I showed you some archery, but Ella, that's nothing compared to real training. And it's only harder when you're our age to train."

"But if I wanted to, would you let me?" Ella leaned forward, watching every feature of his face.

"There are a lot of rules, Ella. I don't have the power to change them."

"So that's a no then," Ella growled. Why had she even bothered asking? She hadn't thought he would say yes, had she? It was history repeating itself all over again.

"Ella—"

"Why did I think it would be any different?" Ella remarked as she stood up and marched towards her door. It had been the same with Charisse, always giving her false promises, raising her hopes, only to crush them. Ella closed her eyes and mind to the pain of that memory.

"It's not that easy, Ella. There are things to take into consideration."

"What is there to consider? It's a yes or no question." Ella stepped into the hall. She needed him out of her room.

"Ella, you don't understand, you never have, even back then—"

"Don't you dare tell me about back then?" Ella seethed as she grabbed her hair, gripping the roots. Better her hair than his throat. All she could see was her eight-year-old self crying in her room, wanting to train with her friends. Ella shoved the memory back down as she turned her gaze on David. "It's not something hard that I'm asking for, David."

"What's going on?" Henry walked out of his room. He stood between the two, just as he always had when they'd argued.

"All I want...all I have *ever* wanted was to learn how to fight. To help protect this kingdom. Why is that too much to ask?" Her eyes glistened. She would not let fall down her face.

"All I ever wanted was you...am I not enough for you? You have always been enough for me." David stepped closer to her, his eyes pleading with her. Henry moved slightly to block Ella from David. David didn't have to understand the gesture, but Ella heard it loud and clear. Henry still didn't trust her not to hurt him.

"And all I have ever wanted was to be allowed a fair chance at chasing my dream. If you can't offer that to me...then I don't know where we stand." Ella shrugged, her voice thick with unshed tears as she held them back. Her throat burned, but she would endure it so long as they didn't see.

"Ella, please—"

"No. Stop it. I hate you. I hate you for doing this to me." Ella spun on her heels and went back to her room. She slammed the door in David's face. She didn't waste any time. Ella quickly put on some plain riding clothes, laced up her boots, braided her hair, and walked out of her room. David and Henry were still there, deep in conversation.

Ella ignored them, running for the stables. She didn't care about Henry's escort rules. She needed to get out...now. It was exactly like last time. But she would not let them see her cry again. Not over this. So she ran, and the ghost of Charisse ran with her.

"Ella, stop behaving like a spoiled child. You don't get everything you want because you demand it." Charisse pulled her squirming and kicking down the hall toward her bedroom in the palace.

"I want to fight. Let me train." Ella cried, pulling against the queen's firm grip.

"Ella, wait." Henry ran after her, his footsteps bouncing off the stone walls as he caught up. "What are you going to do?"

Ella ignored him, quickly saddling Dream.

"You are a lady, Eleanor, and ladies do not behave this way. Not in public."

"Please!"

"Ella, what are you doing?" Henry stepped in front of Dream as Ella climbed up.

"I'm getting away before I do something I regret again. Now, move." She pulled Dream around Henry, kicking her into a trot.

"Please, Rissie...let me train...please." Ella grounded her feet as she begged.

"Ladies are not fighters. They are not knights. You will do as your parents desired and become a lady of this court."

Ella kicked Dream into a faster gait, navigating her to the open fields behind the palace. It would never change here. She would never be allowed to be who she was, only be who they deemed acceptable. Ella broke Dream into a gallop.

"Ella, I know you want it now," Queen Charisse kneeled at face level with Ella, "but in a few months, maybe even days, you'll change your mind about this. For now, you're going to your room."

"I don't want to."

"Eleanor, you screamed in the middle of a ball. You will stay in your room for the night." Queen Charisse set Ella on her bed in all of her finery. Her pale blue dress was crunched in Ella's fists as she looked up at the queen with tears streaming down her face, her long white hair coming out of its braids. "I know it's hard right now. I know you miss your parents. My little snowstorm, please understand this is for the best." Queen Charisse kissed Ella on the head, not minding her pout. She got up and left, her gown a magnificent shade of midnight blue, sparkling in the candlelight.

"Ella?" Queen Charisse whispered.

Ella looked at her out of the corner of her eyes, refusing to face her.

"I love you."

"I hate you!" Ella crossed her arms and turned her back to the queen.

Ella blinked against the wind, ducking her head as she cleared her eyes.

I hate you.

Those three paltry words were the last words she had ever spoken to the queen. Lady Tremaine had gotten her early in the night after the ball, and Ella's new life had begun.

Ella rode without thinking. How could she have been so foolish? Of course, David would never let her follow her heart. He would probably banish her for who she was now. With each step further away from the palace that Dream took, Ella brought her walls back up, strengthened her resolve, and put herself back together.

For she had come undone.

She had lived a fool's dream all of this time with David and Henry. Going in, she had known that she would have to leave once more to stay true to herself, and this had only shown her how right she had been. While she didn't know what her future held, she knew it couldn't be this. She wanted more than the life David envisioned for them, and for a moment, she had forgotten that. So, she would remind herself of who she was, and why she did what she did.

Ella snuck into Aumont, knowing that it was too early in the morning for more than a few people to be up. She slipped into Mira's room, pausing as complete darkness greeted her. Odd. Ella took a step and stumbled over an open chest. Mira usually kept her room clean. Though extravagant, Mira's room never felt ostentatious. Blue bedding covered the large bed with dozens of pillows piled high. Every time Ella saw them, she wondered how Mira could sleep comfortably with so many. Mira claimed it reminded her of home. The walls were painted a light blue, a reflection of her home kingdom Grecia, known for its sparkling blue waters and harbor towns.

"Mira?" Ella whispered as her eyes adjusted to find her friend lying on her bed, swallowed up by her pillows. Her red hair was a gloriously tangled fan around her head.

"Ella? What are you doing here? You need to be at the palace." Mira sat up slowly, rubbing her eyes and wincing as she touched a bruised, swollen eye.

"What happened?" Ella parted the curtains before rushing to her friend's side. Bruises, the shapes of fingers wrapped around her neck. "Mira, who did this to you?" Fire burned in Ella as she gazed upon her wounded friend.

"They're dead now, so it doesn't matter." Mira laid back down in bed. "You need a bath, hon."

Ella remained silent, waiting for her friend's story.

"It was my mark. All I was supposed to do was sleep with him, and leave some items behind for his wife to find. She wanted to leave him and needed proof that he was being unfaithful. Nothing else was meant to happen." Mira swallowed hard, a tear running down her cheek. "He must have suspected, or someone tipped him off...he attacked me."

"Mira—" Ella held her hand.

"I've been attacked before. Typically, they're men who are already known for hitting women, and I get the pleasure of killing them. They don't expect me to fight back because I'm a woman. And the joy I get in seeing the shock on their faces..." Mira quieted, "but he did...he was *good*, Ella. I observed nothing about him in the days beforehand that suggested he hit his wife. Nothing. Then I'm leaving and...he attacks me, starts choking me." Mira's fingers delicately touched her neck. "I got free and killed him. Bloody mess. But I didn't care. I got out of there as fast as I could."

"I am so sorry, my love." Ella lay down next to her, holding her close. "I can stay here with you if you'd like?" Ella looked at Mira's emerald eye swimming in fear.

She scrunched up her face, swallowing back her tears and rubbing her nose. "No, you need to go to the palace. The ball is in three days, and you need to make sure he's alive. Please don't worry about me. I'm going to hide in here for the day," Mira whispered.

"Mira, are you sure you're alright?" Ella brushed the hair out of Mira's face.

"The only other time I've come that close to dying was the day my father found out I had kissed a stable boy." Mira rubbed her good eye, looking up at the ceiling. "He was furious. It took several guards, and my eldest sister, to stop him. She stood directly between us, staring him down. You know how Lady Tremaine has that look that stops you dead?" Mira glanced at Ella for confirmation. "Miranda somehow developed that look by the age of twenty. She's terrifying, and so brave. She knew my father wouldn't hurt her, his heir, so she was my shield. Took me weeks to heal from the beating he gave me."

"All because you kissed a boy?"

"A stable hand. It's seen as dishonorable to my father to sully oneself that way. Even though I was only thirteen, I wanted to know what kissing was like."

"That's why you were sent here," Ella remarked.

"Yes, and now I can't help but feel that my father has changed his mind about keeping me alive." Mira twirled her tangled hair, examining it.

"Is that why you're leaving?" Ella looked at the other chests around them. The slightest flicker of emotions crossed Mira's face as she turned away.

"I'm not sure anymore." She sighed. "I don't know what's better. To stay here or go find Calla and make sure she and Raven aren't in trouble. It feels to me as though Lady Tremaine is building up to something, El. I mean, how often do all of us have something to do? How often does she send out one of the king's top assassins on a spying mission with her best enchanter, while also putting another in the line of fire? While our lives are being threatened, more than usual, she has Lucifer and Anastasia worked up, and you know when her two little pets are anxious that something is going down."

Ella sat up, biting her lip as she processed everything.

"Am I just imagining everything?" Mira turned her eye on Ella.

"I think you should listen to your heart and your gut. Most of the time, if it's telling you something is wrong, then something is."

Mira laughed softly. "You know, I was hoping you would tell me I'm crazy, El."

Ella smiled weakly. She couldn't tell Mira about their oath being a lie. It would hurt her, and she would do something rash. "Me too. Do you think you could do me a favor when you get to our girls?"

Mira raised a brow.

"Could you get this to Raven?" Ella handed over a blank envelope.

"You're warning her?" Mira took the letter written in enchanted ink.

"Yes, I've noticed the signs as well. I need their perspective if we have any chance. Calla might have been able to if she were here. Lady Tremaine did a good job separating us," Ella commented. What had her stepmother done?

"Well, that was probably the first thing she knew she had to do if she was going to do something less than desirable." Mira turned Ella's letter over in her hands. "I'll make sure it gets to our Snow."

"Thank you." Ella began to leave when she stopped and turned back to Mira. She still stared at the ceiling, the bruises on her neck and face more pronounced in the morning light. "Mira, the next few days will be your best chance of getting away unseen."

Ella walked slowly, trying not to piss off her injured leg.

"Ella, please be careful. Don't trust anyone."

"I will be." Ella opened the window and climbed down the side of the building, shaking off the feeling that she wouldn't get to see her friend again. Which was ridiculous. She would be fine, and Mira would get away. They would both be fine.

Ella stripped down as her bathtub filled with delicious warmth. Candles dotted the washroom, lighting the space with a soft subdued glow that was perfect for calming the thoughts raging through her mind. Mira was right, she needed a bath. Ella sighed the second she lowered herself in, the heat enveloping her.

Closing her eyes, Ella waited for relief as her muscles turned to liquid. The serum floated off and covered the top layer of water in a mushy orange paste. Ella drained the water and washed the residue off before refilling the tub and soaking in the smell of lavender and sage. Once she got out, she looked at the serum and grimaced. If she could avoid putting it back on, she would. Ella hobbled over to her healing kit and pulled out a needle, thread, and a small potion that would numb her muscles.

Ella poured the liquid over her injury and on top of her leg, instantly feeling a cool numbing sensation wash over her. It wouldn't last long. The enchanter who had made it had been weak, barely able to enchant a single bottle without draining their reserves. Next was the part Ella always hated, stitching herself up.

She brought a flame to her curved needle and watched it turn red. She started in the center of her injury and worked her way up with a simple running stitch. Each needle poke made her leg feel firm and stable.

Once Ella had finished the first half, she cut more string and started the other. She was halfway through when the numbing from the potion vanished. Ella bit down on her lip. The bottle was empty, and the pain was a blinding light in her head. Ella laid back, absorbing it as she thought of a solution.

She hobbled over to her washing room and rummaged through the drawers until she found the hidden perfect remedy: rum. Ella gulped down a small shot, waiting for the fire that coursed through her throat to take hold. By the time Ella was done stitching herself up, the bottle that had once been full was close to empty and Ella was slumped in her bed. She stared up at the ceiling, numb to more than her wound. She didn't care about anything or...anyone. She was herself and could do what she wanted, say what she wanted, and be who she wanted.

Ella lifted half of her torso off the bed before having to lie back down as her world spun. She tried again, successfully standing, and then walked to the trunk at the foot of her bed. Ella pulled out a ballgown, her mother's ballgown, its golden color bright.

"I'm sorry I was such a failure." She would never be the daughter her father had raised her to be. She was twisted now. What she knew was that she would never make her parents proud.

Ella got the ball gown on half way before she fell back onto her bed, the rum running its course.

"Ella?"

Ella laughed. Laughed at the worry in Luca's voice as he sat down next to her.

"Why are you always so serious, Luca?" Ella questioned. She spoke slowly, trying so very hard to not slur her words.

"You're drunk."

"Yup." Ella smiled at him. "Stay still. I want to look at your handsome face." Ella placed her hands on his cheeks, squishing them as she stared into his eyes. His dark emerald eyes held a sadness so deep she didn't know what to do but continued to stare at them. "You're always so sad, Luca. What do you have to be sad about? I—I have every—everything to be sad about." Ella stood up, dancing on her toes around the room, the top of the dress pressed against her.

"You need to take a cold shower and get some sleep."

"No." Ella pointed a finger at him, stopping him. "Everyone is always telling me what to do. Protect the prince, Ella. Your place is with David, Ella. Stop bleeding all over the fucking floor, Ella. Kill the prince, Ella. Come home, Ella. Your mother needs you, Ella." She laughed. "Your mother is dying, Ella."

Luca walked over to her. Ella swayed in the center of her room, adjusting her feet to remain standing. She moved the bottle of rum to her lips, draining it of every drop. Ella grimaced when no more came out. Luca gently took the bottle from her and set it on the ground by the bed. He moved deliberately as he assessed her.

"You need to stop moving so fast," Ella commented, holding onto him. She sniffled, rubbing her nose. When had she been crying?

"I heard what happened here this morning." Luca gently held her shoulder, keeping her upright.

Ella looked at her feet swaying beneath her, the carpet dancing with them.

"I uh...." Ella paused as she looked around. "I needed to stitch up my wound, but the potion was so old, and made by someone weak, so it wore off quickly. I thought a single drink of rum would work."

"I'm sorry about what happened, Ella," Luca repeated.

"Ha." Ella spun away from David, no Luca...it was Luca in the room with her.

His face was soft, with the smallest amount of lines crinkled between his forehead. Ella spun around again, trying to ignore him. It was so very hard, though, when he looked like that. Ella waltzed over to him and placed her lips on his, leaning into him. Needing him to keep her up. Luca broke the kiss.

"They aren't gone." Ella tried to move her hands up to his forehead to smooth the lines, but his hands held her captive. "What are you worried about? Let me make it go away, that's what I did, and it feels so good to not worry, Luca. You should try it." Ella kissed him again.

She broke out of his hold so that her dress could drop to the ground. Luca stepped back from her, his eyes wide.

"Ella—"

"Come on, Luca, let's have some fun." Ella walked over to him, tripping over her feet. She fell against him. Standing back up, she tried to kiss him, tailing her lips down his neck and to his shoulder. "Come on Luca, I know you want to."

"Stop it, Ella." Luca held her at arm's length.

"Let's forget about everything and just...let go. Please." A sob wracked her voice.

"I'm worried about you." Luca ran a hand through her hair before cradling her cheek.

Ella leaned into his palm. "Don't be. No one else worries about me. No one has been worried about me since my parents died." Ella wiggled away from him. "Did I ever tell you how my mother died? I was only four—"

"Stop it, Ella. Don't tell me something drunk that you wouldn't tell me sober."

"I was out playing with David and Henry. We were on one of our 'missions', back when I was allowed to go on them. Mom was chasing us, playing the evil villain we had to destroy. It was so easy this time to save Henry from her. We complained that she had taken all the fun out of it," Ella slipped away from Luca when his hands loosened on her.

She walked around in nothing but her underclothes, hands balled at her side.

"That was when we found her on the ground. Pretty much right where you found me yesterday. They carried her away and still I sat there. I didn't budge. Not until my father came to me, 'Your mother needs you, Ella'...' We knew this day was coming, Ella'. Only I didn't know. I didn't understand..."

Ella paced, rubbing her eyes.

"I was too late to understand that her sickness wasn't something that went away."

Luca gently moved towards her and guided her to bed. She didn't notice until he slid a tunic over her and lifted her onto the mattress. "Why do they treat me like that?"

"Who?"

"David...Charisse..." Ella stared at the quilted blanket with dark floral patterns. "Why am I not allowed to be who I want to be? Why are they making it so hard to....protect him? To want to protect him." Ella's vision darkened. Luca handed her a cup of water. "I thought...did you know we were sworn to a different crown?"

"I had my suspicions."

"And you didn't...you never said..." Ella slurred her words, her hands blurring. "What did you give me?"

"I'm sorry," Luca whispered as the potion seeped into her and Ella slept.

CHAPTER TWENTY-THREE

Ella woke up gasping. The feel of her mother's lips kissing her forehead lingered as her dream cleared from her mind. Luca had been there too. Ella clutched her swollen pumpkin-sized head. A loud hissing noise blacked out her vision. Ella lay down carefully. Closing her eyes, flickers of her nightmare surfaced. Her mom had been chasing her, and Luca...had been helping. He looked so sad, so worried.

"What happened?" Ella groaned.

"You got drunk."

Ella jumped, shutting her eyes and clutching her head.

"I would apologize, but you did this to yourself." Luca rolled so that he was on his side, his arm supporting his head.

"Technically, it's Henry's fault. How much did I drink?" Ella cracked open a single eye to look at him.

"An entire bottle of rum. What got into you? You're lucky the ball is tomorrow and not today."

Ella remained silent as she tried to answer that question for herself.

"You're so lucky it was me who found you like this, and in the palace, no less! If anyone knew, Ella—"

"I know, Luca. I don't need a lecture right now."

"Are you sure? Because last night you hinted at not protecting him. Not upholding your oath."

"What a joke of an oath. It's a complicated game I'm playing now, Luca," Ella growled, pushing up with her arms.

She ran her hands over her face, trying to rub the headache away. She pressed her hands to the back of her neck, massaging it. "It's just..." Ella sighed. "I don't think you quite understand what this means to me." Ella laid her arms over her knees. She didn't want to tell Luca how she had wanted to lose control, to do whatever she wanted, to not feel...trapped.

Luca hugged her, kissing the top of her head. "You're right. The hate and love you have for David...isn't something I've experienced. But I'm trying to understand." Luca's hand trailed over her arm until he pulled her against his chest, resting his head next to hers. Ella leaned into him, closing her eyes.

"If I don't protect him...I will lose who I am. All that I have worked to become, will mean nothing, and I...I don't know what to do Luca. He will never accept me as I truly am, yet every fiber of my soul is telling me this is wrong. Lady Tremaine is wrong...my stepmother...has used me."

"The Ella I know is strong, willful, and loyal to a fault to those that she loves. And you love David,"

Ella scoffed.

"You care for him," Luca amended. "And you have used the last nine years of your life to hone your skills. I have loved you since the moment I walked through the grand double doors of Aumont, asking to train, to serve. You stood all high and mighty at the top of that grand entrance and demanded I prove myself worthy of protecting the crown in a duel with you. You were confident, radiant, and knew who you were to your core. I think that Ella would be proud of who you are now and have you lean into who she was then for guidance on what to do now."

"Thank you," Ella whispered. She got up and left Luca's embrace to get ready for the day, knowing she would have to face it one way or another.

Ella changed into a dress that would cover the scars on her wrists, hiding herself once more. Morning fog rolled in faster than her horse could gallop. A wall of it towering over Riset, shrouding it in shades of gray. Silently, Ella walked around the palace, noticing the guards changing over from the night shift. She took notice of the gaps, the places she could slip through to escape. Because she would have to escape. No matter what she did, she would need to run. Lady Tremaine would hunt her down for betraying her, or David would. She would need items from Jaq and then she would be set, her large backpack already set.

Henry found her at the training grounds, watching the men work. Luca was beside him. Ella twitched to jump into the ring. It had been too long since she had been in a proper fight. One that challenged her. Well, aside from the one she'd lost to Henry, she acknowledged.

"Ella, you're here—"

"Of course."

"I just figured, after yesterday...well, I was getting—"

"Ready to come kill me?" Ella spoke. Henry nodded. "Well, I'm here, so there won't need to be any of that."

Henry relaxed, his shoulders visibly softening.

"I need a favor."

"Oh?" Henry crossed his arms, looking her up and down. "Why would I do that?"

"Let's say it's an added incentive to keep me from completing my assignment," Ella snapped. "A friend of mine was attacked the other day."

Luca and Henry both stood at attention. Luca stepped closer to her, his brow furrowed.

"She's okay...shaken, but alive. The man...he was killed. But Henry, I'm hoping you can confirm it for me."

"Your friend...she's like you?"

Ella nodded.

"Then shouldn't you be confident in her skills?" Henry frowned.

"I am. But the attack doesn't sit right. It shouldn't have happened. He wasn't even marked to die. It felt too much like a setup. So, will you look into it?"

"I'm going to need more information, El. Do you have a name or description?"

"No, but I'm fairly certain the death would be very violent. Drowning might be involved."

"I'll look into it, though I am pretty busy with everything else, Ella."

"Have one of your assassin hunters look into it, then. I don't care, but I want to make sure I don't need to go on a hunting mission of my own."

"It won't come to that," Henry snapped.

"Good. Now, I'm going to go for a walk. All of us have a lot of decisions to make." Ella left both of them behind, heading straight for the gardens.

Fog soaked the ground beneath her, soaking into her soft shoes and dimming the colors around the maze. Ella had loved running in it as a child, getting lost. Especially after her mother had died. It was her haven, the only place she could go where she knew it would be a while before anyone found her. Ella wandered, not watching where she went as long as it was far away from her life. Her heart pounded with the need to speak with Raven. She would know what to do. She could cut through the emotions and tell Ella the correct thing to do. She walked until she got to a hidden gazebo with a small waterfall fixture that ran into a pond. Wooden benches lined up along the edges, all of them pointing to the pond and the statue that stood in the middle. Ella tilted her head. The statue was new, though she instantly recognized Queen Charisse smiling down at her, a hand outstretched, pulling her in, beckoning Ella to come to her.

Ella stepped up to her, gently resting her hand on the statue.

"I'm so sorry," Ella whispered. "I don't hate you. I hope you knew that." Ella sat on her knees, feet tucked beneath her. "I miss you...so much."

"She missed you too, you know." David sat down beside her. "Ella, I'm...I'm sorry about yesterday. About all of it," David spoke low as they both looked up at the queen.

"David, I—" Ella stopped talking when she faced him. Seeing him for the first time in over a day sent her heart skittering through her chest. She rested her hand on him, his tunic soft beneath her fingers. His spiced magic tangled itself around her. Ella gripped his tunic and brought him to her, closing the gap between their lips. A first and final kiss before the ball tomorrow. David's lips on hers were like coming up for air after being underwater, full of life and passion. There was no going back, and he would never want her near him again.

He broke the kiss, holding her far enough away to gaze at her. "You know that thing people's eyes do when they're trying not to cry?" David whispered.

Ella stood up, maintaining some distance. She blinked rapidly, her heart hammering.

"What do you mean?" She swallowed, taking one more step back, just to be safe.

"They blink their eyes a lot, and they get wide as if somehow that will keep the tears at bay."

Ella squeezed her eyes shut as the tears got to be too much.

"Sometimes, they even shut their eyes for a long time, as though keeping them closed long enough to will the tears from coming out. Then they take deep breaths and control their heartbeat, all so that they don't show what they're feeling."

Ella's eyes snapped open. "I don't know what you're talking about."

David groaned with his entire body as he took a step towards her. "El...these last few days, you constantly look like you're about to cry. Please let me in. Tell me what's wrong. All I want to do is help. Is it about the ball? My engagement? Whatever it is, I want to help."

Ella crossed her arms, the pressure of her nails digging into her skin, grounding her. "There's nothing wrong, David. I'm fine."

"I see you. I see your sorrow. Please, Ella, I know you're not this person who shuts people out—"

"Well, you and your family would know all about that, wouldn't they?" She kept her hands on her hips, chills rushing through her at the words.

"Is that what this is about? I've told you, I didn't agree. Even then, when I was nine, I didn't want you to leave. Neither did Mom. She took it back, but you had already left. I know there's more going on than this one dumb topic. My magic has been going crazy every time I touch you. It knows something is wrong."

Ella raised an eyebrow. "I'm going to put that 'dumb topic' comment to the side for now. What do you mean your magic knows something's wrong?" She was against a hedge wall, and David, he was so close. His lips were so close. All she had to do was lean forward and she could silence him once again.

"My magic...all enchanters, our magic reacts to people who are important to us. Sometimes it develops over years, sometimes it's instantaneous. But whenever we touch that person, or think about them, our magic reacts—"

"And yours is telling you something is wrong?" Ella looked down at his hands that were oh so close to her. Could his magic sense that she had been instructed to kill him? Did it inherently know?

"Sort of...it's up to my interpretation."

Ella scoffed.

"When you first came back, Ella...I almost fell to my knees at the pure joy my magic pushed into me. I almost lost control." David smiled softly.

"I didn't notice...though you were barely there given your injuries."

"Yes....I also needed to get away. My magic was bursting, Henry could tell. I glowed for hours as I reined it in. I enchanted so many objects to keep that control. Ever since then, every time I touch you," David's hand rested on Ella's cheek. She closed her eyes, taking a slow, controlled breath. "It's like fire shooting through my veins, lighting up every nerve in my body, my magic singing. But now," David paused.

Ella opened her eyes and gazed at him through blurred vision. His eyes teared up before her, the shadows slipping back in, darkening the eyes that she adored. Ella reached up, resting her hand on his cheek to rub away the tear.

"Now, my magic...it's clawing to get to you, to...soothe you, let you know that everything will be fine. I swear the last few days I have been battling myself to not lose control. My magic is...pulling me apart. So that's what I mean when I say something's wrong." David moved so that his hand held hers against his cheek.

Ella blinked.

"Nothing is wrong. Something must be wrong with your magic. You should get that looked at." Ella stepped away from David. She turned her back to him, walking towards the archway. The sound of her feet on the dirt roared in her ears.

"I know you, Ella. But if you don't want to tell me you're not okay, then fine. But, I want some time to myself. I have a lot of decisions to make before tomorrow."

So be it. Ella didn't stop walking until she got to the stables, saddled Dream, and took off.

Ella shook her head, clearing her vision as Dream galloped over the open fields. If she never stopped, then she never had to feel. Her heart hadn't stopped aching, weighing more than her body could carry. Claws dug their way in, fracturing everything that she knew, and they were dragging her down, down, down. She didn't know what would happen when she reached the bottom of that black chasm.

Ella screamed at the wind rushing against her. At least here, no one could hear, no one would know. *No one could know.* Not that they had ever cared.

Ells screamed.

And screamed. And screamed.

Ella pulled up on Dream's reins, hard. Dream stood up on her hind legs before stomping down.

Ella jumped off, collapsing. The grass was tall enough to shield her as she lay down and gave in to the shaking. Ella held her head and curled in on her side. The hard ground circled her as everything spun around her.

The grass cut into her hand as she twisted it, holding on tightly. She had to hold on. Ella dug her nails into the dirt until they were caked in it. What was she doing? She had to pull herself together. It was one more day. One more day and she would be on the run. To where she wasn't sure, but that didn't matter. David would be alive, and he would hunt her down for being Cinderella. Nothing else was important, though. All she had wanted was to protect the kingdom, protect the crown. She would do that, and then...she would disappear. Forever.

CHAPTER TWENTY-FOUR

Ella ensured no tears remained as she walked out of Dream's stall. Celeste waited for her, wearing her finest court dress, her hair braided out of her face, tiara on top. She twisted her hands together, biting her lip.

"Pumpkin, is everything okay?" Ella walked quickly to her side.

"Please don't leave him. I don't know what he said, but I know he didn't mean it."

"Celie—"

"He's not himself...not when she's around." Hatred contorted Celeste's voice, her brown eyes darkening.

"Who?"

"Princess Lena." Celeste's face twisted. "She arrived this morning. Forced David to escort her around as though this place was already her home."

"I...I didn't know she was here." One more threat to monitor.

"Please, Ella. I know you just got back, but he's been so happy, and I hope you've been happy being back here...you don't know what she's like. We can't have her as queen. I would rather David break the treaty than marry her."

"Celeste, hush." Ella slapped a hand over her mouth. What was with these two and wanting to break the treaty? She looked at Celeste and the tears that had gathered in her eyes. Celeste balled her hands as her eyes narrowed, tears born of anger falling free. She shook in Ella's hands as Ella continued to silence her. Ella stepped back, retracting her hand.

"I mean it. She's awful, Ella...wait until you meet her. You'll see." Celeste grabbed Ella's hand and pulled her along.

"Well then, I guess we'll have to scheme before the ball tonight," Ella promised. "Walk with me? I have to change real quickly and run into Riset before the ball."

"Wouldn't want you to be in your ballgown on a horse."

Ella laughed. "Can you imagine me riding a horse in a ballgown? I would probably fall off."

The two talked about the ball as they walked to Ella's room, Celeste bouncing up and down as she spoke about her gown. "I can't wait to see yours. It's going to be stunning."

"It will be," Ella agreed. It had arrived already and currently hung on her wardrobe, its golden threads gleaming on the dark green fabric. The design was impeccable, fitting her perfectly. Her debut at court would be worthy of a ballad or two. But Ella knew it would have looked better on someone else. Her hips would make her look too wide in that many layers, and the back...the gossamer fabric was thick enough to hide her scars from a distance. The seamstresses had almost fainted at being requested to add more fabric. But they had acquiesced.

"What do you mean, I'm not staying in the royal hall?" The woman's voice echoed down the hall. Though loud, it was level and controlled. Ella paused before they could round the corner, placing herself between the woman and Celeste. She held them both back, not wanting to meet Princess Lena just yet.

"You are staying in the guest quarters, your highness."

Ella pitied the servant having to inform her. Though they sounded almost pleased at upsetting her.

"I. Want. To. Speak. To. David."

"His Highness, Prince David, is the one who chose your rooms. Now, if you will follow me."

Ella made Celeste wait one minute before turning the corner and slipping into her room to change. She moved fast, talking to Celeste as she got ready. Celeste, however, was occupied with Ella's dress for tonight, fawning over it.

"What do you need in Riset?"

More weapons and supplies. Not that Ella could tell her. "It's a surprise."

"I love surprises." Celeste walked over and hugged Ella. "I've missed you. I know I was so little when you left, but I noticed. I'm glad you're back." She walked out of Ella's room with her, parting ways at the door. Ella forced a weak smile before running down to the stables.

She took Dream straight to the market street. The market bustled with citizens going home and running last-minute errands. She slipped down a side alley and into the back of a shop she knew well. The packs she had requested were there, waiting for her. Everything she would need once she fled to who knew where, was in those bags. Ella grabbed them and went back to the palace, everything ready to go.

Ella held the green organza ball gown against her and faced the mirror as the sun reached its peak the next day. She laid a sleeve against her arm, making sure it reached her wrist. No one had noticed them yet, not even David, and she intended to keep it that way. The gold flowers and vines were exceptional, glinting in the candlelight. Sparks beat violently against her ribcage as she envisioned wearing the gown and walking down the stairs into the grand ballroom. David had practiced his dance multiple times with Ella until it was second nature. It was the dance David would perform with Princess Lena as part of their engagement. As his friend, she had been more than happy to help quell his nerves. As someone who, admittedly, had a small crush on him, it had cut deeper than her largest dagger. And then, during her dance with David, she was supposed to stab him in the heart. At least, that's what Lady Tremaine thought. She would tell him who she was, and he would abandon their friendship. But he would be safe.

Ella's eyes caught on her compact mirror behind her. It was glowing. Odd. Jaq shouldn't be trying to get a hold of her now.

Jaq, what's happened? Ella opened the mirror, frowning at her friend. He ran his hands through his hair and pulled on his tunic.

You need to come here—

Jaq, the ball is in a few hours, I can't—

It's about Raven. Jaq leaned close to the mirror.

What about her? Ella's hand gripped the mirror, threatening to break it.

I have to tell you in person. Hurry here and you'll make it back in time. Jaq closed the mirror.

Ella opened her door, halting when Luca walked up to it. She darted around him, heading for Dream.

"Ella, what's happening?" Luca jogged to catch up to her.

"I have to go to Aumont—"

"El, that's crazy—"

"Raven might be in trouble. I have to find out. I'll be back before the ball."

"I'm coming with you—"

"No, you're not. You're staying here to protect David and to cover for me if I run late," Ella dismissed him.

"Ella." Luca grabbed her arm and pulled, stopping her. "Is everything okay?"

She looked into his green eyes and smiled weakly. "I hope so. But I have to find out. I'll be back before you know it."

Ella left before Luca could protest any further, saddled Dream, and took off.

Ella walked through the doors and shivered at the chill that raced down her spine. She instantly loosened one of her daggers, the hair on her arm standing at attention.

"Ella, Lady Tremaine wants to see you." Lucifer walked out of the shadows, his hands behind his back.

"Not now, Jaq needs me, and then I have to head back to complete my assignment."

"He's with her. Now obey." Lucifer walked down the hall to Lady Tremaine's office, not waiting for Ella to follow. He knew she would. She always did. Ella walked into the room past Lucifer, giving herself as wide a berth from him as possible. The room was dimly lit, with only a few candles lighting the way. A cup of tea was steeped on the desk in front of her.

"Ella, take a seat, have some tea."

As her eyes adjusted, she found Lady Tremaine in a corner near a portrait of her father and Lady Tremaine. Ella remained standing, her eyes darting around the room as she eyed the tea.

"Tell me, Ella, have I done something to upset you?"

Ella paused for a moment, assessing the room. "Not that I can think of. Is there something specific you had in mind?" Ella adjusted her stance, loosening another dagger. She knew why Lady Tremaine moved slowly. She wanted to make sure all of Ella's attention was on her and nothing else.

"Don't be cheeky. I raised you better than that." Lady Tremaine leaned against the edge of her desk. "With this current assignment. You said you would be able to do it. You said you would do anything to protect our kingdom and the crown. Have some tea." She handed Ella a fresh cup and she took a sip.

"And I will. It's all I've ever wanted. Have I given you an indication that I'm not going to?" Who had told her? The only people who knew she would not kill David were Henry and Luca.

"Not to me, though I have someone who doubts your intentions."

Ella twisted and threw one of her daggers at the man behind her. He grunted as two more men jumped out from behind the desk. Ella palmed another dagger before they grabbed her arms. With wide eyes, Ella looked at them. Their eyes were rimmed with red.

"Let me go." Ella struggled against them, impaling one with the other dagger. He didn't let go, and the first one held the door open as both men dragged her out. Ella kicked her legs, trying to get away.

She screamed louder.

"You can't do this."

Lady Tremaine couldn't do this to her. She could not be locked away. Not again. Ella kicked one of them in the groin. He dropped her fast. She broke out of the other's hold quickly, super-slapping him over the ear for good measure.

She was free.

Ella ran as fast as she could through the house.

Until she stumbled against a wall.

Her vision blurred as the floor twisted into a dark hole before her. Ella pushed away, sidestepping the gaping hole that had appeared out of nowhere. Sweat poured down her back and face as she looked at her hands. Hands that become claws. Ella gasped for air, her vision going black with pain as a dagger pierced her back. The lackey grabbed her. He yanked back on her shoulder. Spots erupted in her vision. This time her scream was pure pain, tears rushing to blind her as a dagger, her dagger, ripped into her.

"What did you do to me?" Ella held her hands before her, heart racing.

A fist to the back of her head ended her panic.

Ella woke up in the attic. Her arms ached from the weight of her body. The metal cuffs locked around her wrists kept her body suspended. Her ankles were chained with enough slack for her to stand. Her vision swam with black spots as she moved her head. The floor tilted, her stomach rolled, bile rising. Ella moaned. Every ounce of her shivered as sweat continued to roll down.

"What did I do?" Ella mumbled. She couldn't know. Lady Tremaine could not know she was going to tell David. Ella found Lady Tremaine sitting in the corner, legs crossed, eyes glowing in the shadows.

"You didn't do as I desired, Ella. As your oath required. All the training, all of those years of planning with the queen, wasted in three weeks."

"I am going to kill him; he's a threat to our peace." Ella kept her eyes low as she absorbed the knowledge that Henry was right. Lady Tremaine was working with the Queen of Trudel. Ella risked a glance up at her, swallowing the panic as Lady Tremaine's face morphed into a leopard. "You should have just killed me all those years ago. Why didn't you?"

"I promised your father I would take care of you."

Ella's chuckles dissolved into hysterics. "Good job."

Lady Tremaine the leopard stood up and prowled around her. "All you wanted was to be a knight, a protector. To train, and to win. I gave that to you. They never would have given you any of that. You know that. It's why you chose this life."

Ella's chest heaved hard as the wood floor below her turned to liquid and disappeared. "You expect me to believe that? That you cared for my father or what I wanted? Did you even grieve his death? Or was his death part of your plan—"

"I would never harm your father. I loved him more than you could know." Lady Tremaine flinched as though Ella had slapped her.

"I loved you as a mother. I trusted you," Ella whispered.

"That was the point, dear." Lady Tremaine straightened her back, letting a malicious smile break across her face.

"Did I ever mean anything to you? Did any of us?" She would not cry. Not right now. Ella hadn't realized how much she had been in denial about her stepmother's motivations. How much she had clung to the idea that at least she still had someone who cared for her. Loved her.

"No. You meant nothing to me."

Ella strained against her bonds as the blow truly rocked through her. No one loved her. She never meant anything to anyone. She had only been a pawn in this game. Ella tried to breathe, to see past the red that was clouding her vision, and the tears that had become too much to bear.

Lady Tremaine smiled at Ella, her hands resting perfectly against her cheek. "Are you quite done, dear?"

"How could you do it? How could you do this to me?"

"It's simple." Lady Tremaine circled her, coming to a stop behind Ella. "Revenge. Knowing you're someone your parents would hate. That's why I did it."

"You may have made me into someone they would never love, but at least I like who I am. I will always uphold my oath, no matter how false it might be, and I will find a way out. And I will bring you to King Matthias."

"I doubt that. You will never uphold your oath, hell you won't even get to the ball to try."

"Was the ball even an option? Or was I just another loose end to tie up?" Ella challenged her, staring down at the monster that twisted in the shadows.

"You're all loose ends." Lady Tremaine left as Lucifer walked in, two men behind him carrying a long wooden table.

Ella's arms shook. This was not how it was supposed to go. She was not supposed to be here. She couldn't be here. Not with Lucifer, not with anyone. Ella strained to breathe. The pain in her wrists grounded her as men morphed into cats circled her.

"What did you do to me?" Ella closed her eyes, squeezing tight.

"It's one of my favorite poisons Raven invented, our clever Snow White," Lucifer purred in Ella's ear. "You remember Malice and what it does. Hallucinations, which I would guess are in full effect now, slow heartbeat, chills. Is any of that going through you right now?"

Ella shuddered as they unlocked her feet and lifted her onto the wooden table before locking them down again. The hardwood bit into her, its cool surface a minor relief to the fever on her skin.

"What are you going to do?"

"Lady Tremaine wants to ensure you haven't given away any secrets." Lucifer's cat grin broke his face in two as Ella turned away.

She watched the other two men. Engraved their faces to memory before the hallucinations changed them. She took in everything from the blond hair to the tattoo on his neck that hadn't aged well, a bloated bird that did nothing to inspire fear. He stepped closer, a rolled leather pouch of various devices in his hand, along with a bottle containing the poison known as Malice. Ella would recognize its twisted gray color anywhere. She turned away from him, keeping her mouth shut...at least until he grabbed her nose and more poison was poured in.

Ella pulled away from herself, fleeing into her mind.

She was in Queen Charisse's private study. Light flooded everything. The queen was on her balcony, sitting on an ornately carved chair, an empty one beside her. She motioned for Ella to join her, her dazzling brown eyes, David's eyes, smiling when Ella walked over. She wore the same gown Ella had last seen her in, the silver threads twinkling like falling stars in the bright sunlight.

"You've grown up." She clutched Ella's hand.

"Where are we?" This wasn't right. This wasn't where she was supposed to be.

"Somewhere safe."

"That kind of place doesn't exist."

Queen Charisse sat on the floor, bringing Ella with her. "My little Snow Storm...I never wanted to send you away. We never...we missed you every day. Had I known what was happening to you...I would have torn that place down and taken you home."

"I loved getting to train," Ella pulled away, "and I'm fantastic." She would not cry. "I missed you...but..."

"I know, and you are becoming an amazing warrior." Queen Charisse gripped Ella tightly. "I've never been so proud."

"How can I…how can I survive this?" A single tear rolled down Ella's cheek. *Pounding could be heard in the distance. Someone was coming after her. The room went dark as Malice consumed Ella.*

Queen Charisse's eyes widened as she stood up and put herself between Ella and whatever was on the other side.

"You will survive because you are stronger than they are. You are so brave, my little snowstorm. You always have been, and you always will be."

"I want you to stay with me." Ella looked at the only other person who had been a mother to her. Protected her.

"I am always with you." Queen Charisse turned away when the pounding got louder, her hands glowing with magic. "Now run!"

Ella stood, screaming as the floor beneath her collapsed, and she fell into a dark hole.

She slammed into her body, her legs and arms jolting as she hit the table.

"I don't think so, Ella. You don't get away that easily." The black cat laughed at her as Ella blinked against the candlelight. "Now tell me, are you going to kill the prince?"

Ella nodded as she closed her eyes. Pinpricks of pain laced her arms. What had they done to her? Ella lifted her head enough to look down and see slight scratches on her arms.

"Let me go. I answered your questions." Ella laid her head back down, unable to support it any longer.

"You have answered one question. I have a few more." Lucifer's eyes gleamed in the light as he forced another poison past her lips.

CHAPTER TWENTY-FIVE

The poison Frost crept up Ella's fingers and toes. Lucifer asked her questions as they spread, each little crystal of ice burying deep in her nerves as she refused to answer. Ella dove into herself, fleeing the ice that encased her body, piece by piece.

She opened her eyes as Frost crawled up her legs and hands, coating her skin like frosted dew drops on a cold winter's morning. She broke out of it, rubbing warmth back into her limbs. Ella was in the maze of Aumont. It was dark, everything silent except for the erratic beating of her heart. She closed her eyes for a moment, waiting for the ground to steady. She had survived a night in the forest with David. She could make it through this. Ella swiped at her cheek, her fingers coming away wet. Why was she crying? She was hunting now. This was no time for tears.

A twig snapped, drawing her attention. Ella followed it, keeping low to the ground, stepping lightly. Frost followed her trail, spreading out to the maze, freezing the fog that swirled around her into a wall of mist. Ella located her prey. He was trying to crouch behind a bench, his body too large. He would not survive this hunt, not with Ella as his hunter. His blond hair was greasy, his distorted falcon contrasted starkly against his pale skin.

She snuck up on him, palming a glass dagger in each hand. Nothing would distract her. She didn't kill him quickly, either. Ella thrust her daggers into him, over and over. She smiled as she walked away, covered in his blood. Her mission of revenge was just beginning.

Ella stopped. Her daggers dripped blood onto the frost, as a woman sat on a bench before her, reading. Her white hair blew in the wind, her dress immaculate.

"Mom?" Ella clutched the dagger behind her back. Not that it mattered. The blood that had splattered across her face and torso would reveal her secret. Ice crept out from Ella's feet, covering the ground in a thin layer of frost.

"My little snowstorm." Lady Lyla looked at her daughter, smiling as she walked over to her. Lyla knelt beside Ella, wrapping her arms around her as Ella buried her head into her mom's shoulder, holding her close as she breathed in the fresh snow smell her mom always carried with her.

"What are you doing here? You're in danger. You have to leave." Ella frantically pulled them to their feet and led them through the maze as ice chased them.

Something was wrong. Very wrong.

Plums of Ella's breath iced over in front of her, dropping to the ground. Her heart fluttered weakly against the cold, trying to beat.

"You're so strong and beautiful. I'm so proud of you, Ella."

"You wouldn't be if you knew—"

"I do, my love. I know everything," Lyla gripped Ella, stopping their march through the maze, the ice thickening as they stayed still. "I know she manipulated you, and that all you ever wanted was to protect those you love. I am proud of you for following your heart."

"I miss you...so much, Mom." Ella crumpled against her, feeling four years old again. "I'm so sorry about that day...I was complaining, and you needed me, and I wasn't there to help you," Ella melted in her mom's embrace. "I sat next to you, but I didn't hold your hand, and I'm so...so sorry, Mom."

"You were four years old, my love," Lyla soothed her, resting her hands on Ella's face.

"Can I stay here with you?" She tried to stand, though Ella's legs refused to break the ice that clung to her.

"All of us have a role to play in this life, my snowstorm. Yours isn't done yet."

"What if I'm not strong enough?"

"You have always had more strength in your heart than in my entire body. You will always do the right thing and find that you have the will to face it. Should you stumble, your father and I will always be beside you, guiding you," Lyla stopped talking, her attention suddenly pulled away.

"Mom?" Ella didn't look, her mind refusing to let her see the leopard she knew was growing larger behind her.

"You are radiant, Ella. Shine bright." Lyla kissed Ella's forehead quickly, brushing away more tears. "Remember, the cold is all in your mind." Lyla kissed Ella's hand, the ice breaking free.

Lady Lyla walked into the shadows as Ella watched the ice crawl farther up her body. If it reached her heart, she was dead. She knew deep down that it wasn't real. The dark blue ice that had reached her waist was due to the poison. Same for the ice that had crawled up her arm to her shoulder and near her neck.

Ella closed her eyes and lay down, repeating three words over and over…it isn't real.

"It isn't real." Ella barely moved her lips against the freeze that had taken over, cracking an eye as she took in the attic once more. Lucifer smiled down at her, a whip in his hands.

"I'm sure it feels very real." He walked towards her feet. "I wonder how long the poison will stay in your system with no antidotes. Tell me, has Raven tested that?"

Days. It would be *days.* But Ella kept her mouth shut. She would never betray her friend.

"I see, well at least tell me this. When did you decide you were going to betray Lady Tremaine?"

"I haven't." Ella's vocal cords rasped. "I'm—" She paused again, swallowing as she tried to speak through the pain. "I'm not going to." How long had she been screaming? What had they done to her? Ella lifted her head, and the room spun, along with her stomach.

She turned her head to vomit all over herself. Ella breathed heavily, her lungs burning as she took in the room. Both lackeys were still present as one of them walked over and cleaned her sick off. Ella gazed out the window as evening set in. Had anyone at the palace noticed her disappearance? Had they even cared to check on her? They were probably too busy entertaining Lena to care. That knowledge was a knife that cut deep.

"I think you deserve a break from the poison, don't you?" Lucifer unchained Ella's feet, knocking them off the table. Her body followed, stopped by her suspended arms.

Her head rolled forward, her vision sending her spinning. Sweat coated her in a thick, sticky film. She was going to need a bath after this. Ella looked up at Lucifer and chuckled to herself.

"What's so funny?" Lucifer gripped her by her hair, dragging her to her feet.

"Your face. You should see it while on Malice. It does the craziest stuff to your already horrid profile." Ella laughed more. "It might be an improvement." Ella gasped when Lucifer punched her in the stomach. She coughed. "Plus, you have yet to prove I've betrayed Lady Tremaine. Who was your source, anyway? Anastasia?" Ella spat blood on him. Lucifer wiped it off as he slapped Ella across the face.

"Someone much closer than I think you realize," Lucifer snarled as he locked Ella's shackles to a pillar, suspending her in the air.

Ella paled when she saw the whip in his hands.

"Perhaps this will get you to answer some of my questions." Lucifer petted it like a cat.

Ella tried to stay still, to not show fear.

But the chains wouldn't stop shaking.

"Now, how are you going to save the prince? What's your plan?" Lucifer lightly let the whip touch her, grazing down her spine.

"It's the original plan. Go to the ball, dance with David, stab him through the heart, and run out of there as fast as I can. That's my plan. What's your plan?" Ella could only hope he was foolish or egotistical enough to tell her. Beads of sweat trickled down her back, the smell of her odor triggering fear as it mixed with the smell of dust and rust in the attic.

"Come on, Ella, you're telling me that when you've been asked to go against everything we were trained to do, to protect the crown and kingdom, that you're just going to...fall in line? That's it?" Lucifer slid the whip handle against her cheek and down her chest. "How boring."

"Sorry to disappoint you." Ella swayed on the chains, her arms screaming against the weight.

"Oh well, guess this will all be for nothing, then." Lucifer shrugged as he prowled around Ella until his back was to her. It was then that a breeze licked the skin on her bare back.

She shut her eyes as this whip struck her scarred back for the first time in years.

"We need to go, Ella."

She opened her eyes, the maze of Aumont towering before her.

"Ella."

She stepped back at the voice. Its deep velvet embrace sent shock and dismay down her spine.

"You're not dead. You can't be dead."

Raven winked. "Not yet, anyway. And neither are you. We're in your mind palace, El. Let's get through this together." Raven's deep blue eyes hardened into stone as she looked at Ella. This was the Raven that Ella knew. Strong, confident, protective. Her hair was back to its normal chin-length curls. Her brilliant blue eyes filled with cunning mischief.

"I miss you." Ella hugged her, not caring that it wasn't real. Raven's returned embrace certainly felt real.

"Come on, we have to go," Raven whispered.

They ran. Ella couldn't see who was chasing them as black clouds converged. Raven whipped them around a corner. Ella found two daggers in her hands. Raven's curved sabers were strapped to her back. Lucifer's lackey turned the corner. Ella got behind the one with black hair and jumped on his back, slitting his throat. Ella attacked the next one before he could react. She stabbed him repeatedly until he tumbled down.

She looked up at Raven as she leaned against the hedge, examining her nails, "You could have helped you know."

"I know, but you didn't need it." Raven walked over to her and cradled her bloodied hands. "You've never needed anyone to save you. You've never needed anyone to tell you what to do or who to be. You've always been strong enough to do that on your own, El. You just need to believe it, too."

Ella nodded as she looked away, a mental tug pulling on her.

"Blood in my veins—"

"Bones of my ancestors," Ella whispered.

Ella opened her eyes as Lucifer hoisted her off the pillar. She was set down on the ground, her wrists chained to the pillars above.

More than ever before, Ella wished she were an enchanter. If she were, she would have found a way to be the first enchanter to ever cast a spell on a human and torture all of them.

"Well boys, it's late, and I have a ball to get to." Lucifer smiled. "You know, because of you, I get to be the one to kill David and Princess Celeste. What is it you call her? Pumpkin?" Lucifer forced Ella to look at him as he gripped her hair. "I was going to kill him quickly, but I think I'll make it last. Tell him exactly who you are." The glint in his eyes shuddered through Ella before she could look away.

"Please...let me kill him. I'll do it...just not Celeste. Please."

"Is that begging I'm hearing? From the great Cinderella?" Lucifer laughed. "I'll pass that along to Lady Tremaine."

Only once she was completely alone did Ella let the tears fall. Her body convulsed as her stomach revolted. Everything ached. Her head lolled forward, her white hair dangling in front. Ella breathed, trying to refocus. Her pain could wait. Lucifer was going to kill David, and then her.

Not that her life mattered anymore. All that mattered was saving David. Making sure he lived. That had always been the right move. Lady Tremaine had worked on setting this up for years. It was foolish of Ella to think otherwise.

She took a shuddering breath and looked up at the wooden pillar and down to the metal cuffs around her wrists. She twisted her hands around the chain and gripped it. Ella got to her feet, taking a moment to steady as her vision blurred and the floor swayed. Ella ignored the hallucinations as best as she could. Her heart lurched at the leopard in the wall. It wasn't real.

"It isn't real." Ella looked around the room. There had to be a way out. Another leopard prowled behind her. "It isn't real." Ella ducked when it lunged, pulling hard on a shoulder.

She squeezed her eyes shut.

"It isn't real."

Ella stood up and found a firm footing, as firm as she could, and pulled.

After all of these years, the pillar had to have weakened. She hadn't spent that time up here for nothing. She could never break the chains, but if she could break the pillar, she could break out. So she continued to pull, as the cuffs cut deeper into her scars than ever before. Ella calmed her heart, braced herself, and pulled again.

The pillar splintered, cracking down the middle.

Ella pulled again and the pillar split in two. She crumpled like a doll to the ground, content to lay there...for a moment.

Footsteps reached her ears. Ella tensed as they got closer.

Not yet, not now.

Ella remained on the floor, listening, preparing herself to attack the moment he walked through the door. Metal scraped over metal as the lock was picked. The door clicked and swung open, a cane touching down.

"Ella." Drea's voice ran like cool water over her, instantly relaxing her.

"Drea." Ella moved to get up, her arms collapsing under her.

"Don't get up, let me clean you." Drea knelt beside Ella, her fingers cold as they touched her exposed bloodied back. "It's...not good, Ella, stay still."

"I'll try," Ella whispered as Drea used a wet cloth and bucket to gently clean the fresh whip lashes. They would scar, just like the others, adding to her collection.

"You couldn't have come up a few minutes ago?" Ella tried to joke.

"I had to wait for him to leave...I really shouldn't be here—"

"I know...Drea...what am I going to do?" Ella whispered.

"I don't know—"

"Ella?" The tip of a sword touched the wooden floor in front of Ella's line of sight.

"Henry?" her voice cracked as she jolted, wincing at the lacerations. He couldn't see her like this. No one could.

"What did they do to you?" Henry locked eyes with her.

"What are you doing here? Why aren't you protecting David?"

"He was worried when you didn't show you, so he sent me to find you." Henry's eyes darted to look at Drea. Ella glanced over as well, noticing that Drea had scooted back into the shadows.

"Henry, you have to get to him—"

"Does it matter now? How could she do this to you? We have to get you to a healer right now." Henry unlocked her wrists and gently touched her scars as his eyes darkened. "Why didn't you show these to me?"

"It doesn't matter. What does is—"

"Ella, don't argue right now—" Henry stopped mid-sentence as he took in the room. He saw the pillars and then the opened wardrobe stuffed with weapons. Then his eyes flicked to the ground and the blood on the floor. He followed the trailer back to the blood on her. "What...what is—"

"This is where I was brought if I failed." Ella didn't flinch when Henry's head snapped to look at her. "None of it matters though, Henry, she's going to kill him right now. Someone told her I was going to betray her, so she sent others to finish it."

Henry jumped at her words and moved to the door and down the stairs, not a thought spared for her. As it should be. Ella watched him go as she gingerly walked to the door.

"Ella," Drea whispered. Ella turned to look at her stepsister with tear-streaked cheeks as she hid in the shadows, her hand covering the scar on her face. "Be careful."

Ella nodded and stepped onto the stairs. The wood was rough and splintered, scratching up her bare feet. Her wounded leg seized up. Ella ground her hands into the wood banister, her throat straining against a scream, her arms shaking as she lifted herself. She could do this. She didn't know how she was going to save David. But she would. Even if it killed her.

"Ella?" Henry rested his hand on hers as it shook. He had come back for her.

"I'll be okay." Ella struggled to remain standing, and she knew it was killing him to wait for her. It was killing her to know that every minute she was weak, was another minute closer to David dying. "You remember where my room is?"

Henry nodded.

"Go there and get my daggers. They're sitting on top of my dresser. Also grab my armored clothing from the top drawer, along with the black cloth sack next to it. While you do that I'm going to make it down these stairs."

Henry turned and began his descent.

"Henry."

He looked back, his face grim.

"Kill anyone who tries to stop you."

He nodded, jumping down the stairs.

Each took a step down and shut her against the feeling of needles piercing her skin. Her feet left a light trail of blood. Her legs shook, and when she leaned on the railing…her arms could barely support her. The muscles in Ella's back were useless, protesting each time she stopped and used them to keep herself standing. But she would continue. She would get through this agony. By the time she made it down all seven flights, she had found her way back to Cinderella. She greeted the feeling of an old friend gone too long.

Henry was at the bottom, everything in his arms.

"Did anyone see you?"

"No, it seems empty."

Ella looked around the foyer. "It won't be for long, let's go." She followed Henry out the front doors and to the large covered carriage that was waiting.

Henry pulled out a beautiful blue dress.

"I can't wear a dress, Henry. I won't be able to fight as well."

"You also can't go charging in wearing nothing but a shredded tunic to a ball." Henry motioned to the clothes that hung limply on her body.

"I won't be, I'll wear my armored clothes and sneak in."

"David will be at the ball. Your armor is your room. We don't have the luxury of stealth. You will need to get to him right away. We discussed how we would do this—"

"Until our plans went to shit, Henry."

"Get into the carriage, stop arguing, and start changing. I'll think of something." Henry huffed as he closed the door behind her.

Henry raced the horses as Ella attempted to change. She knew he was right. The second Lady Tremaine learned of her escape she would have David killed. The only way to prevent it would be to go straight to him.

Which meant going along with the plan to announce who Ella truly was. She used her tunic to clean off the remaining blood as much as possible. The blue ball gown Henry had found didn't allow for her to carry too many weapons, but it was enough. It had to be. Going through her black satchel, Ella found an old diamond earring that she quickly put on, hoping to find Jaq on the other side. He would have the answers she needed.

She finished pulling back her hair into a twist. It was as elegant as she could make it. Ella looked down at herself, making sure that she had covered as much as she could. There was nothing she could do about the red mark on her jaw....or the scars on her wrists.

Ella got out of the carriage before it stopped. Had she been coming for any reason, she would have taken the time to admire the dress Henry had given her. It swirled around her, dancing in the torchlight. The bodice was tight, and for once, she was grateful for its support. The stone stairs that lead up to the entrance were lit with torches. If she'd had the time, Ella would have taken in the palace's beauty in the star-covered night lit up by fire, but not now.

"You certainly know how to pick a dress, Henry." Ella turned her back to him. "Would you mind lacing up the back?"

"Remind me to have you tell my intended, Rose, the next time she thinks I don't know how to choose anything." Henry's hands were firm as they pulled on the thick ribbon. His fingertips brushed the scars, causing her to flinch.

"I didn't know you were getting married."

"Not for a long time. If we survive this, I'll tell you all about it. Right now, we need to find David."

CHAPTER TWENTY-SIX

They walked down silent and empty halls, Ella's legs sending splinters of ice into her toes. She could hear the sounds of dancing and laughter, as they approached the doors. Henry didn't lead them through the main entrance, avoiding the crier and announcing Ella to the court. Instead, they slipped into the back behind the throne.

Ella blinked as the throne twisted.

Queen Charisse sat on a throne that cried blood, the crimson river pouring out into the ballroom. Ella blinked, and it was gone, along with the queen. Sweat rolled down Ella's back as she focused. She had to focus and get David off the dance floor.

"Are you alright?" Henry held her hand on his arm, gently patting it.

"No, but I'll work through it. Now, let's get him." Ella walked onto the dance floor and headed straight for David and his partner, clenching and unclenching her frozen fingers as Frost crawled up her again.

Ella stepped onto the dance floor and did her best to ignore the other dancers, and leopards that prowled around her. The dancers parted slowly as the waltz softly drifted over them. Everyone was beautiful, but none compared to the woman in David's arms.

His partner wore a flowing deep red dress with black lace and beading. She had done all that she could to replicate the fashions of Evrotia. Her long blond hair flowed down to her waist, with a beautifully sharp tiara on her head.

If David's life hadn't been threatened, a different type of nervousness would have overtaken Ella. Would he choose her?

Or would he push her away for not being who he wanted?

Princess Lena was the perfect partner for him. Ella knew she was confident in the way she floated over the dance floor, not once looking at her feet. She was one of the most stunning women Ella had ever seen. And she had been trained since birth to rule. Meanwhile, Ella had subverted all of the items that David desired.

But, none of that mattered at this moment.

If he didn't choose her...she didn't think about that. He would choose her. Ella had to believe that. It was at that moment, as Ella smiled and tapped David on the shoulder, that she realized her entire life had been built for this second in time. No matter what, her path had taken here, and she would save the person she had sworn an oath to protect.

But the nerves remained.

David turned to face, and the entire court went silent as they watched. The only sound came from the orchestra that played above.

"I hope I didn't miss our dance. I was a little tied up." Ella smiled. She didn't dare look at Princess Lena.

"Too late, we're dancing now." Princess Lena kept a firm grip on David's arm. She narrowed her ice-blue eyes at Ella.

"Not anymore, princess." Ella smiled as she watched Princess Lena's face flush red, her eyes shooting fire. "David?"

Now was the moment.

"Lady Eleanor." David held out his arm to her, dropping Princess Lena's hand.

The orchestra began a new waltz as David swirled Ella into his arms. Strong supportive arms that kept her standing. As the music continued to play, the rest of the court resumed their dancing. Princess Lena did her best to remain calm in the face of rejection, Ella noted as she gracefully walked off the floor.

"David—"

"I'm glad you're here. I don't know what Henry said, but...thank you," David whispered. He pulled Ella closer, leading them confidently through the steps.

She shut her eyes for a moment, ignoring the shadows that were crawling out of the walls and heading for her. Ignoring the beats ticking in the back of her head that screamed to get him off the floor. This was their moment. Why did it have to be stolen away once again by her stepmother?

Ella opened her eyes and found King Matthias and Celeste standing to the side, smiling. The entire court was smiling as they danced. Yet none of it could be real...not anymore. Not like this. Ella glimpsed Princess Lena talking to Anastasia in the corner, both of them smiling with malicious intent. As the shadows of her hallucinations crawled up out of them and swam toward David, Ella knew it was time to cut her dream short.

"David, we have to get off the ballroom floor. I can't tell you much right now, but please, trust me, we have to get you away from here," Ella whispered in his ear. She played with his hair, smiling as they spun around, but her eyes never stopped moving. She had to spot the assassins before they got close.

David stepped back, his brown eyes dark with concern. "Ella, what's wrong?" He touched her cheek, seeing the red mark for what it was. "What happened?" His eyes traveled down her arms to her wrists. Her exposed wrists with years of scars in the shape of shackles. David's thumb rubbed over one.

"Who did this to you?" David growled. His fingers tightened their hold for a moment. "Ella, please talk to me."

"David, not here. Please, can we go to your room? Can we go somewhere safe?" Ella broke eye contact to survey the crowd. Anastasia and Lucifer were nowhere to be found.

Not good.

The dance ended and Ella curtsied as low as the song demanded, though her legs quaked.

Then she gazed up and spotted movement. The archer. On the balcony. Arrow ready.

This was the moment. She could uphold her stepmother's oath and let it hit David. Or she could follow her dream and protect the crown.

The archer let the arrow fly.

Ella moved.

"David, look out." She spun them, her back to the archer. She positioned herself where David had been as she forced him to step to the side for a moment.

The arrow flew past, slicing her shoulder. It skittered across the dance floor. Everyone parted as they watched it stop on the marble floor. For a moment, there was silence. Just one second.

It was all Ella needed.

As the room erupted and guards poured in, Ella gripped David and hauled him with her. She didn't give him a choice. She was not letting him go, and she was not listening to anything he said as she got them out. Ella didn't even pause to locate Henry or Luca.

She ran for David's room.

That was where they had put everything together for him. The stone pounded against Ella's feet as they ran. She listened for any sound, any indication that they were going to find opposition.

"Ella, stop, you're hurt." David continued to run with her despite his pleas.

"David, we can't. We have to go. You may not have noticed, but that arrow was meant for you, and it would have gone through your heart. Now please, we have to grab some things, and then we have to go." Ella said. She didn't have time to explain everything. If she stopped the pain would overwhelm her and the poisons circulating in her body would pounce.

"Tell me what's going on," David demanded as they got to his room.

"Yes, Ella, tell him what's going on." Anastasia stepped out of this darkness in David's room, Lucifer behind her. Both of them wore their black suits. Anastasia held her obsidian stone daggers in hand, ready to fight. Lucifer wouldn't need any weapons, he had his strength.

Anastasia pouted as Ella remained silent.

Green eyes loomed behind Anastasia and Lucifer. If Ella uttered a single word, she knew Anastasia would hear the quiver in her voice and she could not let that happen.

"Come on now, Cinder—"

"Ana, stop it. It's gone far enough." Ella found her courage as she pushed David behind her.

"Ella seriously—"

"Shut up, David. Please."

"We wouldn't want him to learn anything now would we?" Anastasia purred.

Ella pulled out the only two daggers she had left and launched herself at Anastasia. Her ball gown's skirts tangled her legs. Ella groaned in frustration as she twisted around in them just in time to stop one of Ana's daggers. As they traded attacks, Lucifer watched from the side, yawning. He yawned. Ella ground her teeth. David came into view, sword at the ready, attempting to take her place. She made sure he couldn't get in. David fighting Anastasia was the last thing Ella needed.

She sliced Anastasia's arm and worked her way through her defenses. But it was slow going as ice kept a firm grip on her fingers.

Anastasia knocked her to the ground, pinning Ella between her legs.

"You stupid bitch, you should have done as you were told," Anastasia growled. She pressed her dagger down.

Ella caught it with her own.

"It's too bad you figured it out though. It was fun watching you serve the wrong crown."

Ice crept up Ella's arm. Anastasia's face warped into a yellow cat, her teeth gnashing to get to her.

"Ella." David's voice echoed far away from her. The sound of metal reverberated through her as it clashed with another.

"I won't let you near him," Ella ground out, blinking against the hallucinations.

Suddenly, the room was empty of the shadows. The green-eyed leopard didn't lurk in the corners. The Frost was gone. Malice vanished from her eyes. This was her only moment.

Ella moved swiftly, blocking out the pain that threatened to surge forward. She knocked Anastasia's dagger to the side and flipped them so that she was on top and Anastasia was pinned below.

"You'll never have him." Anastasia grinned as the two of them struggled.

Ella rested her blade against Anastasia's neck, stilling her.

"Do it, Ella, prove you're the girl I trained with. Prove to me that the girl I spilled blood with within service of our true crown still exists. You could still do it. You could still serve your oath." Anastasia's eyes gleamed with the challenge.

David and Lucifer were next to them, drawing Ella's attention for a second. They were evenly matched. For now. Lucifer smiled as they fought, enjoying their game of cat and mouse. He would tire of it soon, and Ella had to get to David before that happened.

"After all of the lies," Ella leaned closer to her stepsister, "all of the 'lessons in the attic', the burns, the whippings—"

Anastasia locked her green eyes on Ella.

"I'm still not going to kill you. My mercy towards you is a greater punishment than any death could be." Ella slammed the base of her dagger into Anastasia's head and left her lying on the floor.

Ella stumbled to her feet, swaying as the poisons reclaimed her body and all clarity disappeared. Lucifer had David pinned against a wall, David's sword pressed between them. Ella leaped across the room. She barreled into Lucifer, knocking him sideways. Lucifer laughed as he stood up. Ella took a defensive stance in front of David. She tightened her hold on her daggers as Frost reclaimed her fingers.

"Ella, get behind me. Let me deal with him—"

"No." Ella kept David behind her.

"Looks like I'll get my wish sooner than I thought." Lucifer prowled towards Ella, his smile widening. "I don't know how you escaped, and I don't care. You're too drugged to put up an equal fight at least, and those lashes to your back, they have got to be hurting. Tell me, just how broken are you?" Lucifer casually paced around the room, forcing Ella to follow his every step. Analyzing everything he did. All that mattered to her was that there was no red in his eyes, not anymore.

"Ella, let me deal with him—"

"No. He's. Mine." Ella snarled. Once again she moved to keep David against the wall behind her.

"Yes, Ella, let your prince defend you. After all, he doesn't think you're capable enough. Though I guarantee that he'll know exactly who you are before I kill you and him." Lucifer stopped moving, blocking them from the door.

"What's he talking about?"

"I'll explain later, I promise David, I—"

"I'm talking about how sweet little Ella turned on oath to save you," Lucifer pounced.

He grabbed Ella and ripped her away from her defensive position. Lucifer squeezed Ella's wrist until she let go of the dagger enough for him to grab it. He wrapped an arm around her waist, pressing her back against him, her dagger against her neck.

Ella froze. Lucifer would wait to strike. He always liked to monologue, and while Ella didn't want him talking, she also wanted a way out of his hold. For now, she couldn't do anything as David positioned himself to fight Lucifer.

"Did I forget to mention that it was a little mouse that gave her up hoping to spare her?" Lucifer taunted.

Ella twisted to look at him. Jaq would never give her up. Lucifer smiled down at her. Ella went rigid. She didn't know what to do with Jaq's betrayal.

"Except he was wrong."

Ella whimpered as Lucifer rubbed a thumb over her throat.

"If you hurt her, I'll kill you," David threatened, his sword firmly grasped before him.

"I don't think there's much more left to her," Lucifer chuckled.

"Don't." Ella trembled.

Lucifer laughed as she shook within his grasp. He would revel in her pain at exposing her to David. Now that she knew everything she had done for the crown...was to the wrong one.

David stepped closer to them, his hands glowing with power.

"I wouldn't do that if I were you." Lucifer moved his blade. A small trickle of blood ran down her neck.

David stopped, his brown eyes locked on hers, reassuring her that everything would be okay. She knew he believed that. With all his heart, he believed he would save her.

But what he didn't know was that Ella was perfectly capable of saving herself.

"Now, Ella, have you told the prince what your other name is? You know the one everyone would *kill* to know?" Lucifer adjusted his grip.

"David." Ella kept her eyes locked with his, pleading for him to believe her too, just like she believed in him. "I didn't do it."

"Ella is better known as Cinderella," Lucifer crowed.

Ella shuddered as she watched those words strike David. He stepped backward into a wall that was now, according to Ella's eyes, drenched in blood.

Blood poured over everything as her hallucinations flourished. She squeezed her eyes, willing them away. *It isn't real.*

"No," David was quiet in his denial. His sword fell, limp at his side as he broke eye contact with her.

"And now that I've enlightened you, I'm sure you won't mind if I do a bunch of horrible things to Ella." Lucifer's hand lowered to her waist.

"I told you Lucifer, you will never have me."

"The shaking in your body says otherwise."

Ella shook as she let him run his hand up her body.

She pushed his arm away from her neck and jammed her elbow into his stomach. Ella spun around and thrust her knee into his groin.

"You're wrong. I'm not broken. I am stronger, and you will never hurt me again." Ella dug her nails into Lucifer's wrist, twisting his arm around until it broke, her dagger dropping from his hand.

Lucifer wrapped his arm around her waist and barreled them both into a wall. Ella's vision darkened as she hit her head. He pulled back, grinning as she stumbled. His arm hung limply.

Ella shook her head free of the shadows that crawled near her.

Blocking them out, she rammed her shoulder into Lucifer's chest, knocking him against the wall.

She thrust her dagger into his heart, smiling as he sunk to the ground, mouth open.

Ella stabbed him again, and again, and again until all she saw was the blood around her and the look of surprise sealed on his face.

Her name whispered through to her, gently coaxing her out of her bloodlust. She blinked, her vision clearing as she found David. He stood over her, his body stiff, dark brown eyes guarded against her. A look of...horror...it was horror on his face. Horror and disappointment.

"He's dead, that's enough."

"We have to uh...we have to figure out what to do." Ella stood up, wiping a hand across her brow, blood smearing over her skin.

"Not until—"

"What the fuck happened?"

Ella swirled to find Henry at the door. His eyes moved faster than a dagger spinning in the air.

"We have to go. Now." Ella straightened her gown, calming her breathing with each second. Sweat broke out on her body, sending shivers down to her toes.

"I'm not going anywhere with her," the words dripped from David's mouth like thick molasses, and she knew he would never trust her.

"David—" Henry approached him, arms open.

"No. I will not go anywhere with her."

"You don't have a choice. They got a fucking archer in the ballroom, David," Ella flung her arms out wide. "We can't trust anyone to get you out of here alive except me and Henry."

"I have questions that need to be answered," David growled.

"I'll answer them later." Ella tossed his packs at him, storming out of his room. She palmed her daggers, clutching them with hands as cold as ice.

Ella? Jaq's voice came through in whispers in her earring.

Jaq, are you okay? Ella paused, making a face at Henry when he pushed her along. Henry took the lead, moving quickly. They passed the servants' stairs, avoiding detection.

Ella, I am so sorry.

She could barely hear him through the diamond.

Jaq, I can't hear you, She motioned to her ear when David pulled on her arm, his eyes demanding answers. "Hold on." Ella jumped in front of Henry as he opened the side door.

Ella stepped outside first and looked around the corner. She threw her dagger into a guard's heart.

"Ella—"

"He's an assassin. I recognize him," Ella snapped.

"How did you know he would be there?" David challenged her.

"If I was planning on killing a runaway prince, I would make sure any escape routes were covered. Now go," Ella retrieved her dagger before positioning herself on the carriage beside Henry, David climbing in behind.

As soon as they were moving, the diamond cracked in her ear. Ella pulled it out, clutching the two pieces in her hand. The enchantment had died.

"No." She dug through the bag Henry had grabbed from her room, finding a small mirror. She opened it, finding Jaq on the other side. *Jaq.*

I'm so sorry, Ella, Jaq was disheveled, his clothing wrinkled and hair disarrayed.

It's alright, Jaq. I'm...okay... she didn't want to go through this. Not now, not while they could hear.

It's not. She promised me...I'm so sorry, Ella.

Jaq, I need you to grab anything of value and pack it up in your mage room. You're going to have to run away.

I went up to the attic...I saw...I touched the pillars up there... Jaq's voice broke.

Jaq—

I felt it...I felt it all...

They're brutes Jaq. I'm used to it— Ella cast a glance at Henry.

You should kill me for what I did.

No one is going to kill you. Just pack up, we have a plan. How's your strength? Ella took a deep breath. She had to remain calm as shadows chased her in the night.

I'm depleted. Lady Tremaine needed me to enchant a lot of weapons and armor today, Jaw paused, turning around. *Hold on, there's movement. Everyone else should be in their rooms.*

Jaq, I'm on my way. I'm going to try to reach Drea. I'll still be here, I'm just going to set the mirror down.

I don't think that will do anything. He was far away, far enough away that he couldn't be seen.

Jaq, where are you?

I'm by the door—

Get away from there. I need you to barricade yourself in, understand?

I understand, Jaq said.

Ella placed the mirror between her and Henry. "Can you scry Drea?" she asked.

"What? No," Henry muttered.

"I need you to scry for her. Now." Ella removed a blank mirror from her pack.

"I can't, Ella. I haven't...I haven't seen her in—"

"You. Saw. Her. Tonight. You just refused to look. Why is that? Is it because of you that she hides away?" Ella challenged him.

"No. Never. I didn't...Ella...you don't know what you're asking—"

"I know you care for her. Think of her."

"Ella—" Henry turned his head away from the road to look at her.

"What is he sorry for Ella? The man in the mirror, what did they do?" David leaned forward.

She ignored him. "Do it now Henry. I can't and my friend...he's in danger...so I need you to scry her."

Henry snatched the mirror from her, eyes narrowed. He muttered under his breath and focused as he whispered an enchantment.

Hello? Henry's hands fumbled to hold the mirror when he saw her. Ella snatched it, noticing Drea's wide eyes.

Drea, Jaq's in trouble. I need you to go protect him. Please. It was a long shot, but maybe she would help. Ella dismissed Henry's glare, a protest on his lips.

I can't.

Ella stopped breathing.

Drea, please...he can't...he doesn't know how—

Hold on. Someone knocked on her door. All Ella could see was the moonlight shining through Drea's windows. *What do you need?* Drea was sharp, and demanding. *No, you cannot borrow it. Go find something else, there are plenty of choices in the armory,* her voice was muffled. *Then I suggest you put your lessons on lock-picking to good use.*

Who was that?

A novice. She wanted to borrow my sword.

Henry choked on his cough.

Drea, please— Ella couldn't get the words past the tears in her throat. She could barely look at the road as everything shifted and she could scarcely tell real from imaginary.

I need to deny any involvement, Ella. I'm so sorry. Truly.

But you helped me earlier—

*I helped my *sister* when she was hurt. This is different. I am sorry.*

The mirror cracked in Ella's hand; the enchantment was gone. Ten seconds. Her world cracked in ten seconds.

Ella picked up Jaq's mirror.

Never leave me like that again, he whispered.

She won't come. Ella rubbed away a tear before Henry or David could see.

You knew it was a long shot.

"How is Drea involved in this? I thought she couldn't walk?" David asked.

Ella glanced at David. He was closer now, leaning forward in the carriage. Henry's hands were clasped so tightly around the reins they were white.

"I don't have time for this, David." Ella turned away, grabbed the reins from Henry, and encouraged the horses to gallop faster. *Jaq, do you have any weapons left in there?*

No, I don't let novices get away with leaving them in here.

There's not a hammer? Something, Jaq, there has to be something. Ella tightened her grip on the reins instead of raising her voice. It wouldn't help.

Ella...

They're going to be coming for you, Jaq. As soon as Lady Tremaine finds Lucifer's body, she's going to send them. They're already searching the house for weapons.

It's a group of novices, I don't think—

It doesn't fucking matter, Jaq. They want to prove themselves. They need the rush. They crave it. You need to find a weapon now! She was minutes away, and the horses were already going as fast as they could.

"How many novices do you have? What kind of place is this, Eleanor?"

"Shut up, David. I need to concentrate."

She couldn't get the horses to pull the carriage any faster.

"Watch the road, Ella." Henry tried to get the reins back.

A bang echoed through the mirror.

How many are there?

He could look. He had enchanted a mirror right outside of his door.

I'm so sorry Ella—

How many are there? Ella's vision blurred.

Seven—

Okay, you have a couple of choices.

Ella, I don't think—

You have a couple of choices.

Henry no longer protested her steering as the dirt roads straightened.

You can fight your way through and run to the closest room. Only a few of them will know how to pick locks. Or you can get to the cabinet on the left. I think I left a dagger in there.

They reached the farmlands. Ella passed them in a blur. Aumont loomed ahead of them. It was so close.

Ella, I—

Jaq, please— Ella broke through the gates and pulled the horses to a stop by the stairs. *I'm here, hold on.*

I don't know how to fight.

I'll do it for—

A door was smashed on the other side of the mirror. Ella launched herself off the carriage, moving faster than her leg or dress would allow.

A girl screamed close by.

Jaq's grunts filled her mirror. She couldn't see what was happening as Jaq dropped the mirror. Only the sound of his ragged breathing made it through.

CHAPTER TWENTY-SEVEN

Ella paused with the mirror in hand as the reflection broke before her. She dropped it. Ella sprinted, skidding to a halt when she got to the stairs. Her father's sword glinted in the torchlight. She narrowed her eyes. That had been hidden in her room. Ella looked up to see Drea limping up the stairs, her hands still glowing from bringing the enchantment on Ella's sword to life.

Any glimmer of pain in Ella's leg or poison in her body vanished as she rounded the corner and took in Jaq's room. He was on the floor. Blood pooled around him. A group of energized novices surrounded him.

Ella rammed the pommel of the sword into the first novice's head, knocking her out.

There was still a way to save him.

She had to save him.

He was her friend, and she'd lost enough.

Her training took over as she dived in.

Ella focused on getting to Jaq, and his wide eyes as he lay on the hardwood floor. His spectacles were cracked, his tunic torn. He would hate that. He moved his head slowly, his hands glowing. The novices had fallen silent as they fought Ella. The looks on their faces revealed they had much to learn.

Ella's heart raced, her mind scattering as she tried to zero in on each opponent and not on Jaq. She resorted to her daggers and fists, finding the lack of room constricting. One novice moved towards Jaq and Ella lunged, cutting them off with a dagger to the shoulder. Another novice ducked beneath her blades. All of them moved chaotically and Ella lost control. Her vision went red, and her mind went blank of every thought but one: get to Jaq.

Distantly she heard her name being called. But that didn't matter.

The loss of control was worse than it had been at the earl's home. She could blame that on Velocity. But now, it was a loss of emotional control. Her heart thundered in her veins, giving her the fuel she needed to take on those who remained. By the time Ella made it through, blood misted the air, and sweat dripped down her back in streaks of pink. Her lungs heaved as she paused, her vision going fuzzy as she swayed.

"Please, don't kill me. I'm sorry, we were only following orders." The last one was on her knees in front of Ella, hands clasped together. "I won't say anything, please."

"All I did was follow orders too." Ella used her dagger to knock her out.

Ella turned to Jaq, her legs collapsing beside him. She pulled him onto her lap, brushing his hair out of his face.

"I'm so sorry." Blood trickled out of his mouth.

"I forgive you. I know you were only trying to do what you thought was best." Ella's voice quivered at what his betrayal had done.

"What they did...you can never forgive me...all that torture."

She looked away from him and found David and Henry watching them. David's face was red, Henry's was calm. The way Henry gripped David though made her think David had been trying to get in the room.

"It'll be alright. Everything will be okay. I'm going to get some of the sealing serum...grab one of your potions." Ella brushed his hair, adding red highlights.

"We both know the serum won't do anything, and we know what will happen if I take my potion." Jaq gripped her wrist. "Stay, please."

"How dark is his mark?" Henry's voice was soft as it rippled over the room.

"We need help. One of you...please..." Why weren't they moving? "David...please..." Her hands shook as they took in Jaq's wounds. "I'm sorry that I didn't get to you faster."

She didn't hold back the tears. Cuts marked his body. The killing blow was a long, deep cut along his stomach. It would be minutes, if not sooner, before he died. Ella curled in on him, holding him closer.

"I'm sorry I didn't trust you." Jaq closed his eyes. "She's planning on framing you—"

"I know."

"Ella, get out of this room," Henry barked, his voice thick with fear.

Jaq's hands glowed as he bled out.

"I'm not leaving him." Ella clutched him closer.

"Not just the prince's death—" Blood choked Jaq.

"Henry...David, please you're a healer." Neither of them moved, remaining outside of the room. "Please don't die."

"I shattered the mirrors for you. No one will see what happened in the palace or here."

"Good work," Ella whispered. She closed her eyes, unable to tell if the pool of blood she'd seen pouring out of him was real or a hallucination.

"Find the Huntsman, Jason, he can help."

"Ella, please, I am *begging* you—" Henry spoke through gritted teeth.

"No." She looked up at them, her face stained with blood-soaked tears. "I'm not leaving him. I've lost enough." Ella turned back to Jaq. "How do I find him?"

"My pack. Only valuables right?" He smiled. "Blood in my veins—"

Jaq slumped in her arms, his hands glowing brighter with his residual power.

"Bones of my ancestors," Ella whispered, her hand shaking as she closed his eyes.

Every bottle of potion exploded.

"You can't leave me. Not now, not when I need you the most. Please." Ella memorized his face, his messy hair, and crooked spectacles. She wrapped herself around him, rocking back and forth, her body trembling.

"Ella, we have to go."

She remained frozen. Jaq had stopped breathing.

"Ella." Henry touched her shoulder.

Footsteps pounded down the hall, the other assassins that had been sent to kill them. She didn't care. Not anymore.

"Ella." His voice was heavy and quiet.

The unconscious novices were scattered around the room. She had never taken on so many at once. She wouldn't have done it for anyone else.

Luca walked over to her as Ella lifted her head just enough to see him delicately step over a body.

"Ella, we have to go. Jaq wouldn't want you to die." Luca said as he rested a finger under her chin.

"It hurts Luca." She held Jaq closer.

"I know." Luca eased Jaq away from her.

"I failed him." Ella shivered as Frost wormed its way into her mind, the red-painted floor laughing at her. Ella didn't stop when Luca pulled Jaq away from her and then pulled her to her feet.

"I can't do this, Luca. Let me give myself to Tremaine. You should run away. Go back to Holodal."

"You know it's not that simple for me." Luca caught Ella as she swayed. "We're close, Ella. I know it doesn't feel like it, but just because Jaq did something—"

"He told her I wouldn't be able to kill David." Ella looked at Luca. How did he not know?

"He...what?" Luca helped Ella over the bodies of unconscious novices.

"It doesn't matter right now, what does is getting David out of here if this is going to work," Henry ordered.

"Right, keep David safe." Ella closed her eyes as everything spun. "I can do this." She walked away from Luca. What was left of her dress dragged after her, the edges soaked purple. She paused long enough to grab Jaq's large pack, his most valuable things inside.

Ella limped out of the room, pausing when Luca stilled her with his hand. He motioned to her leg, his eyes asking permission before he knelt and slid his hand up her thigh to adjust the bandages.

"All good?" David growled. Ella locked eyes with him. They were dark and full of thunder. She ignored him, limping as fast as she could. The hall was getting dark, and the shadows had begun to move.

Ella stopped, as a tidal wave of ice and fire crawled over her, knocking her against the wall. All three men stopped to look at her, waiting for her to move. Ella shooed them ahead.

"Go, I'll catch up." Ella gasped for air as the walls tilted.

"Get to the other side of the maze. We have horses there." Luca whispered, squeezing her hand.

Ella furrowed her brow. What had he planned? Had something changed? Before she could question him further, Luca ran ahead, Henry and David turning the corner. Ella rubbed her hands over her face. The entire hallway morphed before her, its shadows coming to life.

Ella pushed off the wall and walked down the hall, no longer trying to ignore the hallucinations.

The whip cracked next to her ear.

Ella fell to the ground as it grazed her back.

She stood on feet that quivered. Turning she faced Lady Tremaine as she slid out of the shadows.

"You're not leaving this house."

"Yes, I am. Did you think I would go along with your plan once I learned the truth?" Ella widened her stance, her father's sword gripped tight.

"Of course not." Lady Tremaine shrugged. "I expected it, counted on it." She held the whip close to her, caressing it. "I just didn't think it would take you so long to figure it out."

"So everything...holding me as I cried over my dad...being kind to me...it was all part of the plan you and the queen worked on? All to start a war?"

"Not quite, though you are close."

"Tell me, what evil twist am I missing?"

"I'm not going to reveal all of my secrets." She smiled. "Just know that there are multiple pieces in motion now, whose implications you'll never see coming."

Ella blinked, swaying on her feet. The shadows rippled around her and her stepmother. Lady Tremaine had yet to turn into the green-eyed leopard of her nightmares. Yet.

"It looks like you've ingested maybe three too many poisons today. How are you feeling with all of them running through your veins?" Her laughter bounced around the walls.

"Three?" Ella had been forced to take Frost and Malice. What was the third?

"That arrow you so valiantly took for the prince, it was laced as well. You probably won't survive the night. Raven made it after all. You know how powerful she is at twisting potions into poisons," Lady Tremaine took a step towards Ella, her dress twisting into a liquid that spread out and shifted into spiders that scuttled their way toward Ella.

"Stop. Don't move." Ella pressed a hand to her head, squeezing her eyes shut.

"It's too late, Ella. By the time the prince comes back, if he comes back, you'll be dead, like the queen. Maybe this time he'll lose control and kill himself. I had hoped that would happen last time."

Ella's head snapped up to look at her, ice chilling her veins, and it wasn't from the Frost. All of this death, to start a war. A war that the Queen of Trudel didn't want to be accused of orchestrating.

"You took her from me." Ella's voice was thick with grief as she tried to shove the shadows off of her. They continued to converge, crawling up her torso to engulf her.

"I was there," Lady Tremaine gloated. "At least up until the moment before she died. Those enchanters, that burst of raw power when they die—"

Ella cut her off by swinging her sword at Lady Tremaine. She jumped back, snapping the whip at her.

"You had no right to take her from me." Ella moved in rapid succession. She blocked her stepmother's sword as she dipped and slid around her. Ella moved with precision.

"It was a pleasure to watch the light fade from her eyes."

Ella screamed, no longer holding back as she took a more direct approach. Lady Tremaine's last attempt was to send the whip snapping at Ella.

She caught it, wincing against the sting.

"Did you know that every time she saw me, she asked for you to return home? And every time, I told her you didn't want to." She beamed.

Ella gripped her sword tightly.

She pulled the whip and Lady Tremaine closer only to punch her to the ground. Ella's knuckles throbbed with the impact.

"You chose this life, Ella. Remember that, you only have yourself to blame," Lady Tremaine smirked as she gazed up at Ella through hate-filled eyes. Eyes that Ella had looked to for comfort during the queen's death. "She died thinking you hated her, and you'll die knowing David despises you."

Ella gasped as a knife pierced her side. She dropped the whip and Lady Tremaine as she backed away, removing a knife no bigger than her thumb.

Ella staggered backward, looking at the blood on her fingers. She was out of time. All of Lady Tremaine's reinforcements would arrive soon, too soon. She had allowed herself to be distracted. To be manipulated one last time.

"I said you weren't leaving this house."

Ella crumbled to her side. Her hands pressed against her hip. Lady Tremaine was someone who liked to gloat and Ella needed her to let her defenses down. She twisted so that her back was to her stepmother. She wouldn't be able to resist the opening Ella provided.

"You won't get away with this. Henry...he knows everything. The king will find out what you did."

"No one will believe him. Even if they did, they can't touch me. I'm the queen's ambassador, Ella. You should have thought this through better," Lady Tremaine pressed her shoe into Ella's hip. Blinding light clouded Ella's mind, but it was all she needed.

Lady Tremaine was close enough now.

She picked up her father's sword and ran it up and through Lady Tremaine. She stumbled away from Ella, her mouth open as she looked at the blood seeping out of her.

She sank to the ground, gasping for air.

Ella groaned to her feet and stood over her, her father's sword pointing at Lady Tremaine's chest.

"That was for the queen...and Jaq," Ella whispered.

"Ella, we have to...go..." The echo of Henry's voice came to her on a tidal wave of spiders, breaking through the shadows.

She turned as he rounded the corner. Henry had come back for her. Both of them had.

"Ella...what happened?" Henry whispered, horror in his voice as his green eyes analyzed the scene, his brow furrowed.

"She confessed...she told me...she killed the queen. They can't back away from the treaty or start a war. We're okay, right?" Ella blinked against the stars bursting in her eyes.

"Ella...no...we're not." Henry was gentle as he walked her away from Lady Tremaine's body. "You just...you just gave the queen all the motivation she needs to declare war for the death of her close friend. We have to get you out of here. The queen will demand the king hand you over. You have to go with David. Gods...war is coming." Henry walked them out the door, not giving her or David a chance to question anything he had said.

They walked in silence through the maze. Ella did her best to keep her feet moving. But all she wanted to do was lie down and never get back up.

"I...made it worse, didn't I?" She spoke once they got to the end of the maze, four horses waiting for them.

"Yes, you did. You may have bought us more time though, so you and David have to get Holodal to agree to an alliance," Henry commanded both of them, locking eyes with David. It would be up to him in the end to form the alliance.

Luca walked over carrying two packs. He tilted his head at Ella. She must look worse than she felt.

"We've had a change of plans," Henry said when Luca reached them. "Ella has to go with David. It's the only way to keep her alive now."

"What happened?" Luca took her hand in his, looking her over.

"I killed her, Luca..." Ella mumbled.

"You...killed Tremaine." His hands rested on Ella's cheeks, tilting her head up to look at him.

"I killed her..." Ella covered her face as relief flooded her. Every single limb was lighter with the knowledge.

"And now we have to get you two out of here," Henry spoke, his eyes darting around their surroundings.

"My father, what will you tell him?" David kept his distance from them.

"I'll tell him as much as I'm able. You and Ella have gone to Holodal to get an alliance. He and my father need to get ready for whatever is next. I don't know what the queen will do. I don't know if she'll declare war, or if she'll demand Ella's life. She won't be able to reveal anything about what Lady Tremaine has done, and I can't bring any proof of what's happening in this house without breaking all codes of conduct between kingdoms. The queen will most likely place a new ambassador here, and they will deny us access. David and I cannot be seen here. It would be seen as an act of war, so all of us have to get out of here."

"Henry...what will we tell the public? They'll want to know what happened. The attack at the palace—"

Henry pinched the bridge of his nose. "We'll lie. We'll say that you died protecting the prince from an assassination attempt and that David has been sent to the academy until all threats are neutralized."

"It's our only option now, David. You and Ella need to work together to keep each other safe, and bring back an alliance." Henry spoke quickly, tossing every idea he could think of into his solution.

How could they have fucked up so much, so quickly? Ella swayed on her legs. How much longer could she handle all of the poisons running through her? Maybe Lady Tremaine was correct and she would die because of them.

David nodded. He would do it. As the prince, he would do all that he could to protect his people, even if it meant disappearing.

"Let's get you out of that dress," Luca whispered.

"Luca, come with us." She fidgeted in her dress.

"You know I can't. I'll be killed the moment someone recognizes me in Holodal." Luca took over unlacing her dress. "I'll stay hidden. I have places I can go. Besides, shouldn't I be the one to worry about you?"

"I can take care of myself," Ella said, willfully ignoring the blinding pain in her side.

"I know, it's one of the things that makes you amazing. I hope he eventually sees that." Luca motioned to David.

Ella twisted her body, trying to find relief.

"Let me see those wounds."

"We don't have time. I barely have time to change."

"Then hurry," Luca commanded.

While Ella changed, Henry got David to change into a plain pair of training trousers and a tunic, his sword strapped around his waist. Ella slogged her way into a loose pair of training clothes. She stretched out her muscles as she walked over to the horses. The fire continued to radiate out from her injuries, clashing with the ice Frost provided. Though she hid her wincing, she would have to look at the injuries soon. But they could wait. They would have to wait. Her father's sword was strapped around her, her daggers in a pack.

Ella stumbled. Frost crept back, spiking in her legs.

A scream echoed across the maze. Even from the distance they were at, it pierced the night. The reinforcements had arrived, and they had found Lady Tremaine.

"We have to go. Now." Henry pushed David to his horse. "Two months, David. That's what I can buy the two of you. Two months before the queen can either demand the treaty be upheld or start a war. Bring him back in two months, Ella, with the proof we need."

Ella nodded, walking over to a horse. It wasn't Dream. Couldn't be, that would be too obvious. Night, Drea's horse looked at her with curiosity, as Ella held her reins. She turned to Luca, locking eyes with him. His dark brown eyes pleaded for her to stay as he took her hand and raised it to his lips.

"Make sure you come home."

"Only if you're there when I come back."

"Deal." Luca squeezed her hand and turned around to get on his horse.

Ella put her foot in the stirrup, and pushed off on weak legs, unable to swing herself over. She closed her eyes and gave herself a moment. Sweat broke out on her forehead, the fever taking hold as everything blurred.

"Don't take your time now, Ella," David muttered.

Ella took a small breath through struggling lungs. She kicked off the ground again, summoning the last ounce of strength she could find, and mounted Night. Ella looked at David, and even in the dark of night, she could see the distrust and hatred brewing in him. He may have accepted whatever Henry had said, but it would be a long road back before he looked at her with anything but disgust. Ella's heart fissured as she built another wall and urged Night into a trot. Everything would work out. It had to. Luca and Henry took off down different paths as Ella and David rode off into the forest, not once looking back.

The End.

GLOSSARY

<u>Enchanters Potions</u>

Force - red potion – gives you enhanced strength

Velocity – yellow potion - makes you incredibly fast

Insomnia – purple potion - keeps you awake for prolonged periods

Spotlight - green potion - gives you intense focus on a particular goal

Vivifica - blue potion - reduces physical or mental pain

Fray - black potion - enhances skill during combat

Solacium - white potion - heals wounds and illness

Callidus - gray potion – stealth, ability to slip past enchanted mirrors or not be seen

<u>Snow White's Poisons</u>

Mire — induces hallucinations

Fenith — the sensation of bones breaking

Frost — induces hypothermia

Blaze — induces high fever

Malice — cold sweats with hallucinations

Wraith — mindless paralysis

Golden Apple — instant death that turns you pale and makes your lips dark red

<u>Enchanters Mark Power Ranking from most powerful to least</u>

Midnight

Obsidian

Onyx

Black

Dark Brown

Chestnut

Medium

Light

Tan

Pale

ACKNOWLEDGEMENTS

The phrase "it takes a village" doesn't feel like a line that does enough justice for the amount of support and love I've gotten throughout this process. While writing a book can be a lonely business, I found that the process of publishing this book and finalizing the drafts has definitely not been.

I have to start this by thanking my wonderful boyfriend TJ, you have been my rock, my support, and my biggest fan. I probably would have waited another year or so without your unwavering belief in my ability to pull this off. You always lifted me up and encouraged me in my dream to be published. You also knew when to walk me back from multiple spirals when I wanted to do ALL THE THINGS. Things that were definitely not attainable (yet). While this book had been written before we met, it definitely would not have been published without you.

This book can't end without thanking and recognizing my Found British Family. Marie, Tammy, Alex, Harpy, and Todd all of you showed me what the meaning of "found family" truly means. All of us randomly came together through fate or destiny, but definitely not on a horse, in our flat at Roehampton University in Roehampton, London, UK, and little did we know the journey and friendships that would form from those months living together. It's because of that time together, that I began to figure out who I am as a person, and truly feel as though I could be myself, and not have to put up a fake persona for approval. Our family has withstood over ten years of friendship, and I truly don't know where I would be without it.

Thanks so much to my League of Ladies. Arpi, Brittney, and Puneet, the three of you were my sounding board for more social media, cover input, advice, etc. than I could possibly name. Our friendship means more than the three of you could know. It's not often that I find a group of ladies that I have cliqued with so easily and who have accepted me into their group so quickly. I am so thankful for all of the late-night conversations we've had where I'm waffling back and forth over font, colors, etc., and have each of you talk me through it and make the best decision. Love you all so much!

A huge shoutout to my best friend Natalie who has always been my mental break, and Disney partner in crime! Our trips to Disneyland are always a wonderful reprieve for me from work life and writing life. My writing group ladies are the reason I chose to make the jump into self-publishing. If it hadn't been for our latest writer's retreat and all of your encouragement, I wouldn't be here today. Christina our weekly writing sessions, and your support have been more impactful than you could know. Who would have guessed that being in the same new hire group in work would lead to such a wonderful friendship? Lauren, Ashley, and my bonus mom Elsa, the three of you have become more important to my life than you know. Being 'adopted' by Elsa has been the best thing in my life because I also got two sisters out of it. All of your support over this period of my life has meant so much to me.

I have to thank the two people who have been incredibly instrumental and helpful in getting this book created. Beth Gilbert designed this beautiful cover, she can be found on Instagram @bethgilbert_art. Her work is beautiful and amazing and she's one of the sweetest artists to work with. And my beta reader/editor August Head. Your edits, remarks, and comments always impress me and push me to think about my characters and make sure the story is on track to match what I want. Gary, you may not know YA, but you know Fantasy, and your comments in my story were so helpful while I was in my final stages of drafting! Finally, thank you to Erin Young who gave me some of the best edits I've ever had, and really pushed me to examine Ella and her desire to protect the crown.

Lastly, I couldn't end this without thanking my family. Mom and Dad both of you have found ways to support me in my journey to being a writer. Thank you for always encouraging me to be creative and reach for whatever I wanted to grab out of life.

ABOUT THE AUTHOR

Kelsey grew up in a beautiful seaside town where adventures were just a few minutes outside her doorstep. Her hot chocolate addiction keeps her fueled when she writes, along with the sound of rain and cold weather. She loves to create worlds about Dragons, Assassins, and Magic, just not all at once. Though she will admit that sounds like the beginning of an awesome story! When she's not writing or working she can be found hiking, waterfall chasing, and traveling. Or bingeing the next great show like Bridgerton or The Great British Bake Off.